CONCLAVE CONSPIRACY

✳ ✳ ✳

July 11, 2015

To Philip & Maria —

Great friends, the
best of friends!

Thank you for all you
do to make the world
a better place.

Bud

Conclave Conspiracy

✳ ✳ ✳

Burnham Philbrook

© 2009 and 2014 by Burnham Philbrook
Library of Congress Control Number: 2014908360
LCCN Imprint Name: Burnham J Philbrook, St. Paul, MN
ISBN: 9780692211588
ISBN: 0692211586

This book was printed in the United States of America
Interior & Cover Design by: Create Space
Editing by: Ashley Shelby of Mill City Writers' Workshop
10 9 8 7 6 5 4 3 2 1
1. Fiction 2. Suspense 3. Religion First Edition

To order additional copies of this book, go to www.conclaveconspiracy.com or contact the author at conclaveconspiracy@comcast.net.

For Michele: You have supported me throughout our thirty-five years of marriage, and you supported me in writing this book. I love you now and forever!

Acknowledgments

My sincerest thanks to those who offered their insightful suggestions to this novel: Dr. Jim Berry, Deacon Jack Flood, Ms. Ruth Flood, Sister Rosalie Hennessey, OSM, Ms. Hu Di, Rev. Robert Hudnut, Ms. Kathleen Ismail, Mr. John Watson Milton, Fr. Phillip J. Rask, PhD, Professor Raymond Robertson, PhD, Ms. Kate Schwaighart, Mr. Jim Swiderski, Ms. Dorota Wierzbicka, and Col. Warren Williams, US Army Ret.

A special thank-you to Ms. Ashley Shelby, who edited this book, and to Fr. Greg Skrypek, who encouraged me to write it when I thought it was a silly thing to do.

Chapter One

Jimmy Flahvin had no idea why he had been summoned to Rome. Michael Maloney, the vicar general of the Chicago archdiocese and his old friend, had called him at his law office to say it was vitally important that he travel to the Vatican today. Father Maloney couldn't tell him anymore because he didn't know anything more, other than that a private plane would be at Midway's charter terminal in six hours to fly them both to Leonardo da Vinci Fiumicino Airport.

Although he had been to Rome several times, he had visited Vatican City only twice—once on a long layover when he had spent a couple of hours between flights, and again when he had taken his second son, Joe, with him on a business trip. He and Joe had been tourists in Rome visiting St. Peter's Basilica, the Sistine Chapel, and the museums. Jimmy had not been overly impressed. He had later opined to a friend that there were far too many statues in the square and the church, and that the faces on most of the male sculptures seemed unnecessarily stern. They were not, in his less-than-humble judgment, representative of the kind, caring, and gentle Jesus that inspired his life.

It was Wednesday morning. Just picking up and leaving for even a few days was not something he could easily do. This week's schedule was particularly difficult to alter because he was also preparing for a twelve-day trip to Asia, departing Sunday night. Most importantly, he had great tickets to the Cubs play-off game that evening, and he was going with his daughter, Mary. Mary was a pediatric nurse, and at thirty-two, his pride and joy. Nothing could pry him from an opportunity to spend time with Mary.

"Jimmy, you gotta do this. They made it sound as though the whole future of the Church is at stake," Maloney had pleaded.

Jimmy Flahvin was used to this kind of hyperbole; it was common currency in the high-powered world of international business law. However, he wasn't used to hearing it from a Catholic priest. He looked at his calendar on his iPhone and concluded it was simply impossible for him to go anywhere in the next six days, let alone six hours.

"Mike, I'm really sorry, but I can't go anywhere," Jimmy said. "I've got too much on my plate. Tell them I'll see what I can do later in the month. Maybe I could fly to Rome on my way home from Singapore."

"Jimmy, I don't know what to say other than they need you in Rome tomorrow. The words they used were 'vital,' 'critical,' 'imperative.' They specifically told me to tell you that this is the most important thing you'll ever do in your life."

"Who's asking for me, Mike?" Jimmy asked.

"It's Cardinal O'Bryan, Jimmy, but he said he was speaking for all the US cardinals."

Jimmy had known John Cardinal O'Bryan for several years and considered him a good friend. O'Bryan was a very important leader in the Catholic hierarchy, albeit one of a minority of progressives in the Church. Jimmy remembered when they had first met over dinner and recalled O'Bryan's subtle change in attitude when he had learned Jimmy was a successful international business lawyer and a wealthy Catholic. Princes of the Church were drawn to the affluent faithful out of basic financial necessity. As their friendship grew, they would meet in New York or Chicago when one or the other was in town. Jimmy did some pro bono legal work for both the Chicago and New York archdioceses, and the Vatican had sought his advice numerous times. Whenever one of the cardinals asked for money for an important cause, Jimmy always made a substantial contribution.

He and O'Bryan had last met six months earlier in the office of the archbishop of Chicago, Peter Cardinal Schmidt. Schmidt had invited several prominent Catholics to discuss the future of the Church in America. The discussion had run the gamut. How to solve the severe priest shortage and the possibility of married priests and female priests. The continuing priest sex-abuse scandal (could it get any worse?). Welcoming gays and lesbians to the Church without offering same-sex marriages. The Church's failure to effectively oppose recent wars, and how to help prevent future wars. And why the Church found it appropriate to legislatively impose its views on abortion onto non-Catholics. It had been a straightforward meeting, and that was the last time Jimmy had spoken to O'Bryan.

"Mike, if I could I would. I'm honored that they would contact me during this particular time. But I just can't help them out right now."

After hanging up with Maloney, Jimmy turned to CNN on the large-screen monitor in his office. As they had for the last three months, cameras focused on the chimney of the Sistine Chapel in Vatican City, waiting for the signal that the cardinals had elected a new pope.

These had been trying times for the Catholic papacy. Pope Benedict's resignation, the first in 600 years, had caused great consternation. Pope Francis's election was swift, and he helped restore some of the Vatican's credibility by focusing on the Lord's mercy and the faithful's responsibility to embrace the poor, but elected at seventy-seven and with only one lung, his time in office was too short. His successor, Pope John XXIV, was selected on the first day of his conclave. But six months later, he died from a massive heart attack. The next conclave elected Mark II, a cardinal from the Democratic Republic of the Congo, the African country with the largest number of Catholics. Twenty-five days later, he too was dead; his plane had gone down in the Alps on a routine flight to Vienna. The Catholic Church had buried three popes in less than a year. The heartbreaking drama dominated the news cycles and rocked Catholic communities across the world.

Jimmy could only imagine what was going on in the conclave. But he couldn't imagine what he had to do with any of it. He watched the monitor as black smoke billowed from the rooftop next to St. Peter's.

"There will be no new pope today," the telegenic reporter noted. "This is the longest conclave in modern times. During the last hundred years, four days is the longest it has taken to elect any pope. In what appears to be more than two hundred ballots, the cardinals have not agreed upon a replacement to fill the shoes of the Fisherman."

The CNN reporter continued her commentary, although Jimmy had heard most of it many times during the past three months. "After the pope, the cardinals are the highest-ranking officials in the Roman Catholic Church. There are one hundred ninety-two cardinals, each appointed by a previous pope. They comprise the Supreme Council of the Catholic Church, charged with electing the new pope. However, according to the rules of the conclave, only those under the age of eighty can vote.

"Catholics across the world are wondering what is causing the stalemate. Why can't the cardinals agree?" the reporter continued. "Some speculate about the possibility of a pope from the United States; although no North American has ever served in that high office. If an American is in the running, Cardinal O'Bryan from New York is the most likely. However, with the recent exception of the three most recent popes, only Europeans have been elected, and the vast majority of them were Italians."

Jimmy wondered for a moment as the reporter's voice trailed off. Why was he being summoned to Rome? Could the cardinals actually be considering someone from the US, he mused? Did O'Bryan need his legal counsel to help maneuver through the final hours of the conclave? Did he need a financial commitment to help secure a few additional votes? Had he declined Mike's request too quickly? After all, this was a historic period in the Church. In an earlier time, he would have sought advice from his wife, Vicky. But not today.

He was engrossed in a meeting when Maloney called back. Jimmy asked the other three lawyers to give him a moment. As they stood up and left, he answered the phone.

"They need you there tomorrow, Jimmy. We'll do whatever we can to help you so you can get on that plane at 3:30 this afternoon. You gotta do this. You just have to trust me, Jimmy."

There was a long pause—an uncomfortable silence.

"Mike, let me see what I can do. I'll call you back in a minute." As he hung up, he stared at the vivid watercolor portrait of Vicky that had hung on his law office wall for more than twenty years. He wondered—what's this about?

✳ ✳ ✳

Jimmy stared out the oval window of the luxury Gulfstream G650 as the baggage handlers scurried across the Midway tarmac. When he turned back and looked across the aisle at Maloney, his old friend smiled. Minutes later, the ground fell away as the plane became airborne.

After they ordered dinner—filet mignon for Maloney, salmon for Jimmy—the men settled back against the rich white leather seats.

"Mike, I need some details."

Maloney sighed deeply. He had known Jimmy Flahvin for more than twenty years, and he knew he could not put his no-nonsense friend off any longer. Jimmy was always prepared, and while those who knew him well enjoyed his reaction whenever they could catch him off guard, there was no joy in this situation.

"Look, it's strange. I know it's strange. But I swear, I don't know more than what I've told you. I'm a priest, Jimmy. I do what my bishop orders." He leaned back in his chair and looked ahead. "So that's what I've done."

While Maloney slept, Jimmy wrote in his journal about the events of the day, emphasizing how uncomfortable he felt not knowing his function in Rome. Seven hours later the Gulfstream landed at the charter terminal at Leonardo da Vinci Fiumicino International Airport. Jimmy took his hastily packed bag and walked down the metal stairs to the black tarmac.

"*Buon giorno*," an Italian immigration agent greeted them as she asked for their passports and customs forms, which they had filled out en route. She checked the dark blue passports, stamped a blank page, took the customs form, and said in flawless English, "I hope you enjoy your stay in Italy."

Off to the right of the plane, a white Sikorsky S-92 helicopter waited, its rotors already spinning. Jimmy noticed two midnight-blue Cadillac Escalades parked on either side of the helicopter. Nine men, dressed in black fatigues and armed with automatic weapons, stood between the vehicles and the plane. Jimmy and Maloney watched as a middle-aged Italian man dressed in an impeccably tailored dark gray suit, starched white shirt, and deep alizarin-red tie approached them.

"Welcome to Rome, Mr. Flahvin," the man said. "Please, come. We will take you to where you need to go."

Moments later, they were flying over red-roofed hangars. From his seat in the back of the copter, Jimmy studied the well-dressed man's face. Nothing but a placid smile. He thought it curious that none of the planes on the ground were moving, and that he could not see any other aircraft in the sky as they sped across brown fields, green parks, and then the city landscape. Neither he nor Mike spoke during the brief trip; neither did the Italian man in the front passenger seat.

When the helicopter touched down on the pad on the west end of Vatican City, a security guard opened the door and the well-dressed man invited them to get out. A black Mercedes-Benz S-Class was idling nearby. The ride was brief, no more than five minutes. The four-door sedan pulled onto the cobblestone entrance in front of a pair of weathered, ironbound, arched wooden doors.

"Please come with me," the man said, still smiling. They followed him up a steep flight of dimly lighted stairs and down a polished marble-paved hallway. Their footsteps echoed around the vaulted ceiling. Finally, they entered a spacious room with oak floors partially covered by brown, burgundy, and beige Persian rugs. Enormous multicolored tapestries hung on the dark cherrywood walls. Two plush, deep-brown leather couches faced each other in front of a stone fireplace spewing heat from a roaring fire. Jimmy glanced over at the west wall, which was covered floor to ceiling by a bookcase bearing hundreds of leatherbound volumes. He had waited in sitting rooms all over the world, but none quite like this.

"*Buon giorno.*" Both Jimmy and Maloney turned at the sound of a soft, feminine voice. The attractive woman was dressed in a floor-length black habit with a white shawl covering her dark hair. "Would you like some chai, or coffee, or Diet Coke?" she asked. Jimmy couldn't hide his smile; he'd been a Catholic his entire life, but he had never been offered a Diet Coke by a nun. Before he could reply, Cardinals O'Bryan and Schmidt arrived.

"It's good to see you, Jimmy," O'Bryan said, clasping Jimmy's hand with both of his. "Thanks for coming on such short notice."

Jimmy thought O'Bryan looked tired. Haggard, even. There was an odd look in his eyes. But after all, the man was a frontrunner to be the next pope.

Cardinal Schmidt turned toward Maloney and said, "We need to speak with Mr. Flahvin alone. Would you mind?" Maloney looked relieved.

"Not at all."

"Do you have your cell phone?" Schmidt asked.

"Yes."

"Good, we'll call you if we need anything," Schmidt said.

After Maloney left and the sound of his heavy footsteps faded, O'Bryan spoke directly to Jimmy. "As I'm sure you know, we're in the midst of the longest conclave to elect a pope in hundreds of years. We need to fill the shoes of the Fisherman. And our time runs out in less than twenty-four hours."

Chapter Two

Thirteen weeks earlier, cardinals from all over the world had converged on the Vatican to bury Pope Mark II and to elect his successor. Mark's was one of the shortest papacies on record, having ended tragically when his plane crashed. The papal plane had gone down in the Alps. That much they knew. What they didn't know was what caused the crash, and foul play had not been eliminated.

Mark's death was a crushing blow to the Church. Africans especially were devastated because he was the first African pope, and as a cardinal from Kinshasa in the Democratic Republic of the Congo, he was one of them. Elected at sixty-one, Mark's was to be a long papacy after his predecessor, Pope John XXIV, had served only six months.

It had been a chaotic time for all associated with the Church, but the first two weeks of the interregnum, the time between one pope's death and another's election, had proceeded well. The Church celebrated the life of Mark II, conducted his funeral and burial, and prepared for the papal conclave.

Back in Chicago, Jimmy Flahvin's life had been largely untouched by the historic events in Vatican City, although as a Catholic he cared about such things. Nevertheless, church issues took place somewhere in the background of his life, one that was increasingly fast-paced, especially after his beloved wife had died.

"Never stop moving," he told himself, "and the pain won't catch up." He thought from time to time about why Vicky had left the Catholic

Church; she had been disgusted by the Church's inability, or unwillingness, to address the clergy sex-abuse scandal. The church cover-up had made her literally sick to her stomach. Sometimes he too wondered why he remained faithful to such a callous organization.

There were cardinals from seventy-three countries in Rome at this time, but only 120 were eligible to vote due to the maximum age requirement. John Paul II, Benedict XVI, and Francis had elevated the majority of the cardinals young enough to vote, and most of them were quite conservative.

However, when John XXIV had become pope, there were twenty-nine cardinals within a few months of turning eighty, about to become ineligible to vote in future conclaves. So Pope John had immediately set out to fill the ranks to ensure 120 qualified electors. Unlike John Paul's and Benedict's selections, all of John's choices were perceived as being on the progressive to liberal side of the theological spectrum, as were many appointed by Francis. It was not that John XXIV was himself a liberal, or even a progressive. To the contrary, he, like most of the electors during his conclave, was an unapologetic conservative. However, John had experienced the dictatorship of one-party political rule for many decades in his native Thailand and witnessed the perils that accompanied repressed dissident thought. He had concluded that every human institution needed a loyal opposition. To achieve this goal, he created one within the Catholic Church by elevating bishops who were devoted to the Church but disagreed with him on many issues.

Later, when Mark II was elected, there were only 119 electors because a cardinal from the United States had died in a car crash a few weeks before John XXIV's death. One of the few official acts of Mark's papacy was naming Juan Carlos Villegomez, from Arizona, a prince of the Church just five days before his own death. Villegomez was the youngest cardinal at age forty-five, and as a Latino he represented the fastest-growing segment of the US Catholic Church; Latinos accounted for only 16 percent of the US population, but they comprised more than 40 percent of all American Catholics.

✳ ✳ ✳

Rows of young priests lined up on either side of the corridor connecting St. Peter's Basilica and the Sistine Chapel, chanting the litany of the saints, as their predecessors had done on fifty-nine occasions over the past 550 years, approximately once every decade, and as they had done twice in recent months. The cardinals, each wearing his scarlet cassock, white surplice, scarlet cape, and red biretta, processed from the large church to the much more intimate chapel. The Sistine was the pope's chapel; however, upon the death of the pope, it became the venue for the papal conclave. Cardinal Villegomez was attending his first papal conclave. His mentor, Cardinal Schmidt, walked silently beside him.

"Do you think an American might be elected this time?" Villegomez asked. Schmidt did not turn to look at him.

"O'Bryan would make an excellent pontiff," Schmidt whispered. "But some view him as too progressive."

"How can we help?" Villegomez inquired.

Schmidt looked around for a moment, then ducked his head close to Villegomez's ear. "Shhh." He spoke quietly. "This entire process is conducted in reverent, silent prayer. Possibly, over lunch or dinner, we can respectfully remind our colleagues about O'Bryan's superb qualities, but the conclave rules prohibit any campaigning."

"Can we change the rules?" Villegomez pressed.

Schmidt shook his head. "Only the pope decides the rules for electing his successor."

"But the pope is dead."

"Exactly. The rules are what they are. They can only be modified by the next pope," Schmidt said, somewhat irritated.

"Well, that doesn't seem right. What if a super majority of the cardinals, say two-thirds or three-quarters, agree to new rules?" Villegomez asked in a soft voice. "Surely we must be able to correct a problem or take advantage of an opportunity unforeseen by the previous pontiff."

"What do you think this is, a democracy?" Schmidt whispered, annoyed. "The College of Cardinals is not a legislative body. Remember where you are. The pope is supreme. Even in death. And anyway, the last thing the Church needs is even the appearance of disarray or division."

As Villegomez entered the Sistine Chapel, he stopped speaking, awed by the wonder of the room. On this day, the chapel was meticulously arranged for the election of the Supreme Pontiff of the Holy Roman Catholic Church. There were four rows of three long tables, two rows positioned on either side of the chapel. Ten cardinals would fit snugly at each table, thus accommodating 120 electors—sixty men on each side. High-backed wooden chairs cushioned by dense foam wrapped in beige fabric sat close together, partially underneath the tables. Beige cloth, the same shade as the chair cushions and recently carpeted false floor, covered the burgundy-skirted tables. Rigid cardboard nameplates rested on the tables in front of each cardinal's place, and a Holy Bible lay next to paper and pen immediately behind the nameplates. The altar was the focus at the front of the chapel. It was there each man would cast his vote. Directly behind the altar was Michelangelo's *Last Judgment.*

Villegomez followed Schmidt to his place near the rear of the room. With all 177 cardinals present, Cardinal Belosi called upon the Holy Spirit for guidance by intoning the hymn "Veni, Creator Spiritus." Following tradition, each voting cardinal placed his hand on the Holy Bible sitting on the table in front of him and vowed to follow the rules of the conclave, serve God and the Church if elected, and maintain complete secrecy of the proceedings unless dispensed by the new pope. Outside, noisy worshippers, Roman and international media, and thousands of the curious packed the square. Inside, just silence. The nonvoting cardinals—those eighty and over—departed, leaving the 120 cardinal electors in the chapel.

"We share once again an enormous responsibility," Giovanni Cardinal Belosi of Milan addressed his colleagues on the first day of this conclave. "This is especially true now as we participate for the third time in less than a year in this momentous event—the most consequential process in the Holy Roman Catholic Church. I petition each of you to pray for wisdom and to follow the guidance of the Holy Spirit in this vital and irrevocable decision."

Belosi was the cardinal secretary of state under both John XXIV and Mark II and the man in charge of this conclave. In other times, he would have been the frontrunner to become pope. But these times were unlike any the Church had seen. Moreover, Belosi was nearly eighty, far too old except as a caretaker, and after two of the briefest papacies, no one was interested in a "caretaker pope."

"As you contemplate your duty of electing the next Vicar of Christ and Supreme Pontiff," Belosi continued, "neither friendship nor individual ill feelings, neither exchanged concessions nor worldly possessions, neither the pressure of time nor your personal physical comfort can influence your decision. You must be fully open to the Holy Spirit, leaving all vested interests at the outer doors of the Sistine Chapel."

All understood why Cardinal Belosi asked his fellow cardinals to pray quietly, but fervently, for guidance from the Holy Spirit, and why he admonished his colleagues to refrain from engaging in factionalism or other political shenanigans. The Catholic Church was facing a situation that threatened to be more devastating than the Great Schism and the Protestant Reformation combined. The very existence of the Church was at risk.

Catholics in the United States and Europe had been leaving the Church in droves for more than two decades, the sex abuse scandal being the primary trigger. The numbers were staggering. In the United States alone, upward of six thousand priests had victimized more than thirty thousand children. Dioceses across the country had spent billions for victim therapy, legal fees, and settlement expenses. Insurance covered some of the legal and settlement costs, but in most cases, the coverage was insufficient and quickly exhausted. Individual dioceses paid the claims by selling land, liquidating hard assets, and reducing operating expenses by cutting programs and laying off employees. This created more victims—the poor who depended on help from the Catholic Church. When they ran out of resources, dioceses filed for bankruptcy. Although there was no way to accurately measure the terrible pain and protracted suffering experienced by the tens of thousands of victims, all agreed this disgrace had financially ruined the Church and spiritually threatened its foundation.

As a direct consequence of the sex scandal, financial donations from the faithful had declined dramatically. It wasn't just the abuse; bishops had covered up the abuse and moved the perpetrators from parish to parish. And the Vatican hierarchy was incredibly insensitive to the victims. The Mexican founder and longtime head of a Catholic religious order was among the most egregious examples of the Church's failure to even listen to, let alone address this pressing issue. This influential priest had abused boys and minor seminarians, had long-term relationships with multiple women, and fathered several children. Allegations against the priest had first become known in 1976. But the Vatican had done nothing. He was implicated a few years later and again in the late 1980s, but still no action was taken. Due in large part to his directing substantial amounts of money to the Roman Curia from Mexico's wealthy, the Vatican had actually appointed this priest to prestigious church commissions and conferences. In 2002, the Holy See waived the statute of limitations in sex abuse cases involving children, but not much changed on a practical level. It wasn't until 2010, nearly thirty years after the initial accusations against this priest, that the Vatican formally denounced him. Way too little, way too late.

One-third of Americans raised Catholic had left the Church, many due to the abuse and its cover-up. For every new Catholic in the United States, four renounced their affiliation. And less than 25 percent, a record low, attended Sunday Mass on a regular basis. Fewer Catholics in the pews further reduced revenue and deepened the financial calamity. Some suggested that the largest Christian denomination at the time of this conclave was "former Catholics."

The priest sex-abuse scandal was not the only issue that threatened the Church. Religious vocations were down by nearly 70 percent as compared to the 1960s, causing substantial increases in church payrolls. Sisters and Brothers worked more or less for free; the laypeople who replaced them had to be paid living-wage salaries. In addition, the US dollar had fallen against the Euro for nearly two decades, which further reduced revenues because more than a third of all of the Vatican's donations were in dollars, but expenses were paid in Euros. And the Great Recession had taken its toll on every institution.

With substantially reduced donation revenue, the Vatican sold or mortgaged hard assets to keep operating. First, it collateralized land

and buildings, then it sold hundreds of million shares of stock, and finally liquidated its considerable gold reserves. When all of that was gone, the Holy Roman Catholic Church functioned day-to-day—literally hand-to-mouth. Unfortunately however, the Vatican did not offset the ever-waning revenue by sufficiently cutting expenditures. Like many governments, the bureaucracy continued to spend money it did not have, and operating expenses consumed revenue borrowed against the Church's assets and funds previously allocated for charity. Financial advisors recommended the Vatican sell some of its eighteen thousand priceless paintings, tapestries, sculptures, textiles, and furnishings, but the leaders refused, declaring that these "works of art [were] owned by mankind and [were] only held in trust by the Church."

"The Vatican is virtually on financial life support," the president of the Prefecture for the Economic Affairs of the Holy See reported to the cardinals. "There is the possibility of the Catholic Church literally going out of business." With the Church teetering on bankruptcy, no one in the College of Cardinals knew what the future held. The Church was all they knew. How would they fulfill their mission? Who would care for the poor? Where would they live? How would they survive?

But some of the cardinals weren't thinking about this as Secretary of State Belosi passionately begged them to abide by their sacred vows and give way to the Holy Spirit in their decision-making. Many believed in the correctness of their particular view on an issue so deeply that they were utterly unwilling to listen to anything their fellow cardinals might offer. Opposing ideological factions had been jockeying for political position for years, and the influx of the more progressive cardinals elevated by Francis and John XXIV had only complicated matters. Consequently, some excellent cardinals, regardless of their spiritual and financial leadership qualities, and despite any intercession by the Spirit, could never win election because of the faction they represented. They were simply unacceptable to too many and could not achieve the necessary two-thirds majority.

"Jesus entrusted the keys to his church to a fisherman," Belosi concluded, "a man not learned in the Scriptures or educated in rabbinical ways or the procedures of the synagogue. Peter was a most unlikely leader. But Peter believed in his friend, and he understood the ways of the world. Jesus built his church on the shoulders of this common man. The church may once again be well served by a common man who knows the ways of the world."

Many of the cardinals pondered these words, wondering whom among them the powerful cardinal secretary was endorsing. Who was the common man of whom Belosi spoke? Surely, it was not any of the *Preferati*, those considered viable.

The two men most likely to ascend to Peter's throne had been elected, and now both were dead. Still, canon law, the internal ecclesiastical body of rules and regulations that governed the Catholic Church, was clear: any baptized male could be pope, and every cardinal was a candidate. However, in practical terms, only four among the College of Cardinals were *Preferati*.

Giovanni Vincenzo Cardinal Tamborino was one of two Italians among the top tier. Tamborino was archbishop of Brindisi-Ostium in Puglia, in the southern part of the country—sometimes referred to as the "heel of the boot"—the oldest Catholic enclave in Europe. The story is that St. Peter had put ashore near what is now Santa Maria di Leuca, on the southern coast of Puglia, when he had traveled from Jerusalem to teach the Gospel in the heart of the Roman Empire. A metal cross stands to this day at the location where St. Peter landed.

Being Italian, Tamborino had history on his side. Of the 268 popes, 211 were Italian—79 percent of all popes—and many in the Italian church still believed that every pope should be Italian. Those who held that view considered Tamborino the most "electable." He was only sixty-four, educated in Rome, and a humble and good man. But he was extremely conservative and Italy-focused. It would be difficult for many from developing countries or the United States to see him as an acceptable choice, and none of the progressive cardinals could possibly consider him.

Carlos Mario Cardinal Rodriguez Romero was from Lima, Peru. If there was a frontrunner, it should have been Rodriguez because he was a "priest's priest" and represented the largest ethnic group of Catholics. Many viewed him as a younger version of Pope Francis. He had started his career at an inner-city parish where he had quickly become pastor after the sudden death of his mentor, the longtime leader of this urban church. Rodriguez had worked tirelessly for the underprivileged and poor, and his superiors, particularly Pope John Paul II, who had promoted him to bishop, admired those efforts. On his ordination as bishop, John Paul had said, "Carlos Mario Rodriguez Romero represents all the Church ever hopes for in a priest."

Benedict XVI had elevated him to cardinal a few years later. At the time of this conclave, he was president of the Latin American Bishops' Council, had served as chairman of several Vatican committees, and had strong ties to the US Bishops Conference. He was a right-of-center moderate on the conservative-progressive spectrum, and a thoughtful and respected priest by all who knew him. Moreover, Latin America represented 45 percent of the world's Catholics, and Rodriguez had the support of most Latin American cardinals. However, the Latin American delegation was still poorly underrepresented, with only 24 percent of the voting cardinals. Further, many supporters of the developing world believed someone other than a Latin American should have a chance, given the recent pontificate of Francis I from Buenos Aires.

Manoles Franco Cardinal Sicoli was the other Italian and a leading member of the Roman Curia, the Vatican's administrative and governing structure. The Curia was a complex bureaucracy headed by the Vatican's secretary of state. Its purpose was to serve the pope in the administration of the Church, but it had long ago devised its own self-serving mission. In times past, the Curia had played the deciding role in the election of a new pope, but age and death had diminished their influence, so in this conclave they represented only 12 percent of the total authorized to vote.

At sixty-one, Sicoli was the Curia's ideal choice—a fundamental, doctrinaire conservative who was uncompromisingly dogmatic, with a successful career in the Vatican, and who would have a long reign. He knew how the inner workings of the Church functioned, and he was fond of the regal pomp and ceremony of the papacy. While few would characterize Sicoli as a humble man, his Curia colleagues knew he would fiercely and meticulously defend the long-held Roman traditions that many thought were too often disregarded in other cultures. Although respected for his tenacity, many cardinals outside the Curia found Sicoli too divisive. Both critics and supporters agreed he held unyielding hard-line views. That was both his primary strength and major weakness.

While Sicoli was never directly implicated himself, many cardinals were also deeply concerned about corruption within the Curia—rumors of envelopes of cash delivered for Vatican favors, ongoing turf wars among departments, the never-ending embarrassment of the Vatican bank, and general dysfunction within the bureaucracy. They did not want anyone from the Curia on Peter's throne. Sicoli's only chance was as a compromise candidate, and given the makeup of the College, that did not seem likely, even to his supporters in the Curia.

Then there was John Thomas Cardinal O'Bryan, the American Catholic leader. In addition to heading up the US Catholic Bishop Conference, he had also led the last two delegations of US cardinals to Vatican conclaves and was the delegation's head this time as well. He had served as a White House Fellow during President Ronald Reagan's administration and had maintained a close friendship with the president until Reagan was disabled by Alzheimer's. O'Bryan was a writer, focusing his works on the Church's obligation to the poor, which won him support others could not garner.

Moreover, O'Bryan had several other unique strengths. He had become a bishop well after the priest sex-abuse scandal had broken, and had previously advised one of his mentors, Cardinal Law, to speak out on the issue. He had told Law to disregard the advice of the Boston diocese's lawyers, acknowledge the wrongdoing on the part of the culpable priests and those who perpetuated the cover-up, and make a complete and full apology to all affected. Law, to his lasting regret, did not take O'Bryan's advice. When O'Bryan was later elevated to cardinal and put in charge of the New York archdiocese, he did exactly what he had advised Law. That simple act of authentic contrition won him many ardent supporters among both the clergy and laity in the United States and throughout the world. But there were significant misgivings about a "Superpower Pope." Much of the political, cultural, and economic world lived in the shadow of the United States; many cardinals did not want to take the chance of living in its religious shadow as well. In addition, like all of the other "viable" candidates, O'Bryan suffered from his lack of financial expertise and an inability to demonstrate sufficient capacity to raise substantial amounts of money.

Each of these *Preferati* had his cadre of supporters, but none offered the charisma, political skills, or clerical following of either of the two previous and short-lived popes. There were three others with a chance. Cardinal Mbuto was a progressive cleric from Dar es Salaam—only fifty-six, brilliant, and charming. The son of a subsistence farmer and ordained the youngest Catholic bishop in the world, his vivid memories of childhood supplied him with endless compassion for the poor. As a relatively new cardinal, Mbuto was not well known outside of sub-Saharan Africa.

Cardinal Diokno was the longtime leader of the Manila archdiocese in the Philippines. A staunch conservative, he was admired for the instrumental role he had played in resolving the deadly interfaith turmoil between Muslims and Christians in the Philippines. However, at seventy-seven, Joseph Diokno was just too old for this conclave.

Terrance Cardinal O'Faolain from Dublin, Ireland, the Harvard- and Oxford-educated writer, enjoyed the overwhelming support of the liberal Europeans. Much of his writing, however, repelled his conservative colleagues; O'Faolain had challenged the Church to discuss openly the issues of clerical celibacy, birth control, female ordination, and homosexuality. It was unlikely he could garner even a majority of the vote, let alone the two-thirds needed for election.

So, although the likely candidates could be identified, by Wednesday, the day before the electors first gathered to enter the Sistine Chapel, not a single cardinal could say with any confidence who would be the next pope. Moreover, trepidation that this conclave could turn into a protracted electoral fight was palpable. Unlike recent conclaves, when a "frontrunner" had not received sufficient votes in early balloting and the cardinals had quickly turned to an alternative candidate in order to avoid a drawn-out process, this conclave was rife with near-equal factions who would find it difficult to support someone from another side.

Cardinal Belosi, in his role of the *Camerlengo*, or administrator of the conclave, asked this group of middle-aged and elderly men, some looking quite fit, but many overweight, "What is the will of the conclave? Do we want to conduct our first vote now or wait until tomorrow morning?" One hundred nineteen hands appeared. The process was to begin at once.

The election was by secret ballot. Someone handed Villegomez a small slip of white paper. He read the words imprinted along the top: "*Eligo in Summum Pontificem*: I Elect as Supreme Pontiff..." The bottom half of the ballot was blank. He quickly wrote "John O'Bryan." He looked around as his fellow cardinals bent over their ballots, then folded it twice, as prescribed by custom.

The cardinals voted in order of seniority. Villegomez was the last to cast his vote. He attempted to control his emotions as he walked awkwardly to the front of the chapel. The enormity of the occasion caused his hands to tremble, and his eyes watered as he contemplated his actions. He wondered if he had sufficiently prayed for guidance—or was he just voting for O'Bryan because he was a fellow American? He was unsure and hesitated. When he reached the altar, he knew he could not turn back.

So, as all the cardinals who preceded him, Villegomez repeated the sacred words, "I call as my witness Christ the Lord, who will be my judge, that my vote is given to the one whom before God I think should be elected." He held the folded ballot aloft so all could see and then placed it on a small gold plate sitting atop a gold chalice on the altar. As custom demanded, he tilted the plate and his vote slipped into an urn situated directly below Michelangelo's *The Last Judgment*. As he returned to his place, he fervently asked God for forgiveness for failing to seek sufficient guidance before casting his vote.

When all had voted, one of the previously appointed cardinals took a ballot from the urn, unfolded it, recorded the name written on it, and handed it to another cardinal, who did the same. Cardinal Venkatesan from India then took the ballot and read it loud enough so everyone could hear.

"Cardinal Tamborino," Venkatesan intoned. He took the paper and passed a needle and thread through the word *"Eligo"* so the ballot could not be counted twice.

"Cardinal Rodriguez Romero." Venkatesan took the second vote and passed the needle and thread through it as well. Soon, all 120 ballots hung on the thread, pierced by the needle. Venkatesan tied the ends of the thread together and placed all the ballots on the altar.

He read the tally of the first vote.

"Cardinal Mbuto: seven votes. Cardinal O'Faolain: eight votes. Cardinal Diokno: four votes. Cardinal O'Bryan: thirty-six votes. Cardinal Tamborino: nine votes. Cardinal Sicoli: twenty-six votes. Cardinal Rodriguez: thirty votes." The room had begun buzzing before the cardinal finished the count.

"No one has the necessary eighty votes to be elected," Venkatesan said above the growing din.

Villegomez watched as three cardinals reviewed the ballots before depositing them in the small stove tucked in a corner of the chapel; one poured a chemical over the papers, ensuring the smoke would turn black as it spewed out of the chimney. The ballots were torched, and the message began to thread its way up the chimney of the Sistine Chapel so all in St. Peter's Square could see—there was no new pope today.

John O'Bryan awoke early; his bedside clock read 4:30 a.m. This was his fifth conclave. He had voted for Benedict XVI, Francis I, John XXIV, and Mark II, but he had never before voted for himself. Not until yesterday. He had not received even a single vote at a previous conclave.

"And now I'm in the lead," he pondered excitedly.

Then, quickly, he reminded himself, "No, this is not—cannot—be about me. This is about the Holy Spirit. The Holy Spirit, through the College of Cardinals, elects the pope."

Dressed in his bathrobe, he sat in the large brown leather chair next to his bed, where he opened the Bible his mother had given him on his eighteenth birthday. Its black cover worn and gray, its many pages torn and dog-eared, this Bible had served him so well for so many years that he could not imagine replacing it, even though he often read from an electronic version on his BlackBerry.

O'Bryan turned to the Gospel of Mark and read for nearly an hour before dressing. He put on the same clothes that every other cardinal would wear that day and every day until they elected a new pontiff—a black cassock with red piping and a red sash, a red skullcap, pectoral cross, and bishop's ring. He would not emerge from his room wearing anything else until the conclave concluded.

After Mass, Cardinal Belosi explained some procedures. "As you are all aware, we will take two votes before lunch and two in the afternoon, according to the prescribed rules. We will follow this routine until a successful election. In the unlikely event there is no election within the first three days, we will pause on the fourth day for prayer and conversation. Every morning one of you will be asked to celebrate Holy Mass while others will read aloud from Holy Scripture."

They voted four times on this day, but no one received the necessary eighty votes. The field thinned to three candidates as Cardinals O'Faolain, Mbuto, Tamborino, and Diokno all withdrew from consideration, each sacrificing his own candidacy in hopes his supporters would coalesce around one of the remaining aspirants. When O'Faolain withdrew, most of his votes went to O'Bryan; later in the day, Mbuto's support went to Rodriguez. All of Tamborino's votes moved to his Italian colleague, Cardinal Sicoli, and half of Diokno's went to O'Bryan, with the other half split between Sicoli and Rodriguez. The result was still a virtual tie, with O'Bryan at forty-four and Sicoli and Rodriguez each with thirty-eight.

They continued voting the following day, but there was no election. They took the fourth day off, and after voting on the fifth, sixth, and seventh, they took the eighth day off as well.

The tenth day was a Saturday; they were tired and the frustration in the chapel was understandable. Some had been in Rome for four weeks, and they had been voting longer than any conclave in hundreds of years. At times, the evening discussions were difficult and irritability flared. All knew they had long passed the "average" time of a modern conclave. Cloistered for so long, they feared the faithful and the not-so-friendly media would conclude they were at an impossible deadlock, perhaps even a schism.

The traditional voting process contributed to their stress. Each vote required two to three hours due to the established routine of passing out the paper ballots, writing the name, and walking one-by-one to the front of the chapel to state aloud each cardinal's intentions before God, then counting the ballots and announcing the results. Performing this ritual twice each morning and twice each afternoon consumed nearly ten hours every day.

This, and the rest of every day's routine, left no time for discussion, listening, explanation, or developing consensus. Walking from the Santa Marta hotel to the chapel in the morning, back for lunch, back for the afternoon session, and returning to the hotel at the end of the day took two hours. Morning Mass was an hour. Feeding 120 men three times a day took another four hours. Rest and preparing for another day—seven hours. They were all exhausted. Modern conclaves were designed for two or three days—not for weeks long. Even every fourth day reserved for prayer and meditation did not help develop consensus because most cardinals could only rest from the fatigue.

On the second Tuesday morning, the thirteenth day of the conclave and just before the thirty-fourth vote, Cardinal Belosi explained the provision for limiting the candidates to the top two. This was a provision John Paul II had required and subsequent popes made optional. The cardinal from Bangladesh offered the motion, and Belosi ruled it needed sixty-one affirmative votes to pass, a simple majority of the electors.

All three candidates favored the proposal, but too many of their supporters opposed it. Some feared a two-person runoff would favor O'Bryan, and these men did not want O'Bryan as pope because they considered him too liberal. Others believed the change would help Sicoli, and they opposed him because he was too conservative and would return too much power to the Curia. The motion failed on a clear voice vote.

After the fourth ballot of the fifteenth day, Cardinal Venkatesan read the tally. "Cardinal O'Bryan: forty-six votes. Cardinal Sicoli:

thirty-seven votes. Cardinal Rodriguez: thirty-seven votes. No one has the necessary eighty votes to be elected." No one had changed his ballot during the last ten votes. They were hopelessly deadlocked.

On the forty-ninth ballot, two cardinals voted for Bishop Benjamin Kadam from Mumbai, India. However, during the discussion over dinner, the cardinals were reminded of the bishop's mismanagement of funds donated to help alleviate the effects of a devastating flood in his diocese, and on subsequent ballots, he did not receive any votes. During the next thirty ballots, cardinals nominated twelve other bishops and six leaders of orders of priests, but none received more than seven votes. Even Villegomez heard his name called during the voting as he watched in disbelief as the days and weeks wore on.

The fractious debates of the evening conversations provoked quiet disdain and agitated frustration during the daily voting. Personal relationships were on edge, and the edges were extremely frayed, exposing raw nerves sensitive to every perceived slight or misspoken word. Many cardinals retired to their rooms immediately following dinner simply to escape the post meal conversations. Every day made compromise seem less and less likely. Even those who would gladly alter their vote to end the pain could not bring themselves to vote for the other man. The princes of the Church had become inmates in a prison of factions and indecision. Mercifully, the rules called for another day of prayer and meditation, and hopefully a miracle.

Immediately after the first vote of the thirty-third day, Belosi announced to the assembly, "Although silence, meditation, and prayer between votes are time-honored conclave traditions, they are preventing any responsible group discussion that might enable consensus. The canon lawyers have advised me that the rules of the Apostolic Constitution will permit any cardinal-elector to offer to the whole assembly constructive comments about the electoral process and actual or potential candidates. Therefore, any member of this conclave may indicate a desire to address this body by raising his hand. I will recognize you in the order of your request." No longer would the princes of the Church be limited to conducting debate outside the walls of the Sistine Chapel.

How to rectify the Church's fiscal dilemma was the major topic of the vigorous debate and the focal point of contention. What could be done? What type of man did the Church need to guide it out of the morass? Who could save the Church?

One cardinal proposed that the Church needed a pope who could "effectively reach out to the ultra rich and acquire some of their vast holdings to help get through this challenging time and ensure long-term stability."

Others disagreed. "The Church cannot become dependent on the rich and the powerful. Only common people in the pews and their humble donations offer a source of true stability and independence."

"I agree," another cardinal said. "But who can reawaken sufficient confidence in the Church to motivate hundreds of millions to give just a few dollars a year?"

"A charismatic and spiritually gifted pastor like Francis, one who is able to inspire the masses, could do that."

"Perhaps in other times we could elevate a charismatic man, but the Church's current circumstances demand financial expertise above all else."

As they deliberated, it became clear that none of the three candidates sufficiently possessed the required attributes. However, the only members of the assembled body who might have the crucial financial knowledge, charismatic personality, or ample real-world fundraising experience were unelectable because of their views on substantive issues or the faction to which they belonged. There appeared to be no way out. Five weeks turned to six, and then seven. By the tenth week, nearly all were in despair.

"This problem is of our own making," a senior cardinal exclaimed during one of the votes on Thursday of the eleventh week. "We have so much at stake, and yet we all lack financial discipline. We do not have any standardized accounting or auditing procedures. We have no checks and balances. Each diocese can and does what it chooses. Our whole system is susceptible to corruption and abuse."

Others vehemently disagreed. "The independence of our dioceses *protects* the Church from lawsuits!" a cardinal interrupted from the back.

Finally, Cardinal Montego, the soft-spoken prefect of the Congregation for Peace and Justice, rose to speak. Like many of the older cardinals, Montego was disquieted by the tone and tenor of the discussion. Elevated to cardinal by John Paul II, this was his fifth conclave, and he had never previously witnessed any acrimony. Now he sought to calm the factious atmosphere.

"We must rely on the Holy Spirit to guide us," he said. "Prayer is our only option. This economic problem has been brewing for many years and has only grown to this dimension since Cardinal Blandin retired. He had an extraordinary mind for numbers. Unfortunately, none of us here shares his expertise." A murmur of assent rose from the assembled. "And yet, we must choose from among us. So it is imperative that we regard each other with the utmost respect and deference."

An idle crowd remained in the piazza, but it had dwindled to mostly journalists paid to linger until white smoke rose from the chimney. On the morning of the seventy-third day of this, the longest conclave in centuries, Cardinal Belosi led them in prayer as they beseeched the Holy Spirit for discernment and guidance. For the two hundred and thirteenth time, they voted again.

Cardinal Venkatesan, seemingly half-asleep, methodically read each vote aloud. After reading fifty-five votes, he paused for several seconds as he looked intently at the paper ballot in his hands. "Mr. James Flahvin."

Chapter Three

The room fell silent as the leading candidate stood to speak. "Thank you, Cardinal Belosi, for giving me a moment to address the conclave this morning," O'Bryan said. "For the past ten weeks, I've prayed every day, asking the Holy Spirit for guidance. Yesterday, God answered. In response to his answer, I am today withdrawing my name from consideration." The room erupted. O'Bryan raised his hand and silence again descended. "I'm asking each of you to cast your vote for Mr. James Flahvin, a Catholic layman." Remarkably, there was no sound. The quiet was penetrating.

"I realize this sounds radical. It has been more than a thousand years since a layman has been pope. However, after seventy-two days in conclave, I have concluded that the next pope is not in this room, or among the other leading clergy of the Church. The one thing we all seem to agree on is that the Church must survive and thrive. We must broaden our reach in proclaiming the Gospel. We must expand the essential services offered by Catholic schools, colleges, hospitals, children's homes, day care centers, feeding programs, orphanages. We must establish fundraising mechanisms and fiscal policies to ensure we never face this financial threat again. The new pope must provide the leadership to ensure these results, and it is the sacred responsibility of this conclave to identify and elect that man.

"Many in this chapel have declared that the Church needs a compelling man who can restore confidence in the Church. Someone charismatic. Others advise that a financial expert is the solution, noting that experience and expertise are essential. Still others have suggested that we require someone who can relate to the rich and powerful because they single-handedly could right our sinking ship. Well, I submit to you today that James Flahvin embodies all these qualities."

Some cardinals turned to one another and asked, "Who is this man?" Others asked if he was the American lawyer who sometimes offered legal advice to the Vatican hierarchy. "How could we elect a layman?" someone called out from the back.

"I've known James Flahvin for many years," O'Bryan continued, "and many of you know him as well. He is a devote and faithful Catholic who is also an international business lawyer and world-renowned financial manager. He rescues large multinational companies from fiscal collapse. Been doing it for thirty-five years, all over the world. He is a product of Catholic schools. He's provided pro bono legal services to the Church both in the United States and in Rome."

"He's not a priest?" another cardinal asked aloud.

"No," O'Bryan said. "He's not a priest or a bishop. He is a dedicated servant of the Church. He receives the sacraments, he serves the poor, and he is one of our most generous supporters. He is a man of peace—he was a conscientious objector during the American and Vietnam War and spent time in prison because of it."

"So you've given us his résumé," Villegomez said, his awe worn away by the endless conclave. "Tell us what he believes."

"James Flahvin believes what Jesus taught, and he walks the talk of the modern Catholic man. And he may be the only one who can save the Catholic Church."

O'Bryan sat down quietly. As he slumped in his chair, there was initially hush in the historic chapel. Then the gracious quiet offered while O'Bryan spoke erupted into spontaneous chatter among the bewildered cardinals. His supporters were stunned. Not only had their candidate withdrawn, he had proposed in his stead a layman. An American lawyer. O'Bryan had not advised or consulted any of them in advance of his vote or remarks. Some key advisors thought he was just trying to move the conclave forward by demonstrating what might happen if they did not act decisively and soon. Others concluded this was a strategic ploy on his part to define himself to the conclave in a clearly unconventional but powerfully effective manner. And he hadn't voted for one of the other candidates. That, they told themselves, was the good news.

The bad news was that O'Bryan had withdrawn. How could that be considered a winning strategy? John O'Bryan was an honest, thoughtful, humble, and holy man. If he truly believed the Holy Spirit was guiding him to promote this layman, what did that mean about his own candidacy? Furthermore, the idea of a lay pope was unacceptable given a thousand years of tradition, and that did not reflect well on the thoughtfulness or competence of their candidate.

The majority of O'Bryan's supporters decided to disregard his words of withdrawal and continued to vote for him. The cardinals voted three more times that Saturday, and the final vote of the day was only slightly different from the first morning vote, but the difference was significant: O'Bryan 45, Rodriguez 34, Sicoli 35, Flahvin 5, and one blank ballot. Although Flahvin only received five votes, all found it quite amazing that five cardinals had voted for a noncleric. Equally astonishing, one cardinal had decided to cast his vote for no one. It was unprecedented in recent conclaves that an elector cast a blank ballot. Cardinal Venkatesan announced once again, "No one has the necessary eighty votes to be elected."

*** * * ***

O'Bryan did not join his colleagues for dinner that evening. After dismissal, he immediately retired to his room, where he removed his cassock and shoes, methodically consigning them to the closet. He slumped into the large leather chair and embraced the quiet. There was no question: John O'Bryan wanted to be pope. Although he believed it was a long shot for anyone from the United States to be elected, he recognized he was highly qualified, and he was confident he would make an excellent pontiff. On the other hand, he admitted the financial crisis posed unique challenges with no easy fixes.

As the conclave had progressed, he had come to the disappointing conclusion that this was not his time. He did not have the necessary skills, experience, or knowledge needed to effectively address the financial problem. Even if he was elected, by this point the conclave had become so factious, after eleven weeks of difficult and argumentative discourse, that it would take years for any of the three cardinal candidates to mend the divisions and hurt feelings.

The more he prayed, the greater his clarity and the stronger the message from the Holy Spirit: he was not to be pope. He was to cast his vote for a man who could successfully cope with the urgent and complex situation, a man who could save the Church temporally so it could continue to serve spiritually.

Saturday evening, Sicoli met with his key supporters. "We need to end this absurdity immediately," he told them. "We cannot consider a layman of any ideology, but if he is O'Bryan's comrade, we know he is a liberal. The Church will never accept or recover from a liberal layman." Turning to his friend Cardinal De Luca, an Italian colleague, he said, "Put an end to this, Andre."

On Sunday morning, as the cardinals gathered, a heavy rain pounded the clay rooftop tiles. Intermittent thunder stole the cardinals' attention as they contemplated another day of divisive debate and voting.

Prior to the first vote, Cardinal De Luca rose to be recognized. As he swept his gaze across the assembly, he spoke deliberately but softly. "Electing someone who is neither a cardinal nor a bishop, not even a priest, is outside the parameters of canon law. Even if it were permissible, electing a layman with children would put the question of married priests on the table in a way it has never before been considered."

De Luca straightened his shoulders and adjusted his thick glasses. Looking directly at O'Bryan, he continued. "Cardinal O'Bryan, your gracious and generous withdrawal from consideration is clearly in the best interest of the Church. Now, with only two candidates to choose from, we should get very close to a two-thirds majority on the next ballot."

Venkatesan read the results of the day's first vote: "Cardinal O'Bryan: thirty-three votes; Cardinal Sicoli: thirty-four votes; Cardinal Rodriguez: thirty-five votes; Mr. Flahvin: eleven votes; and seven blank ballots." Rodriguez was in the lead for the first time, but twelve cardinals had changed their votes overnight, six more deciding not to support anyone.

Cardinal Tamborino stood and called on his colleagues to respect Cardinal O'Bryan's principled decision to withdraw from consideration, as he and many others had already done. "Moreover," he said, "those of you who are voting for this layman are throwing away your vote and unnecessarily prolonging this conclave. It is neither judicious nor practical to fill the shoes of St. Peter with a noncleric."

Cardinal De Luca asked to be recognized again. He cleared his throat but failed to hide the irritation in his voice. "The law presumes anyone who will be elected pope must first be an ordained priest. That is why the canons explicitly state if the man elected is not a bishop, he shall immediately be ordained a bishop. It is not possible to ordain a layman a bishop, because only priests can become bishops. Canon law does not allow for any intervening act prior to ordination. Therefore, it is not possible to elect a layman to this sacred office."

Cardinal Diokno, an O'Bryan supporter, stood. Belosi acknowledged him. "I have the utmost respect for my dear friend and colleague, the eminent cardinal from New York. I am aware that Mr. Flahvin has offered important and helpful legal advice to the Vatican, and I know of his reputation as an effective business lawyer and a charismatic speaker. However, I must admit, I too find Cardinal O'Bryan's proposal to be outside the bounds of tradition and common sense. A noncleric cannot and should not become pope. Turning over the keys of the Church to a layman is a recipe for disaster. And this particular layman knows nothing about the inner workings of the Church, and I presume precious little about Scripture or theology."

Cardinal Mbuto then addressed the conclave. "I also know James Flahvin. We met many years ago when he and his wife volunteered in a remote village in my diocese. I remember him quite clearly now, even though I do not know why I should, it being so long ago. I recall he was a sincere man, driven to serve out his Christian faith. He asked me why the Vatican did not commit more of its resources to helping the poor become self-sufficient. I must admit, I had no adequate answer."

He paused for some time, his hands clasped in front of him and his eyes looking down. Then he added, "After prayerful consideration, I have decided to vote for Mr. Flahvin."

"I find this idea to be most preposterous," Cardinal De Luca said irritably. "If the next pope changes the rules of the conclave or the precepts of canon law allowing the possibility of a lay pope, then the College of Cardinals would be permitted to consider a layman; however, until that time, it is not possible."

Cardinal O'Faolain rose quickly. "Cardinal De Luca, I believe you are misstating canon law. As Cardinal O'Bryan has rightly stated, this and any other conclave can elect as pope any baptized man. Any suggestion to the contrary is simply wrong."

"I take offense at both your insinuation and your tone," De Luca stated heatedly. "You are not a canon lawyer, and you are in no position to correct me on my interpretation of the law."

Belosi recognized that the conversation was deteriorating quickly. He called for a recess, and the cardinals streamed out of the chapel. O'Bryan, however, remained in his chair. He knew that if James Flahvin was to have any chance of election, the misgivings of the electorate must be fully addressed. O'Bryan spent the next two hours carefully crafting answers to each objection. He focused his arguments toward his supporters and those who might consider his recommendation. If he could persuade all of his voters and 80 percent of Cardinal Rodriguez's backers, Flahvin would have the required two-thirds majority.

When the conclave resumed, Belosi recognized O'Bryan to speak.

"Many legitimate questions have been raised about whether we can elect any layman. I too raised those questions when this radical idea first came to me. Initially, I dismissed the notion as absurd. But as I prayed, answers appeared to me.

"First, St. John Paul II confirmed the possibility that someone other than a cardinal or bishop can be elected when he wrote, 'They shall give their vote to the person, even outside the College of Cardinals, who in their judgment is most suited to govern the universal church in a fruitful and beneficial way.' Some might conclude this requires, at a minimum, that the person be an ordained priest. However, St. John Paul II was always precise with his words, and he did not use the word 'priest'; he used the word 'person.'

"Second, some have suggested that a man with children should be disqualified. However, St. Peter was a married man with children, as were many popes who followed.

"Third, Mr. Flahvin lacks knowledge of the workings of the Church. But most of us would have much to learn about the inner workings of the Vatican's bureaucracy and how to manage the Church. One thing Mr. Flahvin will not need to learn is how to save the Church from bankruptcy. He has proven himself a charismatic fundraiser and a renowned expert at turning around financially troubled institutions.

"Fourth, in the past the College has elevated those who held specific expertise when the Church was in great need. Now is such a time. We've spent the past seventy-three days acknowledging that none of us, and no one we have considered, has the necessary credentials to lead us out of our financial morass.

"And finally, it is true, we don't know Mr. Flahvin's positions on any issues other than war and peace and the Christian requirement to serve those in need. However, many popes have been elected because their electors thought they knew the man's positions on the critical issues facing the Church at the time. Very often, they later discovered they were mistaken in their belief, or upon becoming pope, the pontiff's positions evolved or outright changed.

"I urge those of you who have so graciously and courageously supported me, to please cast your vote for James Flahvin. And I call on all others in this holy chapel to consider this devoted Catholic layman in this time of great and unique need."

No one else offered to address the conclave prior to the next ballot, so the cardinals voted. Cardinal Sicoli led for the first time with thirty-six votes. Twelve more electors switched from O'Bryan to Flahvin, giving the layman twenty-five. Far more important, several additional cardinals chose not to vote; there were twenty-nine blank ballots.

After the totals were announced, Cardinal Montego stood so all could see him. The array of expressions on the faces turned toward him betrayed anxiety, confusion, anger, excitement, even resignation.

"Historically, the Holy See has relied disproportionately upon donations from the faithful in the United States to meet its needs. While other countries have contributed generously, none has the capacity of America. For that reason, it behooves us to listen carefully to Cardinal O'Bryan at this time to help ensure the commitment and loyalty of the Americans. I encourage each of you to be open to the possibility that the Holy Spirit may be moving us in a direction none of us might have ever even considered."

Cardinal Tamborino stood up suddenly and exclaimed, "This whole layman thing is ridiculous! I don't even know why we are considering O'Bryan's proposition. A layman cannot and should not be elected pope at this point in the history of the Church, no more than a Protestant minister or Jewish rabbi should be elected. O'Bryan has withdrawn. We have two excellent candidates in Manoles Sicoli and Carlos Rodriguez. We should limit our votes to them. I petition the cardinal secretary to either rule that we must restrict our votes to those two cardinals or put the question to a majority vote."

When Belosi ruled Tamborino's proposal out of order, Cardinal De Luca jumped out of his chair and angrily accused Belosi of running a failed and irresponsible conclave.

"The conclave is in recess," Belosi said sharply. "We will resume at nine tomorrow morning." For the first time in the course of the conclave, there was no second afternoon ballot.

That evening, Belosi asked for the consensus opinion of the lawyer-electors—the canon lawyers among the cardinals—on the question of whether a layman could be elected pope, and if so, under what circumstances. The next morning, prior to the first vote, they reported.

"The fact that only cardinals have been elected for the past one thousand years is grounded in tradition, but it is not prescribed by canon law or the Word of God," the dean of the lawyer-electors said. "Because there were laymen selected as legitimate popes during the first millennium, we have concluded that, although the proposition is extremely unusual and contrary to second-millennium tradition, a layman can legitimately become pope because what has happened in the Church in the past can happen again." Belosi sat back in his chair. "However," the lawyer-elector continued, "if a layman is elected, he must be immediately ordained a priest and then a bishop, and if he agrees to serve, he becomes pope upon becoming a bishop. If there are any impediments that would prohibit him from being ordained, then the election will be null and void." This invoked widespread mumbling throughout the chapel.

✳ ✳ ✳

The first vote of the day showed more movement toward Flahvin; he now earned twenty-seven votes. There were even more blank ballots—forty-two.

"Given the condition of the Church today, I agree with Cardinal Montego that perhaps the Holy Spirit is presenting us someone with skills none of us have," Cardinal Schmidt said to the assembly. "We have considered every other possibility to no avail. We must give due consideration to this option, even as extreme as it may seem. Through prayer and reflective meditation, we will hear the guidance of the Holy Spirit."

Cardinal De Luca raised his hand, indicating to Belosi he wanted to speak. "I wish to address my dear brothers in Christ who just voted for Mr. Flahvin. I understand your frustration with this process. All of us are worn out. We all want to move to a constructive conclusion as soon as possible. However, casting your vote for someone who cannot possibly get enough votes to become pope only prolongs our difficulty and increases the divide among us. We have been at this for so many weeks. Now it is time to coalesce around one of the remaining viable candidates. Cardinal O'Bryan has withdrawn. So I beseech you, in the name of God the Almighty, please choose between Cardinal Sicoli and Cardinal Rodriguez."

Cardinal O'Faolain stood. "I take umbrage at the suggestion that those of us who voted for Mr. Flahvin are adding to the divisiveness of this conclave. We have a sacred duty to consider all options put before us. With all due respect to cardinals Sicoli and Rodriguez, we have offered them our consideration on two hundred twenty ballots, yet neither has garnered even fifty percent of the vote, let alone the two-thirds required. Perhaps it is time for them to withdraw as Cardinal O'Bryan and all the others have so appropriately chosen to do."

No one else asked to be recognized, so Cardinal Belosi called for the ballot. After everyone had voted, the totals were, "Cardinal Sicoli: thirty-six; Cardinal Rodriguez: fifteen; Mr. Flahvin: thirty-two; and thirty-seven blank ballots. No one has the necessary eighty votes to be elected."

Prior to the next vote, the electors were startled to see Cardinal Rodriguez rise to speak. "I, like all of you, have been praying for wisdom and guidance. I ask God why, after two hundred twenty-three ballots, you have not seen fit to elect me, but rather over the last few days, my number of votes has consistently decreased. God has answered my prayers. In response to that answer, I am withdrawing my name from consideration. I will vote for Mr. Flahvin. I ask each of you to prayerfully consider Mr. Flahvin's candidacy."

As Rodriguez sat down, the buzzing in the chapel swelled. De Luca whispered in Sicoli's ear, "This means you are the only legitimate candidate. You'll win on the next ballot. You are the next pope, Manoles." Cardinal Sicoli smiled knowingly at his friend. He too believed the protracted contest was almost over. The other Italian members of the Roman Curia were also visibly pleased by this turn of events. They all believed that a Sicoli papacy would restore complete power to the Vatican. Moreover, he would reaffirm the historic Italian leadership of the Church, which had been lost several decades before with the election of Karol Cardinal Józef Wojtyla of Poland.

But the final vote of the day did not meet Sicoli's supporters' expectations—Sicoli: thirty-five votes; Flahvin: thirty-four votes; and fifty-one blank ballots. Nearly half of the cardinals had simply chosen not to vote. The conclave had reached the depths of disarray and despair.

Tuesday was a day for meditation and prayer, but Cardinal O'Bryan used the break to visit with many of his supporters who wanted to know, from him, what it might mean to have a noncleric as pope, and how they could explain his election to the faithful. Every conversation ended with agreement to pray for guidance from the Holy Spirit.

Cardinal Sicoli's supporters also worked the electorate. They collaborated in their effort to extol Sicoli's virtues and spread fear about the possibility of electing an American liberal with no connection to the institutional Church. The existence of the Church was at stake, they told the undecided electors, and it was irresponsible to put it in the hands of an American lawyer who, without doubt, would change the Church in ways unimaginable.

On Wednesday morning, the seventy-seventh day of the conclave, after all were gathered in the Sistine Chapel, Cardinal Belosi prayed aloud once again.

"Dear Father, provide each of us with the wisdom of the Holy Spirit so we will know your will and abide by it. Give us the strength to do that which you require of us. Provide us the grace necessary to protect your church as we contemplate the unknown and prepare for the future, in the name of your Son, Jesus Christ. Amen."

Belosi asked if anyone had anything to say prior to the first vote. He looked out onto a sea of exhausted, drawn faces, but from among them, Cardinal Alonso Martinelli indicated his desire to speak. Nearly all of Sicoli's supporters had publicly spoken in favor of their candidate, but not Martinelli, a Sicilian who had served in the Curia since he was a young priest. With a master's degree in accounting, and as the protégé of the deceased Cardinal Blandin who had so deftly managed the Vatican's financial affairs in previous decades, Martinelli was responsible for all church finances, and his colleagues turned to him with interest as he rose to speak.

"I'm concerned that too many have not fully grasped the severity of our financial position. The Holy See and the Vatican will dissolve as viable entities unless we do something immediately. We have insufficient revenue and numerous creditors who expect payment. We have lost money every year but one since 2007. We've never recovered from 2012 with the internal leaks, all the rumors of corruption, power struggles, money laundering, and mismanagement. Or in more recent years, when diocesan leaders in America and Europe were tried, convicted, and imprisoned for their involvement in the cover-up of the sex abuse scandal. We have mortgaged virtually everything and can no longer pay the interest on the loans, let alone repay any of the principal. We are now so far in the red that we will be forced to dissolve before Christmas. An American, who understands finance, fundraising, and the ways of the world, may be exactly what we need in order to survive."

"I'm sorry if this is obvious," Villegomez said, "but why can't we hire the financial expertise we need? There must be thousands of financial firms owned and run by Catholic men who could help us get out of this mess."

"No doubt there are many such firms," Cardinal O'Faolain replied. "And I suspect we will need to employ several regardless of who is elected. But what we need now is a leader who is a strategic financial thinker and has the charisma to raise several billion dollars in the near term."

"Does this man even speak Italian?" one of Sicoli's supporters called from the back, disregarding all decorum of the proceedings. "As Bishop of Rome, he must speak Italian so he can address the parishioners and converse in the language of the Vatican State."

Cardinal Hoffman rose momentarily, then waved his hand, indicating he'd changed his mind. He returned to his chair and no one else spoke.

The first ballot of the day commenced. Venkatesan confirmed the tally. "Cardinal Sicoli: thirty-five votes; Mr. Flahvin: fifty votes; and thirty-five blank ballots. No one has the necessary eighty votes to be elected."

Flahvin had taken the lead. Belosi immediately ordered the second vote to commence. Each cardinal once again took a ballot, wrote a name on it, walked to the front of the chapel, and put it in the golden urn. When the last of the 120 electors completed this ritual, Cardinal Venkatesan started reading the votes aloud so everyone could hear.

"Cardinal Sicoli." He read a second ballot, "Cardinal Sicoli." He read the third, "Cardinal Sicoli." He read the fourth, "James Flahvin," the fifth, "James Flahvin," the sixth, "James Flahvin," the seventh, "James Flahvin." When he finished, Cardinal Venkatesan verified what everyone in the room had already tallied in their minds. "Cardinal Sicoli: thirty-six; Mr. Flahvin: sixty-four; and twenty blank ballots. No one has the necessary eighty votes to be elected."

Cardinal De Luca leapt to his feet. "We are on the brink of major catastrophe. We are within a few votes of electing to lead the Holy Roman Catholic Church a man whom only a few of us even know! We have a sacred obligation to protect the Church and ensure her future. If you are attracted to this man because you believe he can save us from our financial distress and from ourselves, I ask this question: How do you know he has the ability to raise the necessary hundreds of millions dollars? We cannot fulfill our duty without some knowledge of whom we might entrust with the sacred role of sitting on Peter's throne. I therefore propose we invite Mr. Flahvin to this conclave so we might interview him and determine his qualifications for this most vital responsibility."

The dean of the canon lawyer-electors and a renowned church historian rose to speak. "Candidates for pope have never been interviewed during a conclave. Moreover, the rules clearly state there may be no outside influence on the electors. Bringing anyone from outside these walls to speak with us while we are still voting would irreparably alter that fundamental and well-established principle. In fact, I suspect it would negate the entire conclave and we would be required to start the election process all over again."

"Well, the least we ought to be able to do is ask Mr. Flahvin if he would even serve if elected. Otherwise, we are just wasting our time," De Luca responded.

"If Mr. Flahvin is elected, only then may he be asked if he is willing to fill the shoes of the Fisherman. Any contact with him before that event will put the entire conclave into jeopardy," the lawyer stated emphatically.

Cardinal Diokno arose. He spoke slowly, deliberately, and softly, unintentionally forcing all to strain to hear his words. "I've reconsidered my view on this proposition. If we truly believe the Holy Spirit guides us in this selection, then it is not necessary to interview any of the candidates. Nor is it necessary the pope speak Italian. There is no requirement he be a priest. It is not necessary he understand the inner workings of the Curia. If we genuinely believe the Holy Spirit inspires our decision, then the man we select need only be a baptized and practicing Catholic. God will take care of the rest."

During the lunch break, Sicoli and Flahvin supporters feverishly worked the undecided voters, most of whom were well-known by now, even though every ballot was secret. That afternoon, Belosi called the conclave to order and the balloting commenced.

At the end, Cardinal Venkatesan confirmed the results of the 227th ballot. "Mr. James Flahvin: eighty-two votes; Cardinal Sicoli: thirty-six votes; and two blank ballots. We have a new pope."

Sicoli turned to De Luca. "We cannot let this stand," he whispered. "This reckless and despicable action will result in the demise of the Church as we know her."

"What do we do with the ballots?" Villegomez asked Belosi. "We cannot send up white smoke until Mr. Flahvin acknowledges his willingness to serve."

Belosi turned to O'Bryan. "How long do you think it will take Mr. Flahvin to get here?"

"If he's in Chicago, he could be here tomorrow," O'Bryan replied.

Belosi addressed the assembly. "Now that the election is concluded, we can no longer be influenced by external sources. We also must inform James Flahvin of his election, but we are still bound by our oath of secrecy. Hearing no objection from the lawyer-electors, I ask for a show of hands of those willing to authorize Cardinals O'Bryan and Schmidt a dispensation from their vows of secrecy given the proven and urgent necessity to speak with Mr. Flahvin." More than two-thirds of the cardinals agreed. Belosi looked toward O'Bryan and ordered, "Well, John, you and Peter should get started immediately."

Belosi continued. "Cardinal O'Bryan and Cardinal Schmidt will locate Mr. Flahvin and summon him to the Vatican. However, they will not advise Mr. Flahvin of his election until he is safely inside the city walls. We will recess until James Flahvin joins us in this chapel and responds to the question of whether he will accept the papacy. We have already burned the ballots from the unsuccessful votes this morning.

We will not burn the ballots from the successful vote until we learn of Mr. Flahvin's decision."

Cardinal Schmidt turned to the canon lawyers present. "After we advise Mr. Flahvin of his election, how many days can he have to decide?" The lawyers conferred among themselves for a few minutes and then reported to the conclave.

"Under the rules of the Apostolic Constitution, the one elected must make his decision the day he is notified."

"I understand that a voting member of the College of Cardinals would be expected to announce his decision upon notification of election," O'Bryan said. "He would have had time to consider and pray about the possibility throughout the electoral process. But how can we expect anyone who has not been a party to these proceedings to make such a momentous decision without prayerful consideration?"

The lawyers deliberated a bit longer, and then reported. "The Apostolic Constitution requires that the one elected make his decision known on the day he is elected. It is our unanimous judgment that the decision must be announced within twenty-four hours of notification of election in order to be within the bounds of the constitution. The church believes that time has a different dimension in the realm of the Holy Spirit. And we are now in the realm of the Holy Spirit."

"How are you going to explain that to James Flahvin?" Villegomez whispered to Schmidt.

"Let's hope he is in communion with the Spirit. Otherwise it's going to be a tough sell."

✳ ✳ ✳

O'Bryan and Schmidt conferred. "We shouldn't contact Flahvin directly," O'Bryan said. "But isn't your vicar general a friend of Jimmy's?"

They decided to call Maloney and instruct him to locate and speak with the pope-elect. However, they agreed they could not betray their intentions to Maloney—only that it was a matter of grave Church business. Once they located Flahvin, they would send one of the Vatican's jets to pick him up.

It was already past two in the afternoon in Rome and seven in the morning in Chicago when Schmidt called Maloney at the Chicago Archdiocesan Chancery Office.

"Good morning, Mike," Schmidt said when Maloney answered. "I need you to do something very important."

Maloney immediately recognized his boss's voice. "Your Eminence, aren't you supposed to be in conclave? I thought you weren't allowed to make phone calls."

"I have a limited dispensation," Schmidt replied. "Mike, if my memory serves, you know James Flahvin, the attorney in Chicago."

"Sure. Jimmy's an old friend, although I haven't seen him for a while."

"I need you to find Mr. Flahvin and ask him if he would please come to the Vatican today. I'll send a jet to fly him here," Schmidt said. There was a long pause on the other end of the line.

"I know where to find him, assuming he's in town. But I'm curious: What's all this about?"

"Please, just get a hold of him and tell him we need him to come to Rome. We need him here tomorrow."

"There has to be something I can tell him," Maloney said. "The guy's almost always on the road, Peter. He's not going to drop everything without some explanation." Schmidt looked over at O'Bryan, who had been listening to the conversation on the speakerphone.

"Father Maloney, this is John O'Bryan." There was no sound. O'Bryan waited and then motioned to Schmidt that there was no one on the other end.

"Yes, yes, Your Eminence," Maloney eventually stammered. "How may I help you?"

"Michael, when you reach Mr. Flahvin, tell him his presence at the Vatican is vital. Insist he arrive tomorrow. He will question why. Tell him this request is from all the US cardinals, and there is nothing more important to the Catholic Church than his being here tomorrow."

"I'll call him right away," Maloney said, as Schmidt looked at O'Bryan and threw up his hands.

"Thank you, Michael," O'Bryan said. "Call us back as soon as you speak to him. Good-bye."

"Your Eminence," Maloney asked, "what do I tell him?"

"Ask him to trust you. Tell him the Church urgently needs him in Rome tomorrow, and I personally need him here as well." O'Bryan paused and looked over at Schmidt. "Tell him there is nothing of greater consequence in his life than his being at the Vatican tomorrow."

That night, O'Bryan called Cardinal Belosi in his room. "Mr. Flahvin will be here tomorrow morning, Giovanni," O'Bryan said.

"He'll have questions," Belosi said. "When he arrives, you and Peter should meet with him to provide the details. Leave nothing out. I expect he will respond with shock and confusion. Remind him that God works in mysterious ways, but that God is always with each of us on our journey."

Chapter Four

There are only a few times in a man's life when the events of one day change everything, forever. This was one of those days for Jimmy Flahvin.

He got up at six forty-five and started his daily routine. He turned on *Morning Joe* on MSNBC, relieved himself, exercised his back, washed his hands and splashed warm water on his face, shaved, weighed himself—188 this morning—showered, combed his thick brown hair, brushed his teeth, put in his contacts, applied some Metrogel on his chin to control his rosacea, and got dressed. The whole process took forty minutes. Today he wore a handsome blue suit with a starched white cotton shirt and blue rep silk tie, a gift from a friend at Hanyang University in Seoul.

He lived all alone now, ever since his wife had died. At one time, this big five-bedroom colonial house was a loud and bustling, cheerful home for four kids, Vicky, and him. Now it was just him. He had thought about moving downtown into one of the high-rise condominiums over-looking Lake Michigan and forgoing the daily commute. But he loved this house and could not bear the thought of leaving his home, where he had spent so many years with his family. There were just too many wonderful memories.

Besides, the children were grown and all lived in the Chicago area. They came home every holiday, and often stopped by during the week or to barbecue on the weekend. That is, if he was home. His international business law practice took him all over the planet. Ever since Vicky had died, he had increased his trips, logging 150,000 flight miles already this year. Loneliness often crept into the empty house, and he missed his wife deeply.

He ate a bowl of Cheerios and blueberries with some dry wheat toast while he read AP stories on his iPad, then left for work at 7:55. Several days a month, he would ride the commuter train into the loop, but most often, he drove the Edens Expressway south from his home in Winnetka and then east onto the Kennedy to his law office in the Willis Tower. Today he decided to take the more leisurely and scenic route through Evanston and then down Lake Shore Drive to the city.

On the way in, he stopped for gas at a BP station on Tower Road and then took Sheridan Drive south, traveling through Northwestern University. His alma mater was over 150 years old and stretched for more than a mile along Lake Michigan. It was a beautiful campus and held a very special place in his heart because it was here he had learned his profession and met his Vicky. He drove along the shore past the elaborate Baha'i House of Worship, the Evanston Art Center, Grosse Pointe Light Station, and Loyola University, where he had earned his bachelor's degree in world history.

As he drove, he listened to classical music by Jonathon Marcus. He had met the pianist at the Minneapolis airport where Marcus had been playing on a grand piano in the main reception area. Struck by the beauty of the compositions, he had purchased the entire set of ten CDs and downloaded them to the car's audio system. Both Vicky and Jimmy had enjoyed Marcus's music. Now when he listened, it reminded him of her. It was soothing, and it comforted his deep grief. The music was especially poignant when he drove her dark blue Toyota hybrid, which he had started using shortly after her death.

He loved this drive along the shore; it was serene and relaxing. He liked the activity on the street—students going to class, workers repairing homes and buildings, men selling newspapers on street corners, women pushing their babies in strollers, the college campuses, parks, high-rises, and buzz of city life. It was always beautiful and predictable;

the eighteen-mile trip to the loop took forty-five minutes. The freeway was far less predictable, and he liked predictability.

Jimmy drove into the Tower's executive parking garage at 8:47, parked in his reserved spot, and took the elevator to the busy lobby. He hiked through the three-story atrium past columns of shiny stainless steel over polished granite floors to elevator security. After placing his right hand over the palm reader, the turnstile opened and he put his briefcase on the X-ray conveyor belt and stepped through the metal detector. Retrieving his brief case, he waited for an elevator. He got in and pressed 90.

His law firm occupied the entire eighty-ninth and ninetieth floors. When he got off the elevator and entered the firm's welcoming executive-level reception area, Lori, the receptionist, advised him that Father Michael Maloney had called several times that morning.

"He said he tried your cell but there was no answer," she said.

"Yeah, I turned it off for the drive in. If he calls back, put him through."

Jimmy was one of three senior partners in a successful law firm that he had cofounded and helped build over the last thirty-one years. Levin, Flahvin, and Peterson specialized in business law—finance, mergers, tax, employment, and contract law. Most of their clients were based in the Chicago metropolitan area, but he had established an international business practice representing prominent clients on five continents as well as Chicago companies that conducted business around the world. As a business counselor, his specialties were helping ultra-large companies weather grave financial challenges and take advantage of significant financial opportunities.

He walked down the cherrywood-lined hall into his spacious office on the northeast corner of the building. The panoramic wall-to-wall bronze-tinted glass windows revealed a splendid view from more than a thousand feet high. The northern windows displayed the impressive city below, and he could pick out celebrated landmarks including Wrigley Field, the home of his beloved Cubs. To the east, he could see Lake Michigan and Navy Pier, Millennium Park, Grant Park, where former President Obama had given his acceptance speech in 2008, Shedd Aquarium, and Adler Planetarium. It was spectacular!

Despite the incredible vista, what struck visitors most about this simply decorated office was the lack of a traditional oversized executive lawyer desk. In fact, there was no desk at all. Instead, he had assembled six chestnut-brown leather chairs encircling a polished marble table situated in the middle of the room. It was there that he conducted business with clients all over the planet.

With a wave of his hand, soft classical music filled the room through speakers high in the ceiling. Relaxing comfortably in the chair that most directly faced a micro thin sixty-inch computer/TV monitor that hung on the west wall, he reviewed his schedule for the day and pressed a button on his phone.

"Christine, could you please come in for a minute?"

"I'll be right there," she chirped.

Christine was thirty-seven, an extremely bright paralegal, completely dedicated to her boss. During the fifteen years she had worked for him, she had grown quite protective, especially since Vicky's death. She entered his office and sat down across from him. As she sipped black coffee and he drank Diet Coke, they went over his schedule for the day. He had a 9:30 meeting with several lawyers from the firm to discuss a financial deal they were putting together in London; an 11:00 conference call with a major client in Tokyo; lunch with the CEO and general counsel of a Chicago client at 11:30; a law-firm budget committee meeting at 1:30; a 3:00 call with a lawyer in Sao Paulo; and a meeting with Christine to finalize his Sunday trip to Singapore at 4:00. Then dinner and a Cubs game with his daughter, Mary. It was a typical day.

The game would be the best part. He enjoyed the practice of international law, even though it had grown old. But he loved going to Wrigley Field, one of the longest-standing ballparks in major league baseball, with its charming scoreboard and outfield walls covered by deep green ivy. Tonight, he had reserved club box seats right behind the Cubbies' dugout for a division play-off game.

But most important, he was going to the game with his little girl. He was so proud of Mary and her commitment to nursing and caring for children, and he loved her company. It would be a delightful evening.

As he and Christine finished, the phone rang. It was an old friend, Mike Maloney. He told Christine that she could go, and he would get back to her later. He spoke with Mike for about five minutes. When they finished, he turned on CNN and watched for a few minutes, then lingered for a while, looking out at the great lake through the expansive window, awed by Mike's unusual request.

A knock on his door interrupted his thoughts. His 9:30 meeting had arrived. He and the other three lawyers immediately got down to business discussing the London deal. About a half hour into their conversation, Christine called.

"It's Father Maloney again. Do you want to take it or call him back?" she asked.

"No, I'll take it."

"Sorry, guys," he said to his colleagues. "I need to take this call. Christine will reschedule for later today."

He and Maloney spoke again for a few minutes, although this time the priest did most of the talking. He listened intently. When Maloney finished, Jimmy paused, staring out at the horizon. Then he said, "Mike, let me see what I can do. I'll call you back in a minute."

He needed to clear his calendar, so he called his law partner, David Levin. David was a longtime friend, as was the third senior partner, Jerry Peterson. They had all met in law school and remained close during their first few years after graduating. David had worked downtown for a major firm in its corporate division, while Jerry had gone to the Illinois Attorney General's Office. Jimmy had worked for Chicago Legal Assistance, a nonprofit organization providing free civil legal service to low-income and elderly folks in Cook County.

Five years out of law school, they had formed Levin, Flahvin & Peterson, Attorneys and Counselors at Law. David was a few years younger, quite a few pounds heavier, and brought a peculiar sense of levity to partners' meetings with his sharp wit. But he was a fine man and a highly respected lawyer. In fact, they all had excellent reputations as outstanding business lawyers. Most of their growing client base came as referrals from current clients and members of the Chicago bar.

"David, I have to go to Rome for a couple of days on very short notice. I'm going to need some help covering my schedule. Do you have any problem with Christine asking some of the junior partners to cover for me?"

"Not at all, Jimmy," David replied. "Why the short notice?"

"I think it may have something to do with the election of the new pope. Although I'm not exactly sure. Papal elections are inordinately secretive. They won't tell me anything until I get there. I need to meet with a couple of cardinals at the Vatican."

"Why you, Jimmy?"

"I'm not sure. I've done some pro bono work for the Chicago diocese and the Vatican over the years. I suspect they need legal counsel," he answered.

David was a Jew, and although the two of them had shared basic information about their respective religions over the years, David really did not know much about Catholicism.

"Well, Jimmy, if you can help them get this election thing over with so it's not on the news every night, that'd be a good thing."

"Thanks, David. I'll make sure Christine keeps you informed."

He made a list of his appointments for the next three days and the partners he wanted to cover for him. Then he asked Christine to come in.

"I need to go to Rome on business today," he explained.

"The airfare will be very expensive given the short notice, but I'll get right on it."

"No, that's not necessary, Christine. I'm taking a private jet. I'll do the Tokyo call and the lunch meeting today," he said, "but I need to clear everything else through Friday."

He gave her a list of assignments and asked her to call each of the partners to brief them on the appropriate files.

"Sure, boss. I've got it covered."

He knew she did.

As she left, he called Maloney back.

He had lunch with his client as planned at the private, members-only Metropolitan Club on the sixty-seventh floor of the Tower. He did not return to his office. He took the elevator to the parking lot and drove home to pack a few things. Because he traveled extensively, he always had a bag ready to go. He checked his mail, phone messages, and personal e-mail and was on his way to Midway by two thirty. Taking the interstate, he arrived with time to spare. As he boarded the private aircraft, he had no comprehension of how this flight would forever and so dramatically change his life.

Chapter Five

When Father Maloney left the room, the three men sat on the worn leather couches, O'Bryan and Schmidt facing Jimmy. He could hear the crackling from the fireplace. As he gazed at his old friends, the looks on their faces—exhaustion mingled with hope—reminded him of the way his wife, Vicky, had looked in those final weeks. Even now—two years after those grueling last days—loneliness could steal in unannounced. He caught himself calling after her when he bounded up the basement stairs. "Vicky?" he had heard himself say just the other night in his sprawling kitchen. How that raw spot in his stomach ached when he realized his slip a nanosecond after calling out her name. At other times, he would speak to her directly, telling her about his day, bringing her up to date on their children's lives, and asking her for advice. Sometimes he thought she responded. Most of the time he knew she was gone. He was painfully alone.

"What I'm about to tell you may seem unbelievable," O'Bryan said. "But put your trust in the Holy Spirit and remember that God calls each of us to service in different ways, sometimes in very mysterious ways." He looked over at Schmidt, then said, "After prayer, meditation, and substantive discussion, the College of Cardinals has elected you the next pope of the Roman Catholic Church."

There was quiet, and then, "What did you say?"

"The College of Cardinals has elected you pope."

There was no sound save the crackling of the fire. His loud chortle broke the quiet.

"That's absurd," Jimmy said, laughing. "I'm not even a priest, let alone a cardinal. Now tell me why you brought me here."

"Every Catholic man is eligible to be elected pope," O'Bryan responded.

Jimmy felt his body go slack as his laughter died away.

"This is the real thing, Jimmy," Schmidt said.

Jimmy stared at the glowing embers. It was an uneasy stillness for the two clerics.

"I don't understand," he at long last said, in a half whisper. Without looking up at the cardinals, he asked defiantly, "Who's in charge of this process?"

"Cardinal Belosi, the cardinal secretary of state," Schmidt answered. "He is in charge."

"I'd like to see Belosi."

"He'd like to see you as well," O'Bryan replied.

As Cardinal Schmidt left the room, Jimmy fixed his gaze just above the blue tips of the flames. A large coal dropped into the air path. His thoughts returned to Vicky. What would she think? What on earth would she think? A few moments later, Schmidt returned with Cardinal Belosi. The two men had worked together on numerous occasions when Jimmy had provided legal advice to the Vatican.

"Your Eminence," Jimmy said, "please help me understand."

As the cardinal described the conclave process, the Church's desperate financial situation, the conclave's inability to elect anyone from within the College of Cardinals, or any ordained man for that matter, and why Jimmy's particular skills, experience, and leadership were so needed during this critical time, Jimmy listened intently as he continued staring into the fire.

The more Belosi spoke, the more Jimmy felt his confusion fade away, replaced by his usual, comfortable, lawyerly confidence. He could fix this.

"I can help you," Jimmy finally said assuredly. "I've helped many clients in difficult financial circumstances. Now, yours is among the most challenging, but that doesn't mean we can't work this out. I'll do this on a pro bono basis, and I can assure you that all the resources of my law firm will be put at your disposal."

"Jimmy," his friend O'Bryan interrupted softly, "the College of Cardinals doesn't want you as a consultant. We've elected you pope."

Jimmy Flahvin's short-lived comfort ebbed. He grew despondent as the three cardinals continued their explanation of the situation, and he began to grasp the impossible decision that lay before him.

"Pray intensely about this," O'Bryan counseled four hours later, when the conversation finally ended. "And let Cardinal Belosi know your decision in the morning."

"I'll need much more time to consider this, several weeks at a minimum," he said emphatically. "This is a major decision. There are many considerations."

"The rules of the conclave require an immediate response from the one elected," Belosi explained. "Only the pope has the authority to change the rules, and until you accept, there is no pope. Given the unusual circumstances of your election, we can legitimately extend the time for your response until tomorrow morning."

"Tomorrow morning? That's simply not possible," he said, aghast.

"Those are the rules. There is nothing any of us can do to change them."

Jimmy ruminated for a moment and then said, "We need to be very clear about something. If I decide to do this, and that is a very big and unlikely 'if,' I will do it on my terms, much as Pope Francis did. Apparently, the traditionalists didn't like much of what Francis did during his short tenure. Well, I doubt they will approve of anything I might do either. I don't know much about how this institution operates or functions. But I would conduct the office in a manner very different from most previous occupants. I won't be imprisoned in Vatican City, or anywhere else. Advise the other cardinals of this. They might want to reconsider and change their votes before it is too late."

"Every pope does it his own way," Belosi said soothingly. "All anyone can ask is that you pray, asking the Holy Spirit for guidance, before you act."

"You can bet I'll pray. I give you my word, I'll pray. I'll pray very hard."

"Now, take my hand," Belosi said, rising. "Let us ask the Holy Spirit for guidance." The four men stood in a circle holding hands.

"Dear God, we petition you for wisdom and guidance. We ask you to offer our brother, James, the strength to accept your call to lead your church. Grant him peace of spirit and clarity of mind as he contemplates his duty. And provide every cardinal and all the clergy the energy and understanding to support James on this journey. We ask this in the name of your Son, Jesus Christ. Amen."

✳ ✳ ✳

Jimmy awoke five hours later. He was hungry; his last meal had been on the plane almost twelve hours earlier. He lifted the phone. A Vatican operator answered.

"May I help you, Mr. Flahvin?" she offered.

"I'd like to go out for dinner. Can you please make a reservation for me?"

"I'll have dinner sent to your room, if you like."

"No, that's not necessary," he replied. "I'd prefer a local restaurant."

"There are many good restaurants just outside the Vatican walls. I'll be pleased to make a reservation for you. What time would you like to dine?"

He checked his watch. "Seven thirty, and I'd like to walk a bit. Although somewhere close is fine."

"I'll call you right back, Mr. Flahvin."

Jimmy considered asking Maloney to join him, but decided he needed to be alone on this momentous night. Besides, he couldn't talk to Mike about this anyway. A few minutes later, the phone rang.

"Mr. Flahvin, I've made reservations for you at Ristorante da Cesare for seven thirty. It is located on Via Crescenzio, about a fifteen-minute walk. It's easy to find, and the guard at post at Sant Anna's Gate will give you directions when you leave."

The service certainly cannot be faulted, Jimmy thought. As he left his suite and walked to the guard station, he wondered how anyone could call this place home. Outside, the streets teemed with people, but uncharacteristically, he did not notice. He was in deep contemplative thought.

Ten minutes later, he was accepting the Ristorante da Cesare's maître d's invitation to sit outside at a sidewalk table. The waiters were elegantly dressed in white coats, crisp black trousers, starched white shirts, and black bowties. There were several white-draped tables aligned outside, each nicely adorned with half-burned flickering votives. Jimmy noticed he was the only patron. People strolled up and down the sidewalk on their way to their various destinations, but he was pleased that the dense chest-high green hedge pleasantly obscured the vehicles on the busy street. Oblivious to the pedestrians, his thoughts masked the noisy traffic.

"What could possibly be before me?" he wondered aloud after ordering a full-course meal. He knew it was impossible to make this decision in the time allotted, especially without outside counsel. Nevertheless, as he was apt to do with any important decision, he rolled the pros and cons, the plusses and minuses, over in his mind.

He was healthy, sixty-seven years old, and a widower. His children encouraged him to date; he was a good-looking man—tall, slim, and fit. His hair was dense, graying at the temples, but he looked a decade younger than his age. The kids thought dating might mitigate his intense loneliness. But regardless of their encouragement, he had no desire to become seriously involved with other women. It was not that he wasn't attracted; he just was not interested in any long-term relationship.

He enjoyed the practice of law, but it no longer offered any authentic challenge; and he was tired of helping the rich and prosperous make even more money. The children were well on their own, albeit at varying degrees of maturity. He owned substantial financial assets and had no debt. Money, now or in the future, was not an issue for him or his kids. Ever since his Peace Corps years, he had contemplated living in another foreign country, although southern Europe was not on his short list. He had zero interest in retiring. A successful executive, he had often mused about the intrinsic rewards of leading a large, elaborate, complex corporation.

Being the CEO of the Catholic Church offered a splendid opportunity to meet all his personal interests, he thought as he picked at his *insalata mista*. And that's how he viewed this offer. The Catholic Church constituted a multinational corporation in serious financial trouble. He had always envied the power, authority, and autonomy exercised by CEOs of major international companies. This job would be the ultimate position because the pope did not report to a board of directors, and the stakeholders did not expect profits.

The church's current financial trouble was not a deterrent. In fact, he saw it as a stimulating challenge. Jimmy relished the opportunity to creatively deal with serious corporate fiscal issues. Besides, the Vatican was actually in much better shape than the cardinals suggested. The Church might be cash poor, but it had enormous assets. And not just physical assets. The Church represented Jesus the Christ. If it genuinely reflected the teachings of Jesus, and reached out to the faithful forthrightly as it sought their support, he was certain the response would be more than sufficient. Besides, the mere fact that he would be the first pope from the United States would in and of itself generate enormous sums from American Catholics.

But that's not what most intrigued him. This job would allow him to make a genuine and positive difference in the lives of millions, perhaps billions, of people worldwide, he mused. As leader of Catholics across the world, he could focus the energy and priorities of the Church to address the needs of the poor, serve social justice, and stand in solidarity with the abandoned, unheard, and forgotten. Additionally, he could constructively change the Church in ways that a conventional insider never could. As pope, he could engage the heads of Protestant and Orthodox churches in discussions about collaboration and Christian unity. As the Vicar of Christ, he could initiate personal conversations with leaders of Islam, Judaism, Hinduism, and Buddhism, and encourage theological understanding and mutual respect. As the political head of the Vatican state, he could meet with world leaders and promote peace among all nations while speaking to the critical global issues of the day. Very heady stuff, he thought.

However, the negatives abounded. The idea of being celibate for the rest of his life was a definite drawback. Even though he had no desire to remarry, he was not prepared to forgo totally the intimate companionship of a woman. While he had been faithful to Vicky during their marriage, he had been tempted to stray more than once. Before Vicky, he'd been with many young women. And since her death, he'd found himself in bed with a few women—but never in Vicky's and his bed. Sex was just one part of his life he'd have to give up. He also drank—Chivas Regal scotch whiskey on the rocks was his preferred drink, and he preferred it often. He suspected he might be encouraged to give that up as well. It was true he was lonely at times. But wouldn't he be even lonelier in a far-off European city away from his children, grandkids, and friends?

Trying to lead a group of bureaucratic administrators in Rome and a worldwide organization of priests, bishops, and cardinals, about whom he knew precious little, was another negative. He would be the outsider's outsider. He pondered the possibility that some might want him to fail, perhaps even help him to fail. He had no internal constituency, no relationships with the major players, save Belosi, O'Bryan, and Schmidt. He had no ability to speak the organization's language. He was, in fact, the most unlikely candidate in modern papal history to assume these responsibilities. More, he was likely to become anathema to those who expected the leader to come from within the hierarchy—a nonconservative in an extremely conservative and traditional enterprise. A layman in a structure of clerics.

"Popes were men of unbounded and transcendent faith," he said to himself, almost audibly. "They rendered a solemn commitment to the Church and lived dedicated lives of prayer." Jimmy remembered seeing images of John Paul II on his knees, deep in prayer and meditation. He, on the other hand, only attended Mass on Sundays, and not every Sunday. His "prayer life" consisted of reciting the Lord's Prayer before he went to sleep at night. When others asked him to pray for someone who was sick, he always agreed and then paused momentarily to ask for God's help for whoever asked him. But that was it. He could not remember the last time he had actually prayed on his knees, except at

Mass. That, Jimmy thought, was a prescription for total failure, and the Church would not survive failure.

He straightened in his chair and tried to eat. He was hungry but his stomach was queasy. The whole idea was ridiculous. Absurd. Beyond the realm of any reasonable person's imagination. The Church had to be desperate, collectively gone insane. "Why in God's name would anybody think I'm qualified to be the leader of the Catholic Church?"

Further, he ruminated, he had a genuinely comfortable and good life. It was not the law that kept him practicing; he truly enjoyed his colleagues and clients. He loved living in Winnetka, seeing his kids and grandkids whenever he or they wanted. They were his world. They kept him grounded and they kept him young. Why would he want to change any of this, he asked himself repeatedly. "How could I possibly do this and not have my entire world turned upside down?"

Then his thoughts returned to Vicky. She was the love of his life. They had met thirty-nine years ago, when he was in law school and she was working on her bachelors. They had married three years later. She was an extraordinarily beautiful and accomplished woman, exceptionally intelligent and passionately determined. He often said she was smarter than he was, and no one questioned that. She could hold a room full of lawyers hostage with her engaging conversation and radiant smile. She had borne his children and given him a loving home. She had supported him in whatever he wanted to do. He had not always taken her advice, but he had agreed she was nearly always right. After decades of being a faithful Catholic, her Church had abandoned her and its basic teachings by covering up priests' diabolical sexual offenses toward children. How could he become the leader of an institution she so despised?

And yet, there was a nagging voice that reminded him that the Holy Spirit inspired the electors of the pope. While he could not rationally explain it, he did believe it. How else could God ensure that the Church would endure?

It was not much different from the writers of the Gospels being inspired by the Spirit to record the Word of God. If the Creator chose to speak to the people, someone would have to convey the message. But because of man's utter unreliability, it was necessary for the biblical writers to be incited to convey the truth. That's why the Church taught that even the New Testament authors who had never met Jesus could accurately reflect the Word of God. God had inspired their writings. Although some passages might be open to interpretation, and translation often posed a challenge, the general message was crystal clear: love God above all things, love your neighbor, love your enemies, put others first, sacrifice, serve, do good works, repent—repent was huge—and pray for God's help and blessing.

Was this simple message all he needed? His thoughts turned to a moment while on business in New York City, when an African American man had stopped him on the street, hoping for help.

"Is there a church nearby?" the man had asked him.

Never breaking stride, Jimmy said, "I'm not from here. I don't know where anything is."

But the man called out to him. "You're the first person who's spoken to me today."

Jimmy slowed his pace and then stopped. He turned and looked at the man. "How can I be helpful?"

The man's eyes filled with tears. He told Jimmy that he was out of work. He had recently burned his hand in a fire. He had two kids—a six-year-old boy and a four-month-old girl. They had no food. That morning he had hiked three miles on foot to the city welfare office, having not even enough money for subway fare. The government worker could not help him. There were forms to fill out. Time periods to wait. His kids needed help today. Jimmy asked the man what he needed to get through today.

"Some food and diapers for my baby," the man said, "that's all I need. There's a Walgreens right up the street."

"Well, let's go, then," Jimmy said.

The two of them marched into Walgreens. The man moved quickly, as if he needed to get this done before his benefactor changed his mind. Jimmy distinctly remembered what the man selected from the shelves, because it surprised him so. He got two boxes of cereal, two half gallons of milk, a loaf of white bread, a jar of peanut butter, a twenty-four count of disposable diapers, baby wash, a container of soft soap, two boxes of laundry detergent, a package of bar soap, and some Vaseline for his burnt hand.

As they strolled out of the store, the man turned and said, "I have to ask you for one more thing."

"What's that?"

"Could you give me some money to put me on the bus?" Jimmy took two twenty-dollar bills out of his pocket, gave them to the man, and said, "This will get you a ride home and a meal for you today."

The man stood staring at him for a moment, then broke into a huge smile. He embraced Jimmy and said, "Thank you, brother."

"You're welcome."

The man began walking to the bus stop, then turned back and said, "I guess I did find the church today. God bless you."

✳ ✳ ✳

Jimmy decided to return to Vatican City via a different route, along the River Tiber. Crossing over the river on a cobblestone pedestrian bridge, he briefly felt a bit alarmed, concerned that someone was following him. But he couldn't see anyone behind him. He sauntered along narrow back roads for about fifteen minutes, when he saw a woman on the corner across the narrow moonlit street. She was young and attractive, dressed in a remarkably short red skirt and a black top with a deep-plunging neckline. His eyes were drawn to her cleavage as she smiled openly at him. He looked at her intently. Under other circumstances, he would have just walked by, not paying her any attention. But he realized if he were to take this job as offered, this would be the last night for the rest of his life that he could even contemplate being with a woman.

He looked at her long legs and moved his eyes up her torso to her round breasts. When he glanced at her enchanting face, she was still smiling. She appeared to be in her early thirties, brunette, gorgeous, sexy, inviting, and probably expensive. Jimmy grappled with the temptation.

"*Buona sera*," she said.

"Hello," he stammered.

"You look like a nice man. Would you like some company tonight?" He thought carefully before he spoke. He would enjoy nothing more than to be in the arms of a skilled, soft, gentle, attractive woman on this night. He was certain those who knew him well would understand if he succumbed under these improbable circumstances. He even believed Vicky would excuse him, because it would just be sex, not a violation of their love. Most important, he knew God would forgive him as God had forgiven him for so many past transgressions. Yet, as Jimmy looked deep into her dark, alluring eyes, he realized he could not violate her dignity, even if she invited him to do so.

"God loves you and God blesses you," Jimmy heard himself say. "He will not forsake you. With God's help, you have the power to live the life you want to live."

His words surprised him, as they seemingly came from somewhere outside himself. He smiled at the woman now; she stared at him as he turned and stepped away. As he walked, he knew he had decided. He would accept the offer from the College of Cardinals.

✳ ✳ ✳

Sitting alone at a wine-stained table in the rear of a traditional Italian bar, Jimmy ordered Chivas on the rocks. He dialed Christine's number at the law office. It was after two thirty in the afternoon in Chicago, and she would be back from lunch.

"Hello, Christine. I need you to do a few things for me this afternoon." He gave her the names of the people with whom he wanted to speak and gave several specific instructions. After they hung up, the waiter brought him the scotch. He took a sip and slumped back in the comfortable cordovan leather chair. A few minutes later, his cell phone rang.

It was his partners, David and Jerry.

David asked, "What do ya need, Jimmy?"

"Hey, David. Is Jerry there with you?"

"Yeah, I'm here, Jimmy."

"You guys alone?"

"Yup," David replied. "It's just the two of us in my office. What do ya need?"

"I, ah..." he started and then stopped. "Um, I, ah..." and he stopped again, exhaling deeply. He felt his chest tightening up. Tears welled in his eyes, and his voice quivered. He took a deep breath and blew it out.

"I need to resign from the firm." He paused. "I, ah...I don't know how to tell you guys this, other than that something's come up, and I need to resign."

"What's going on, Jimmy?" Jerry asked. "Are you OK?"

"You know, next to Vicky and my kids, I love you two guys more than anything," he said, as his voice cracked and his eyes filled with tears. "Working with you for the past thirty-one years has been pure joy. You've helped my family and me so much. You've always been there for me," he gasped. "And I am eternally grateful."

"Jimmy, please, please tell us what's happening," David pleaded.

"I'm sorry, David. I can't right now. I wish I could, but I just can't," he sighed.

He took a gulp of scotch, wiped his eyes, cleared his throat, and composed himself.

"It'll all be clear tomorrow morning. I've asked Peter Jaworski to meet with you at the office at seven thirty. I suspect it'll be on CNN by eight. Reporters will probably descend on the firm. They'll want to know things about the firm and me. Peter will be able to help you respond. Just tell the truth—no embellishments, no lies. I'll send Christine an e-mail tonight instructing her to inform the employees and my clients tomorrow morning. Everyone will know what's going on by eight. I gotta go, guys."

Again, his voice trembled as he spoke. "I just didn't want you to learn about this on the morning news," he quietly cried into the phone. "I wanted to tell you myself."

He fought to regain his composure. He took another deep breath and a swig of the scotch. "But don't worry. It's not a scandal. I haven't committed any crime. It's nothing like that. I'll talk with you soon. Thanks, guys."

He hung up.

David and Jerry just stared at each other, wondering what was possibly happening to their law school classmate, law partner, and best friend.

Levin broke the quiet.

"I'm completely baffled. In all our years together, even during Vicky's illness, I've never heard him this distraught."

Peterson shook his head.

"I don't have a clue, David. I don't have a clue."

✳ ✳ ✳

Half an hour passed before Christine called back. He picked up his cell phone as soon as it rang.

"I've arranged the conference call with your kids for four o'clock, and I made their flight reservations," Christine reported.

"Thank you, Christine. You always do such a wonderful job for me."

It occurred to Jimmy that this would probably be the last time she would assist him in this way. It saddened him. He thought about all the years they had worked together and how enormously supportive she had been. "Christine, I want you to know how grateful I am for all you've done for me these past fifteen years, especially since Vicky died. I've grown to depend on you for so many things. It just won't be the same without you."

"Why do you say that, Jimmy? I'm not going anywhere," she said.

"I just want you to know how much I appreciate all you do," he said, as his eyes once again grew moist.

"Is everything OK, Jimmy?" she asked with deep concern.

"Yes, Christine, everything is fine. You are the best assistant anyone could ever hope for. Good-bye." Jimmy hung up before Christine could reply.

Promptly at 11:00 p.m., he called the AT&T conference number and punched in the PIN. Matt and Mary were already on the call.

"Whaddya need, Dad?" Matt asked.

"Let's wait for Joe and Pat," he responded. A moment later, Pat joined the call, and then Joe.

Matthew was the oldest, a thirty-five-year-old computer whiz who worked as the director of Management Information Systems for the State of Illinois in the Department of Administration. In his free time, he built customized gaming computers. Matt was married to Katy, a tender and sensitive woman in her late twenties. They had twin eight-year-old boys. Mary was single, a devoted nurse and an electrifying pianist. She had studied at the Jacobs School of Music at Indiana University for two years before transferring to the nursing program at the University of Illinois Chicago. His second son, Joe, was thirty-one and had just completed his master's at The Theatre School at DePaul University, one of the most esteemed schools of fine arts in the country. The youngest was Patrick, twenty-eight and still trying to figure out what he wanted to do with the rest of his life. Pat was as bright as the others were, but his was a difficult challenge, given his overachieving father and older siblings. He currently worked at an Exxon gas station, but hoped to go back to college or a technical school in the near future.

After they exchanged pleasantries, Jimmy started. "I have been offered a wonderful opportunity with the Church in Rome. I've decided to take it. It'll change all our lives, although mostly for the good. I can't say much right now, but I'd really appreciate it if you would all come to Rome to be with me for a few days. It's a pretty big deal."

"Well, that sounds exciting," Mary said.

"When do you need us to come, Dad?" Matt asked.

"Can you be here tomorrow?" he asked, softness in his voice. "I've taken the liberty to book each of you, as well as Katy and the boys, on a flight out of O'Hare tonight."

"Gee, I'm sorry, Dad. I've got a presentation tomorrow that I just can't miss," Joe explained.

"I understand, Joe. But if I told you I had only a few days to live, would you come then?" he asked.

"Dad, come on..."

"Well, this is as important as that," Jimmy said emphatically.

"You're not sick, are you, Dad?" Pat asked with tender yet anxious concern in his voice.

"No, no, Pat. I'm perfectly fine," he assured him. "I just want you to know how comforting it will be if all of you are here tomorrow. Next to marrying your mother, tomorrow is the most important day of my life. And Joe, I'll guarantee you, your boss will understand."

"What time's the flight, Dad?" Mary asked.

As he returned to Vatican City and approached the Swiss Guard on duty at Sant Anna's Gate, Jimmy realized he didn't have any badge or pass that would permit him entry. He started to take out his passport to show the soldier at post, but before he did, the guard said, "*Buona sera,* Mr. Flahvin," and opened the gate. "Do you know how to get to your room, sir?"

"I'm not sure."

"That's all right. The Captain will show you."

Jimmy heard someone say, "Just follow me, Mr. Flahvin." He turned around and saw two men dressed in dark casual clothing coming out of the shadows behind him.

He thought to himself, "So there was someone following me. Of course. They wouldn't let me go out on my own in Rome at night, the evening before I'm to become the leader of the Roman Catholic Church."

✳ ✳ ✳

Jimmy woke at four the next morning. Two hours later, he picked up the phone and dialed Belosi's room. Belosi answered.

"Your Eminence, I've decided to accept your offer."

"I'm very pleased by your decision, Mr. Flahvin." Belosi was intensely relieved. He could not imagine reconvening the conclave and starting the electoral process all over again. The past three months had exacted an enormous toll on the cohesiveness among the cardinals. Moreover, the Church needed to take immediate action regarding the financial situation. Further delay would have devastating effects on the Church.

"This was a very difficult decision, Cardinal. In fact, I'm not sure I even made the decision. I almost feel as if it was made for me."

"The Holy Spirit guides each of us who are open to the will of God in the way that is most helpful to us at the moment," Belosi said assuredly.

"Your Eminence, I'm going to need a lot of help. I'm a successful guy, but I know there's no way I can do this alone. I'm not naïve. This is not going to be easy. I suspect there are some in the College of Cardinals who are not supportive of my taking on this role."

"You are correct. As I told you yesterday, it took many ballots, but you did receive more than two-thirds of the cardinals' votes," Belosi said.

"I suspect many priests, bishops, and laypeople simply will not understand how a layman can become pope. They will question my authenticity and authority. If we are going to have any chance at success, I'm going to need every cardinal's help. Especially yours. You are deeply respected by Catholics worldwide. I'm going to need you to run interference for me. You'll need to coordinate the effort to bring the reluctant on board. I'm absolutely clear, Cardinal Belosi, in the absence of your abiding support, my election will result in failure."

"I give you my word, as God is my witness, I will devote all of my prayers and all of my strength to helping you on this journey that the Holy Spirit has called you to," Belosi replied.

They concluded the phone call agreeing that Belosi, O'Bryan, and Schmidt would join him in his suite at seven.

Replacing the phone in its cradle, Jimmy knew it was done. He had terminated his partnership at the law firm; he had arranged for his family to come to Rome; and now he had told the cardinal secretary of state that he would do it. There was no going back.

Chapter Six

Jimmy put on a Maya-blue cotton shirt, a light blue and tan striped tie, and a dark beige suit. He looked in the mirror. He certainly did not look like a pope, but he did look good. Minutes later a waiter brought his breakfast and a copy of *L'Osservatore Romano*, the Vatican City newspaper. It was in Italian, so not of much use; but the food was good. Almost as soon as he'd finished his meal, the cardinals were at the door.

"The day will start at nine in the Sistine Chapel, where I will ask you if you accept the decision of the College of Cardinals to become the Supreme Pontiff," Belosi explained. "You answer yes. Then I will ask you by what name you will be called, and you respond.

"Cardinal O'Bryan will then ordain you a priest. That ceremony will take about half an hour. Then I will ordain you a bishop. That too will take a half hour. As soon as you become a bishop, you immediately become pope. Then we will burn the final ballots and white smoke will go up the chapel's chimney. Bells will ring throughout Vatican City signaling that the Holy Roman Catholic Church has a new pope."

"What time will that be?" Jimmy asked.

"About ten thirty. At this time, you will retire to the sacristy, where you will put on the papal robes. Then you, I, and three other cardinals will step out onto the balcony of St. Peter's. This is when the world will be told you are pope, and you'll be greeted by the faithful." Jimmy noticed O'Bryan was watching him carefully, looking for signs of hesitancy.

"Then what happens?" Jimmy asked.

"You return to the Sistine Chapel to say your first Mass with all the cardinals. That will formally conclude the conclave." Jimmy began to balk, but O'Bryan stopped him.

"We've written out all the instructions on how to say Mass, what you do when, what you say. It is all in a liturgical book that will be easy to follow. If you just stay on track with the book, you'll look like a pro."

"What happens after Mass?" he asked.

"You will receive the cardinals from the papal throne," Belosi explained. "Each cardinal will pay you homage and vow obedience. Then you will retire for lunch with the cardinals of the Roman Curia, and later you will rest. While we are engaged this morning, the papal staff will arrange your few belongings in the papal apartment. This evening, I will introduce you to your personal staff. Tomorrow, we will—"

"Excuse me a moment," Jimmy interrupted. "First, I cannot be introduced as pope until eight in the morning, Chicago time. That's three in the afternoon here."

Belosi glanced over at O'Bryan and Schmidt. "We can arrange that," O'Bryan assured him. "We can start at 1:00 p.m. rather than 9:00. You can step out onto the balcony at 3:00."

"Second, I don't want to wear papal robes. I plan to wear a simple white cassock on a daily basis and plain vestments that a regular priest would wear when I say Mass. On more formal occasions, I will wear a light beige business suit with a clerical collar. I'd like to start that today." Alarmed, Belosi leaned forward to speak, but Jimmy cut him off.

"Third, I want to celebrate my first Mass in St. Peter's. I would like nuns, priests, brothers, and regular people invited and interspersed with the bishops and cardinals in the pews. Please make sure there are some nuns and brothers seated in the first couple of rows. If there are Servite sisters or Christian brothers in Rome, make sure they are invited. I intend this as no disrespect to the hierarchy. It's simply an acknowledgement of the role some wonderful sisters and brothers played during my formative years. I'll say more about this during my comments."

"These are highly unusual requests," Belosi said. "But we will do as you wish."

The three cardinals knew that his proposed attire would cause the most difficulty. Popes had been wearing ornate robes embossed in gold for centuries. Francis had shunned the glitter, but a pope in a business suit?

The church regulated official clothing and its color based on rank. The cassock, a floor-length wraparound piece with neck-to-toe front-center buttons, often tied at the waist, was the principal clerical garment. The priests' day-to-day cassock was black with black buttons, while bishops and archbishops wore black cassocks with amaranth red buttons and trimming. Cardinals wore black cassocks with scarlet buttons and trimming. The pope's cassock was all white—actually, ivory. In addition, each clerical rank wore different levels of ornamental vestments for Mass and other sacraments. Priests, bishops, and cardinals all wore black Western-style business suit coats and trousers with a standard clerical shirt and Roman collar, but no pope had ever worn a business suit.

O'Bryan quickly chimed in, catching Belosi's eye. "The mere fact that you were elected is highly unusual. We are not surprised that you may conduct your papacy somewhat differently from your predecessors."

"I fully respect and intend to honor the theological and liturgical traditions of the Church. However, I also intend to demonstrate to both Catholics and non-Catholics alike that the Church is absolutely committed to the simple message of Jesus the Christ. While I may not be a theologian, I am quite clear about his commandment to love God above all things and to love our neighbors and our enemies as ourselves. That is what the Church must focus on and emphasize. Anything that detracts from that message needs to be changed. That is why I do not want to wear fancy papal robes. From my perspective as a layman, when the pope wears gold braid, red shoes, and flowing silk robes, his garments unintentionally interfere with the central message of Christianity."

Schmidt responded, "I think your attitude will have a very positive effect on all Catholics."

"Fourth, I will not receive anyone from the papal throne. I am neither a king nor royalty. I will not be treated as such. Jesus specifically said, 'My kingdom is not of this world.' I am a common man, a lowly sinner, whom God plucked from obscurity for reasons none of us can fully explain. I will continue to behave like and be treated as a common man—a common man with extraordinary responsibilities. So I will not sit on a throne."

There was another moment of uncomfortable silence. Then Belosi repeated an observation he had made the previous afternoon, saying, "Every pope conducts his papacy according to his own understandings. You've assured us that you will pray about your decisions, and that is all any cardinal or bishop will ask."

"One other thing," Jimmy continued good-naturedly. "I need someone to assist me today. Perhaps there is a bright young English-speaking priest who could be conscripted into service?"

"I know just the fellow," O'Bryan said, relieved to be on to matters more mundane. "Father Jeremiah Canyon is a young lad from Long Island, studying in Rome. I'll have him here in fifteen minutes."

"That's all for now. We can deal with the rest tomorrow," Belosi said. "We'll be back at twelve forty-five to escort you to the Sistine Chapel."

✳ ✳ ✳

Jeremiah Canyon, a relatively short and slightly overweight young cleric, knocked on the door. "Good morning, Mr. Flahvin," Canyon said as he entered.

"Good morning. Have they told you what this is all about?"

"Cardinal O'Bryan called and instructed me to meet with you and do whatever you ask," Canyon replied. "He said I'd have whatever resources and authority I need. I was quite surprised to receive his call because they are in the midst of conclave. Cardinals aren't supposed to have any contact with anyone during this time."

"Well, I appreciate your help," Jimmy said. "I need you to pick up some friends and family at Fiumicino today. They expect you to meet them just outside the baggage-claim area." Jimmy gave the young priest the details of who was coming and when. Two people from a Chicago PR firm would arrive first at around eight thirty and should be through immigration and customs by nine, so Canyon needed to hurry. An hour later, Father Greg Keegan would arrive from St. Paul, and he was to be brought to the suite as well. Ten members of his family were scheduled to arrive in the early afternoon. Jimmy explained he would not be able to see them until evening, so Canyon should take them to the Atlante Star Hotel on Via Vitelleschi—easy walking distance to St. Peter's.

"There is an event scheduled in the piazza at three, and I want you to escort my family to the VIP section of the public seating area," Jimmy instructed.

"What's the event?" Canyon asked.

"Well, you'll have to wait and see. But if you take good care of my family, you'll get a front-row seat."

"I'll take care of it," Canyon assured him. They exchanged cell phone numbers. Jimmy opened the door, and Canyon understood it was time to leave.

"Good-bye, Mr. Flahvin," he said. "Today will be a great day for the Catholic Church in America," he added as he moved into the hallway, intimating he was aware of more than he let on.

✳ ✳ ✳

Canyon brought the PR folks to his suite, and Jimmy invited them in. MDB was one of Chicago's oldest and most prominent public relations firms and a client of his law firm for twenty years. The election of any pope was big news, but Jimmy knew instinctively that managing the media coverage of his election would require top-flight professionals. So he had arranged with MDB's managing partner, Peter Jaworski, the previous evening to get two of their best people on a flight so they could be in Rome this morning.

Cynthia Meyer was a senior partner and a well-known media strategist. She had worked in increasingly responsible positions for the *New York Times*, *Newsweek*, ABC News, and CNN before joining MDB twelve years earlier. She understood major mass media, and she had many friends in the industry. Tough and straightforward, she was usually the smartest person in the room. Cynthia was a product of eighteen years of private Catholic schools—elementary, high school, university, and graduate school—and, unlike many of her classmates, was still a practicing Catholic. She considered herself a moderate Republican, but had never been politically involved in her attempt to maintain journalistic and client objectivity.

Then there was Larry Cooper, a man in his early forties who had earned his spurs in Democratic politics. He had been a young campaign staffer for Al Gore in 2000, primarily doing advance. Later he had worked for several US Senate campaigns as media-relations director. He was a graduate of Columbia School of Journalism and had earned his MA in Social Media from Yale. Together, Meyer and Cooper represented exactly what Jimmy believed he needed.

"Our boss said you need some assistance. How can we be of assistance, Mr. Flahvin?" Meyer asked.

"The College of Cardinals has elected me the next pope," he stated matter-of-factly. "I assume the papacy at midday. The Vatican will announce this to Catholics worldwide at three this afternoon. It's been many centuries since a layman has been elected pope. And there's never been a pope from the United States. I need the two of you to develop a media strategy that will help allay the natural apprehensions, concerns, confusion, even fears that my becoming pope will evoke. And I need you to do this without getting the Vatican office staff bent out of shape."

The two guests sat in stunned silence. They looked at each other for a moment, and then Meyer said to Jimmy, "If we weren't meeting inside Vatican City, I'd assume this was some kind of hoax. But it must be a hoax, because you have to be a cardinal to become pope." She paused. "Don't you?"

"This is no hoax," Jimmy responded. "I almost wish it were. The rules provide that any baptized man can become pope," he explained. "When a layman is elected, he is ordained a priest and a bishop. Then he immediately becomes pope."

"So laymen have been elected in the past?" Meyer asked.

"It's been nearly a thousand years since someone other than a cardinal has been pope," he responded.

"So why hasn't there been any black or white smoke for the past couple of days?" Cooper asked.

"They couldn't discharge any smoke until they knew if I'd accept. They'll send up white smoke at around one this afternoon."

"So—you're the new pope?" Meyer asked hesitantly.

"I will be this afternoon."

"Wow. This is incredible!" She paused briefly, and then exclaimed enthusiastically, "This could be the story of the year, maybe the decade! All right. Let's get started."

They spent an hour discussing the situation. Jimmy explained what he knew about the election process and the scheduled events of the day. The three of them kicked around several short- and long-term ideas, discarding some while putting others into the "possibility pile." They decided that as soon as the white smoke and bells signaled there was a new pope, the Vatican would leak that the new pontiff was an American. That would be 2:00 p.m. in Rome, 8:00 a.m. in New York, and 7:00 a.m. in Chicago. A half hour later, while he was preparing to speak from the balcony, they would have the Vatican media people leak the fact the new pope was a layman from Chicago and offer background on how a noncleric could be elected.

Meyer would put together a two-page bio, making it available to the media immediately upon the announcement of his name. This would also be the basis for the initial Vatican website and Facebook postings. Later in the day, with the help of Jimmy's family and law partners, she would put together a lengthy biography. Cooper would work on a list of interviewees—people who could be interviewed on various US, European, and international television talk shows. Jimmy's brother and sister who were still in the United States, as well as the three siblings who were on their way to Rome, his two oldest children, and his two law partners would be the primary candidates. They would reduce the number of people offered to the media, depending on who did the best jobs during this first interview round.

Meyer suggested arranging a media-prep conference call for 8:15 a.m. central, about the time Jimmy would leave the balcony in St. Peter's Square. Jimmy's two kids, brothers, and sister would meet with them at the Vatican Information Service conference room, where they would participate in a conference call. During the call, Meyer would get everyone's agreement to participate in media interviews, provide advice about how to successfully conduct a media interview and respond to questions, explain the key talking points each should make about Jimmy, and answer their questions. The Vatican Information Service would then advise the worldwide media of the contact information for those who could provide personal information about the new pope.

"Won't the Vatican media service be disgruntled with Cynthia and me usurping their turf?" Cooper asked.

"We have to get this right. Just don't step on toes you don't have to," Jimmy said.

As they were leaving, Meyer turned to Jimmy and said, "I think you should consider doing a TV interview with one of the world's top journalists in the next forty-eight hours. A wide-open exchange where you can tell the world who you are, what you believe, and what you plan to do. Give the world an idea of what you will do as the leader of the Catholic Church. Popes never do that type of thing with major international media, so it would get enormous coverage."

"I'll think about that," he replied.

Jimmy sat in the large leather chair and considered the rest of the day. He had called Father Greg Keegan the night before, and he would arrive from the airport any minute. Keegan was easily one of Jimmy's oldest and dearest friends. They'd met forty-five years earlier during Keegan's initial assignment at St. Edna's in Arlington Heights, Illinois.

St. Edna's was in a typical western suburban Chicago community—upper-middle class, primarily Republican, conservative, and virtually all white. Keegan, on the other hand, had grown up on a small family farm in the far southwestern part of the state. His family was Democratic to the core. As a priest, Keegan was apolitical; however, he shared the social values of his parents and grandparents, aunts and uncles, and brothers and sisters.

Keegan was only twenty-six when the archdiocese had assigned him to St. Edna's, but he had been clear about his mission and purpose.

He was a burly guy, five foot ten and 185 pounds of solid muscle. His deep black hair, dark, shaved face, and baritone voice easily drew the attention of even the most casual observer. On Keegan's first Sunday at St. Edna's, he had given the homily at every Mass.

After thanking the pastor for introducing him to the parishioners, and telling the congregation that he was pleased the archbishop had assigned him to St. Edna's, he had held up his chalice for all to see. "This cup will hold the consecrated wine—the Blood of the Christ—and represents the vessel used at the Last Supper," he said. Normally, a chalice was made of silver, preferably gold. But not Keegan's.

"My chalice is black," the new priest declared in his deep voice, "because where I grew up, the soil was black, and when you put your hands in it, you knew you were rich. More importantly, most of God's people are black. This chalice represents those people—the impoverished, the forgotten, and the disenfranchised."

Many in the pews were offended. Others just sat in wonderment, questioning, "Who is this strange young priest, and why is he here in our parish?"

Not long after arriving at St. Edna's, Father Keegan had gotten involved in an ongoing boycott of Tarrington, Inc., a men's clothing manufacturer, because the company had successfully prevented its largely Mexican immigrant workforce from forming a union. St. Edna's wasn't home to any Mexican Americans, but Keegan was not swayed by who was or was not in his parish. He focused on justice issues, and the boycott had not yet achieved its objective. Keegan was frustrated. So he had convinced several well-known Chicago celebrities, including a starter for the Bears football team—a high school classmate—a well-known successful Illinois businessman, and the famous conductor of the Chicago Symphony to join him in his cause. A week before Christmas, the boycott leaders once again asked the management at McGuire's, Chicago's largest department store, to stop selling clothing made by the Tarrington Clothing Company. When management refused their appeal, Keegan arranged for the three celebrities to join him on the sidewalk in front of McGuire's with their trousers rolled up to their knees and red and green painted cardboard barrels hanging from their shoulders over their torsos and bare legs. The barrels read, "I'd rather wear no pants at all than wear Tarrington." Keegan had advised some friends in the media of what these celebrities intended to do if McGuire's once again refused the boycott organizers' request.

The *Chicago Tribune* and the local TV evening news covered and ran the story. Both the AP and UP wires carried the *Tribune*'s photo of these prominent men not wearing trousers in the middle of winter on the streets of Chicago. It was an extraordinarily successful tactic. Newspapers all over the world printed the photo, along with a caption about immigrants being denied the right to unionize. Not long after, McGuire's capitulated and stopped selling Tarrington's clothing, and within weeks, the clothing company agreed to negotiate with the workers union. Keegan became somewhat of a star to those who supported justice issues.

It was through this media coverage that Jimmy had first become aware of Father Keegan. He then learned that Keegan was also active in the yet-to-be-effective but impassioned and articulate suburban Vietnam War opposition movement. The young priest marched in war protests and wrote letters on behalf of young men who sought conscientious objector status. Keegan really did not care if the boys met all the legal criteria for CO status. It was enough if they simply did not want to fight. In Keegan's judgment, the war was unjust and morally wrong. Anything he could do to end it, or to help young men from having to participate in it, was morally right. To his dismay, the government denied CO status to most of the boys he tried to help. Some fled to Canada. Most joined the National Guard or succumbed to the draft and went off to war. But a couple got through. That, he concluded, made his efforts worthwhile, even though his bishop had objected to his involvement more than once.

Jimmy had reached out to Father Keegan. Having just graduated from Loyola University, Jimmy was no longer eligible for a student deferment, and he wanted to contest his draft board's decision denying him conscientious objector status. Like many young men at the time, he had judged America's involvement in the Vietnam War as morally wrong because the Vietnamese had never threatened the United States and the United States had no right to interfere in their internal affairs. Moreover, he could not justify killing others except in self-defense. Politically and religiously opposed to the war, Jimmy told Father Keegan he was ready to go to prison for his beliefs because the war was immoral.

When he informed the priest that his draft board had refused to grant him CO status, Keegan encouraged him to appeal their decision. "Ask the draft board specifically why they denied your claim," the priest recommended. Keegan carefully walked Jimmy through all the steps. The law required local draft boards to hear appeals in person if a young man so requested. So when Jimmy's appeal hearing came up, he did as his new friend had advised.

At the hearing, Jimmy asked the men sitting around the table, "Can you explain why you decided I do not qualify for conscientious objector status?"

"Each member's reasons are individual and personal," the chairman said. "All of us looked at your file individually, and our reasons for denying your claim are of a personal nature." Based on those reasons, the board members refused to answer any other questions.

Undaunted, Jimmy asked, "Did you conclude that my objections to the war are not religious in nature?" The chairman refused to answer. "Do you think I'm not sincere?"

"We have nothing more to say about this matter," the chairman said. That was the end of the inquiry.

"Ah, this could be helpful," Keegan had said when Jimmy told him about the hearing. "By not telling you why they denied your claim, they may have denied you your constitutional rights." At Keegan's urging, Jimmy appealed the local draft board's decision to the national board. His appeal was denied. He then appealed to the president of the United States, but this appeal was also denied. A few weeks later, Jimmy received his draft notice.

Jimmy Flahvin reported to the Federal Office Building in downtown Chicago on the designated morning printed on his Order to Report for Induction into the Armed Services of the United States. As the officer in charge began filling out his paperwork, Jimmy advised him that he would cooperate fully in all preinduction activities, but that he intended to refuse induction.

The officer stopped writing and looked up. "Are you sure you really want to do this, son?"

"Yes, I'm absolutely sure."

"This is a very serious decision. It could result in very grave consequences. I hope you have thought it through carefully."

Jimmy stood his ground, so the officer told him to participate in the regular schedule for the day, but not join in the final event.

After a full day of tests and a complete physical, government personnel escorted all the inductees into an ornate room with soft brown walnut paneling and multicolored flags of the United States and all the armed services. The young men were lined up in a single row, facing an army colonel in dress blues who was about to issue them their oath of service. Before delivering the pledge, standard procedure called for each inductee to take one-step forward to demonstrate his willingness to serve. The colonel instructed the men to step forward. When they did, Jimmy stood still.

The colonel had been advised of Jimmy's decision not to comply, so when he did not move, the colonel said simply, "Mr. Flahvin, you may go home." All the other young men turned and looked at Jimmy incredulously. Some uneasily wondered if that was all they'd had to do to avoid going to war—just not take that step.

Jimmy knew that draft resistance was a federal felony and that he would be arrested. A few weeks later, as expected, the FBI picked him up at the factory where he worked and took him into custody. The federal government charged him with failure to comply with the draft board's order of induction. He was fingerprinted, processed, and placed in a dreary vacant cell in Cook County Jail. The rules permitted one phone call. The only number he always carried with him was Keegan's. The priest arranged to bail him out the next day.

Jimmy's parents were supportive but fearful and frantic; they did not know what might happen or what they could do. Jimmy had always been independent and self-assured. Nothing they said could dissuade him. Jimmy was saddened that he had brought such pain and concern to his parents, especially his mother. All he could do was tell them not to worry and that everything would work out all right.

Like all similar cases, the government fast-tracked his criminal trial. Judge Michael Olson, one of the most conservative federal judges in Chicago, convicted virtually all "draft dodgers" who showed up in his courtroom and sentenced them to the maximum penalty—five years in federal prison. Jimmy's attorney told him that the cost of a jury trial was prohibitive, and, regardless, his odds for an acquittal before Olson were one in a thousand at best.

"If you go through with this trial, Jimmy, you should be prepared to go to prison," the attorney advised. "And with Olson as trial judge, you should plan on five years." His lawyer thought it would help his case if Jimmy took the stand and testified. Jimmy agreed. He wanted to explain why he opposed this war.

At trial, Jimmy's lawyer asked him several questions to lay the foundation for his religious beliefs, his opposition to the war, his knowledge of the just-war theory, and the manner in which his draft board had responded to his request for an explanation as to why they had refused his claim.

"Can you explain the principles of the just-war theory and how they relate to the Vietnam War and your decision to refuse induction?" his lawyer asked him.

"There are five tests that must be met before a war can be determined just. If a war cannot meet each of these tests, then the war is immoral and Catholics cannot fight. The first test requires all the parties be duly constituted and recognized governments. It is clear the Vietnam War meets this test."

Jimmy then explained why the Vietnam War failed the remaining four tests and concluded, "It's clear that the Vietnam War does not meet all of the five tests. If any one of the five is not met, then the war cannot be justified. That is why I refuse to fight in Vietnam."

The prosecuting attorney vigorously cross-examined Jimmy in an effort to make his argument to the judge. "Are you suggesting that all wars are wrong—that there can never be a just war?"

"No. I believe World War II met the just-war principles."

"Do you know the official position of the Catholic Church regarding the Vietnam War?" the federal prosecutor asked.

"I know that the Catholic Church subscribes to the just-war principles," Jimmy responded.

"But is that the official position of the Catholic Church?"

"I don't know if the Catholic Church has an official position. I do know that the Old Testament instructs that we should not kill. Jesus teaches we should love our enemies. The Catholic Church teaches that we should abide by the Ten Commandments and follow the teachings of Jesus," Jimmy replied.

"You've testified that you are Catholic and that you base your opposition to the war on your Catholic faith. Yet you cannot tell me the Catholic Church's official position on the war?" the prosecutor asked, feigning incredulity.

"I am Catholic. But I base my opposition to the war on the teachings of Jesus the Christ, not on the teachings of men. Scripture clearly lays out Jesus' official position regarding war. He tells us to love our enemies as ourselves, to feed our enemy if he is hungry, and to give him water if he thirsts. I do know that Pope Paul VI told the United Nations, 'If you wish to be brothers, let the weapons fall from your hands.'"

"How do you reconcile the teaching of Jesus to 'love your neighbor as yourself' with the fact that when you refused to be inducted, one of your neighbors had to go in your place?" the prosecutor asked.

"It is a moral outrage that anyone be conscripted to fight in this unjust war. I am truly sorry that any man be required to go in my place. However, any man drafted because I refused had the same opportunity to refuse as I did. If everyone who opposed this terrible war refused to go, there would not be enough men to fight. The government would be forced to change its policy."

"But if every person had the right to question the government and refuse to fight, how could the government ever effectively defend our country?" the prosecutor asked.

"If this war was about defending the United States, it would be a wholly different situation. That is not what this war is about. History will bear that out. Thirty or forty years from now, there will be very little question that the Vietnam War was not about defending the United States."

"Even if you are right," the government attorney continued, "we don't know that today. All we know today is that your country, through the president of the United States, has declared, 'We need you,' and you refused to answer the call. How can any patriot not obey the call of his country?"

"I am subject to an authority higher than the president of the United States. I believe you are too. God does not permit us to live by the motto, 'my country, right or wrong.' We're all obligated to live by the law of God to love our neighbors and our enemies."

The prosecutor realized he was not making any progress with this draft dodger. Moreover, he had made his points to the court. He ended his cross-examination.

Then Father Keegan testified on Jimmy's behalf. He told the judge about Jimmy's commitment to his faith and devotion to his family. He explained that the principles of the just-war theory, originated by St. Augustine and further developed by St. Thomas Aquinas, St. Thomas More, and other Catholic theologians, was the basis for the Catholic Church's position on war. "St. Thomas More wrote that war could only be waged in defense of one's country and that there is no evidence that the Vietnam War is a defensive measure to protect the United States."

Jimmy's attorney asked the priest about the Catholic Church's position on the Vietnam War. "The Catholic Church does not have an official position on the war," Keegan said. "But all Catholics are bound by their conscience. The Second Vatican Council wrote the Constitution on the Church in the Modern World. One paragraph is specifically relevant to your question. May I read it?" Judge Olson agreed. Father Keegan read from the Constitution.

In the depths of his conscience, man detects a law which he does not impose upon himself, but which holds him to obedience. Always summoning him to love good and avoid evil, the voice of conscience, when necessary, speaks to his heart: do this, shun that. For man has in his heart a law written by God: to obey it is the very dignity of man; according to it he will be judged. Conscience is the most secret core and sanctuary of man. There he is alone with God, whose voice echoes in his depths. In a wonderful manner, conscience reveals that law which is fulfilled by love of God and neighbor. In fidelity to conscience, Christians are joined with the rest of men in the search for truth, and for the genuine solution to the numerous problems which arise in the life of individuals and from social relationships. Hence, the more right conscience holds sway, the more persons and groups turn aside from blind choice and strive to be guided by the objective norms of morality.

"That is what the Catholic Church teaches about Catholic men participating in any war. It is a matter of conscience. If a Catholic man objects to war based on his conscience, he must follow his conscience and cannot fight. Jimmy is not permitted by his Catholic religion to participate in this war because it is offensive to his conscience. Therefore, he should have been granted legal status as a conscientious objector."

Father Keegan's words lingered in the courtroom long after his testimony ended. In the meantime, Jimmy's lawyer prepared his final argument: that because Jimmy's draft board declined to advise his client of the reasons they denied Jimmy's claim, the draft board's ruling was invalid because it violated specific rights protected by the Constitution of the United States of America.

"James Flahvin was denied his constitutional right to appeal. He could not make an effective appeal because he did not know why the draft board refused to grant him CO status. Furthermore, this court cannot adjudicate one way or the other whether the local board acted properly. The local board not only refused to tell my client why they decided to deny his claim, they refused to advise this court as well. The board provided no basis for their decision in their record, thus denying this court the necessary information to determine if they acted properly."

Several weeks passed before the judge informed Jimmy's lawyer that he had been convicted of a felony under federal law and sentenced to five years in prison. Jimmy had expected the verdict and had made appropriate preparations. But Father Keegan was devastated and incensed. The priest may not have been a lawyer, but he understood basic fairness and justice.

"How could anyone appeal a ruling when the deciding body refused to explain why they rejected the claim?" Keegan asked over and over again.

Jimmy served his time at the Federal Correctional Institution in Pekin, Illinois, a low-security facility for males located just south of Peoria on the Illinois River. He was scared for his safety when he first arrived, but as time passed, he overcame his trepidation. The days were long and often monotonous. He had a job in the bakery, but earned literally pennies an hour. The warden allowed the inmates to watch TV news occasionally, and whenever the Cubs, White Sox, or Bears were televised, they could watch the game. But most of the time Jimmy was just plain bored.

Jimmy did his absolute best to be a good prisoner, and he was well-liked by both staff and inmates. He was polite and courteous to all, stayed out of trouble, interacted appropriately, and kept to himself when necessary, which was most of the time. He felt utterly alone and isolated, but he reminded himself that he was "just doing time." If he kept his head low and mouth shut, he would stay alive, and maybe get early parole.

Prison became more bearable after he learned about the Bureau of Prison's Inmate Education Program. Although the program was intended to help young men get their GEDs and finish high school, one curriculum offered opportunities for college and postgraduate courses. He persuaded the prison staff to let him apply for a Master's in Business Administration degree at a nearby campus of the University of Illinois. When accepted, the warden allowed him to spend up to eight hours a day studying, researching in the library, and taking exams. Once a week, a member of the local faculty visited for a couple of hours to discuss what he had missed in class. He finished the degree requirements in three years and graduated in the top 10 percent of the students, which was quite remarkable, given he had never attended a single class.

Greg Keegan drove the 182 miles every month to visit his friend. The visits meant a great deal to Jimmy; it was hard time, and any contact with old friends meant the world to him. They met in the visiting room, a drab, colorless, open space filled with gray metal chairs. All visitors and inmates sat together in easy view of the guards. The lack of privacy was intentional. Greg and Jimmy sat across from each other as they discussed the war, his classes, the Church, politics, Jimmy's family, and prison life. His brothers and sisters came to visit occasionally as well, but it was too difficult for his mom and dad to see him locked up. Jimmy sent messages to his parents through Father Keegan, and all were grateful. When it was time to part, the priest encouraged him to keep the faith and pray every day.

"Just don't give up, Jimmy," Keegan would tell him. "Don't let the turkeys get you down."

Five years is a long time to be incarcerated. However, there was opportunity for parole and time off for good behavior. But before Jimmy was eligible to apply for early release, the 7th Circuit Court of Appeals reversed a conviction in a case nearly identical to Jimmy's on the grounds that the local draft board had failed to explain why they denied the defendant's request for classification as a conscientious objector.

That ruling resulted in overturning several convictions, including Jimmy's. As Keegan had thought, the local draft board was obligated to tell Jimmy why they denied his claim. To the heartfelt joy of all, including many of the prison staff, Jimmy was released within a couple of weeks after the trial court heard his motion to overturn the conviction based on the 7th Circuit's decision.

Later, and partially because of Keegan's many visits to Jimmy in prison, the priest applied and was hired as a chaplain by the Minnesota Department of Corrections. The Chicago archdiocese transferred Keegan to the archdiocese of St. Paul and Minneapolis, where he was assigned as a part-time assistant pastor at a quiet, inner-city parish, and full-time at a state prison. Later, Keegan became pastor of St. Mary's parish. Even though he continued to fulfill his responsibilities at the prison, the archdiocese regularly assigned him to help prepare newly ordained priests who were high on the list to become pastors early in their careers.

Jimmy and Keegan had stayed in contact throughout the ensuing years, so when Keegan received the call from his old friend, it was not completely unexpected. That Jimmy called from Rome on behalf of the leadership of the Church in the midst of a secret conclave—that was totally beyond mysterious.

✳ ✳ ✳

"What are you doing here?" Keegan asked after embracing Jimmy.

"Sit down, friend." Jimmy explained the events of the past thirty-six hours and what would happen during the rest of the day. Keegan was speechless.

"I'm going to need you close by my side," Jimmy said to Keegan as his friend absorbed the astonishing news. "So plan on being in Rome for a while."

"OK, Jimmy. Anything." He shook his head. "Should I be calling you 'Jimmy'?"

"We'll figure that out later."

"What will you do as pope? I mean no disrespect, Jimmy, but this is remarkable. What's your plan?"

"You ask too many tough questions," Jimmy responded. "Quite frankly, I don't know. I haven't had any time to really think about it. Cardinals Belosi, O'Bryan, and Schmidt convinced me that this isn't about me. It's about the Holy Spirit. I am just a vehicle—a servant. I will try to do what I think God wants me to do. I guess I'll pray a whole lot for wisdom and grace. But I'm pretty sure if I demand too much clarity on this deal at this point, I'll just get my briefcase and catch a plane home."

"Don't do that, Jimmy. You'll make a great pope. I was just curious about what you are going to do first. You have my word; I will do whatever you ask. If you're the servant of the Holy Spirit, then you can count on me to be your servant."

"Thanks, Greg. That means a lot to me. You can do something for me today. Find Mike Maloney. I'm meeting with my family later this evening and I'd like both of you to join us. Afterwards, I want the three of us to visit a bit."

"OK."

"I gotta go. I need to get ready for the Sistine Chapel. I'll see you this evening."

Chapter Seven

Five cardinals and two Swiss Guards in full regalia escorted the pope-elect to a black Cadillac Escalade. A second Escalade was parked nearby. Opaque windows concealed the inside of the vehicles. They rode a short distance to a private entrance to St. Peter's Basilica, and then walked a winding corridor to the Sistine Chapel. Jimmy found it interesting that he did not see another human being anywhere along the way.

As he entered the side door to the chapel, all the cardinals stood; most applauded. The applause lasted for what seemed an excessively long time. Belosi led him to the altar in the front of the sanctuary and motioned everyone to sit down. O'Bryan initiated the sacrament of ordination. It was a beautiful ceremony resplendent with tradition, prayer, song, scripture readings, and reflections. Cardinal O'Bryan laid his hands on Jimmy's head, prayed for the outpouring of the Holy Spirit upon him, and declared him a priest. There was thunderous applause.

Next, Cardinal Belosi ordained him a bishop. Again, it was a beautiful traditional ceremony. Belosi acknowledged that he was ordained a bishop and immediately asked, "Do you accept your canonical election as Supreme Pontiff?"

"Yes," Jimmy replied softly.

"By what name do you wish to be called?" Belosi asked. Jimmy knew a pope could take whatever name he chose. The tradition of popes changing their names was not common until after Octavian became John XII in 955. Even then, some popes kept their given names through the eleventh century. However, for the past thousand years, every pope had chosen a distinctive name upon his election. Jimmy Flahvin chose "James." No other pope had ever been called James, so he was James I.

The Master of Papal Liturgical Celebrations took a prepared parchment certificate that acknowledged that James Thomas Flahvin accepted his election and papal ministry, and that he would be called "James." The master signed the document, two cardinals witnessed his signature, and the master embossed it with the seal of Vatican City, certifying that Jimmy Flahvin was Pope James I.

Cardinal Belosi presented James to the College of Cardinals, proclaiming, "I present you Pope James I, the Bishop of Rome, Vicar of Jesus Christ, Successor to the Prince of the Apostles, Supreme Pontiff of the Universal Church, Sovereign of Vatican City, and Servant of the Servants of God."

Again, the cardinals applauded vigorously. Jimmy Flahvin—father, brother, husband, lawyer, American—now possessed full and supreme power over the Catholic Church. No event in modern Christianity was more extraordinary or more profound. James was overwhelmed. He understood the legal implications of what had just taken place, but the emotional impact took his breath.

He coughed to mask his feelings. Then he said, "I take the name James because it is the name my mother gave me at my baptism. More important, Scripture records that James often accompanied Jesus on his most challenging excursions. Now I pray that Jesus will accompany me on this most challenging excursion."

The previous day's newspaper and blog headlines had declared "Church Divided" and "Conclave Cannot Elect." It had been two days since the last communication from the chimney of the Sistine Chapel. Now, even supporters of the Church were questioning. Something else must be going on if they were not voting or not burning the ballots.

Perhaps they had taken a multiday break for prayer and discussion. Perhaps it was something more menacing.

Dedicated groups of people still lingered in St. Peter's Square, waiting for white smoke. Many were journalists, but some of the faithful also stood sentry. Cable news channels remained around the clock; print media and broadcast correspondents came and went, chasing rumors that first spread throughout Rome and then around the world. One story opined that the voting had stopped because the leading candidate had died during the conclave and the cardinals were starting over. Another insinuated that someone had been elected, but the chosen cardinal refused to take the post. An international cable news show reported that because of the length of the conclave, the cardinals had decided to take several days off so that their minds could clear and they could regroup.

When Thursday came and went without any smoke from the blackened chimney above the sun-bleached, red-tiled chapel, the buzz in the piazza and on television and the Internet across the world reported possibilities even more sinister. Had voting stopped because the conclave had disintegrated into irreconcilable factions? Was this a sign of a schism? Was there evidence of serious wrongdoing or moral indiscretion on the part of one or more leading candidates?

Friday's morning headlines read "Cardinals in Disarray," "No Votes, No Pope," "Conclave Factionalized," and "Why No Smoke?"

No one on the outside had any idea what was going on inside the Sistine Chapel, and the Vatican media-relations office was unable to stem any of the rumors. Complicating matters, the cardinals had no idea what was being reported. They did not have access to any public media or private communications, pursuant to the rules of the conclave. Moreover, any cardinal who broke the code of secrecy or initiated contact with the outside world, without the unambiguous consent of the conclave, would be automatically excommunicated.

Now it was after noon on Friday, and there had been no signal from the chimney since eleven thirty Wednesday morning. The reporters in the piazza knew the rules; there should have been several additional ballots during this time, and at least four markers of smoke, be they black or white. Most media outlets appreciated that the peaceful and orderly replacement of a supreme monarch was not an insignificant task. Some reported it that way. However, others were not as generous.

At long last, Cardinal Venkatesan took all the ballots from the final vote, sprinkled them with the chemical ensuring the smoke would turn white, and put them in the sacred furnace in the Sistine Chapel. He lit them with a wooden match and then ignited the special canister. As soon as the smoke curled through the chimney, bells throughout Vatican City rang aloud. The Swiss Guards waited for this signal. The entire regiment immediately assembled and assumed their positions around St. Peter's Square in preparation for the new pope, who would march out onto the balcony of the celebrated basilica.

The message was loud and the message was clear. The Catholic Church had a new supreme leader. People throughout Rome hurried to the piazza to see the pontiff and receive his blessing. Tens of thousands swept into the square from every direction. Local radio and television stations and international cable news channels announced the Catholic Church had a new pope. Based on Meyer's strategic leaks, some news outlets reported the new head of the Roman Catholic Church might be an American. This news spread quickly, but Romans did not believe someone from the United States could possibly have been elected. Within an hour, CNN International suggested that the new pope might even be a layman.

For nearly 220 years, the Gammarelli family had made the pope's clothes in their small shop in downtown Rome. Prior to the commencement of the conclave so many weeks before, one of the Gammarellis had delivered three boxes of papal garments to the Vatican—a small, medium, and large—to ensure the correct size for the unknown pontiff. Each box contained a "zucchetto" or skullcap, two floor-length light ivory cassocks, a white sash with a gold border to go around the waist, a scarlet mozzetta, a mitre—a traditional pointed bishop's hat—and red leather shoes. One cassock was made of silk, the other wool with silk cuffs. The new pontiff was able to choose the size and fabric he wanted to wear. The mozzetta was a beautifully fashioned cape that fit over the shoulders to the elbow and buttoned in the center. Historically, the pope wore three versions of the mozzetta—scarlet satin for summer, scarlet velvet adorned with white ermine fur in winter, and white silk with white fur during the Easter season. Each was stunning, especially against the cassock. The Gammarellis, however, did not know that this pope would wear more humble vestments.

In a third-floor sacristy adjacent to a chapel in St. Peter's, James removed the dark beige business suit he'd worn throughout the day, chose the wool cassock, and decided not to wear either a mozzetta or a mitre. He didn't even consider the red shoes. Promptly at three, Cardinal Belosi bounded out onto the central balcony of St. Peter's, a small alcove situated three stories above and looking directly out at the piazza. With evident pride, he announced to the tens of thousands in the square, "*Habemus Papam*! We have a pope! He is James Flahvin from the United States of America. He shall be called Pope James."

There was thunderous applause and chanting. "*Viva il Papa, Viva il Papa, Viva il Papa.*"

James followed behind Belosi and stood in front of the chanting crowd. He looked out at the faces of faithful as they repeated the Italian mantra and applauded exuberantly. "This crowd is huge," he said to O'Bryan.

As he looked around at the mass of humanity below, he saw his family off to the left, near the front, and then Keegan, Meyer, and Cooper standing next to them. Tears streamed down his children's faces. He waved in their direction. He felt the warmth of the masses' affection and embraced the excitement.

As he glowed in the moment, he also sought to steady his bearings. They were not honoring him, he thought, as the din from the cheering and clapping continued. His election was not like that of a US president, in which the people roared their approval for someone they had selected. This applause was for the high office he now occupied. If he was to gain the people's support, he would have to earn it by relating to them on the things they all had in common—their humanness, their belief in Jesus the Christ, and their commitment to loving God and loving neighbor. An interpreter stood next to him, ready to translate his every word simultaneously through a microphone.

He blessed the crowd, tracing the sign of the cross over them.

"In the name of the Father, and of the Son, and of the Holy Spirit. Amen." He turned to his right and blessed them again, saying, "In the name of the Creator, the Savior, and the Sanctifier. Amen." He turned to his left, and a third time he traced the sign of the cross, saying, "In the name of Creation, in the name of Salvation, and in the name of Sanctification, you are blessed by Almighty God, maker of heaven and earth." The crowd fell completely silent.

"*Dio vi benedica*. God bless you all," he said. "I apologize that I do not speak Italian; but nor do I speak Kikongo, Thai, German, Polish, Kiswahili, Spanish, Chinese, Pilipino, Gallic, Tamil, Portuguese, Japanese, or any language other than English. Fortunately for me, English has become an international language." There was light laughter from the crowd.

"If you are looking for my name on the list of cardinals, you can stop now. You will not find me there. Two days ago, the College of Cardinals elected me pope of the Roman Catholic Church. They invited me to come to Rome. I flew from Chicago yesterday. Cardinal Belosi, the Vatican's secretary of state, asked me if I would agree to step into the shoes of the Fisherman. After prayer and reflection, I said yes. Today I was ordained a priest and a bishop. Then I came immediately to speak to you.

"You may be asking yourself, 'How can someone who is not a cardinal become pope?' Please believe me, I asked myself the same question. You may be asking, 'How can someone who is not learned in Scripture and theology become pope?' Please believe me, I asked the same question. You may be asking, 'How can someone who is not even a priest become pope?' I too asked that question.

"When I was a little boy, my mother told me, 'God works in mysterious ways.' Well, I tell you today, my election as pope is among those mysteries. What is not a mystery is that God calls each of us to serve others. We are obligated to answer God's call. Sometimes our call may seem indirect or puzzling, difficult to figure out or confusing. At other times, it hits us on the head like a brick falling from the sky. Regardless of how God calls us, we are obliged to answer. God calls each of us to love our brothers and sisters as well as our enemies. God calls us to serve those in need—the children, the abandoned, the destitute, the lonely, the sick, the elderly, the imprisoned, and all those who are placed in our path. Today, God has called me to serve God's people through the Church. I intend to answer that call to the best of my ability."

Enthusiastic applause interrupted him, and the crowd chanted again, *"Viva il Papa, Viva il Papa, Viva il Papa."*

"I am from Chicago, Illinois, in the United States of America. I grew up there. I was married there, raised a family there, and worked there. I will always be an American. However, now I am also a Roman. I want to assure you that I will not take the Vatican out of Rome. Nor will I take the Romans out of the Vatican." Again, there was spontaneous applause.

"Two years ago, my wife, Victoria, died. It was the saddest day of my life. I was alone for a while. Today I am no longer alone. Now I am yours." Again, vigorous applause reverberated across the square, and the chant, *"Viva il Papa, Viva il Papa, Viva il Papa"* continued for some minutes.

He finished by saying, "I ask you for one simple favor. Every day when you say your prayers, please include a prayer for me. I need your prayers and God's help. If you pray for me, God will answer your prayer. And I will pray for you. I pray today that the blessing of Almighty God, the Father, the Son, and the Holy Spirit, will descend on you and remain with you always." After gazing out at the enormous crowd for one last moment, James turned and disappeared into the basilica as the crowd roared with approval.

✳ ✳ ✳

James put on the simple vestments of an ordinary priest in preparation for his first Mass. He chose a green chasuble—a large, loose-fitting, sleeveless outer vestment worn by every priest at Mass. Many popes wore gold, gilt-edged, and highly ornate chasubles. This one was unadorned—emphatically plain, as he had requested.

Closing his eyes, he prayed to God for help in this new role. He placed a green and white stole around his neck so that it hung over his shoulders and down the front of his torso. Sitting down on a worn, straight-backed wooden chair, he reviewed the book appropriately titled *How to Say Mass*, which O'Bryan had assured him would make him "look like a pro."

James understood the importance of the Mass to the Catholic faithful. It was the primary worship service, celebrated in hundreds of thousands of churches all over the world every day. The book divided the Mass into two parts—the Liturgy of the Word and the Liturgy of the Eucharist. Even though he'd had sixteen years of Catholic education, James did not recall that the Liturgy of the Word was taken from the rituals of the Jewish worship service performed in synagogues more than two thousand years ago. Of course, he knew that the Liturgy of the Eucharist recreated the Last Supper.

As he prepared, Swiss Guards ushered preselected bishops, priests, brothers, and sisters into St. Peter's Basilica, interspersed in the pews with the College of Cardinals. Common folk filled nearly half the church, some plucked from the square where he had just spoken. Within minutes, the enormous medieval church was completely filled. The people waited in exhilarated anticipation for this historic event. His children and grandchildren sat near the front, looking around wide-eyed at the great church in rapt amazement.

At three forty-five, the church bells rang. A parade of eleven cardinals processed from the left side of the Basilica up the center isle to the sanctuary. The cardinals were dressed in all their splendor—each in scarlet cassocks, elaborately adorned white lace surplices, and white linen mitres each embroidered with their individual and unique coat of arms. Several steps behind, a tall, unpretentious-looking priest, in plain green and white vestments and wearing a white skullcap, followed. The entire church rose, and stayed standing, as they tried to get a glimpse of the new pope.

Cardinal Belosi announced in a loud, clear voice, "It is my high honor and great privilege to present to you the Bishop of Rome and the Supreme Pontiff of the Holy Roman Catholic Church, James I."

James moved to the center of the altar and motioned them to sit down, although more than half decided to kneel. He began Mass as any priest would, but he felt way outside his comfort zone. Even Cardinal O'Bryan's book and the fact he had attended at least three thousand Masses during his life did not offer him confidence or reassurance. He stumbled several times and frequently lost his place in the "easy-to-read" manual. He knew he looked like anything but a "pro."

After he read the Gospel for this day, he stepped away from the pulpit and walked directly into the area of the pews where the people were sitting. Now, this was where he was comfortable—speaking directly to people in his own words and voice. He had a strong voice that carried a great distance, but in this venue, he used a wireless mic attached to his vestments, due to the huge church being just too large. A translator stood at the elevated pulpit and spoke into a microphone, providing simultaneous translation in Italian.

"For most of my life, people have called me Jimmy," he started. "I guess now I will be called James. That's what my mother called me—especially when I was in trouble." There were broad, affirming smiles and laughter from the crowd.

"I won't tell you much detail about who I am or my background. I suspect the media will provide all that information over the next few days. However, I hope you will not believe everything you hear or read, whether it be good or bad. The good men and women in the media sometimes get things wrong," he said as he flashed his twinkling eyes toward the PR execs.

"I can tell you this. I was born in a suburb of Chicago, Illinois. I was raised in an Irish-American Catholic family. I attended Catholic grade school, high school, and university. My mother and father, and the Servite Sisters and Christian Brothers, taught me the Gospel, my values, and the love of God and his Son, Jesus the Christ. My parents were parents like many of you. My teachers were sisters and brothers, just like those of you here today. These men and women imprinted a profound and indelible mark upon who I am. That may be all you need to know about me.

"The most important thing these good people taught me was that the purpose of life is to serve others. That is what Jesus teaches each of us throughout Scripture: Love God. Love your neighbor. Love your enemies. Help those in need. Care for the sick." Looking directly at Father Keegan, he continued, "Visit the imprisoned. Share what you have with others. Do to others as you would have them do to you. It is not a complicated message. It is something each of us can do. It is not easy at times, but it's not complicated. It is doable.

"My only prayer is that during the time I walk in the shoes of the Fisherman, we, all of us together, will serve God's people as fully as we are asked. I believe God asks us to devote our talents to primarily three tasks. First, to protect the vulnerable and those in need, especially children. Second, to eliminate the false divisions that separate God's people. Third, to spread the message and Word of Jesus the Christ."

The people in the pews sat in rapt attention. Many of the cardinals, bishops, priests, nuns, and brothers were awed by the clarity of his message and the simplicity of his words. Some of those who had not voted for him were inspired by his homily, but most of Sicoli's supporters were not impressed. To them James I was one of, if not the most, egregious errors the Roman Catholic Church had ever encountered.

"It's helpful if we see what's before us in context," James continued. "This papacy is one of hundreds. Each pope is the successor to Peter. Each is accountable to God. I am number two hundred sixty-nine. I suspect there will be at least two hundred sixty-nine more—perhaps two hundred sixty-nine times two hundred sixty-nine. Therefore, this will not be the reign of James, as some might characterize it. This papacy will simply be an attempt by one more man to do his best. In community with all the faithful, I will work to ensure that the church Jesus built on the Rock will continue to fulfill its reign.

"In order to do that, I will need your help and your prayers. I ask each of you to pray for me every day. Ask God to grant me wisdom, so I will know what I am called to do. Ask God to grant me strength, so I will be able to do what God wants me to do. And ask God to bestow upon me grace, so that I'll be able to do well that which I am to do."

He turned and walked back to the altar. Resuming where he had left off, he followed his manual as best he could, paragraph by paragraph, but he repeated one entire prayer and unintentionally skipped over another. "This is going to take some time getting used to," he thought to himself.

After the consecration of the bread and wine, he paused for several moments. He was in complete wonderment that through the power of God, he had just turned simple bread and wine into the body and blood of Jesus the Christ. He closed his eyes and prayed he would never become complacent about this miracle of miracles. He then said the essential prayer of offering that followed, but modified the script when it came to the Lord's Prayer. He led the congregation in the traditional prayer as recorded in the Gospel of Matthew, but concluded it in a way not very familiar to Catholics.

Our father, who art in Heaven, hallowed be Thy name. Thy Kingdom come, Thy will be done, on earth as it is in heaven. Give us this day our daily bread, and forgive us our trespasses, as we forgive those who trespass against us. And lead us not into temptation, but deliver us from evil. For Thine is the Kingdom, the Power, and the Glory, now and forever. Amen.

Many in the church did not know how to react. The Catholic pope had just prayed what many considered the Protestant version of the Lord's Prayer. He anticipated some consternation, so he looked out upon the people, remained silent for a moment, and then said in his loud, booming voice, "If we are to eliminate the false divisions that separate God's people, we first must learn to pray together. By adopting this version of the Lord's Prayer, we begin our journey to pray together. While we honor Catholic tradition and culture, Scripture teaches that Jesus prayed that we all be united."

The Lord's Prayer was a symbolic gesture because Catholics did pray this doxology, the final stanza of the Lord's Prayer. However, Catholics prayed the words, *"For Thine is the Kingdom, the Power, and the Glory, now and forever"* after the priest first invoked an interlude. By saying this most important Christian prayer as Protestants did, an unmistakable message was sent that this papacy would be unlike any other in recent history. And it confirmed among his adversaries that this man was dangerous.

James took his first meal as pope with the College of Cardinals. While eating, he asked each cardinal to introduce himself by name, country, and religious title, and to describe what he considered the most formidable challenge facing the Church today. Each responded in turn. They identified many difficulties, burdens, and concerns confronting the Church. The issues most often raised were the acute financial instability and uncertainty from the local parish all the way to the Vatican, the severe shortage of priests, and the growing lack of confidence in the Church among Catholics around the world. James personally took copious notes as each cardinal spoke, intending to make it clear to all in attendance that he would be fully engaged in helping resolve the ills of the Church. When dinner ended, he thanked them for their candid and reflective responses.

James retired to a spacious suite in the Santa Marta, which had been tastefully prepared for the new pope. There he met with his children, his brothers and sister, Greg Keegan, and Mike Maloney. They were all overwhelmed by the events of the day, not fully comprehending that their father, brother, and friend was now the supreme leader of their church, the largest religious institution on earth. Although suffering from jet lag, they reminisced late into the night, telling wonderful stories about Vicky, growing up with an international lawyer dad, the challenges of attending Catholic schools, the delights of living in a Chicago suburb, the tribulations of being a Cubs baseball fan, and their unbounded love for Grandma and Grandpa. Some tales were witty, humorous, and entertaining—others more tender, stirring, and inspirational. They laughed, they cried, they hugged—and they laughed some more. They consumed several bottles of fine Italian Primitivo red wine before they ended this joy-filled and memorable evening.

Earlier that day, on the other side of the Atlantic, Chicago reporters had descended on the Willis Tower in hopes of interviewing someone from Jimmy Flahvin's law firm. It seemed like every local journalist in the city showed up, as did stringers for CNN, BBC, ABC, CBS, NBC, FOX, and NPR. Worldwide media wanted to know everything about this first-in-a-millennia lay-pope and the first ever pontiff from the United States.

Meanwhile, the Vatican Information Service was inundated with media requests. Thousands of reporters and media outlets from throughout Europe, Africa, Asia, and the Americas asked to be credentialed, and it quickly became apparent to the Vatican staff that this number of journalists was beyond their management capability. Although initially miffed that an American PR agency had been called in to help do what they had done effectively for decades, and had successfully managed for two new popes just within the previous year, they became sincerely grateful for Meyer's and Cooper's assistance as they quickly discovered this pope was quite different.

Cardinals O'Bryan and Schmidt were offered up for interviews, and the Information Service reluctantly agreed to include the pope's family members and former law partners as secondary possibilities, as the media pros had suggested. Meyer, for her part, coached the family and James's former law partners to answer questions by telling real but positive stories about Jimmy Flahvin.

"Even though you know Pope James is a great man, there will be plenty of people who will want to tear him down," Meyer instructed. "Modern-day popes are often treated like political figures, even though we prefer to consider them as the most prominent religious leader. You will need to tell the best stories possible. Nothing negative—his opponents will take care of that. They have to be true stories; you cannot make stuff up. If the media catch you in a lie or making stuff up, they will rip you apart and make the pope's life miserable.

"You offer the world its first look at our new pope. As the old saying states so well, 'You don't get a second chance to make a first impression.' Go do him proud."

His daughter, Mary, was interviewed on CNN. "Our mom died two years ago, and, as you can imagine, it was a really difficult time for all of us," she reported. "But when Mom was first diagnosed with terminal pancreatic cancer, Dad told her he would stay by her side every day until the end. And he did. The doctors gave Mom six months to live, and during those last few months, Dad took her to the cancer clinic, bought her medicines, cooked her food, bathed her, dressed her, read her Scripture, and prayed with her every day. During that entire six months, he went to his law office only four times and worked for only an hour or two each of those days. We were all very proud of Mom, and the grace she showed throughout her illness and death. But we were absolutely amazed at the love, commitment, and dedication Dad showed to Mom throughout all her life, but especially during those last six months."

The *New York Times* wrote about James's law practice and quoted his law partner, David Levin. "Jimmy is a remarkable lawyer and an even more remarkable business partner. He is absolutely dedicated to our clients and the integrity of the law. In thirty years, he never took a sick day, until a couple of years ago when his wife, Vicky, was dying of cancer. Other than annual family vacations and weekends, he was always there, every day working hard, serving our clients."

NBC's Today Show interviewed Matt Flahvin. The host asked Matt what the new pope was like as a father. "Dad was always there for us kids, always available, even when he was traveling," Matt said. "I remember when I was about nine and dad was in France on business. Mom was out grocery shopping, so I called him on his cell phone and asked him if I could go to my friend Tommy's house. Dad asked if Tommy's parents were home and how long I'd be gone. After I answered appropriately, he said, 'That's fine, Matt. Just make sure you tell your mother I said it was OK.' Then Dad told me that there was a seven-hour time difference between where he was and where I was, so he was on his way to dinner. When Mom got home, I told her that Dad said I could go to Tommy's. She said, with a tone that made me think she did not believe me, 'Your father is in Paris, Matthew.' I said, I know, I just called him. She exclaimed, 'You called your father in France to ask him if you could go to Tommy's?' And I said, 'No. I called Dad on his cell phone and he just happened to be in France.' We kids never thought it was anything unusual to call Dad anywhere or anytime. He always responded in a loving and caring way, no matter how many time zones away."

James's friends, colleagues, and family offered the world an intimate portrait of this layman who had just become pope. The people liked what they heard. Editorials in several US newspapers asserted how wonderful it was to have an American pope. *Newsweek, US News and World Report, People*, and *Time Magazine* all put him on their covers and wrote flattering accounts of his life. European, Asian, and African journals also wrote lengthy and encouraging stories.

However, just as Cynthia Meyer had predicted, not every commentator was so gracious or positive. The *Wall Street Journal* argued that any man who refused to fight for his country was unfit to be the leader of the Catholic Church. A former law firm employee alleged to a *Chicago Tribune* reporter that Flahvin had fired her unfairly when he was the firm's managing partner. Some conservative Catholics criticized him for refusing to wear official papal garments, not sitting on the papal throne, and saying a Protestant prayer.

It was not long before the gossip grew even more sordid. A caller on a US national radio talk show claimed he had known Jimmy Flahvin in college and insisted he often drank until he was so drunk he could not walk or talk straight. A woman called in on a similar radio show and alleged she'd had sex with Jimmy on several occasions. "Was this recent?" the show's host asked.

"Oh, no, we were in our twenty's; it was before he was married," the woman replied. "But he led me to believe that we were gonna get married, and then he dumped me without so much as a good-bye. He's not a nice man."

James let Cynthia worry about the press. He understood the role of the media. Every public figure was treated the same. He could not expect to be dealt with any differently.

Chapter Eight

"**W**hy would anyone want to kill me?" James asked the commander of the Swiss Guard, somewhat naïvely.

"There have been death threats made against many pontiffs over the centuries; it's just that in your case the numbers are much greater," Colonel Lukas Meire explained.

"Do you think they're real?"

"We take them all very serious," Meire replied.

"Is there anything I can do to help lower the probability?"

"Every significant leader on the planet today is exposed to possible assassination. We will protect you. You can help us by doing what we recommend."

"This is a bit disconcerting," he confided to Belosi as the meeting ended. "I didn't anticipate this."

Historically, papal inaugurations were lavish affairs. However, James's instructions were to make this observance as simple as possible, knowing that simplicity was rare in papal rites. This elaborate, time-honored religious ceremony was filled with joyful song, chanted prayer, and magnificent regalia. As is the case with all papal rituals, sacred tradition dictated the magnitude, scope, and formality of the celebrated event. So he had decided not to make any major waves about the traditions of the ceremony, given the early stage in his papacy. However, as he had done at his ordination, he rejected the usual glistening, gold-trimmed royal papal robes and throne. Instead, he wore a light ivory cassock with a wide white, silk waistband, an ivory mozzetta, a clerical collar, a wooden pectoral crucifix, polished black wingtip shoes, and a white skullcap. He chose to stand throughout the service.

The entire College of Cardinals remained in Vatican City for the solemn observance. On the day of the inauguration, dignitaries from across the planet—presidents, kings, queens, prime ministers, senators, governors, business executives, international lawyers, United Nations officials, and bishops, priests, sisters, and brothers, as well as prominent leaders of several Protestant denominations—filled St. Peter's Basilica. Several Jewish rabbis and the imam from the Grand Mosque in Rome also attended. To the dismay of some members of the Curia, James reserved half the seating in the famous church for common folk and the poor. In addition, tens of thousands of faithful stood outside in the piazza. Every major news outlet was present with cameras rolling, devices recording, and writers chronicling.

The following day, James was shown his residence on the fifth floor of the Apostolic Palace, a sixteenth-century baroque structure within a short walking distance from St. Peter's. Michelangelo's biblical frescos covered the ceilings, and multihued rugs cushioned the floor. It was a splendid Vatican City residence, but James found it cold and medieval— not a place where he'd want to live. He understood why Pope Francis had decided to stay at the Santa Marta. As he strolled through the urban gardens and parks of Vatican City, magnificently designed with fountains and sculptures, he discovered a vacant two-bedroom apartment in a secluded area on the west end near the heliport. James asked to have the dwelling repainted in simple earth tones and carpeted in dark brown. It became a comfortable home with a well-equipped kitchen where he often prepared his own meals. In the living room, he had a large flat-screen television installed so he could watch the Chicago Bears and the Cubbies play on the satellite sports channel. The study offered a relaxing space where he read and wrote. He turned the second bedroom into a small chapel to meditate and pray. He enjoyed living next to his nonclerical neighbors—Vatican employees—and their children.

✳ ✳ ✳

"Good evening, Your Holiness," Maria Lopez, a well-known CNN celebrity-journalist, started her televised interview.

"Please, just call me Pope James."

"Let me start with the most basic question. How does a layman, a lawyer from Chicago, become pope?"

"The news media has reported on this quite extensively and mostly accurately. Any baptized man can be elected pope. However, how I was personally elected is still mystifying to me."

"What did you think when the cardinals of the Catholic Church asked you to become pope?"

"Words cannot capture the extent of my thoughts and emotions. However, I have been comforted in the knowledge that God works in mysterious ways," he responded.

"Are you saying God selected you to be pope?" she asked.

"The Church teaches that all of us are called by God. The Creator asks each of us to serve our brothers and sisters through love and justice. I believe the Holy Spirit inspired the cardinals to select a pope outside their numbers. For reasons I cannot explain, they elected me."

"The Vatican reports that the cardinals met for eleven weeks, but they could not agree on a single candidate. Apparently, they split their votes among several cardinals, with no one receiving the two-thirds required. The rumor is that Cardinal O'Bryan nominated you. Do you know if that is true, and if so, why he did that?"

"You'll have to ask Cardinal O'Bryan those questions."

"I interviewed Cardinal O'Bryan. He would not confirm that he put your name into the running, but he did say there was broad understanding that the next pope was not among the one hundred twenty cardinals assembled. He also told me that he knew you quite well, and that he had worked with you on several Church-related projects. He distinctly remembered how impressed he was when you first met and how his admiration grew over the years. He said you had all the qualities of being a great pope except you were not a priest. I asked him if he ever thought that you, as a layman, would be elected pope. He said no. Does it bother you that he didn't expect you to be elected?"

"Not at all. For more than one thousand years, every pope has come from among cardinals and bishops. It should not surprise anyone that the cardinals did not expect to elect a layman."

"Our information is very limited. We do not know who or how your name was put into consideration, or how many ballots it took before you were elected. After your name was read as one of those for whom a vote was cast, it has been reported that many of the cardinals asked, 'Who is this man?' Then our information runs dry. We do not know any more after that. What else do you know?"

"The conclave is a confidential proceeding, much like an executive session of a US congressional committee. What goes on behind those closed doors is seldom known. I know very little of what happened during that time. What I do know, I cannot report. I've agreed to honor the confidentiality of those proceedings," James said.

"There have been reports that you are an unlikely candidate for pope—"

"The most unlikely of all."

"Yes, the most unlikely. There are allegations that as a young man you drank alcohol to excess, had many female companions—"

James interrupted again. "I've committed many sins throughout my life. Yet the Holy Spirit inspired the cardinals to elect me pope. That is a message of hope for all sinners. However, it is not a license to sin. It's a message that shows every sinner can repent and be saved. I have repented and continue to repent for my sins. God forgives me."

"Pope James, many Catholics are reported to be very concerned about a layperson being pope. What do you say to them?"

"St. Peter was a layperson, and he was the first pope. I do not suggest that I possess the qualities of Peter. Yet Jesus did select a layman to lead his church two thousand years ago. So I don't think we should be afraid of a layperson leading the Church today."

"You were married for many years; what is your position on married priests?" Lopez asked.

"There has been a long tradition of celibacy among the clergy in the Catholic Church. However, Peter was a married man, as were many of the early Church leaders. I assume there will be substantial conversation about this issue. My personal view is that God calls some of those among us to become a priest, sister, or brother. Church law should not get in the way of God's calling."

"Are you saying you support the concept of married priests?" she pressed.

"There will be plenty of time for consideration of that issue. All I am saying is that God calls each of us. The Church should not interfere with anyone's calling."

"Birth control is another issue the Church has dealt with over the past several decades. What is your view on that?"

"Life is sacred because God creates life. We must always honor that. The questions I pose to the Church are these: Which is the greater sin—a destitute married couple with five children living in abject poverty in a developing country, using birth control, or a wealthy couple with no children, using birth control? Which is the greater sin—a husband who has HIV giving the disease to his wife, or using a condom to protect her?"

"You suggest you pose that question to the Church, but as pope, aren't you the Church?" she queried.

"The People of God are the Church," he replied. "The priests, bishops, and pope are merely God's instruments in service to God's people."

"What about homosexuality?" she asked.

"The Church has a long-standing opposition to homosexual behavior. However, my father taught me not to judge others, even when we may think others are committing bad behavior. As Pope Francis asked, 'Who are we to judge?' Further, my mother taught me to love everyone. Consequently, I believe we cannot discriminate against homosexuals or treat homosexuals differently than we do heterosexuals. St. Paul says we are all sinners. The Church accepts the basic proposition that sinfulness is part of the human condition. That is true for heterosexuals and homosexuals. The Church must not discriminate against homosexuals based upon what they do in their private lives. What we do or don't do in our private lives is for God to judge."

"Are you suggesting homosexual behavior is the same as heterosexual behavior?"

"I'm only suggesting that it's important to recognize God creates homosexuals and heterosexuals. Straight or gay, we are all children of God. And every child of God is a precious gift. As Christians, we must respect the intrinsic dignity of every person."

"But the Church does not treat homosexuals the same as heterosexuals when it comes to marriage. Are you proposing that be changed?"

"Marriage is a sacrament of the Church. It is a sign of the sacred. Marriage is a public statement about the loving union of a woman and a man collaborating with the Creator as they conceive and raise children. Homosexuals cannot receive the sacrament of holy matrimony because it is not possible for homosexuals to collaborate with God in the process of creation."

"But the Church doesn't just deny gays and lesbians the right to marry; the Church also opposes all forms of homosexual civil unions. Why should the Church try to impose its religious beliefs on the public through government entities?" she pressed.

"The Church has supported laws that are consistent with the teachings of Jesus the Christ. That is why she opposes capital punishment and abortion. However, I believe the Church exerts greater influence when she teaches the Word of God and encourages men and women to live out the Word. That is more effective than attempting to impose the Word. I don't believe it's helpful to expend limited resources trying to counter every law that is contrary to the Word."

"How does that affect homosexual marriage?"

"The Church reserves the sacrament of holy matrimony for the union of a woman and a man. However, if a government authorizes contracts between individuals that some call civil unions or civil marriage, the Church need not oppose that law. There is a major difference between marriages blessed by the Church and civil unions created by the state."

"Do you see one of your goals as pope to convert people to Catholicism?" she asked.

"Conversion?" James smiled widely. "Oh, no, conversion is God's job. Our job is to love our neighbors and our enemies. To love God above all else. We are to follow the teachings of Jesus. Live the Gospel. And help lift people out of poverty and despair. We do this by working to ensure that everyone has the opportunity to realize the fullness of their God-given potential."

"Some have called the pope the Antichrist. What do you say to them?"

James chuckled briefly. "I am not the Antichrist. Jesus the Christ is my Lord and Savior."

"Do you pray often?" she asked.

"I pray a whole lot more now than I used to."

"There are reports that there have been many threats on your life. Can you confirm those reports?"

"I've recently come to understand that threats go with the territory of belief and leadership. I pray for and forgive those who might threaten or injure me. Jesus taught us to love our enemies and to do good to those who would harm us. So I pray for those who might wish me harm."

"Does it frighten you that people out there want to kill you?"

"It is disconcerting—we all want to live a long life, don't we? But a life worth living is a life worth dying for. When I die, I will join the Creator, the Savior, and the Sanctifier in life eternal. Life is a gift from God. However, I do not fear any person who might want to take my life. All of us can enjoy life eternal. Just love God, love your neighbor, love your enemy, repent for your sins, and do as Jesus teaches."

"Are you suggesting that anyone can get to heaven—that you don't have to be Catholic?" she asked, incredulous.

James hesitated a moment, then he replied. "In Matthew, Jesus teaches that to attain eternal life, there are some things we should not do. Do not kill. Do not steal. Do not commit adultery. Do not bear false witness. He also identifies things we should do. Honor our father and mother. Love our neighbor as our self. Feed and clothe the poor. Welcome strangers to our homes. Visit the sick and imprisoned. Love our enemies. Rid ourselves of worldly distractions.

"St. John writes that whoever believes in God shall have eternal life. So if you believe and do the Lord's work, you will have life eternal. But there are many roads. Only God gets to determine who is saved."

"So you don't have to be Catholic to get to heaven?" Lopez pressed. James smiled again.

"There is an old story about a Jew, a Protestant, and a Muslim who all died together in a car accident. When they arrived at the gates of heaven, St. Peter welcomed them and showed them around. As they were touring, they saw a massive wall. One of them asked St. Peter, 'What's that wall for?' Peter responded, 'Oh, that's where the Catholics are. They think they're the only ones up here.'"

Lopez started to laugh and then caught herself. Had the Catholic pope just told a joke about Catholics, she wondered. She didn't know how to respond, so she simply concluded the interview. "Thank you, Your Holiness," she said, and then corrected herself. "Ah, Pope James."

Several staff and clergy had watched the interview on monitors just outside the taping room. As he walked out, Cardinal Sicoli approached him, smiling; but his grip on James's arm told a different story. He pulled James into an alcove.

"We're not going to change two thousand years of tradition just because you have an agenda to push. Married priests? Out of the question. The Church will never permit it. Artificial birth control is now and always has been a mortal sin. There are not different levels of sin based upon the circumstances of the sinner. Homosexual marriage is an abomination because all homosexuality is objectively disordered."

The pope listened calmly as Sicoli stated his litany of objections. When he finished, James asked, "Cardinal Sicoli, are you available to come to my office tomorrow morning at eight thirty?"

"No," he responded, "I have Mass at eight."

"Then be in my office at nine."

Sister Rosalie, the papal secretary, buzzed the pope on his phone. "Cardinal Sicoli is here to see you." It was 9:08 a.m. Ten minutes later James told Sister Rosalie to show the cardinal in. The papal office was a room Sicoli had visited hundreds of times during the reigns of previous popes. He was quite comfortable in this space, unlike many others who often entered with trepidation. Nevertheless, he immediately recognized the layout had changed considerably. The large, ornate cherrywood desk was gone, as were the two white guest chairs that sat facing the Holy Father's desk. The comfortable white leather couches in the sitting area were also absent. In their place sat six brown leather chairs encircling a round marble-top table, all set atop a muted Persian rug in front of the fireplace. A large, dark walnut cross—not a crucifix—hung on one wall, and a collage of family photos filled another.

James watched Sicoli take it all in.

"Sit down, Cardinal," he said. Sicoli took his time choosing a seat, and then in due course sat down.

"Cardinal Sicoli, you and every other cardinal may come to this office at any time to express your concerns about what I say or do. But if you ever criticize or instruct me in public again, you will no longer wear the cardinal's cassock or reside in Vatican City."

"I just wanted you to know the correct position of the Church on some very controversial issues that you raised during your television interview," Sicoli said. "Which, I hasten to add, was unprecedented in itself."

"Allow me to repeat myself so there is no misunderstanding," he said. "I invite you and every other cardinal to speak to me in private about any concerns you may have about me or how I am conducting the papacy. However, if you publicly criticize me again, you will be reassigned as a parish priest outside the walls of Vatican City. That is all." The pope stood up. After a brief moment's hesitation, Sicoli got up and left the room.

As he walked down the hall, Sicoli raged. "How could this lawyer—this *American*—have the audacity to speak to an esteemed cardinal that way?" he thought to himself. "Having the legal authority to do something was one thing; but the nerve to be so brazen, especially to a member of the Curia leadership, who has faithfully and honorably served the Church for so long, was beyond the bounds of all Church decorum."

Later that day, the pope asked Sister Rosalie to invite every cardinal and bishop who was in Rome to a meeting the following morning in the Hall of the Pontifical Audiences. More than two hundred cardinals and bishops were already in the conference room when James entered. All rose.

"Good morning, everyone," James said once everyone was seated. "Thank you for coming on short notice. I need your advice. Cardinal Sicoli has advised me that it is inappropriate for me to raise the possibility of married priests. He says that is something the Church will never permit. I want to know what you think."

There was prolonged silence. Many had heard about Sicoli confronting the Holy Father after the television interview, but they felt uncomfortable being asked about a colleague and a senior member of the Curia in such a public forum. After nearly a minute, Cardinal Tamborino from Puglia broke the quiet and said meekly, "The Church has a long and cherished tradition of celibate priests."

Cardinal Bērziņš of Latvia quickly added, "However, the Church has ordained married men throughout the centuries, and there are several hundred married priests serving today in the Latin Rite due to specific and unique circumstances. And of course there are many married priests in the Eastern Rite."

"My question is quite straightforward," James said. "Is Cardinal Sicoli correct when he says, 'The Church will never permit married men to be ordained priests'?"

Again, there was no response.

Then Cardinal DeLuca rose and said, "Perhaps Cardinal Sicoli was simply stating that it would be better for the Church if priests were never allowed to be married."

"Perhaps," James responded. "But that is not how I understood his words."

Eventually, Cardinal Rodriguez spoke up. "Your Holiness, the question you pose seems illogical because only you have the authority to decide if married men will be ordained or not."

Bishop Garcia from Mexico City stood. "In our archdiocese, as in most archdioceses throughout the world, we have many deacons who are married men. We are prepared to ordain these men priests if and when the Holy Father authorizes them to receive the sacrament of Holy Orders."

Cardinal O'Faolain added, "Many of us would welcome the opportunity to ordain married men, especially given the shortage of priests throughout the world."

The pope's question was answered, and all in the room understood the penalty for publicly challenging this pope.

James reviewed his e-mails in his office at the Papal Palace. Then he celebrated eight o'clock Mass in an unimposing chapel, which was packed with clergy, Vatican City staff, Romans, and tourists. Without any notes, he delivered a succinct homily based on the Scripture reading of the day, incorporating the themes of service to others and love of the Creator. After Mass, he had a full schedule with meetings regarding Church finance and administration, international matters, promotions of priests to bishop and bishops to cardinal, and human and economic development in the poorest areas of the world. This had become his daily routine, although he also held audiences with world leaders, celebrities, major donors, pilgrims, and children. Youngsters from all over the world came to see him at the Vatican, and he never disappointed them. Sometimes he would spend an hour or more with a group of youth just visiting, singing, praying, and telling stories.

It was not long in this new role before Jimmy realized that he had not fully grasped the loneliness that accompanied the job. He grieved deeply for his wife, although that would have been the case wherever he might have been. Her death had left a gaping void in his heart and his whole being. That emptiness would not be filled by anyone. Still, what he had not calculated was how much he would miss regular contact with his adult children. Although his relationship was different with each, he missed them equally. Not being able to regularly enjoy their company left a deep chasm.

Moreover, he longed for his former life. He yearned for his home, where he and Vicky had raised their children and where she had died. He often thought about his law partners and the work in which he had been engaged for so many years. He missed his neighborhood, the local restaurants, the drive into the city, the walks along Lake Michigan, the serenity of the city parks, the congestion along the freeways, the comfort of living in the space he had known for more than thirty years, and time that was his and his alone.

And he had no friends in Rome. Cardinals O'Bryan and Schmidt had returned to their archdioceses in New York and Chicago, Keegan had gone home to St. Paul, and Maloney was back in Chicago with Schmidt. He enjoyed the interaction with his personal staff, but they were not friends. They could not fill the void. Nothing consoled his aching soul and pained heart. He concluded he had chosen a life of complete desolation—one in which he would always be active and engaged, but never serene, happy, or at peace. The mental and emotional anguish overwhelmed him. This was a torture he had never before experienced— self-inflicted and emotionally crushing.

He found himself medicating the pain with his only reliable friend— Chivas Regal scotch. After long days of meetings, speeches, worship services, and presentations, he would retire to his apartment and pour himself a tumbler of scotch on the rocks. On many evenings, one glass led to a second and too often a third. He tried to soothe his anguish with some of the finest liquor made. But no matter how much he drank, he never escaped isolation and sadness.

If he had that third scotch, in the morning he'd often be hung over. His body would ache from the debilitating effects of the booze. The headaches were the worst part; his skull would throb with raw pain. He did not drink every day, not even every week, and he never drank when he was travelling—only in the confines of his small apartment in the smallest city-state on the planet. But when he did have that second and third drink, he always woke up the next morning feeling the same way. He swore to himself that he would imbibe less so the hangovers would be less intense, only to discover that after he took the first drink, he no longer cared about the quantity.

CHAPTER NINE

"**W**hat if the evil one had infiltrated the conclave?" Sicoli mused. "What if there were among the cardinals those who were weak, those who had allowed the evil one in? What if the temporal and spiritual enemies of the Church had orchestrated the unprecedented number of ballots? What if the prince of darkness had outsmarted the cardinals into believing that this American imposter was the salvation of the Church, when in fact he was chosen to destroy the Church? What if there was a conspiracy among the evil one and unfaithful cardinals? And what an enormous success for evil itself if the prince of darkness was responsible for the selection of the leader of the Roman Catholic Church."

Manoles Cardinal Sicoli was a proud man, but he was also a dedicated servant to the Roman Catholic Church. Although considered an ultraconservative, he loved the Church and was willing to sacrifice everything to protect her, including his reputation and his life. Sicoli was well aware of past conclaves electing men who had not been sufficiently qualified to be pope and the subsequent serious harm they had brought to the Church. Church history lamentably acknowledged popes who had been a disgrace to the Chair of Peter. Some had allegedly consorted with mistresses during their pontificate, while others had been suspected of having male lovers. One had even held the throne at three different times. However, the election of Jimmy Flahvin was far more damaging than simply electing an incompetent or a degenerate. This conclave had elected someone who was ineligible to be pope. Sicoli had concluded Flahvin was not legitimate; he did not possess the right to the unbroken, lawful succession to the shoes of the Fisherman.

In quiet conversation, in places where he could not be overheard, and only with those he knew well, Sicoli carefully broached the subject.

"So what are your thoughts about the conclave electing a layman?" Sicoli would ask with apparent innocence. If the reply tended to be positive or neutral, he listened, and then changed the subject. However, when his question elicited a negative response, he probed further.

"Do you think the cardinals had the authority to elect a layman? Doesn't two thousand years of tradition electing only members of the clergy prohibit the election of a layman? How could it be possible to elect someone who is ineligible to be elected? Who would want to undermine the very foundations of the Church by putting an illegitimate on the throne? What force would have the power to thwart the inviolability of the Church through the actions of men?"

Through these efforts, Sicoli identified four cardinals, nearly a dozen bishops, and a cadre of young priests who were equally incensed by Flahvin's election. He met with them individually and in small groups. "Flahvin has already moved the Church to the left and thus, by definition, toward sin," he proclaimed during one of the meetings, deriding Flahvin's organizational pronouncements and calls for ecumenism.

"Requiring the Protestant version of the Lord's Prayer is disgraceful," one of Sicoli's lieutenants declared.

"The talk of married priests and birth control is beyond the pale," Cardinal De Luca stressed.

"Equating homosexuality with heterosexuality is an abomination," a young priest contended.

"Flahvin's lack of commitment to promoting conversion to Catholicism, and suggesting those who were not baptized in the Church could enter heaven is frightening, and it greatly angers me," a bishop asserted.

The more they reflected on the events of the conclave and contemplated the potential disaster for the Church, the more they questioned

Flahvin's right to be pope, and whether the forces of evil had played a role in this convoluted and illegal election.

"The prince of darkness and his band of evil angels are powerful creatures whose main purpose is to lure the faithful away from the Church," Sicoli avowed emphatically. "Life itself is a struggle between good and evil—a war that the lord of evil is intent on winning. The evil one conscripts the weak, even those claiming to be committed and faithful."

Sicoli ranted and raved to his sympathetic audiences. "Liberal thinking in the Church toys with the boundaries of good and evil. Abortion, homosexuality, birth control, premarital sex, and adultery represent evil incarnate, and the liberals are all too ready to cozy up to those who advocate these abominations. Now they have their man on Peter's throne. The outcome will be disastrous."

Sicoli grew obsessed by the thought that the conclave may have elected an Antichrist. "St. John writes of those who would be Antichrists—the deceivers who deny 'Jesus Christ has come in the flesh,' and those who do not 'abide in the teaching of Christ, but go beyond it.' St. Paul uses the terms 'man of sin' and 'son of perdition' to describe these people. True believers can identify the Antichrists by their actions—they sit in the temple, claim divine authority, espouse heresy, perform fake miracles, and do all types of sinful deeds. That describes this American lawyer precisely.

"Whoever exhibits these characteristics is evil incarnate. True believers are unconditionally obligated to rid the world of their wickedness. It is the Christian's duty to purify the Temple of the Holy Spirit of iniquity. It is our duty!"

The more they met and discussed, the greater their indignation and outrage grew. Many of Sicoli's followers also concluded Flahvin was an Antichrist—the Son of Perdition. Still, they were disheartened by their unanswered question: What could they do? This was out of their hands. The College of Cardinals had voted.

Chapter Ten

"**D**ispatches from dioceses throughout the Americas and Europe report the number of people attending Mass has increased significantly," an aide to Cardinal Martinelli reported. "And the collection plate is up as well. In some places attendance and contributions have increased by over fifty percent."

"That's very good news," Cardinal Martinelli, the Curia administrator in charge of Vatican finances, responded. "Over what time period has this occurred?"

"It started almost immediately after Pope James's election and inauguration," the young aide said.

Cardinal Belosi and other leaders of the hierarchy were pleased by this turn of events. But it only increased their sense of urgency to put the new pope on a fast-track papal-training program. His instructors tutored James in Church history, Holy Scripture, fundamental doctrines, sacred traditions, and long-held customs. The new pope was a quick study, but the cardinals and bishops were a collection of uncompromisingly conservative men.

James chafed at many of their views, especially those relating to social issues and the meager role the Vatican and the College of Cardinals played in providing genuine assistance to the economically poor. As they explained, he questioned. When Cardinal Hoffman detailed the Church's opposition to artificial birth control, James pressed him on the historical and scriptural foundation.

"Didn't Pope Paul VI appoint an esteemed commission of bishops and theologians to advise him on the scriptural basis for the Church's opposition to birth control?" he asked Hoffman, as if cross-examining a witness.

"John XXIII first appointed a commission of non theologians to study the issues of both birth control and population growth," Hoffman answered. "After John's death, Paul VI continued the inquiry and added bishops, cardinals, theologians, physicians, and even women to the commission."

"Did not a majority of the commission find that artificial birth control is not 'intrinsically evil'?"

"That's correct," Hoffman responded, uncomfortable with both the tone and manner of the pope's questioning.

"And the commission also recommended to Pope Paul that each Catholic couple rely on their own conscience to determine the morality of artificial methods—is that correct?"

"Yes. But Paul VI rejected the majority recommendation and accepted instead the minority report, which was partially the basis for his encyclical, *Humanae Vitae*," Hoffman replied defiantly.

"There were seventy-two members on the commission, correct?"

"Yes."

"And sixty-eight agreed with the majority report that artificial birth control was not 'intrinsically evil.' Only four dissented, correct?"

"Yes, Your Holiness."

"Only four of the seventy-two voted that contraception was a mortal sin under all circumstances. Is that right?"

"Yes, but they weren't just any members. One was the commission's president, and another was the papal theologian."

"But weren't the other sixty-eight members respected cardinals, bishops, laymen, and theologians?"

"Yes, of course."

"Well then, please help me understand how the pope could reject the majority opinion. The vote was overwhelming. The majority was comprised of highly respected members, many of whom he personally appointed."

"It is not complicated, Holy Father. The pope has the sole authority to decide. The pope was not required to adopt the majority opinion."

This explanation baffled and disappointed James. Given his collaborative style and democratic propensities, it was outside his comprehension how one man could make a decision contrary to the clear advice of the vast majority of Church leaders and trusted advisors on such a critical moral issue affecting so many lives. Further, he did not appreciate the rationale for this concentration of power in one man. However, it was dawning on him that he now possessed that power.

✳ ✳ ✳

Although James's first impression of Vatican City had suggested this was not a place he would want to spend much time, now he found contentment in the terraced rock beds, illuminated, gushing fountains, and the centuries-old Vatican Gardens that encompassed more than half of the city-state's territory. He was most comforted by the countless shades of living green that spanned the bucolic enclave from one end to the other. The paved walkways were his to stroll, and he rediscovered the pure joy of being alone amid God's natural creation.

However, the joys of embracing nature were short-lived. In subsequent days, members of the Curia taught him about the complicated functioning of Church administration and the workings of the vast bureaucracy. When they addressed Church finances, the tone turned gloomily pessimistic. The financial reports were not complicated; they simply showed there was no money.

In addition, insufficient numbers of men were applying for the seminary—progressive thinkers were not encouraged to join up, and being a priest no longer held the social status it once did—and the sex scandal had substantially reduced donations to the Church at every level.

Neither of the obvious options to correct the financial situation was good—sell works of art to generate cash for daily expenses, or declare bankruptcy. For several hours at a time, James probed his briefers in an effort to appreciate the totality of the financial crisis. He quickly realized there were tens of thousands of different church accounts in thousands of financial institutions in hundreds of countries worldwide. However, much of the wealth was pledged as security for loans and other indebtedness. There were valuable endowments, but nearly all the proceeds were either legally restricted or controlled by bishops and religious orders outside the Vatican.

As he reviewed volumes of financial statements, James concluded he needed professional auditors to investigate the Church's fiscal condition and discern its financial status. One of his former clients was an international accounting firm. He immediately sought its counsel. A senior partner was Catholic, and the firm agreed to provide its services pro bono.

This team of top accountants and auditors attempted to identify every account within the Vatican and assemble a set of reliable financial documents. They also solicited pro bono independent accounting firms in every major Catholic diocese worldwide to do the same thing. While many dioceses were in serious financial trouble, the accountants and auditors found hundreds of millions of dollars squirreled away in accounts controlled by cardinals, bishops, and priests all over the world.

James grew more disillusioned. Cardinals and bishops were well aware of the Vatican's financial challenges, and yet they did not come to its aid. He ordered all this money frozen until the auditors got a handle on the total picture. A few bishops recommended the Church become transparent by submitting annual financial reports at every level and adopting the best practices of preeminent public companies. James quickly heeded their advice.

Next on his list were expenditures. In some dioceses, Church leaders had wasted money on extravagant homes, cars, boats, vacations, and religious jewelry. He demanded an end to all of it, informing the College of Cardinals and the Synod of Bishops that materialism in any form could not be allowed to obstruct the focus of God's church. Whatever assets the accountants found, he seized, selling most of it. Those who presumably "owned" the accounts were not happy.

Then there were the Popemobiles: twenty four-ton armored vehicles dispersed throughout the world to ensure their ready availability to the pope wherever and whenever he traveled. In addition, there were six in the Vatican garage. The bishop in charge explained to the new pope that various auto manufacturers had donated all the Popemobiles.

"We don't really know the cost or value of the vehicles, but they didn't cost the Vatican anything. Many companies want to give things to the pope. So we've never seen it as a problem," the bishop explained.

James retorted, "These vehicles cost the Church in the form of contributions lost. Automobile manufacturers who want to contribute to the Church could donate something we need, like four-wheel drive jeeps or vans for our work in developing countries. More important, these vehicles cost each of us in our own understanding of what is valued in life. Jesus teaches that if we try to save our life, we will lose it. We must lose our life to be saved." Within a month, all but two of the Vatican Popemobiles had been sold to museums.

Chapter Eleven

"**P**lease cancel all my appointments today. I'm not feeling well."
"I'm sorry to hear that, Your Holiness," Sister Rosalie replied
sympathetically. "But just as a reminder, you have meetings with
Cardinal Xavier from South Africa at ten, Cardinal di Amico, prefect of
the Congregation for Bishops, and Archbishop Ricter at eleven, and a
special blessing at noon for the children of St. Ignatius from Colon. And
this afternoon you are scheduled to meet with the prime minister of the
Philippines at two, Mr. Bianca regarding Vatican finances at three, and
you have a working meeting with the poverty task force at four. This
evening, you have a requiem prayer service for Bishop Mancini at St.
Francis Church at seven." James put his head in his hands as he listened
to his secretary. "Do you want me to cancel all these appointments?"
she asked.

"No, perhaps not," he replied. "Keep the ones with the children
and the prime minister. Cancel everything else. I want to see Cardinal
O'Bryan in my study. He's here for a few days for meetings of the audit
committee. Please find him and tell him I need to see him as soon as he
is available."

James had a terrible hangover accompanied by a crushing and
sobering sense of dread. After calling Rosalie, he stumbled through his
morning routine and made breakfast in his apartment. He had been
pope for three months, and he was deeply despondent.

Sister Rosalie called Cardinal O'Bryan on his cell phone, but there was no answer. She then called the office of the audit committee secretariat. Sister Mary DeLourdes, the executive assistant to the secretary, answered.

"DeLourdes," she asked with an obvious sense of urgency, "do you know where Cardinal O'Bryan is? Has he arrived for the audit committee meeting yet?"

"Yes, he just arrived, Rosalie," she said. "What's wrong? You sound upset."

"I need to speak to him."

"Is everything OK?"

"Everything's fine, DeLourdes. I'm sorry. Just been a stressful morning. I need to speak with the cardinal for a moment."

"Right away, Rosalie," DeLourdes said. A moment later Cardinal O'Bryan picked up the phone.

"Hello."

"Cardinal O'Bryan, this is Sister Rosalie. His Holiness would like to see you in his apartment at your earliest convenience. Will nine thirty this morning work for you?"

"Of course. Do you know what this is about?" O'Bryan asked.

"I'm sorry, I don't know. I'll tell His Holiness that you'll be there at nine thirty."

When Cardinal O'Bryan arrived, the pope's assistant greeted him and walked him up a flight of stairs to the door of the pope's study. He knocked lightly on the door before ushering the cardinal into the room.

Dressed in a blue sweater and khaki Dockers, the pope slouched in one of the four leather chairs around a polished coffee table near the fireplace.

"Thanks for coming on such short notice," James said as he rose to greet the cardinal.

"Your Holiness, I am at your service."

"Don't call me that, John. Please."

"I have to," O'Bryan smiled. "What can I do for you?"

"John, I can't do this anymore. I am not cut out for this. Making me pope was a huge mistake. I'm not a theologian or a pastor. I haven't figured out how the Vatican or the Church bureaucracy works. All the archaic traditions, vestments, and rituals make me extremely uncomfortable. And being called 'Your Holiness' is absurd, given the life I've led."

"Your Holiness," O'Bryan started.

"Please, John. I beg you. Just call me Jimmy."

"OK," O'Bryan replied hesitantly. Choosing his words carefully, he said, "I appreciate your concerns. Every pope is challenged by the enormous transition in becoming pope. John Paul II once told me it took him three years before he fully grasped he was pope. He said the enormity of the responsibility was too great for any man to accept and that only with God's blessing could any man fill Peter's shoes. Many popes have felt this way and questioned whether they were sufficiently holy to lead the Church."

"John. I'm a smart guy," James interrupted. "I know when I'm outside my element and in over my head. Believe me, I am way outside my element and barely treading water. This is not an issue of the job being too big. I can handle any job. I have no doubt that I'd make a good president. This is an issue of not being right for this job. I am simply not the right person to be pope. I learned very early in my law practice the value of cutting losses early. It's like that old Kenny Rogers song—you gotta know when to hold 'em and know when to fold 'em. It's my time to fold 'em."

Cardinal O'Bryan paused, drew in a deep breath, and responded slowly but deliberately.

"You are the only person who is right to be pope at this time in history. It is clear from the way the faithful respond to you. Catholic churches in the United States, Canada, and Europe are overflowing on Sunday mornings. Baptisms in developing countries are way up. You give people hope that the Church will change and respond to their needs. You have brought hundreds of thousands, maybe millions, of people back to the Catholic faith. They believe you will make changes that will put the Church on the right path. Whether you like it or not, they have put their spiritual lives into your hands. You know you cannot let them down.

"And furthermore, you'd make a lousy president."

"Why's that?"

"Because you couldn't kill anyone, and presidents always end up killing people." Stillness divided the men.

Finally, the pope asked, "John, is it better for someone's hopes to be dashed or for them to believe in a fraud?"

"You are no more a fraud than any other man. We are all broken. We are all subject to self-doubt. There is an old saying that 'God does not call the qualified, God qualifies the called.' Any man who does not question his justification to be pope should never have been elected. Jesus puts us all back together. Furthermore, the people do not believe in you, Jimmy; they believe that you, as pope, will help bring them closer to Jesus. This is not about you. This is about you being an instrument of the Holy Spirit. God called you to do this job."

Again, there was reverent quiet.

"John, I need you to hear me," James pleaded calmly. "The Church operates like a medieval monarchy. The clothes, the hierarchy, the buildings, the statues—they're all out of the Middle Ages. And while I might be the king, there are a whole lot of princes running around here with their own portfolios. I'm a twenty-first-century guy, John. I'm just not cut out for this fifteenth-century shit."

"Jimmy," O'Bryan tried to interrupt.

"And Sicoli. He makes this situation intolerable. He's all over me every time I say anything contrary to his ultraconservative views. While he hasn't castigated me in public since I told him I would turn his red cassock black, I'm well aware he undermines me at every opportunity. The Curia publicly vows their allegiance to me, but they follow Sicoli in whatever he says. Belosi is a good and loyal man. But he is too old to run the Vatican. Sicoli consistently outmaneuvers him."

O'Bryan looked at him in surprise.

"Oh, I have my spies, John," James said. "I know what happens around here. Look, the bottom line is Sicoli does not believe I am a legitimate pope, so he thinks he can rightfully thwart anything I do or say. He has several protégés strategically spread throughout the Curia to ensure his views are implemented. This is a political battle, John. I know how political battles are fought. I know who wins and why and how. I cannot win this one. I do not have a constituency here. I believe the people in the pews are supportive of what I'm trying to do, but they don't run the Church. Right now, Sicoli does."

A lesser man, especially someone who had dedicated his life to the Church, might have taken several years to arrive at the same conclusions, O'Bryan thought as he listened to his friend. John XXIV and Mark II had both struggled with the same issues, but they had been denied sufficient time to fully understand the current reality of the situation with this level of clarity, let alone effectively address it.

"If you see this as a political battle, then contest it as such," O'Bryan said. "Move Sicoli out; send him to New York as my coadjutor. I will ensure he does not cause any more trouble. Belosi has to retire in a few months due to age. Select a young cardinal who will make a good secretary of state and put him in Sicoli's job for the time being. Let him learn the ropes for the next six months, and then when Belosi retires, make him secretary of state. We can identify Sicoli's protégés and reassign them to dioceses outside of Vatican City. The tougher ones can be sent to Paris and Dublin, where they'll be under the watchful eyes of those who want you to succeed."

Jimmy listened intently to his friend. "You've thought about this?" James asked.

"Your power comes from three sources, Jimmy. First, you are the direct successor of Peter, not the successor of Benedict, or Francis, or John, or Mark. This means you have the same responsibility Jesus gave to Peter, and you have the same authority Jesus granted Peter. You're not bound by the actions of your predecessors; you're the Vicar of Christ. That's what's so great about the Catholic Church. If one guy screws up, the next pope can fix it. If the majority of one College of Cardinals thwarts the Holy Spirit and elects a pope of their own choosing, the Spirit will renew the Church with the election of subsequent popes. This is the Peterine guarantee, and it is your primary source of legal power. Every cardinal and bishop values and honors this power. It's so prominent in our belief that it's inscribed in Latin around the dome of St. Peter's."

"The primacy of Peter. How does that pertain to me?" James asked.

O'Bryan smiled to himself; he thought about his lectures and recalled his students asking similar questions when he was a professor of theology, but he never thought he'd be explaining it to a sitting pope. "First and foremost, Jesus specifically made Peter the head of his church when he stated, 'You are Peter and upon this rock I will build my church, and the powers of death will not prevail against it.' All the apostles were vital to the early Church in their own right. But Peter was special. Numerous scriptural references unambiguously identify Peter as the leading apostle. Whenever the apostles are listed in the New Testament, Peter is always named first. His name is mentioned nearly two hundred times; the next-closest apostle is John, at less than thirty! When Jesus asked the apostles, 'Who do you say that I am?' it was Peter who answered that Jesus is the Messiah, 'the Son of the living God.' Jesus said to Peter, 'Flesh and blood did not reveal this to you, but my Father who is in heaven.' Jesus invited only Peter to walk with him on water. Jesus foretold Peter's suffering and death on a cross. Those things set Peter apart in a very special way. He was the first leader of the fledgling church, the first pope."

"But how does that translate into me or any other pope receiving Peter's responsibilities and power?" James asked.

O'Bryan smiled. "As a lawyer, you'll appreciate that some of the evidence is circumstantial. Nevertheless, there's overwhelming evidence that Jesus not only selected Peter to lead his church, but Jesus also expected Peter's successors to lead his church as well. We know Jesus intended to build a church, because he said so. Then Jesus gave Peter 'the keys to the kingdom of heaven.' He said 'the powers of death will not prevail against' his church. Based on this, it's not reasonable to conclude Jesus expected his church to be fulfilled during Peter's lifetime.

"Moreover, it doesn't make much sense that Jesus would want Peter to return the keys to heaven when Peter died. The keys are eternal. Someone had to receive the keys. So the most logical conclusion is that the Church had the responsibility to pass the keys to Peter's successor."

James hesitated. "I don't know, John. That sounds a little thin to me. I'm not sure I'd want to take that case on a contingency fee. What's the opposing argument?"

O'Bryan weighed his options before he replied. He needed to be straight with this lawyer-pope. He could not pull any punches or disregard any contrary arguments. "Peter never specifically asserted supremacy. Moreover, none of the apostles claimed the authority given to them by Jesus would pass on to their successors. The doctrine of apostolic succession—the concept that the authority of the twelve passed on to their successors—is not found anywhere in Scripture. Other than Matthias, there is no record of passing apostolic authority to anyone. In addition, even if apostolic succession can be inferred from Scripture, there's nothing to suggest Peter's successors would have authority over the other apostles' successors.

"The opposing side concludes that apostolic succession is not necessary to ensure the growth and stability of the Church. The Church is founded on the Word of God. Scripture is the authority; there's no need for a successor to Peter.

"Moreover, the Gospel advises that false prophets will arise from among the leaders of the Church, and it's incumbent upon each Christian to compare all teachings with Scripture in order to know the truth."

"It's a good argument. What's the rebuttal?"

"In the absence of apostolic authority, there is only chaos. Doctrinal misunderstanding, sacramental uncertainty, and theological confusion reign. Scripture does state that false teachers will come forward. That is exactly what has happened, as demonstrated by the countless non-Catholic denominations and the numerous interpretations of Holy Scripture."

Both men sat quietly for a few minutes. Then James said, "You said the pope has three sources of power. What are the other two?"

"You can harness the power of the people, especially when they respond to your spiritual message and humility. This hasn't always been the case, but it is today. The role of the pope has shifted over the centuries. What's vital today is what you say, where and how you say it, what you do, and how you do what you do. Your words and actions determine your authentic power, because if the faithful respond, your personal power is enhanced enormously.

"You have the potential for tremendous effectiveness, Jimmy, because you speak to the needs of the people in words they understand. They hear you. Forgoing the trappings of the office, wearing simple vestments, publicly acknowledging your sinfulness, and speaking in clear, uncluttered language all bring you closer to the people. They believe you have fully assumed the role of the servant. That's why Francis was so loved by the faithful. The cardinals and bishops see this, too. Even those who might disagree with you or oppose you know this strengthens your effectiveness. That's why some are so keen on stopping you."

James thought for a moment. "And the third?"

"If you are faithful to God, you have the power of the Holy Spirit. That is your third and preeminent source of power. The Holy Spirit is always present in the Church. The Holy Spirit guarantees the authenticity of the Church's teachings on doctrine and morals. The Holy Spirit inspired the College of Cardinals to elect you as the leader of God's church. Now the Holy Spirit will guide you as you lead. You are simply an instrument. All you need is faith."

O'Bryan surmised that he had not convinced James about apostolic succession and the principle that every pope is a direct successor to Peter. But he did think the pope grasped the argument about the Holy Spirit.

"Some cardinals aren't sure you realize how powerful all this makes you," O'Bryan said carefully. "Sicoli and his cronies take advantage of this. His attempts to browbeat you into adopting positions that are more conservative fulfill his twin goals. Anytime he moves you to the right, it's good for him. He knows the more conservative you are, the less power you have, because the people won't respond as positively. And without the people, your authority wanes. As you say, you don't have a constituency in the Vatican. Your constituency is in the pews and with those who have not yet returned to the pews."

The pope silently pondered O'Bryan's words. Sitting back on the soft leather chair, he watched the glowing fire. He cleared his throat, and without removing his eyes from the jumping flames, he said, "So we move Sicoli and his people out. How do we ensure the next guy isn't just as rigid and dogmatic?"

"There are cardinals, bishops, priests, nuns, and brothers who have prayed every day for a pontiff who will focus on the words of Jesus as they relate to the needs of the poor. They found this in Francis, but it was too brief. They want someone who will take the Church well into the twenty-first century, and ensure the Church has sufficient priests—a man who will see beyond the temporal traditions, pomp, and ceremony. They support you because you emphasize the fundamental issues of war and peace, wealth and poverty, reconciliation with other denominations, and protecting God's creation—both children and the planet. Other popes have done great things, but no recent pope has dedicated his papacy to the plethora of issues as you have led them to believe you will. Some of the hierarchy believe their prayers were answered with your election. They are not a majority, but they are good and strong people. You need to select from this group."

"But what if I just don't want to be here anymore?"

After a brief silence, O'Brien asked, "May I speak candidly?"

"Of course."

"Suck it up."

James's head snapped up at his friend's words. They looked at each other for a moment, and then shared a hearty laugh.

"God requires you forgo the familiar and the comfortable, Jimmy."

"You know that's not what I wanted to hear."

"I know," O'Bryan said. "But we both know it's true."

James felt rekindled. He decided to give it another try; after all, he had never quit anything before, not even the most hopeless case. He spent the remainder of the day, save blessing the children and meeting with the Filipino prime minister, fashioning a strategy to make a genuine, constructive, and lasting difference in the Church, and considering how he might increase his comfort level so the job might be at least tolerable. Although the pope had supreme power, he had learned the universal college of bishops was the source of the actual power in the Church. They decided which policies to carry out and which ones to deemphasize. If James was to make any real difference, he would need to work successfully with this group of men, even if they were part of the problem.

However, James believed an exclusive group of celibate, conservative men could not effectively represent the diverse people of God. The momentous issues facing the Church required comprehensive insight into the ways of the world. On one hand, it was wonderful that men would abstain from sex and marriage, and dedicate their lives to prayer and obedience to God. However, by limiting leadership to such a narrow demographic, the Church may well have planted the seeds of the multiple scandals and unnecessary challenges it had endured over the centuries.

James pondered in silence. "A broader, more representative group of bishops and priests might be better equipped to ferret out the negative and expose potential greed, pride, lust, and arrogance. What if the college of bishops and cardinals were composed of married men and women, as well as celibate men and women? Collectively they might more effectively lead the Church. It may not matter if they were conservatives or liberals. Their life experiences and devotion to the Gospel of Jesus, their love of the Creator, and the command to 'love your neighbor as yourself' are most important," he thought to himself.

James decided to bring together a small cadre of people to develop a comprehensive long-term strategy and identify specific short-term tactics. He asked Rosalie to cancel his appointments for Friday and Saturday.

"Please make the necessary arrangements for Cardinals O'Bryan, Schmidt, O'Faolain, and Mbuto, Fathers Greg Keegan and Mike Maloney, and Peter Jaworski and Cynthia Meyer from MDB Group to meet with me Friday morning," he instructed. He included O'Faolain because of his reputation as one of the most progressive cardinals, and Mbuto because he remembered meeting him years ago when he and Vicky had volunteered in Tanzania.

Late Tuesday evening, after Rosalie had invited Father Keegan to the Friday meeting, the priest called the pope from his home in St. Paul to recommend that Fr. John Simmons, a young cleric who was currently his assistant, join the Friday morning meeting.

John Simmons had been born and raised in St. Paul, Minnesota. He was a bright and talented student—first in his class at Cretin-Derham High School, St. Thomas University, and St. John Vianney Seminary. He was high-energy, often working twelve to fourteen hours a day. A kind and thoughtful fellow with a clever sense of humor, he was not conservative, as most young American priests tended to be during this time. He understood and embraced Jesus' command to love one another and serve the poor. He was not hung up on the sixth commandment or the strict rulings and traditions of the temporal Church. In fact, Simmons often wondered how the Church could be so preoccupied with human sexuality while billions of people did not have enough food, nutrition, health care, or education to live full and productive lives. However, he was politically savvy and did not openly express his personal views during his academic years. Suspecting his superiors would not fully recognize his other abilities if he were perceived as a "liberal" in this conservative church, Simmons kept his mouth shut about any issue that might be considered controversial or edgy.

After a priest was ordained, his bishop generally assigned him to a parish as an associate pastor until he gained sufficient experience to handle his own parish. However, because of John's class rank and his work ethic, the archbishop offered him the unique and coveted opportunity to work in the archdiocese chancery office as assistant to the vicar general. If he did well in this position, he would be in line to succeed the vicar general. Then he would be on his way up the hierarchical ladder. Although tempted by the opportunity, Simmons politely turned down the offer, asking instead to be assigned to one of the local parishes, preferably in Minneapolis. His fellow newly ordained priests told their friend he was crazy not to take the chancery job; he might never have a chance like that again.

John Simmons was then assigned to St. Mary's, an inner-city parish in St. Paul. It was at St. Mary's that Simmons met Keegan, who quickly became his mentor. The young priest found Keegan to be a friendly fellow with both a deep sense of justice and a sly sense of humor. He also learned that his teacher was openly independent and did not follow all the rules or toe the line as often instructed by the hierarchy.

Some thought the archbishop put up with Keegan's independence only because of the severe shortage of priests.

The stories about Keegan were legend, like when he and a new associate priest would do a communal penance together. Just before they started the sacrament, Father Keegan would announce from the altar to the church full of people, "My associate is quite young and new at this. So he will only take venal sins today. I'll handle all the mortal sins." Everyone would laugh, and the assistant priest's face would invariably turn red.

Nevertheless, being the associate pastor at St. Mary's turned out wonderfully for John Simmons. Keegan was so often at the state prison that Simmons needed to fulfill most of the pastoral duties. This provided him genuine, hands-on work with parishioners, many of whom were struggling economically, physically, emotionally, and spiritually.

For five years, Simmons and Keegan worked together. They became close friends, and the older found the younger to be the most brilliant student he had ever encountered. So Greg Keegan recommended him to his old friend, the new pope.

"I think he'd make a good assistant," Greg said over the phone. "You can get a good look at him on Friday. If you like him, you are ahead of the game. If you don't, you'll still have a young and brilliant mind sitting around the table."

"Bring him with you," the pope said.

Vatican City is like any small town. Everyone knows everybody and everything. When members of the Curia learned of the pope's impending meeting with select cardinals and American media consultants, they became anxious. It was unusual for leaders of the Church's administrative and theological departments not to be invited to important meetings. Why were Mbuto and O'Faolain requested to attend when none of the other papal candidates were on the list? Why was a woman invited to such a gathering? They could only hope her presence did not forecast their gravest fears about this layman for whom few of them had voted.

James kept all his appointments on Wednesday and Thursday. However, during every spare moment, he considered multiple strategies and tactics affecting personnel, policy, procedure, and finances. He knew intuitively he would need to identify the progressives, moderates, and conservatives within the College of Cardinals and among the theologians and bishops throughout the Church. And he would need reliable inside advice about who was trustworthy and who was not.

On Friday morning, the invited guests gathered in the pope's study in the papal apartment. After introductions, a short prayer, and an explanation of why they were there, they discussed in detail how James could make a real, constructive, and lasting difference in the Church. They concluded their conversation at eight forty-five Friday evening and resumed at nine sharp Saturday morning. By four that afternoon, they had agreed on ten actions.

First, James would appoint a close and trusted friend as chief of staff and immediately elevate him to cardinal. He named Greg Keegan to this post. "This is not an offer, Greg. It is an assignment. I need you." All agreed this was the correct decision.

Second, he would recruit a cadre of young, bright, and dedicated international staff and spread them throughout the Vatican. John Simmons would be the first of this group and become the pope's principal assistant.

Third, the group put together a list of the most intelligent and influential cardinals, bishops, and theologians, loosely categorized as conservative, moderate, and progressive. He assigned Simmons to gather their writings and homilies. The pope would review the writings, interview those he thought would be most helpful, and appoint the best and brightest to major Curia posts.

Fourth, and among the most difficult challenges, the Church needed to increase vocations of priests, brothers, and sisters so that the pope had a sufficient number of working clergy at the grassroots level. Priests posed the greatest problem. During the previous decade, the number of priests had grown by only 2 percent—far less than the increase in Catholics worldwide, especially in Africa and Asia. This raised the issue of married and female priests. Cardinal O'Faolain argued most vehemently and articulately in favor of maintaining celibate priests, even though he was among the strongest advocates for married priests in his public writings—writings that had often gotten him into hot water with previous popes.

"The rule of celibacy is not dogma," O'Faolain explained. "It is a facet of canon law. Thus, it is subject to change by the pope in the Church's quest for the fullness of Truth, as the Holy Spirit inspires. Nevertheless, if you were to make that significant change, it would be a change of many centuries of tradition." The group discussed this issue at great length, as the pope listened intently.

"Many will argue that it would be imprudent to precipitously change the rule requiring celibacy," O'Faolain contended. "And they have compelling arguments. Paul writes in First Corinthians that 'the unmarried man is concerned about the things of the Lord, how he can please the Lord. But a married man is concerned about worldly things, how to please his wife.' Paul continues, 'He who marries the virgin does right, but he who does not marry her does better.' He clearly states that it is better for the one who is committed to spreading the Word not to marry. In large measure, this is because marriage requires total and complete commitment to the other. When a man is ordained a priest, he becomes married to the Church and devoted to his flock. He cannot afford to be distracted by a second complete and total commitment to a wife and children."

Cardinal Mbuto politely disagreed. "St. Paul did preach that chastity is the higher calling and encouraged unmarried men and widows to remain unmarried. Paul also taught that chastity was a gift, and that God grants different gifts to different people. Paul never advocated that anyone had to be celibate in order to serve God or preach the Gospel of Jesus Christ. Moreover, several scriptural references suggest priests need not be celibate. Timothy wrote that a cleric should be the 'husband of one wife,' and Hebrews admonishes that 'marriage should be honored by all.'"

"Jesus was celibate," O'Faolain continued. "Every priest is called to be like Jesus and follow his example. In large measure, that is why the Second Lateran Council disseminated a universal promulgation that definitively prohibited married men from becoming priests and banned priests from marrying. This was not a new decree. Centuries earlier St. Augustine, St. Cyril, St. Jerome, and others supported a celibate priesthood. Moreover, there is evidence that this tradition reached as far back as apostolic times. Two thousand years is a long tradition to overturn."

Mbuto countered again. "But early Church history tells us that St. Peter, most of the apostles, several subsequent popes, and many bishops and priests were married and fathers of children during the first three centuries. In fact, until the mid-twelfth century, deacons, priests, and bishops regularly married and legitimately fathered children."

"There are other reasons to require celibacy. In the modern world, a world preoccupied with sex, the celibate priest is a powerful example to men and women of all ages. Celibacy demonstrates that sexual urges can be restrained and that life need not revolve around that which is 'sexy,'" O'Faolain argued.

"Yes," O'Brien agreed. "Celibacy can be a positive example; however, every priest need not be celibate to demonstrate it. Committed marriage can also exemplify God's love, and married priests offer that example as well. Besides, the most recent sex abuse scandal has taken a huge toll on the value of mandatory celibacy. Moreover, we've all seen the data that suggests celibacy inhibits emotionally healthy men from even considering a vocation."

"If you want to change the rules on celibacy, you must first clean out the Curia. Supporting celibacy is a litmus test for even being considered for any significant position in the Curia," Cardinal Schmidt warned.

When the discussion subsided, James thanked everyone for their thoughts and contributions. He made a special note of thanks to Cardinal O'Faolain.

"I'm greatly moved and impressed by your arguments against married priests when, based upon your writings, I know you favor the proposal," he said to O'Faolain.

O'Faolain responded. "Thank you for your kind words, Your Holiness. However, if your papacy is to have long-term constructive and positive effects on the Church, you must be certain that any changes you make are fully vetted and that you've heard all the arguments, pro and con."

"I'm very grateful to you, Terrance," he said. He looked around the room. "I've been praying about this issue from the day John and Peter advised me I'd been elected pope. I am deeply concerned about the severe priest shortage. Merges of parishes in North America, due to insufficient priests, have had devastating effects on Catholics. Our priests are old, and getting older. The situation is only going to get worse, and fast. In Asia, Africa, and South America, even in areas where vocations are on the upswing, large percentages of the population cannot attend Mass or receive the Eucharist because there are no priests. How can the Church fulfill its essential mission and responsibilities if it cannot ensure the faithful have ready access to the Eucharist and other sacraments? It's a question I've asked myself countless times."

James reminded his colleagues of the thousands of Catholic men who had left the priesthood in the past fifty years to get married. Under current law, they could not return to the priesthood. He, like many American Catholics, had several friends in this situation. Furthermore, he suspected there were hundreds of thousands of men who were called to the sacrament of ordination but were also called to the sacrament of marriage. The rules forced them to choose one over the other.

"I have not heard any rationale, either today or previously, that adequately supports the current convoluted policies on married Catholic priests. In the Eastern Rite you can be married, but the Latin Rite prohibits it—that is, unless you're a married Protestant minister who converts to Catholicism. Then you can be ordained a priest and be married. It makes no sense to me.

"Consequently, I have decided to amend canon law. The Church will continue to emphasize the value and gift of celibacy. However, married men called to the priesthood will be ordained. In addition, current priests and bishops, in both the Latin and Eastern Rites, will be allowed to marry. We will encourage all single priests to consider celibacy. However, we will no longer prohibit the combination of the sacraments."

For a moment, the only sound in the room was the crackling of the fire. O'Faolain was visibly moved as he wiped tears from his eyes. He had quietly argued for this change for decades. Now he only hoped he had adequately argued against his longtime position so that the pope was sufficiently informed. The others in the room were unanimously pleased by this result. However, the quickness, decisiveness, and clarity of the decision surprised them all.

That brought the pope to the question of female clergy. He acknowledged that he had wondered for years why the Church prohibited women from becoming priests. Clearly, God could call women to the priesthood just as he calls men.

"Greg, do you recall what you said to me a decade or so ago when I asked you why the Church prohibited women from being ordained?" he asked rhetorically. "You told me, 'The Catholic Church is the last great bastion of male dominance. If women can be ordained priests, then what's to prevent them from becoming bishops and cardinals? God forbid, someday one could become pope. The men of the Church will never allow women priests because they fear a woman pope.' I have never forgotten your words. I said then and believe now, that's a shame.

"However, two thousand years is a long time. There is no credible historical precedent of women priests as there is for married priests. Two decades ago, St. John Paul II stated unequivocally that women could not be ordained to the priesthood. Authorizing women priests will require substantial conversation, reflection, and prayer." They moved on to the next subject.

Fifth, they all agreed the Church had to send the message that this pope took the priest sex-abuse scandal and its cover-up seriously. Given all that had transpired in the last twenty-five years, the question was how to do that in a way that was believable and credible.

"John, you were in the middle of this when you were in Boston. How did the Church find itself in a cover-up?" James asked his friend.

"It snuck up on them, in a way. At first, many bishops really didn't believe that priests could or would commit such dastardly acts. That turned out to be naïve. History shows that the Church has struggled with sex scandals for centuries. So then they started sending the predators to Church-run treatment centers, and after their 'successful therapy,' they returned to parish work because they needed the priests to run the churches. That didn't work because the recidivism rate was too high. Then they thought the abusers could remain in the priesthood if assigned to restricted ministries. That proved false as well. They really didn't know what to do."

"So while all this was going on, no one informed the police," Keegan commented. "Why was that?"

"The bishops knew about the abuses for years, but they were overly concerned about the scandal, the effects on the Church, and the welfare of the priests. Too often, the potential victims weren't on the radar screen. They knew that every case was going to cost a lot of money, and the lawyers advised them not to do anything that would adversely affect their defense. You know how that works, Holy Father."

"Yes. Unfortunately, I do."

"The victims' complaints were often settled quietly and the files locked away. The financial settlements prevented the victims from ever saying anything to anyone, so the perpetrators were never charged because the authorities didn't know anything. When a new complaint was brought, there was an unwritten admonition never to admit that there were other cases, and so secrecy became the culture. People thought they were protecting the Church and forgot about the kids. The abuse and the cover-up was so widespread, we'll never know the full extent of it."

"Didn't anyone see through all this?" Simmons asked incredulously.

"Eventually. But it took a public outcry to get them motivated, and then it took a while for the bishops and the Vatican to develop a workable policy that would actually protect children. Finally, in 2002, the US Conference of Bishops unanimously approved a 'zero tolerance' policy for abusers—the Charter for the Protection of Children and Young People. So now, whenever there is an allegation of abuse, the church alerts the government authorities, removes the accused from duty, and conducts its own internal investigation. We've trained millions of children to recognize and report abuse, and we run criminal checks on virtually everyone today. Then, in 2010, the whole thing blew up again, only this time in Europe. The Europeans didn't seem to learn anything from the mistakes we made in the United States."

"What's happened to the perpetrators?" Cynthia Meyer asked.

"Some were eventually charged and convicted, but only a small percentage. Statutes of Limitations got many of these guys off. Some have resigned or been defrocked. Some have died; others are in assisted living facilities. Some are still active in the Church."

"What's been the effect of the zero tolerance policy?" James asked.

"It's helped a great deal. There are far fewer abusers today, but I have no doubt it continues. And those who have an interest in keeping it under wraps will continue to cover it up."

James was quiet—thinking. Then he said, "Raping or otherwise sexually abusing a child is a crime against humanity. Covering up that crime compounds the heinousness of the wrongdoing. Jesus spoke specifically about this. In Matthew he says, 'If anyone shall offend one of these little ones which believe in me, it would be better for him to have a millstone hung about his neck, and be drowned in the depths of the sea.'

"We can only surmise the number of children who would have been protected from abuse if the Church had just done the right thing from the beginning. This is the most vital issue facing the Church. A much bigger deal than the financial crisis. We must take effective action to rid the entire Church of all abusers, and all those who protect them. We must protect the children, and we must protect the Church. I want to be proactive, not reactive. How do we do that, John?"

"We throw the perpetrators out headfirst. Just throw them out, every one of them. No second chances. No opportunity for recovery. Put real teeth into the zero tolerance policy. You emphatically tell every cardinal, bishop, priest, deacon, brother, sister—you tell them all—if you sexually abuse a child of God, now or in the past, or cover up someone else's abuse, now or in the past, you're out. Gone. Finished. And every time there is even a whisper of a complaint, we turn that information over to the authorities. We let all the clergy know that if you sexually abuse anyone, or cover it up, God may forgive you, but you are no longer a member the clergy."

Previous popes had apologized for the great harm perpetrated on the young. Pope Benedict XVI had enacted successful steps that greatly reduced the incidence of sexual abuse well below that of other denominations and occupations dealing with children. But the public was still wary. James would go further and require the resignation of every sister, brother, priest, bishop, and cardinal who either abused children or, more importantly, concealed abuse. No one would be immune. Those who voluntarily resigned would remain eligible for their pensions. Those who requested Vatican trials and were convicted would forfeit their pensions and be defrocked. Furthermore, the Church would turn over to local government authorities all evidence it possessed, regardless of how old it was, letting the chips fall where they might.

"How will this affect the shortage of priests?" Simmons asked.

"There are four hundred thousand priests, bishops, and cardinals worldwide," Keegan said. "The percentage involved is relatively small, although we can't afford to lose anyone. But we cannot allow any of the perpetrators or those who concealed the perpetration to continue serving in the Church."

This decision was unprecedented. They realized several cardinals would resign; apparently, there was little doubt which clerics had participated in or condoned the cover-up. As painful as this would be, it would also offer James the opportunity to elevate young progressive and moderate men to the College of Cardinals. He would select some from the first group of the most experienced and qualified married priests.

Sixth, James would make children the focus of this papacy. Jesus had taught the value and importance of children and severely admonished those who might harm or injure children. By focusing positively on children, James would stress Jesus' teachings and directly counter the Church's dismal failure to protect children from priests' sex abuse. James genuinely believed that it was everyone's duty to help all children, especially those in need, and he wanted the Church to set the example for all to follow.

Seventh, he would travel extensively throughout the world. He suggested he begin in a Muslim country in an attempt to build bridges with Islam and to demonstrate that Christians could be respected and trusted." He would take his first trip as soon as feasible.

Eighth, he would engage and embrace the mass media. They all agreed he had made a positive first impression with his interview on CNN International. He would continue to submit to media interviews and simply speak the truth as he saw it. The chips would fall, but they assured him that most would fall in his favor.

Ninth, they easily convinced him he needed to spend time with family and friends. He could establish an "American Vatican" in Chicago. Schmidt, Keegan, Maloney, and Meyer would work out the details.

Finally, he would assign Sicoli to the New York archdiocese to work under the direction of O'Bryan. Although Sicoli had not been involved in the sex abuse cover-up, some of his lieutenants had participated, so they would be gone. Sicoli's remaining supporters would be dispersed throughout the world, placed under the watchful eyes of the pope's most trusted bishops.

✳ ✳ ✳

On a dank and drizzling Monday morning, Cardinal Belosi's office phone rang.

"Good morning, Your Holiness," Belosi said as he recognized the pope's voice. James had called to advise the secretary of state of the decisions made the previous Friday and Saturday.

"I'd appreciate your input regarding how we might implement these decisions," James said. They spoke for nearly thirty minutes, and Belosi was grateful for being kept in the loop.

Later that morning, O'Bryan and Keegan met with the pope in his study. "Managing the Sicoli situation requires some finesse," he advised his two friends.

"I recommend you be quick and direct," Keegan said. "Perhaps Secretary Cardinal Belosi should deliver the news to Sicoli, so you can stay above the fray."

O'Bryan agreed.

"No. I have to do this myself. It's not in my interest to permit any question in Sicoli's mind about my commitment to do what needs to be done."

Early that afternoon, James invited Belosi, Sicoli, and O'Bryan to the papal office. He asked Belosi to come fifteen minutes early so he could advise him of the decision to reassign Sicoli to New York.

"That's a wise decision," Belosi responded. Then, after a beat, he added, "But Cardinal Sicoli has many supporters in the Curia. Cutting off the head of the snake may not be sufficient." James explained the plan requiring all those involved in any way in the sex abuse scandal or its cover-up to resign and to reassign Sicoli's remaining key lieutenants. Belosi mused that might not be enough.

"Not every holy man is a bishop, and not every bishop is a holy man," Belosi counseled. "It will be difficult to know who is loyal to the institution and who is loyal to you. Each may be loyal to the Church, but they are loyal in their own way. Some may believe that supporting Sicoli is the best way to support the Church, especially if they think you might advance radical or far-reaching change. Some of Sicoli's people in the Curia are good and honest men. You can win them over. Others need to reside in Siberia, far away from anyone to whom you delegate authority."

"How do I do that?" asked the pontiff.

"It's not easy to identify the wheat from the weeds," Belosi advised. "Jesus instructs us that's best done at harvest time. I can help you to some extent, but even with a lifetime of working in the Curia, I cannot be certain of every man's intentions. The most dangerous are easy to spot. They should be spread out to churches in remote communities in developing countries where communications are challenging and Internet access is not readily available. Otherwise, they will conspire with each other and it will make no difference if they are together in Rome or separated in cities around the world. You must do your best to win over the others."

"How soon must I act?"

"When you reassign Cardinal Sicoli, you must simultaneously reassign the others," he replied. "But equally important, I recommend you appoint cardinals and bishops who recognize you are pope because the Holy Spirit inspired the conclave to select you. You must construct a community of supporters within the hierarchy as soon as possible.

Most popes take too long to do this, and it prevents them from moving the Church in the direction where she needs to go."

"How long will it take you to identify those who are 'most dangerous'?" James asked.

"They're very obvious," Belosi responded. "I'll have a list to you by day's end."

The phone rang. Rosalie announced the other cardinals had arrived. After everyone was seated, James said to Sicoli, "I need to have my own people in leadership roles in the Curia. You have served the Church and previous popes well. However, I have decided to make Cardinal Mbuto prefect of the Congregation for Divine Worship and the Discipline of the Sacraments. I am reassigning you to New York, where you will be coadjutor of the New York archdiocese. You will report to Cardinal O'Bryan. I wanted to advise you of this personally because I respect the role you have played in the Church. I hope we'll be able to work together in the years to come."

Sicoli failed to hide his surprise. He thought for a moment and then said, "Coadjutor generally implies that after a year or so I would take over as bishop of the archdiocese. Is that your intent?"

"No," James replied. "While that is often the case, it will not be in this situation. You and Cardinal O'Bryan will work out how you will best serve the New York archdiocese. But John will be in charge."

"When is this effective?" Sicoli asked evenly, yet tersely.

"Immediately. Cardinal Mbuto arrives on Monday. I'd like you to introduce him to your staff and advise him of the major issues you are working on. You should travel to New York the following Monday."

Sicoli did not immediately respond, but then said, "I'd like to take a couple of my longtime assistants with me."

"That won't be necessary. There is a fine support staff in New York. Working directly with the Americans will help you acclimate to your new responsibilities." Sicoli looked at Belosi, hoping for some signal that perhaps this could be negotiated.

"This is best for everyone, Manoles," Belosi said. "New York is a wonderful diocese, and there are a lot of Italian Catholics."

Later in the day, Belosi delivered a list of three cardinals, seven bishops, and twelve priests. Their reassignments or resignations were announced the following day, and within six weeks, all the young priests had been scattered to rural village parishes throughout Africa, Asia, and Latin America, in dioceses where there was no question about the local bishop's loyalty to the new pope. Two of the identified cardinals and most of the bishops decided to retire early, several retreating to European monasteries and the others relocating to their private estates in Italy. Cardinal DeLuca was assigned to Dublin, where he would be monitored by his nemesis, Terrance Cardinal O'Faolain.

There was no question in anyone's mind what had gone down. Those removed had made little effort to cover their displeasure with the new pontiff. Everyone knew Sicoli was their leader. Once he was gone, there was no hope of retaining the former power structure. What was so surprising was that past popes had allowed years to lapse before they had removed adversaries. No recent pope had ever moved so quickly and decisively. James was a tenacious and determined leader with little allegiance to the status quo, one who would not permit insurgencies.

James's new kitchen cabinet implemented the rest of the plan. Members of the Curia were advised of most actions in advance, and in some cases, they too were asked for their input prior to execution.

Both Keegan and Simmons immediately moved to Vatican City. Keegan was ordained a bishop, elevated to cardinal, and made chief of staff. This was a new function within the Curia; the secretary of state had previously fulfilled many of Keegan's new duties. Belosi understood; he turned eighty in a few months and was past retirement age—and he was ready to retire. However, Belosi did counsel James to appoint a more experienced cardinal than Cardinal Keegan as secretary of state. Simmons became James's executive assistant.

According to the strategy, the pope interviewed the thirty-seven brightest and most influential clerics. He was quite impressed with all of them, although troubled by the depth of conservative views held by most. James wondered about the opinions of those in the hierarchy whom he did not interview. Nevertheless, he identified six men, in addition to Cardinal

Mbuto, with whom he believed he could work well, including the young Juan Carlos Cardinal Villegomez, from the United States, and appointed them to key leadership positions in the Curia. Mbuto would take Sicoli's post until Belosi retired, and then he would become secretary of state.

After the Vatican published the retirements and reassignments, James confronted the challenge of advising the Curia, the College of Cardinals, and the faithful of his decision to amend canon law to allow married priests. Given the deep-seated conservative views among the Curia and the College, and the strong opposition to any change, he was struck by various polls showing a majority of parish priests and nuns generally supported ordaining married men. Moreover, he was aware that the vast majority of the faithful favored married priests as well.

James gathered Cardinal Belosi and the cardinals whom he had recently appointed to Curia leadership positions in his office. After explaining his decision and reasons to allow married priests, he asked for their comments. Several expressed their personal misgivings about how this dramatic change would affect the Church, but none expressed disagreement with the decision. To express disagreement after the decision was announced would be a bad choice.

James later met with all the cardinals and bishops from greater metropolitan Rome at Paul VI Auditorium, and included many cardinals and bishops around the world via video conference. Again, he told all participants of his decision and his rationale.

"I honor the value of, and calling to, celibacy," he told the clerics. "Jesus was celibate, and that speaks volumes to its import. Among other things, it demonstrates that normal human sexual desires can be controlled and constrained. I believe this is especially helpful to young men and women who are not yet married. However, in the minds of many Catholics, the sex abuse scandal has clearly outweighed many positives generated by celibate priests. While that does not devalue celibacy, it does put it in context—just as marriage is not for everyone; celibacy is not for everyone, not even every priest."

With these meetings concluded, the press office issued a two-page statement informing Catholics worldwide of this change in canon law. The news release closed with a quote from Pope James.

"This is not an edict I enjoin today. Rather, I offer this change in canon law in hopes it will be useful to Christians around the world. I ask all Catholic men and women to pray about how this might affect their lives. Women, ask yourselves if your father, brother, husband, uncle, grandfather, sweetheart, or friend might make a good priest. Men, ask yourself if God wants you to serve humanity through the priesthood. If you ask God this question in prayer, God will answer you."

Catholics throughout the world were taken by surprise. Few had believed this change would occur so quickly. While many of the faithful applauded the decision, Sicoli and his kind were enraged. Not only had the charlatan removed Sicoli from the Curia, which was the Italian cardinal's rightful place, given all his years of service to the Church, but now this American lawyer had nullified one of the most important and long-standing traditions of the clergy. To this lifelong Church bureaucrat, married priests were an abomination. Sicoli was convinced that sex was the root of most sin—even if it was unavoidable for procreation—and was not to be partaken of by religious leaders.

"The man is an imposter," Sicoli said to a gathering of his most ardent followers at the private estate of one of his supporters on the outskirts of Rome, on the eve of his departure to New York. "We cannot let this stand. He will put the Church into utter ruin before he's finished. Something must be done!"

"But what can we do, Your Eminence?" a bishop asked. "He is the pope. He is supreme. All power rests with him."

"The American lawyer is a fraud, not a pope," Sicoli stated vehemently. "The evil one is the source of his power. He is the Antichrist. O'Bryan and the other liberals duped many good cardinals into electing him. This was the work of evil incarnate. There's no other explanation."

He continued his ranting. "Under any other circumstances, the conclave never would have chosen an American capitalist lawyer, let alone a non cleric, to be pope. We have to stop him now, before he sanctions birth control, abortion, and euthanasia, bans the Latin Mass entirely, authorizes homosexual marriage, totally decentralizes the Church's power outside the Vatican, and approves the ordination of women."

"How can we stop him if you are in New York?" one of the young priests asked. "If they can remove you and Cardinal DeLuca, they can remove all of us."

Sicoli offered consolation. "Belosi cannot identify all of you. As long as you are careful, you will be able to act."

"Cardinal Sicoli will continue to give us direction from America through a clandestine website we have established," DeLuca said. "Let there be no mistake, we must eliminate the Antichrist. When we do, the College of Cardinals will see the error of their ways, and at the next conclave, they will elect Cardinal Sicoli pope."

"We have a responsibility to Holy Mother Church to be rid of him. It is our duty as princes and clergy," Sicoli concluded.

Chapter Twelve

"Colonel Meire says the Secret Service will provide protection while you are on American soil, so he thinks you only need two Swiss Guardsmen to accompany you to Chicago," Simmons reported to the pope.

"Why the Secret Service?" James asked.

"Apparently that's what they do for all heads of state. We can bring our own security if you want, but it is a lot cheaper if they do it, because the United States requires that you have significant security protection. So pending your approval, I have made flight arrangements for you, two Guardsmen, and me on Alitalia business class for August 3. Of course, you could take one of the Vatican jets, but if it's just the four of us, it's far less expensive to fly commercial, and the effect on the environment is much less when compared to using a Vatican jet."

"That's fine, John. Whatever works best and is environmentally friendly. I'm just glad to be going home to see my family and friends. I don't want to cause any fuss with the other passengers. Arrange it so I get on first and off last."

They flew from Vatican City to Fiumicino Airport on the same helicopter that had ferried Jimmy Flahvin to the Vatican months earlier. No pope had flown anywhere with the public on a commercial aircraft in many decades. In the modern papacy, it was unprecedented.

Lieutenant Colonel D'Amore made arrangements for James and his three companions to secretly board the Boeing 797 Dream Cruiser in

advance of other passengers. As they settled in, the senior flight attendant, hands trembling, asked Pope James if he needed anything. He
thanked her and said he was fine. A moment later, the captain walked
back to James's seat and told him what an honor it was to have him
onboard. He thanked the captain and said to him, "Have a safe flight."
They both smiled.

As the other business-class passengers boarded, they immediately
recognized James, but none approached, out of respect for his privacy.
Of course, they wondered why in God's heavenly name the pope was
travelling on their plane. Shortly after they were airborne and the seat-
belt light turned off, James got up to walk around. He acknowledged
each of the flight attendants, and then, out of the corner of his eye, he
caught a glimpse of a young girl sitting in coach in an aisle seat next
to her parents. She waved at him, and he walked over to her. Kneeling
down so his eyes were level with hers, he said, "Do you like flying in
airplanes?"

She replied somewhat shyly, "Yes."

"So do I. How many times have you flown on an airplane?"

"Just once, when we came to Rome."

"Really. And why did you come to Rome?"

"To see the pope. Are you the pope?"

"Yes, I am," he replied.

"I thought so. Only the pope wears all white clothes. We saw you at
St. Peter's. You were far away. It's nice to see you up close."

James looked past the girl at her parents, who were staring on in
amazement. All over the plane people were standing, some on their
toes, trying to capture a glimpse of him and taking photos.

"What's your name?" he asked the girl.

"Kathleen."

"Kathleen what?"

"Kathleen Marie Hanson."

"My mother's name was Kathleen Marie. What a coincidence."

"What's a coincidence?" she asked.

"That's when two things are almost the same, but for no obvious
reason. It's like both you and my mother having the same name."

"That's cool we have the same name," she said.

"Yes," he laughed. "It's very cool."

As he stood up, the entire coach section burst out into applause. Most people on the plane were Catholic tourists returning home from Rome. There were also several priests and nuns and a couple of bishops. They all applauded for an extended period. James acknowledged the applause and then placed his hand on the girl's head and asked God to bless her. He shook the hands of her mother and father and told them, "You have a lovely daughter. God bless you. And God bless you, Kathleen Marie."

They landed at O'Hare International Airport outside Chicago on Saturday morning. Simmons took the pope's and the Swiss Guards' passports and deboarded before any of the other passengers. He processed through immigration in the diplomat line, collected all the bags, and cleared customs. When all the other passengers were off the plane, four US Secret Service agents came on board and invited Pope James and the two Swiss Guards to follow them off the plane and through a series of special exits. They led him to the garage, where a contingent of Secret Service agents and Cook County Sheriff officers waited. They got into a black SUV and followed a motorcycle detail to James's home in Winnetka.

The Flahvin home was on Bryant Avenue, not far from Sheridan Road and Lake Michigan. Winnetka was a wealthy residential suburb of families of highly educated and hard-working professionals. Although this was a safe community with little crime, the pope continued to get death threats. At the urging of the Swiss Guard, Father Maloney, the pope's son, Matt, the director of administration for the Chicago archdiocese, the Cook County Sheriff, and the Secret Service had arranged for the installation of several security and privacy measures at the house in preparation for James's return. They asked the neighbors for their input to ensure they would not offend or anger anyone by the various provisions. The Village of Winnetka granted the necessary permits and variances.

Concrete barriers along the roadway shielded the front of the house, and a black wrought-iron fence protected the entire front and side perimeter, including the driveway. A fingerprint-activated system controlled the gate. All the windows and doors of the house were replaced with bulletproof glass, and the exterior walls were reinforced with bomb-resistant steel. A twelve-foot high cedar fence covered a thick concrete wall, which encircled the back and side yards, and they upgraded all the electrical and communications wiring to the highest security level. No one particularly liked the fortress look, but all understood the need.

James had not been back to Winnetka since that eventful day ten months earlier when he had been summoned to Rome. It was good to be home. He and Vicky had always considered Winnetka an ideal place to live and raise a family. The local park district managed several recreational areas along the shores of the enormous glittering lake, and Jimmy and Vicky had strolled for hours down Sheridan Road and in nearby Lloyd Park. During the summer, they would sail off Lloyd Beach, and on warm summer days when the kids were young, they would swim at Tower Road Beach. Sacred Heart Catholic Church, where they were parishioners and where the kids had been baptized and attended school, was just a mile west down Tower Road.

James put the cassock aside that day and wore khaki shorts, a blue and white polo shirt, and cordovan leather sandals. All of James's kids, grandkids, and brothers with sisters-in-law and sisters with brothers-in-law showed up that first Saturday. As in any large family, there was no monolithic thinking about Jimmy's decision to become pope. While most were supportive, his youngest son was deeply disappointed and sad that his dad had moved so far away. He had already lost his mother to cancer, and now his father was gone, too.

Kathleen, James's sister who was named after their mother, was downright angry with her older brother. Taking him aside and out of earshot of others, she said, "Jimmy, I just don't understand how you could do this. Vicky was the love of your life, and you know how she hated the Catholic Church. How could you become the leader of the church she so despised? I just don't get it. Leaving your kids and law practice and all of us. How could you do this?"

"Ya know, Kathy, it was a difficult decision, and it's a difficult job. I am sorry you feel this way, but I think in my heart of hearts that Vicky would understand. I did not seek this out. This was not something I campaigned for or schemed to do. God called; I simply answered. I know Vicky would understand, and I know Mom and Dad would be proud."

"Well, Jimmy, I think it's just plain wrong. I always thought Vicky was right about the Church, and I think she's crying in her grave. I've never felt so let down by you. It is so selfish to just pull up and leave your entire family for a bunch of old men that don't have a clue. I'm sorry, Jimmy, I can't stay today." With that, she walked out of the house to her car. Her older brother watched her drive away as he wiped tears from his eyes.

James's other sister found him in the foyer, and they embraced. "Kathy will come around," she assured him. "She just needs time."

The rest of the day was low-key and relaxing. James's son Joe and Simmons showed the two Swiss Guards how to barbecue steaks and chicken over mesquite briquettes. The women brought a variety of salads and chocolate bars. Everyone ate well, enjoyed some fine California red, and shared the pleasure of one another's company.

He wrote in his journal that night about the great joy he felt visiting with his kids and other siblings. He was amazed by how much his twin grandsons had grown since he had seen them last, and how his children got along so well. Family had been everything to him in the past, and he realized how much he missed being with them on a regular basis.

✳ ✳ ✳

"Pope James Home in Winnetka," the headline read. Somewhat surprised and simultaneously proud, though a bit embarrassed, he looked at his picture on the front page of the *Chicago Tribune*. The story was about how a Chicago lawyer had become the improbable leader of the Roman Catholic Church. It was a flattering account, but he was still deeply hurt by his sister's words of the previous day. That dampened any fulfillment engendered by the article.

Cardinal Schmidt had arranged for James to celebrate Mass at his former parish in Winnetka. Secret Service agents drove him to the church in a black Cadillac SUV, accompanied by a motorcycle detail. They parked in the lot on the east side of the church, next to the rectory. The Sacred Heart complex was a substantial facility, and the church looked rather massive from the outside. However, it only sat about five hundred people and actually seemed quite small once inside.

James had specifically instructed Schmidt to provide no advance notice that he would be saying Mass. However, when he arrived at the rectory to meet the pastor, Father Jack Thielin, the parking lot was packed, and cars lined up on the adjoining streets. Knowing that few people attended early Sunday morning Mass, James suspected word had leaked out.

Father Jack welcomed James warmly. As the priest attempted to kneel to kiss his papal ring, James held his hand tightly and with a strong pull prevented him from lowering his body.

"No need to do that, Jack," he said politely. "How have you been?"

They had known each other for more than six years, ever since Thielin had become pastor at Sacred Heart. The pastor asked if he could introduce him at the beginning of Mass, even though everyone in the parish knew who he was.

"I'd appreciate that, Jack," James said.

"Would you like to wear the vestments we use for special celebrations?" Thielin inquired, hoping he would agree, although Cardinal Schmidt had advised the pastor the pope would bring vestments.

"No, thanks," he replied. "I have my own."

On this Sunday, he wore a white chasuble, which had a wide cobalt-blue band with the Greek letters for alpha and omega sewn in chartreuse on the front, and a simple outline of a fish on the back, symbolizing Christianity. Alpha and omega are the first and last letters of the Greek alphabet, representing the Almighty and Eternal God who was in the beginning, is now, and ever shall be.

"I think we should get started, Jack," James said. "We can visit after Mass." The two priests walked down a narrow interior corridor to the church sacristy. Several people had gathered there. James greeted them, preventing them from kneeling and kissing his ring.

More than a thousand people had crowded into the church. They squished into every available seat, while others stood along the side and back walls and packed the balcony with overflow in the foyer and out onto the sidewalk. At the rear of the church, two lectors in suit and tie, two altar girls wearing crimson cassocks and white surplices, the pastor, and the Supreme Pontiff of the Roman Catholic Church gathered as they waited for the appointed time.

The service began promptly with the choir singing "They'll Know We Are Christians by Our Love," and the congregation stood. Father Jack nodded to the lectors, and they processed up the center aisle to the front of the church. One of the lectors carried a bulky crucifix, and the other carried the lectionary. Altar girls and priests followed. As they reached the front, James stopped next to the person in the first pew while Thielin walked up the three steps to the top of the platform, turning to face his parishioners.

"We are blessed by Almighty God to have in our presence today the Holy Father. Many of us have known him and his family for many years, and I am deeply honored to welcome him home to his parish. Please give a warm Sacred Heart welcome to our dear friend, Pope James."

The church nearly shook with deafening applause as he walked up the steps to the altar. He stood facing the people, thanked them for their welcome, and quietly gestured for them to stop, but they kept applauding. After another minute of applause, he spoke loudly into the microphone.

"In the name of the Father, and of the Son, and of the Holy Spirit. Amen." The applause lessened, but did not end.

"You're not even supposed to know I'm here this morning," he said to laughter.

"Cardinal Schmidt was instructed to tell no one. So if you don't want to get your good cardinal in trouble with the pope, I suggest we simply celebrate Mass as we would any other Sunday." The laughter continued. "So let's try this again. In the name of the Father, and of the Son, and of the Holy Spirit. Amen." And Mass began—he was familiar with the liturgical routine now and no longer needed his special instruction manual.

The congregation was spellbound as they watched James's every move. After reading the predetermined Gospel for this particular Sunday from the pulpit, James walked down the steps to the center of the main isle and addressed the congregation.

"Thank you for welcoming me home," he started. "I apologize to those of you who live in my neighborhood. Unfortunately, you have to put up with the inconvenience of all the security measures of the Cook County Sheriff and Secret Service. As pope, I am also head of state of Vatican City. Because of that, the US federal government requires that I have protective service while I am in the United States. I cannot decline this protection. It is a precondition to my coming here. I ask that you have patience with the officers. They are only doing their jobs.

"Recently I announced a change in canon law. Married men with a vocation to the priesthood may now be ordained. In addition, priests called to married life can marry. This, as you know, is a major change in modern Catholicism. The Church has always encouraged and cele-brated celibacy among the clergy. However, a married clergy is not new. St. Peter was married, as were many of the apostles. Furthermore, bish-ops and priests were married during the early centuries of the Church.

"The Church continues to honor and promote celibacy among the clergy. But we also honor and promote marriage. Married life is a won-derful calling. Many married men and women have served God well. Even popes, some of whom were canonized, were married men. The church recognizes marriage as a sacrament because Jesus honored marriage. He spoke about marriage in the Gospel of Matthew. Jesus said, 'A man will leave his father and mother and be united to his wife, and the two will become one flesh. So they are no longer two, but one. Therefore what God has joined together, let no man separate.' He hon-ored marriage again at the wedding in Cana, when he turned water into fine wine at the behest of his mother.

"I know from my personal experience that loving a woman need not interfere with loving or serving God. I also know that loving God need not interfere with loving a woman. I know too that after loving God, family should always come first in a man's life. One's vocation should always take second place. Nevertheless, family can enhance a person's work by giving it focus and offering a more genuine understanding of life. Scripture teaches all that God created is good. Physical intimacy is good. It is granted by God and enjoyed in love. My life without my wife, Vicky, is less today. It is less because of the loss of the emotional, intellectual, spiritual, and physical intimacy we shared together.

"St. Paul suggests in Corinthians that life might be easier as a single clergyman. However, 'easier' does not mean more fulfilling or more spiritually enriching. And being single is not necessarily easier. Several years ago, a friend of mine from this diocese retired from the priesthood after nearly forty-three years. I took him to lunch in celebration of his retirement. I asked him what it was like to be a priest for so many years. He said, 'It was lonely.' I don't know what I expected him to say. But I was surprised when he said he had been lonely for all those years. I do not believe God wanted him, or any of us, to live our lives in loneliness.

"Some men are called to the priesthood. Others are called to marriage. However, God calls some to both. Some married men sitting in this congregation today, and others throughout this parish, the archdiocese, and the world are called to both. Some of you know who you are. Others may not yet know. Through prayer, it will be revealed to you. Trust me, if I can be called to the priesthood, anyone can be called." People in the pews smiled back at James.

"The need for priests today is enormous. The Church cannot fulfill its sacramental responsibilities if we do not have enough priests to serve God's people. The Eucharist is central to the Christian life. However, in Asia, Africa, and South America, large percentages of the population cannot attend Mass or receive the Eucharist because there are too few priests. In the United States, and in this archdiocese, parishes are forced to merge because of insufficient numbers of priests. In some cases, those mergers are corrosive and drive people away from the Church rather than enhancing their spiritual lives.

"So I ask every man in this church today to ask Almighty God if you should dedicate the rest of your life to serving others—the poor, the forgotten, the imprisoned, the homeless, the children—by serving God through the Church. And I invite every woman to encourage the men in your life to pray for guidance and to heed God's call." James returned to the altar and continued the celebration of the Mass.

Just before Mass ended, Father Jack announced that Pope James would greet parishioners at the front entrance to the church. The pastor explained the Pope's wishes that they neither kneel nor kiss his ring, despite the ancient practice by which Catholics honored religious hierarchy. The closing hymn was an Irish piece, "The Lord of the Dance." After the third verse, the altar girls, lectors, pastor, and pope walked back down the central aisle and out of the church.

It was a captivating morning, the sun already high in the cloudless powder-blue sky. They stood on the weathered concrete sidewalk in front of the ornate Christian building, greeting friends and parishioners. The black SUV and motorcycle escort waited a few yards away at the curb while the line of people wrapped around the building. Standing immediately to James's left was one of the plainclothes Swiss Guards, while the other stood directly across from the parade of people. Secret Service officers were always close by. Simmons remained at James's side, taking notes of the requests people made and the pope's responses. The young priest would later guarantee any commitment the pope made was fulfilled.

One of Vicky's best friends moved up in line, and when it was finally her turn they embraced. "It's so good to see you," she said.

"It's great to be home," he responded.

"I don't know what Vicky would say about you becoming pope, but I think it's great. What you are doing for the Church is wonderful. What a breath of fresh air you've brought to this stodgy institution."

"Thank you. I appreciate that. Not everyone agrees with you. Not even everyone in my family."

"I know. I've talked with Kathy. You can't please everyone. I think what you have done about married priests is right on the mark. Now you just have to include women. If you do that, you might even get Kathy's vote."

"Female ordination—that's a tough one."

"I know. But you'll do what's right."

"Pray for me?"

"Every day, Jimmy. Every day." She smiled, gave him a kiss on the cheek, and squeezed his hand.

Winnetka Police and Cook County Sheriff officers surrounded the area. Word had gotten out, and a cavalcade of media photographed his every move and attempted to record each conversation. For an hour, James shook hands and visited with everyone who greeted him.

Returning to the sacristy, James changed into his light ivory business suit, thanked Father Jack and the altar girls, waved good-bye to all those who were still at the church, and hurried to the SUV. The media followed as closely as the police allowed. He was expected at the Winnetka Presbyterian Church for the nine forty-five service.

✳ ✳ ✳

Rev. Robert Jacobson, a renowned religious author and a leader in the International Presbyterian Church, waited outside for James as the motorcade arrived. The senior pastor wore a black floor-length robe and a black stole with magenta and white embroidered Christian symbols over his shoulders.

"Thank you for allowing me to be here this morning," James said.

"You are always welcome in the House of God," Jacobson replied.

Before they walked into the church, Jacobson gave James a wireless microphone. The faithful filled three-quarters of the church, and members of the media occupied most of the remaining seats. The crimson-robed choir, sitting behind the altar and facing the congregation, quietly awaited the service. Upon gaining the attention of the choir director, the pastor nodded. Music immediately burst forth, lyrics uplifted, and the worship service got underway. The two men strolled down the center aisle, and Jacobson showed James to his front-row aisle seat. The pastor continued up to the communion table as the members of the congregation whispered to one another about the man in the white suit and white skullcap who was in their church.

Turning to the assembled, Jacobson said, "You may have noticed we have a special friend with us today. Many of us know him as Jimmy Flahvin. He has a new name now. All across the world, he is known as

James the First. Please help me welcome our dear friend, Pope James." Unlike at Sacred Heart, no one in the church, other than Bob Jacobson and the cadre of reporters had any advance notice he would be worshiping with them today.

Speaking to the people in the pews from the center aisle, James started. "I come here this morning to publicly thank each of you for all you did for my wife, Vicky. You befriended her and gave her a spiritual home when she had no place else to go. As those of you who knew her know, Vicky was raised Catholic. She was baptized, made her first communion, confirmed, and married in the Catholic Church. Vicky often told me she was totally Catholic. She really did not know how to commit to anything other than one hundred percent. The priest sex-abuse scandal broke her spirit. She simply could not comprehend how a priest could take advantage of, and so abuse, a child. Vicky was devastated, as were many Catholics. When the media reported that there were hundreds of priests involved and thousands of children victimized, she fell into despair. However, it was not the sinfulness of the priests, or the horrific harm perpetrated on the children, that drove her from her Catholic faith. The cover-up by the Church hierarchy ultimately severed her relationship with the Catholic Church. Vicky was so disappointed, so disillusioned, so betrayed, so distraught that she could no longer even walk into a Catholic church. Her faith in God was not weakened. Her Christian beliefs were not in jeopardy. However, her connection to Catholicism was gone.

"For many months Vicky was without a place to worship. It was a spiritually difficult time for her. Then she found you. You took her in. She became a part of this wonderful Christian community. Her spiritual life was whole once again. She loved worshiping here. She loved each of you. She would often come home after Sunday worship and tell me how welcoming this community is. She'd tell me about Bob's profound sermon. She'd tell me about all the good work you do in serving those in need in the city and around the world. She even convinced me to read Bob's books—all fifteen of them." That evoked laughter and a sheepish grin from Pastor Jacobson.

"Then Vicky got sick. The diagnosis was stage-four pancreatic cancer. Your response was remarkable. You loved her, supported her, prayed with her, and cared for her. And you were a huge support to our children and me." As James spoke, several in the pews wiped away tears.

"We buried Vicky from this church. It was the saddest day of my life. You filled this sanctuary with love. Many of you told stories about my wife that filled my heart. I cannot thank you enough for the tenderness and support you showed our family.

"I still long for Vicky every day. I know that she is eternally happy in the presence of Almighty God. But I miss her terribly. However, I am so grateful in knowing that in her final years and during her last days, friends from this Christian community surrounded her. Thank you. God bless you."

There was not a dry eye in the church as everyone stood and gave him booming applause. He sat down in his seat, put his head in his hands, and cried.

✳ ✳ ✳

Media vans and reporters deluged Winnetka. Stories of James's interaction with passengers on the flight from Rome, and his inspiring and heartfelt homilies at the Catholic and Protestant morning worship services, had reached the mass media with the speed of a text message. As James and his family and friends enjoyed one another's company inside what had become a compound, tens of thousands of people from all over the greater Chicago metropolitan area drove to Winnetka in hope that they might visit with, or at least catch a glimpse of, the hometown pope. All the roads leading in and out of the village clogged to a standstill. People parked their cars wherever they could find a spot and attempted to walk to the pope's home.

The chancery office and the Cook County Sheriff had agreed that the sheriff's department would provide round-the-clock protection of the pope's home when he was not in Chicago. However, when he was at home, they blocked off the entire surrounding area with gray steel barricades all the way from Humboldt Avenue on the south to Tower Road on the north, and Sheridan Road on the east to Prescott Avenue on the west. Only residential traffic was allowed in or out, and that was limited to members of households issued special passes. James's family and guests were also issued passes. Cook County Sheriff officers and Secret Service agents were stationed in their squad cars at every intersection. Passersby could not linger for even a moment. If they did, they were sternly told to keep moving. The police answered no questions about which house was the pope's or where he might be. The crowds came and dispersed quickly—the police were forcefully aggressive in moving people along so there was nothing to see and nowhere to go. The Illinois governor and Chicago and Winnetka mayors encouraged people not to go to Winnetka. By early evening, the roads were back to normal.

During the next six weeks, James enjoyed his respite from the Vatican. Although he could not escape Church business, the time at home offered a needed vacation. To his great dismay, he was unable to leave his home, except for occasionally venturing out for dinner at a local restaurant and for Mass on Sunday morning. He had hoped to take leisurely walks along Lake Michigan and to visit his old law office, but the Secret Service advised against it due to the significant number of death threats. It was a small price to pay, given he was able to spend quality time with his children and grandkids.

One morning, Matthew approached him in the living room. "Dad, the Democratic Congressional Caucus has asked me to run for the US Congress. I presume it's because Catholics are a strong plurality in the district and I'm the son of the pope. So this is probably much more about you than it is about me. But still—"

"Congratulations, Matt!" Matthew smiled, embarrassed. "Politics can make for a difficult life, Matt. I suspect it can also be very fulfilling. You could make a genuine difference in people's lives. Still, power can be an aphrodisiac that only the most well-grounded can resist."

"Do you think I should run, Dad?"

"Only you can answer that, son. But as you contemplate that question, I encourage you to dig deep into your soul. Ask yourself whether your faith is strong enough to withstand and endure the enormous temptations that elective office poses. Remember what your mother used to tell all of you. 'Bad company corrupts good character.' Jesus stated it clearly when he asked, 'What good does it do for a man to gain the whole world and lose his soul?' You are a very good man, Matt. I am extremely proud of you. But only you know if you have sufficient character and strength of purpose for this." He put his hand on his son's shoulder.

'I think I'd like to do this, Dad."

"Then do it. I will support you any way I can. But you know I cannot do anything publicly."

"Pray for me, Dad."

"I already do pray for you, Matthew—every single day."

Later that week Mary stopped by the house for dinner with her boyfriend, Kerry. During the meal, they told James they intended to marry and asked for his blessing.

"Well, that's wonderful," he said. Turning to Kerry, he asked, "Do you love Mary?"

"Yes, of course I do," Kerry responded. "I love her with my whole heart, my whole being."

"In marriage, love is not just about the heart," he told Kerry. "Love is not a feeling; it's a covenant. It is the decision to be present to and care for your spouse during both the best and the most difficult times. It is a resolution to support, sustain, and befriend another human being, another child of God, every single day of her life, even when she's on your butt—even when it may seem like she doesn't love you. And love means that she will do the same for you.

"So I ask you again. Do you love my Mary?"

"Yes," he replied.

"Mary, do you love this man?"

"Yes, Daddy, very much," she replied.

"Then you have my blessing."

"Will you marry us, Dad?"

"I'd be thrilled."

Chapter Thirteen

"I 've got good news and bad news," Cardinal Mbuto reported one day after the pope had returned to the Vatican. "Which would you like first?"

James had become quite fond of his secretary of state, Jacob Cardinal Mbuto, and they had developed an easy working style. The pope found Mbuto unique in that he was unusually bright, loyal, and creative, and exhibited tireless energy. The pope fully depended on Mbuto to keep him fully informed and to successfully execute any assignment.

Mbuto grew up in a poor farming village in the highlands of south central Tanzania. It was a life far removed from James's experience. Jacob didn't start school until he was eight because his father needed him to take care of the family's goats and sheep. Then he broke his leg when he was ten and lost a half year of schooling. The local rural medical aid was not equipped to mend his fractured bone, so his father carried him on his shoulders eighteen kilometers down the long, winding mountain path to the public bus that would take them to the hospital in Iringa. Mbuto stayed at the hospital for six weeks while his leg healed. When his father returned to get him, he put his son back up on his shoulders and carried him up the mountain to their village, so as not to strain the newly healed but still weak limb. It was another six weeks before he could walk with confidence. Cardinal Mbuto often told this story as an example of the committed relationship he and his father shared.

Mbuto attended elementary school in his home village and then was fortunate to get a full scholarship to a Catholic high school in a community about fifty kilometers away. Jacob was a gifted student—curious about everything, a prolific reader, a promising writer, and a results-oriented, energetic worker. He excelled and was able to attend the University of Dar es Salaam on a full scholarship. Then, unexpectedly, after only two years at the university, he enrolled in the Catholic seminary in Arusha. No one was more surprised by his decision to become a priest than his eleven brothers and sisters, none of whom had ever thought of Jacob as religious. After he was ordained, Father Mbuto served fifteen rural village parishes in the Iringa diocese, riding his motorcycle from church to church every weekend, starting out on Friday evening and saying his last Mass at four on Sunday afternoon.

At thirty-six, he was ordained one of the youngest Catholic bishops in the world and proved himself to be a natural and inspirational leader. He later studied in Cape Town, Rome and Milwaukee, Wisconsin, where he earned a Ph.D. in Scripture at Marquette University. He spoke several languages, and his Italian and English were impeccable. John XXIV elevated him to cardinal only a few months before he died.

Cardinal Mbuto saw James as both a friend and a mentor, someone who could teach him about a world that he did not know. He was extraordinarily grateful for the opportunity to work with this American lawyer-pope, but even more grateful for the ease with which they interacted and the confidence the Holy Father placed in him.

"You know I always want the good news first because I have no choice about getting the bad news," James responded.

"OK," Mbuto said. "Nearly forty thousand married men have responded to God's call to ordination. Men who left the priesthood to marry are returning. Dioceses are fast-tracking married deacons because they have already had much of the necessary instruction. Seminaries have increased their capacity to encourage new vocations of married men, and some dioceses are even offering evening and weekend classes in order to accommodate working aspirants. Special classes are being designed to help new priests cope with the challenges of a married clergy."

James interrupted. "That's terrific. But if that's the good news, what can the bad news possibly be?"

"Forty thousand is too small a number. Our hope that married priests would compensate for the severe shortage has vanished. We need a couple hundred thousand priests; forty thousand won't come close to addressing the problem."

"I should always get the bad news first." James was greatly disappointed. He suspected it had been wishful thinking that ordaining married men would resolve the shortage. The Eastern Rite had a married clergy, and there was no surplus of Eastern Rite Catholic priests. The obstacles to the priesthood were just too intractable—low pay, centralized control, an aggressive "pulpit committee," and many years of required study—too overwhelming for most men to conquer. And allowing priests to marry affected other aspects of the clergy. Although most priests remained celibate, some now dated in the hope of finding a meaningful relationship and loving partner. It was difficult, though, because these men had little or no adult romantic experiences.

There were plusses, though. James elevated thirty-six family men to the rank of cardinal, and one hundred were ordained bishops. About half had been married priests for many years in the Eastern Rite or ordained Protestant ministers who had converted to Catholicism. The rest were men who had left the priesthood to marry and now returned. However, five of the married cardinals were new priests, all of whom had enjoyed successful secular careers—a president of a prestigious American Catholic university, a CEO of a multinational corporation, a former prime minister of a European country, a renowned Asian heart surgeon, and a Latin American lay theologian. Each of the five had resigned their previous positions to serve the Church more directly.

James wanted to fully engage the enormous experience of these men as he conveyed to all the faithful that everyone was welcome to, and could lead in, the Roman Catholic Church.

Nevertheless, every time James made a progressive decision that affected married men, there was a cry from women asking when they would be recognized for their gifts. When would they be allowed to heed God's call to unconditionally serve the Church? This caused him considerable consternation. James believed in his heart that Jesus would not discriminate, and he was certain female ordination would resolve the significant shortage of priests. All the same, while the people in the pews favored women priests, Church history only supported the inclusion of married men, and the hierarchy was not ready to ordain women. Married cardinals offered some hope. They were far more open to the possibility of, and the opportunity presented by, a female clergy. Yet it would take time. How much time was the question.

Within a year of James's inauguration, the cash-flow bankruptcy the Church had been experiencing when he had assumed the role of Peter was effectively rectified. The impounding of individual clergy bank accounts, the tremendous increase in the Sunday collection plate, and massive amounts of private contributions offered in his name though Peter's Pence provided the necessary revenue to pay the bills and move the Church forward.

Many clerics seethed when their accounts were confiscated and material possessions seized; but the newly discovered assets provided financial infusions that quickly got the Church off life support. The money was helpful, but James was incredulous that Church leaders all over the world found it acceptable to control large amounts of money and amass lavish Church wealth while hundreds of millions of God's people suffered in desperate poverty.

As Catholics responded positively to the new pope, parish enrollments mushroomed and Sunday Masses filled churches. Historically, more people in the pews always resulted in more money in the collection plate. However, this was special. The number of contributors went up and the amount per donor grew as well. Peter's Pence generated the real money and offered the pope new flexibility. A nineteenth-century practice meaning "pennies for the pope," Peter's Pence encouraged Catholics worldwide to donate directly to the pope without any percentage taken off the top by local priests or bishops. After John Paul II's election in 1978, he had substantially increased donations through Peter's Pence by calling on all Catholics to give to an annual collection for the pope. His campaign had been a great success, with the faithful from the United States contributing more than a third of the total donated.

However, after the sex abuse scandal gained public attention in the mid-1980s and the cover-up broke wide open in the late '90s, donations to all Church programs had suffered, including to Peter's Pence. In 2010, when the media disclosed Pope Benedict's questionable actions regarding the scandal while he had served as a cardinal in Munich, many viewed the pope as condoning the cover-ups, and Peter's Pence took a direct and fatal hit.

James's freshness and common approach revived Peter's Pence. MDB Group created an inviting and compelling website and social media content that stimulated record support for Peter's Pence. They mimicked successful US political campaign fundraising techniques, engaging tens of millions of small donors who generated over ten million dollars daily, most coming from Europe and the United States. Increased income offered expanded opportunity to serve the Church, which James translated as serving the poor.

"I want to establish a human and economic development department staffed by priests, nuns, and laypersons with experience working with local people in developing countries," he told Mbuto. "Identify advisors from the Jesuit Corps, Maryknolls, Franciscans, Catholic Relief Services, Caritas, Voluntares Globales and other nonsectarian NGOs who can help us understand how the Church can best use our newfound wealth for the benefit of the vulnerable and those in need."

James remembered an Irish priest in Indonesia whom he had met when he and Vicky had volunteered there years before. Father Charlie Martin had dedicated his life to liberating people from poverty. James believed Father Charlie was the ultimate example of sound Christian "liberation theology" in action, and his community-based projects were the epitome of what works in advancing developing communities.

Indonesia, the largest Muslim country in the world, was one of the pope's favorite places. He especially enjoyed Sumatra—the quiet and serenity of the rural villages, and how peaceful he had felt during his and Vicky's brief times there. The people were economically poor, but like other impoverished areas where James had served, their generosity of spirit overcame the day-to-day economic challenges and engendered deep happiness. It was a beautiful nation. The scenery was fascinating—impenetrable tropical bush; tamarind, bamboo, banana, palm, and coconut trees; flamboyantly adorned birds; and primitive dugout canoes dotting the sea, some motorized and others with paddles or flapping, tattered sails. Of course, there were the radical fundamentalists who had so disrupted the country, its economy, and its tourism industry by acts of terrorism. However, these people represented just a tiny, albeit fanatic, minority. The vast majority of Indonesians were kind, thoughtful, considerate, and loving.

Father Charlie preached and practiced the simple presupposition that local people must be in charge of their own development efforts. "Free people will decide for themselves what they will and will not do," he would say. "It's only when local people take the leadership role in the creation of their development projects that they have any chance of success."

Charlie and his staff reached out to all people in the region, most of whom were Muslims, and they always cooperated with local government officials and the military. Results were tangible and effective. That's what got James's attention. Charlie's development organization managed nutrition and education programs for pregnant women and new moms, preschools, and elementary, middle, and high schools, and administered major hospitals and village clinics. Perhaps most important, from a religious perspective, the majority of the mothers and children in these Catholic schools, and nearly all of the patients at the Catholic hospitals and clinics, were Muslim. Father Charlie had even built the foundation for a mosque, which happened to be adjacent to a Catholic church. His objective was not to convert the Muslims, but simply to serve the economically poor. To do the work of Jesus the Christ.

James recalled the Irish priest advising the volunteers in his Irish lilt, "Put aside your American results-oriented mindset. Appreciate the plain reality that by just showing up here in this small, remote village, you are contributing directly to the future of these children. The mere fact that you've come all this way, reaching out to those in need, providing your assistance and care, making an effort to know the people, and offering your friendship, is more than enough. In the Sumatran value system, human relationships and interaction are much more important than specific goals, objectives, or results."

It was with these thoughts in mind that James called Father Charlie Martin one morning and asked him to come to Rome to head up his human and economic development efforts.

"You don't want me for this job, Holy Father. I get in too much trouble," Charlie said, a laugh in his voice.

"How's that?"

"You remember when I was cut off from Catholic Relief Services because of some powdered milk?"

"Yes, I remember," James said.

"That was a long time ago. Your law firm represented me, and you tried to bail me out, but even you couldn't help. Remember?"

The US Department of Agriculture had had a surplus of powdered milk and had given some of it to Catholic Relief Services in Indonesia. Charlie had received several truckloads of the milk for impoverished children in the Bandar Lampung region. His staff nutritionist had told him not to take the milk because it was a one-time donation and would not help the children. The nutritionist had informed the priest that once you start a young child on cows' milk, it is necessary to keep giving it to them. Otherwise, it can have serious adverse side effects.

"Our parents were too poor to buy milk after the free milk was gone, and we didn't have any money to continue a milk program," Charlie reminded the pope. "But the powdered milk had financial value. I knew wealthy Indonesians would buy it. So I sold the milk and used the profits to pay for a new school. When CRS learned what I'd done, they went ballistic. You later told me it was against US law to monetize donated goods, and CRS feared that USDA would come down on them hard. So I was cut off from all future donations, regardless of their origin."

"I do remember," James said, smiling, "and that's exactly why I want you to coordinate this ambitious effort, Charlie. I need your vision and wisdom. I need your expertise. Most important, I need your commitment to the poor and underprivileged."

A week later, Father Charlie Martin moved to Rome and became the Catholic Church's development czar. He and James were a formidable team. They raised enormous amounts of money and engaged hundreds of thousands of volunteers in serving the poor. Focusing on pregnant women and young children, they provided food, nutrition, and protection from infectious disease so that infants' and toddlers' brains could fully develop and those children could realize the fullness of their God-given potential. Working under the direction of local community leaders, they built, supplied, and staffed facilities and educational programs for pregnant women and new moms, preschools, health clinics, and community centers. They constructed homes and apartments for the homeless in the rural countryside and urban centers, and created caring facilities for the orphaned, abandoned, and disabled, ensuring sufficient nutritious food, healing medicines, quality education, and appropriate clothing. They recruited volunteer physicians, nutritionists, dentists, therapists, and nurses to provide health care and nutrition and hygiene education to children and their parents; supplied seeds, fertilizer, and water-conservative irrigation and farming technology for school and household gardens and to small family farmers; and trained entrepreneurs and offered low- and no-interest loans to small businesses all over the world. The results were significant. No previous effort, public or private, had ever made such a positive and lasting effect on poverty and human development.

"Truth be told, I didn't know much about theology, the catechism, or Church history when I was elected," he confided in John Simmons. "Yet it quickly became clear that I needed to learn. I studied Scripture and the history of the Church. Researched one chapter of the Bible every night, concentrating on the New Testament, but reading from the Old as well. I studied several theologians from different denominations, to get their take. I had read much of the Bible while in prison years ago.

But I had no idea how it would hold such meaning and purpose at this stage in my life."

In the second decade of the twenty-first century, Christianity was the largest religion in the world, claiming one-third of the planet's nearly eight billion people. There were five major Christian churches, and more than 50 percent of Christians were Roman Catholic, with about 40 percent members of a multitude of Protestant denominations.

James wondered why Christianity had divided into so many factions. His curiosity brought him to the history of the Nicene Creed, a proclamation of Christian belief promulgated in AD 325; the Great Schism of 1054, when the Eastern and Western churches had split, due in part to the interpretation of the Nicene Creed; the sixteenth-century Protestant Reformation, which had further divided the church of Jesus the Christ; and the lives of the popes, some of whom were partially responsible for these divisions.

One scriptural passage struck James particularly profoundly. In John 17, Jesus says,

> I pray also for those who will believe in me through their message, that all of them may be one, Father, just as you are in me and I am in you. May they also be in us so that the world may believe that you have sent me. I have given them the glory that you gave me, that they may be one as we are one: I in them and you in me. May they be brought to complete unity to let the world know that you sent me and have loved them even as you have loved me.

These prayerful words of unity concerned James. The current situation among the Christian denominations hardly resembled the vision of unity Jesus had prayed for to the Father—"that they may be one as we are one: I in them and you in me."

As James pondered these words, he sought the wisdom of Catholic theologians, as well as Protestant, Anglican, and Orthodox. Most agreed that Scripture emphasized the importance and value of church unity. However, none could recommend an easy or practical way to achieve it. James gained an increasingly sympathetic appreciation for Patriarch Michael Cerularis and his followers in the eleventh-century schism, and Martin Luther and the sixteenth-century Protestant reformers. While no denomination could escape blame, James concluded that some Catholic leaders had significantly contributed to Christianity's rifts. He considered the argument that the pope was a major obstacle to bringing denominations together—not James as an individual, but as an institution, along with the Roman Catholic claim that the pope was the rightful heir of Peter and the supreme leader of all Christianity.

James looked to Cardinal O'Bryan as his personal mentor on such issues—a role that O'Bryan relished. Whenever the New York cardinal was in Rome, the pope invited him to his apartment, and they would discuss Church history and theology over dinner and a bottle of Italian Primitivo.

"What's your take on John 17, where Jesus prays to the Father for unity among his followers?" the pope asked during one of those meals.

"Many theologians interpret that as a directive to all Christian believers that we be united as one church."

"Is that widely held throughout the various denominations?" James asked.

"I believe so. Of course, there are always the dissenters."

"Is that your interpretation?"

"Yes," Cardinal O'Bryan replied. "I think Jesus hoped that all believers would be united in one body, as Paul writes in Ephesians."

"What's preventing that from happening?"

"It is very complex, Holy Father."

James chuckled. He knew O'Bryan was not being disrespectful. Theology, Church history, and Holy Scripture were O'Bryan's areas of expertise. It was understandable that O'Bryan would instinctively conclude that he couldn't understand these complexities; he was just a lawyer. But he wanted O'Bryan's insight and expertise. "So humor me, John. Describe the complexity."

"I'm sorry, Holy Father. I meant no disrespect."

"I know, John," he said with a wide smile.

"The human condition is so complicated," O'Bryan explained. "The Great Schism was a result of theological disagreements, but it was also caused by church politics, jealousies, ethnic conflicts, clerical material-ism, and even misunderstandings due to differences in language. The reasons for the Reformation are equally convoluted. And unfortunately, we've found that once the glass is broken, it is very difficult to put it back together."

"What role has the Vatican played in these divisions?" James asked, assuming his cross-examination mode.

"We've made our mistakes. But we can't beat ourselves up over things that happened hundreds or thousands of years ago. I don't think it's possible, or even helpful, to ascribe blame to any one group, a single individual, or a specific issue."

"So you agree that the Holy See has not always had clean hands."

"Yes, Holy Father. Pope Paul VI said as much when he asked other denominations for forgiveness for the role the Catholic Church played in the separations."

"Wasn't the Protestant Reformation primarily caused by clergy sell-ing indulgences to quicken safe passage out of Purgatory?"

"That was one of the causes."

"Now that was a clear indicator all was not well in the Universal Church," the pope said sarcastically. "But Martin Luther, John Calvin, and others broke away not just because of theological differences. Weren't they also motivated by the immorality, greed, and abuse of power by bishops, cardinals, and even some popes?"

"Yes, Holy Father."

"I know how this can happen, John. My wife was a devout Catholic until she learned about the child sex-abuse cover-up. As terrible as the priests' sex abuse was, she could forgive those men for their sins. However, she could not fathom how men who claimed to be devoted to the teachings of Jesus the Christ could knowingly put children in harm's way. She could not comprehend how Church leaders would not hold those priests accountable for their misdeeds and instead protect the perpetrators. Vicky concluded that men who failed to protect chil-dren could not possibly be God's chosen representatives. So she left. When leaders don't walk their talk, it's almost impossible for the faith-ful to follow."

"I know," O'Bryan replied. "I know. I tried very hard to prevent the cover-up in Boston. But I failed."

"We need to turn this around, John. We have to do all we can to foster the unity that Jesus prayed for. Paul VI, St. John Paul II, and Francis were deeply committed to this. I am as well. On the theological front, I can't think of anything more important."

"I agree," O'Bryan said.

"The questions are: What do we do? How do we do it? I've been giving this some thought. What if I publicly apologized for the mistakes of the Catholic Church? Made a big deal out of it. Then bishops and cardinals all over the world followed my lead. What if we acknowledged that Luther and Calvin were men of great faith and committed to the word of Jesus the Christ? What if I rescinded the excommunications of the Reformation leaders?"

O'Bryan winced. He supported the concept of Christian unity. But there were limits. "Both St. John Paul II and Benedict apologized for mistakes. So doing that would be OK," O'Bryan said. "But retracting the Protestants' excommunications? That would be most distasteful in the mouths of many Catholics. After all, those guys left the Church. They questioned apostolic authority. They renounced the role of the pope. I don't think it would be helpful. First, it wouldn't bring many Protestants back, and second, it would put into question your and every other pope's authority. Furthermore, the Curia and bishops the world over would be terribly offended."

"Paul VI rescinded the excommunications of the leaders of the Great Schism," James reminded his friend. "That went a long way toward restoring communion between the Orthodox and Roman churches. Why can't I do the same with Protestants?" He did not give O'Bryan the chance to answer. "We're obligated to address the divide within the Christian church. Jesus prayed for unity. He said there shall be one flock and one shepherd, and referred to himself as the Shepherd. On the organizational front, how can anything be more important? Our resolve cannot be influenced by offended feelings among Catholic clergy or hierarchy. The stakes are too high. The rise of all these denominations is the work of man, not the Holy Spirit. And it appears that on more than one occasion members of the Roman Curia, even popes, were among the culprits."

O'Bryan remained silent. He knew his friend was right, but if James pressed this issue, he also knew there'd be hell to pay.

James understood serious and fundamental disagreements among Christian denominations were widespread, particularly about the sacraments, the style of worship service, and apostolic succession. Major differences regarding the Eucharist, Scripture, and Church history, culture, discipline, and traditions caused the appearance of irreparable division. However, James was convinced that Christian denominations had far more in common than what separated them.

Like popes Paul VI, John Paul II, and Francis before him, James committed himself to complete Christian reunion through prayer, mutual respect, and understanding. Theologians agreed that most Christians believed the precepts laid out in the Nicene Creed, the product of the fourth-century unity council convened by the Roman emperor Constantine. The interpretation and translation of certain words and phrases of the creed had been the cause of division for many centuries. However, in 1975 several leading denominations had adopted an ecumenical version of the creed, which helped move meaningful reconciliation forward. In the twenty-first century, many Christian denominations included a common testament as part of their Sunday worship service. Although some of the words were slightly different, the theological understandings were the same:

I believe in one God, the Father, the Almighty maker of heaven and earth, of all things visible and invisible. I believe in one Lord Jesus Christ, the only begotten Son of God, born of the Father before all ages. God from God, Light from Light, true God from true God, begotten, not made, consubstantial with the Father; through him, all things were made. For us men and for our salvation he came down from heaven, by the Holy Spirit was incarnate of the Virgin Mary and became man. For our sake he was crucified under Pontius Pilate; he suffered death and was buried, and rose again on the third day in accordance with the

Scriptures. He ascended into heaven and is seated at the right hand of the Father. He will come again in glory to judge the living and the dead and his kingdom will have no end. I believe in the Holy Spirit, the Lord, the giver of Life, who proceeds from the Father and the Son, who with the Father and the Son is adored and glorified, who has spoken through the prophets.

I believe in one holy, catholic, and apostolic church. I confess one baptism for the forgiveness of sins, and I look for the resurrection of the dead and the life of the world to come. Amen.

These words were the foundation of James's Christian belief and the basis for his grand optimism and commitment for ecumenism.

With the help of his Chicago PR firm and his closest advisors and staff, James embarked on a campaign to establish an ecumenical organization called One God, One Church. He invited leaders of every major Christian denomination to Vatican City to participate in a Christian Unity Summit.

In his opening Summit remarks, James said, "On behalf of Catholics worldwide, I apologize for every wrong, every indiscretion, every injustice, and every sin perpetrated by the Catholic Church during the past two thousand years. Jesus commands that, 'If you are offering your gift at the altar, and there remember that your brother has something against you, leave your gift before the altar and go first be reconciled to your brother.' In that spirit and in the spirit of the Lord's prayer for unity, I offer to you, my brothers and sisters in Christ, my personal apology and the apology of the Catholic Church. We ask your forgiveness.

"Jesus prayed to the Father that 'all of us be one.' We in this room have no alternative but to do all humanly possible to abide by his wishes. We have made progress. We have enjoyed many successes in recent decades, upon which we can build. There is widespread conformity on the Nicene Creed. Orthodox and Catholic churches have reconciled issues relating to the Holy Spirit. We have also recognized that man cannot make 'definitive assertions about the inner life of God.' Lutherans and Catholics have agreed on the way of salvation. This was one of the dividing issues that moved Martin Luther centuries ago.

"But while progress has been made, we need to do much more. We can become one body in Christ," James told his non-Catholic friends. "Through the Holy Spirit, our differences can be reconciled. We need only cleanse our hearts and acknowledge regret and repentance for past wrongs. We all can resolve to work toward a common understanding and expression of Christian faith. With God's help, we can reach full communion of faith, fraternal accord, and sacramental life. This is required for the greater good of all believers and the coming of the Kingdom of God. With prayer, humility, and commitment, we can realize Jesus' prayer."

Turning to his own cardinals and bishops in the auditorium, he said, "Jesus' petition for all his followers to be as one will require each of you, and all our clergy, to help heal the terrible wounds of the past. We must all be open to, and accepting of, different and unfamiliar worship services and church-governing structures. That is why I included the doxology, traditionally used by Protestants when ending the Lord's Prayer, at my first Mass in St. Peter's. It was a prayer for unity.

"In the spirit of unity, I have directed this doxology be included as a continuous part of the Lord's Prayer at all Catholic Masses throughout the world. In the spirit of unity, the Roman Catholic Church will join the World Council of Churches, overturning our long-standing policy to go it alone. I am instructing every diocese to become actively engaged in their local Council of Churches chapter.

"In the spirit of unity, I have today rescinded the excommunications of Martin Luther, John Calvin, and all the leaders of the Protestant Reformation. These were men of great faith and tremendous commitment to Jesus the Christ.

"In the spirit of unity, I pray that all Protestants will join all Catholics in one communion."

This was an unprecedented statement by a Catholic pope. The response from other denominations was extremely positive. Many leaders joined the One God, One Church ecumenical movement and initiated significant interdenominational collaborations. Nevertheless, as O'Bryan predicted, many in the Catholic hierarchy were offended and angry. Although the pope had conferred with the Council for

Promoting Christian Unity, several members of the Curia opined that he should have sought their advice before making such a radical decision. And this was not James's first offense.

DeLuca telephoned Sicoli from Ireland the following evening. "On what grounds could he revoke the excommunications of those who were responsible for dividing God's church in the first place?" DeLuca asked rhetorically. "It was Luther who started the whole mess, and now he was singled out by the pope as a man of 'great faith and commitment to Jesus Christ.'"

"This is getting way out of hand," Sicoli replied. "He is undermining positions the Roman Church has preached for hundreds of years. We may need to move quicker than we originally thought."

Chapter Fourteen

In his darkened quarters at a local seminary outside Vatican City, Father Bonn practiced putting the bomb components together. He had rehearsed the exercise so many times in his cramped room that he could have performed it in his sleep. An engineer by training, Bonn understood the mechanics of the device, but he questioned the morality of taking human life—anyone's life.

Sicoli had meticulously planned every detail. Getting the bomb-making material into Vatican City had been relatively easy. Learning how to assemble and use the bombs presented the most difficult challenges. Explosive training was not something Catholic priests had on their résumés, and there was no opportunity to practice. However, the Internet offered a source of abundant and valuable information, and a video game allowed Sicoli's lieutenants to learn how and where to place the bombs on the papal helicopter.

Access to the aircraft created the most obstinate hurdle. The Swiss Guard was impenetrable. No one could infiltrate it. Even though Guardsmen wore strange-looking uniforms for a military force—a diagonal jerkin, yellow, blue, and red trousers, and black berets—and appeared to arm themselves with antiquated lances, halberds, and swords, no security force in the world was more dedicated to its principal. Theirs was a half-millennium-old tradition of defending the life of the pope, if necessary by giving their own. For more than five hundred years, this elite group of Swiss men had sworn to faithfully, honestly, and honorably serve the supreme pontiff. It was impossible to contemplate turning even one of them. Moreover, if any of the guardsmen suspected anything, the immediate ensuing investigation would foil the plot.

Sicoli needed to design and execute the deed without raising any suspicions. Carrying the bomb-making material onto the helicopter, piece by piece, over several months, was the answer. His coconspirators obtained a copy of the maintenance timetable, studied the aircraft's cleaning and inspection schedule, and identified windows during which they could plant the components undetected. Getting some of their own onto the helo took a high level of coordination and chicanery. Security measures permitted no one other than guardsmen and mechanics aboard a papal aircraft, unless they were on the flight manifest. So Sicoli's lieutenants devised legitimate reasons to fly without drawing attention. This would have been simple if Sicoli or one of the other cardinals or archbishops made the request. However, Sicoli was in New York, DeLuca was in Dublin, and the others either reassigned outside the Vatican or retired. The few remaining high-ranking clerics in the Vatican needed to stay well undercover until the plot concluded. Using their internal network, they learned when a nonsuspecting cardinal or archbishop was traveling and arranged to have one of their working-level priests assigned to the entourage or hitch a ride. That is how they got the bomb-making elements onto the aircraft.

Prior to boarding, every passenger was examined by a metal detector and hand searched. Consequently, each collaborator was restricted to carrying limited amounts of contraband. Metal parts imbedded in belts, plastic explosive wrapped in clerical collars, and electronics concealed in cell phones, tablets, and laptops got them past the detectors. It took fifteen separate trips over a four-month period to get all the necessary materials onto the helicopter and safely placed where only Father Bonn could locate them.

✳ ✳ ✳

Turkey, one of the most important Muslim countries in the world, was a nation James had not previously visited. He met with Grand Imam

Mehmet Ali Burakgazi on his first afternoon in Ankara. Catholics' and Muslims' reactions were mixed when the media published the impending visit between these two renowned spiritual leaders. Some thought it was a conversation long overdue. Others felt offended that their leader would break bread with an "infidel."

James was concerned about the ever-growing divide between Muslim and Christian communities throughout the world. Some Christians had concluded Islam was a religion of terror and violence. James knew better. Muslims were devout, religious, and God-fearing people. Some Muslims viewed all Christians as infidels. That was not true either.

James was absolutely convinced there was no chasm too wide to bridge among believers. Reaching out to Muslims by offering his hand in friendship would be an unmistakable signal that Christianity, the Catholic Church, and this pope respected Islam. This would state far better than any words his belief that both Christians and Muslims were devout believers in the same Creator.

The two men met at one of the grand imam's offices in the center of this modern city. It was an impressive workspace in a room attached to a historic mosque. Minute indigo, gold, black, and magnolia geometric marble tiles set in adjoining concentric circles wrapped the four-meter-tall office walls. A complex chandelier dangled from the center-arched ceiling. As in the pope's office, there was no desk. A glorious crimson, gold, and sapphire rug covered the center of the cream-colored marble floor. Several artistically hand-chiseled wooden chairs—seats and backs covered in ruby-red silk—encircled an inlaid, polished granite table. A gigantic world map and a smaller map of Turkey and the surrounding area hung on the main wall.

A waiter offered the pope tea served in crystal tulip glasses and an assortment of tropical fruits. In the beginning, they employed translators; Grand Imam Mehmet Ali Burakgazi spoke in Turkish, and Pope James I in English. After less than ten minutes; however, they both felt a comfortable chemistry, a mutual awareness, as if they had known each other for some time. The grand imam dismissed the translators and spoke impeccable English.

The conversation delved into personal issues concerning their families, faith, prayer, life, and the value of sacrifice. The grand imam was stunned to learn that the pope prayed multiple times each day, as did all faithful Muslims across the world. The pope was surprised when the grand imam told him he had volunteered for several years in a remote, impoverished village in the northern part of the country near the Black Sea before becoming an imam.

The conversation turned to children. "I believe the needs of the children are where our greatest responsibilities lie," James said. "This is not simply because they are the future, but because children are the innocents. They most resemble the image of God."

"That too is my view," Burakgazi responded. "It is vital we treat and teach our children correctly because Allah so commands. We have a children's program in the cities, which we conduct during the summer between school terms for primary- and secondary-school children, intended to expose youth to the diversity of our culture. We focus on economically poor children in an effort to enhance their pride and self-concept. Our university students work with the disadvantaged, teaching art, culture, sports, and music on two days, and then they take the children on field trips to museums, parks, and zoos on the third day each week. We try to enlighten them on both Islamic and Western traditions. Our goal is to provide a deeper and more genuine appreciation of Islam and a more accurate depiction of the West. We want to move them from being drawn to fundamentalism."

After their initial conversation, the two men enjoyed dinner at one of the government palaces. The menu was typical for Turks—feta cheese, flatbread, olives, yogurt salad, peppers and tomatoes in extra virgin olive oil, sardines rolled in grape leaves, dried apricots, hazelnuts and filberts, and roasted lamb kebabs, with melon and fresh berries for dessert. Over dinner, the grand imam raised the issue of Palestine and Israel. While his comments were pointed, it did not appear he was making a political statement. Rather, he was genuinely asking the pope for his thinking on what the solution might be.

"Violence is seldom the answer and rarely justified," James said between bites. "The people of the Middle East need to come together as brothers and sisters. They are all children of God with common ancestry in Abraham. It's not an easy task, but we all must work toward that end."

"I agree," Burakgazi responded. "But what's the mechanism for achieving that end?"

"The governments need to sit together and negotiate the resolution. However, that cannot and will not happen until the people of Israel and Palestine come together and break bread. I believe that in this situation the leaders must be the followers, and the followers must become the leaders."

"What do you mean by this?"

"The local people in the villages and neighborhoods must conclude that those they see on the other side of the fence are their friends and neighbors. Local people must take the initiative and establish the exchange. If they do, the government leaders will follow."

"That is an intriguing proposition, but again I ask, what is the mechanism?" he pressed.

"Perhaps the mosque and synagogue are the venues. Perhaps Islamic and Jewish religious leaders from outside Palestine and Israel could be the facilitators." He fixed a meaningful look on the grand imam. "Perhaps you are the key leader to create the opportunity for facilitating the conversation."

"What exactly are you proposing?"

"People need to find a way to discover they are far more alike than different. They need the genuine opportunity to realize that their differences pale in comparison to what they have in common. Look at you and me. We have discovered this in the midst of a single meal."

"How can we, as outsiders, influence that?"

"You are a highly respected and important Islamic leader. I think you could play a critical role in this effort."

"Ah, the politics are very difficult."

"I understand."

"And it's virtually impossible to deal with the Jews. They are set in their ways, and determined to maintain a stranglehold over all of Palestine," he said, with irritation. "There is nothing I can do to change that. That is the root of the problem. Allah commands us to seek peace with our neighbors, but it's impossible with the Jews."

"Are you able to have conversations with Jewish leaders?

"No, it's impossible."

"I have a friend, a neighbor in Chicago, a highly respected rabbi. Perhaps the two of you could meet to discuss your differences and your similarities."

"I've always been willing to meet with anyone who is sincere in their efforts to resolve conflicts and disputes. However, I've had no success with the Jews."

"This might be an opportunity to seek peace with at least one Jewish neighbor."

"And if we did this, what role would you play?"

"I could host. Offer neutral ground."

The grand imam stroked his beard and closed his eyes as he contemplated the pope's offer. Meeting with a rabbi, anywhere, could pose serious political risks, but this Muslim cleric of great faith understood that if risks were not taken, the already perilous situation would continue to deteriorate.

"It would be necessary that any meeting be held outside the view of the media, in a private, confidential place," Burakgazi said.

"A friend of mine has a villa in southeastern France. I'm sure we could meet there without anyone being aware."

"What you are asking is very problematic," Burakgazi said into his fist.

"Life is full of problems. How we deal with the opportunities to address the problems is what makes the difference," James replied. The men sat quietly for a few moments.

"Let me give this some thought. I'll get back to you."

As dawn broke the next morning, the *adhān*—the Islamic call to worship—awakened the pope. As he lay awake listening to the melodic voice from the nearby mosque, he contemplated the gift of a community that wakes her people by calling them to prayer.

James spent the next two days in Istanbul, where he met with the ecumenical patriarch of the Orthodox Church of Constantinople, visited with Turkish Catholics, and celebrated Mass at outdoor venues. For a Muslim country, the crowds were substantial. On the fourth day, shortly before he was to leave for the airport, Grand Imam Mehmet Ali Burakgazi telephoned Pope James I at his hotel to advise that he would be willing to meet with the American rabbi, provided the pope could guarantee absolute secrecy. James assured him and thanked him for his trust.

✳ ✳ ✳

"David, this is Jimmy Flahvin."

"Jimmy, great to hear from you. How you doin'? Enjoying your new job?"

"I'm fine, David. Not sure I'd use the word 'enjoy' to describe how I feel about this responsibility. 'Overwhelmed' might be more accurate."

"You've never met a challenge you couldn't conquer, Jimmy. We both know that."

"I appreciate your confidence, my friend." After a short pause, James continued. "David, I need your input. If I asked Rabbi Goldman to speak with me about something in the strictest of confidence, and he agreed, could I trust him?"

"My Rabbi Goldman?" David asked, incredulous.

Isidore Goldman was the senior rabbi at Mount Sinai Temple, David Levin's synagogue. Throughout the two lawyers' friendship, whenever there was an event at temple that involved David and his family, Jimmy and Vicki had always attended.

"If Goldman gives you his word on something, it's like platinum," David assured him. "If you spoke with him about a confidential matter, he wouldn't even share it with his wife. He is one of the most honest and trustworthy men I know. What's this all about, Jimmy?"

"Lawyer-client privilege, David," James said.

David laughed. "Say no more."

After hanging up with his former law partner, James asked Sister Rosalie to place a call to Cardinal Montego, the prefect of the Congregation for Peace and Justice. Montego owned a family villa in the French countryside. James asked if he could use the home for several days for a private meeting, toward the end of the following month. He did not explain the purpose of the meeting, but invited the cardinal to join him. Montego accepted without hesitation.

Next, James instructed his scholars at the Vatican who focused on Judaism to provide background information on Goldman. Two days later, he received a comprehensive dossier, which he read immediately. Then he asked Rosalie to arrange a telephone conversation with Rabbi Isidore Goldman for the following afternoon.

"You understand this conversation is to be kept in strict confidence," James said to the rabbi after exchanging pleasantries.

"You have my word," the rabbi said.

"A few days ago I met with Grand Imam Mehmet Ali Burakgazi in Ankara. I found him to be a sincere, thoughtful, and genuinely caring man. He is committed to his faith and a devout and faithful believer. We discussed the potential value of Islamic and Jewish clergy getting to know each other better. We both believe clergy could play a more positive and constructive role in resolving the Israeli-Palestinian dispute. I told him about you, Isidore. I explained that you too are a sincere, thoughtful, and genuinely caring man. That you are committed to your faith. That you are a devout and faithful believer. I would like to invite both of you to join me at a villa in southern France as my guests. The objectives would be to simply visit and get to know each other over the course of a couple days. Would you be willing to do that, Isidore?"

The silence on the other end of the line went on for so long that James checked his phone to see if they had been disconnected. Finally, Goldman said, "Can I have a few days to think about it?"

"Yes, of course. But you can only seek your own counsel. You cannot discuss this with anyone."

"Of course," Goldman said.

A few days later, Rabbi Goldman advised the pope that he would be willing to join the pope and the grand imam. The three men agreed to meet in southern France in five weeks.

✳ ✳ ✳

"I am ready to die if necessary to save the Catholic Church, but I'm uncomfortable with participating in the killing of another human being," Father Bonn said to his mentor.

"He is the Antichrist," Sicoli countered. "We must defend the Roman Catholic Church."

"But God commands that we shall not kill."

"It is no sin to protect the Church. It would be a sin not to protect her. This is a war against evil, and there are always casualties in war."

Bonn's concerns were quieted, but not vanquished. Cardinal Sicoli was persuasive.

"I've given you the most important assignment—the final step of assembling the device. Your responsibility is clear. You arrive at the west pad sufficiently early on the designated morning to be first onboard. The pilots will be going through their flight checklist, so they will not pay you any attention. Before any of the other passengers arrive, you carefully remove the hidden components and assemble them. Can you do this, Eric?"

There was quiet, and then, "Yes, Your Eminence. I will do this in order to protect God's church."

On the designated day, Father Eric Bonn arrived at the helipad before anyone else. He cleared security and boarded the helicopter. Preoccupied with their checklists, the pilots were oblivious to the young priest as he moved through the aircraft, collected all the components, assembled the bombs, and placed one device directly underneath the chair where Flahvin would sit, attaching it to the seat bottom with duct tape. He put the other under the sink in the tiny restroom near the fuel tank. Bonn was to hitch a one-way ride with the pope to Paris and return a week later after visiting extended family in France. Sicoli informed Bonn that another conspirator would remotely detonate the explosives before Flahvin returned from Paris, thus diverting suspicion away from Rome.

Shortly, the other passengers arrived. After going through the necessary security measures, they too boarded. There was small talk among them as they waited for the pope.

✳ ✳ ✳

Running late for his flight to Fiumicino Airport, James hurriedly put some things into his travel bag. He was to leave Vatican City at 8:20 that Thursday morning, and then take a papal jet to Paris. At 8:15, he was still getting ready. Mary had called unexpectedly a half hour earlier. She and her fiancé were having a quarrel, and she needed to talk with her dad.

After the call, as he was about to leave his apartment, there was a deafening explosion that shook the building. He dashed to the window and saw fire and dense black smoke billowing from the helicopter pad. Within seconds, two Swiss Guards who were at sentry outside his door rushed into his residence.

"Holy Father," the corporal said, struggling to remain calm. "There's been an explosion. Our security protocols require we escort you to a safe location."

"What happened?"

"We don't have any information yet," the guardsman responded, taking him by the arm. "We'll tell you everything as soon as we have information. But you must come with us now."

As they exited the building, two additional halberdiers met them at the door. The five of them got into two white golf carts and sped away, in the opposite direction from the rising smoke, along the winding walkway through the Vatican City gardens. Three minutes later, they stopped at the rear of the government building. Priest and nuns, bishops and lay workers rushed out of the building to see what was happening. They stood in shock as they watched the Holy Father and his security guards jump out of the carts and enter the building through the large bronze doors. They quickly descended three flights of stairs, where they found several other Swiss Guards standing in front of an oversized, reinforced steel entry. As he reached the bottom, one guard opened the heavy door and ushered him into the "safe room."

"The helo exploded," the sergeant major said as soon as the door closed. "It was completely destroyed. We don't know for sure, but it appears all onboard were killed."

"Who was onboard?" James asked, his heart racing.

"We verified the manifest," the sergeant major responded, "and we believe everyone who was scheduled to travel with you this morning was on the aircraft when it exploded." James slumped onto the couch, his legs giving way beneath him.

"Cardinal Montego, Cardinal Chavier, Father Simmons, and Father Bonn are listed on the manifest."

"The pilots?" James asked.

"Juan and Josef," the guard replied.

"Anyone on the ground injured?" James asked quietly.

"We're not sure yet, Holy Father."

"Let's pray for the repose of their souls," James said, his voice breaking. The Swiss Guards and the pope joined hands, standing, and recited the Lord's Prayer. Then James said, "Dear God, if any of these men survived this explosion, we ask that you heal their bodies and give them strength to endure their pain. For those who have died, we commit them to your mercy and ask for consolation for their families, in the name of Your Son, Jesus the Christ. Amen."

A moment later, the door to the safe room opened and Colonel Lukas Meire, the commander of the Swiss Guard, and cardinals Mbuto and Keegan rushed in.

"Holy Father, you're alive!" exclaimed Keegan. "We thought you were on the helicopter."

"Thanks be to God!" Mbuto exclaimed.

"Do we know who was on the chopper, Holy Father?" Keegan asked.

"Montego, Chavier, the pilots." He paused, and then added, "John Simmons."

"Oh, no," Keegan sighed.

James was despondent, more for his dear friend Keegan than for himself. Simmons was a remarkable young man, a good priest, his faithful assistant and trusted friend. He had served him well and died in that service. But for Keegan, Simmons was like a son.

In a time of crisis, the Vatican's standard operating procedure was to hunker down and say little or nothing to the media, especially about events that occurred within Vatican City. However, anyone near the Vatican on this otherwise tranquil Thursday morning was aware something frightfully grave had happened. The Swiss Guard immediately requested the Roman police and fire departments' assistance. Screaming emergency vehicles arrived within minutes. The lieutenant colonel of the guard informed the press office and the Curia that the pope was not onboard when the papal helicopter exploded. The thundering blast, the columns of black and grey smoke, and the presence of Rome security officials prevented the Vatican from any attempt to maintain its standard cloak of secrecy. The press office simply reported there had been a serious malfunction in the helicopter and that several people had died, but that the Holy Father had not been onboard.

The media wanted to know more. Who died? Why were others on the helicopter? Was the pope scheduled to fly this morning? If so, why wasn't he onboard? Where was he going? What caused the explosion? Was there any evidence of foul play? Was this an assassination attempt? What security measures were standard? Were those measures in place? Who had access to the helicopter?

The press office refused to answer any questions, so reporters filled in the blanks for themselves. "Eyewitnesses" gave their accounts, although the only genuine eyewitnesses were Vatican clergy and Swiss Guards, and they were not speaking to the media. However, that did not stop all sorts of "information" and "news" from being reported.

As various television news shows, radio talk stations, and blogs ran with the story, conspiracy theories abounded and tweeted across the planet. Several reporters left little doubt in the minds of their viewers, listeners, and readers that this was a failed assassination attempt. What other explanation was there? As one analyst on CNN said, "Rumors abound about the death threats James receives regularly, and helicopters don't just blow up, especially while they're still on the ground."

Vatican watchers and "Vatican experts" were interviewed: "Who would want to kill this well-liked and popular pope? Who would benefit from his death? What explosives might have been used? Who had access to the helicopter pad? Was this an inside job?"

The guardsmen, cardinals, and pope waited in the safe room for several hours. They watched local and international news coverage of the explosion on a large flat-screen TV. James was deeply disturbed by insinuations this might have been an "inside the Vatican" assassination attempt.

Political and religious leaders from around the world called the Vatican to share their concern about the incident and their joy at the pope being alive. Grand Imam Mehmet Ali Burakgazi telephoned en route to Paris to express his condolences for the lives lost. He assured the pontiff that he was willing to reschedule. Rabbi Goldman, also on his way to France, called to convey his deep sadness. He too promised the pope that his decision to meet with the grand imam was unfazed. Throughout the morning, Colonel Meire received phone calls and text messages updating the situation.

James pulled the colonel aside and whispered, "Is there any evidence this was anything other than a serious malfunction, Colonel?"

Meire dropped his voice and leaned closer to the pope. "Lieutenant Colonel D'Amore reports the preliminary findings suggest there might have been a bomb planted on the helicopter." James's insides lurched, but he conveyed calm.

"Why would anyone want to do that?" he said. The colonel had no answer. "Please keep me personally posted on the progress of your investigation," he directed.

Later in the day, there was wonderful news. Simmons had not been on the helicopter. Due to his concern for the rarely tardy pope, he had disembarked just moments before the blast in order to check on the pontiff. As he was rushing away from the aircraft, the force of the violent explosion had hurled him to the tarmac and knocked him unconscious. When the Rome paramedics had found him, they had immediately taken him to a hospital just outside Vatican City. When James learned about this, he asked the guards to take him to the hospital. As the pope entered Simmons's room, he saw his young assistant lying in bed, entangled in life-saving tubes. He kissed the young priest on the forehead and said, "So my dillydallying saved your life."

"Apparently, it saved both of our lives," Simmons retorted.

James called Simmons's parents in Minnesota, reassuring them their only son was alive and healthy. "You deserve to be very proud of raising such an extraordinary young man. John's contribution to the

Church is immeasurable. His love of and commitment to the Creator is remarkable. Thank you for sharing him with me."

✳ ✳ ✳

He had been warned about the threats on his life, but he had not paid much attention. "Crazy people always threaten international leaders, but they very seldom take action," he had thought to himself. The probability of assassination was far less than an airplane falling out of the sky. And the chance of that was minimal. But now fear struck deep. Intellectually he grasped that death was a daily possibility, spiritually he looked forward to worshiping God in heaven, but emotionally he had not signed on for this. The lawyer in him wanted to know the facts: How did this happen? Was this an attempted assassination? If so, who was involved? Why did they want to kill him? Why would they kill others to get at him? The questions seemed endless.

The last assassination attempt on a pope had been nearly four decades earlier, when John Paul II was attacked by Mehmet Ali Ağca, a Turkish murderer. That plot had failed, although John Paul was seriously injured. If this was an attempted assignation, it appeared to come from within the walls of Vatican City, and that caused distress and consternation. It was well known that ultraconservatives and fundamentalists within the Church were outraged at some of James's decisions and concerned about his vigorous outreach to other denominations and non-Christian religions. However, those differences among the hierarchy could never justify killing the Vicar of Christ. Bishops and cardinals across the spectrum decried the attack. Rumors about who was involved, and why, ran rampant within Vatican City and throughout the world.

With the approval of Cardinals Mbuto and Keegan, Colonel Meire requested assistance from the FBI and MI5 to investigate the helicopter explosion that had killed five people. They reviewed hundreds of electronic messages and interviewed everyone who had seen, heard, or had any knowledge of the event. In order to provide a just process, the Vatican provided each interviewee legal counsel. To ensure posterity, the interviews were videotaped.

The investigators concluded that a small, isolated, but hostile group of clerics within the Vatican, with the help of some unknown financial backers, had conspired to assassinate the pope by blowing up his helicopter. Based on the testimony of several witnesses and many e-mails and text messages, they construed that the conspirators believed James was the Antichrist. Their apparent objectives were to end James's "evil policies" and return the papacy to an "orthodox pontiff." The most shocking finding was the significant involvement of a leading member of the College of Cardinals, and the possibility he may have masterminded the conspiracy.

The three investigatory agencies submitted a joint report to the Vatican's secretary of state. Mbuto carefully read their account, wincing at parts, painfully distressed by others. He then shared the report with Keegan. The two of them presented it to the pope. Cardinal Keegan did the talking.

"We have very sad news, Holy Father. The investigation concludes that there was a conspiracy of young priests under the guidance of two bishops and the supervision of a cardinal to assassinate you. The effort was apparently funded by a wealthy European layman."

James was taken aback. How could Catholic priests, bishops—even a cardinal—be involved in murder and the assassination of the pope, he wondered to himself. Shocked, he finally asked, "Who was involved?"

"The evidence couldn't identify the layman; the money was untraceable. Other than Father Bonn, I don't think you know any of the priests. Bishops Kiesler and Franco managed the operation here, and we are very sorry to report that Cardinal Sicoli conceived the plot and orchestrated its execution from New York."

There was a long silence as the pope rested his chin against his closed hand and stared at the floor.

"What do you want us to do, Holy Father?" Mbuto asked. James did not respond as he continued staring at the Persian rug. Tears welled up in his eyes, which he eventually brushed away with his fingers. After an excruciatingly long time, he spoke.

"How are felonies prosecuted here?"

"There are two options," Keegan explained. "We can handle this internally, where all the proceedings are confidential, or we can ask the

Italian government to take the case. Our internal system starts with a trial by a judge. There's only one, so everyone is treated the same. If a defendant is convicted, he can appeal to a tribunal, then the appeals court, and ultimately the Supreme Court. All of these officials are appointed by the pope, and you can reassign any of them at will. And, of course, you can intervene at any time and exercise your supreme judicial authority."

"Cardinals are handled differently," Mbuto interjected. "They can only be judged by their peers or by you directly. So Sicoli would skip the preliminary courts and be tried before the Vatican Supreme Court."

"But most cases tried internally are civil matters," Keegan continued. "There are many complications with trying criminal cases within the Vatican. We don't even have a place to incarcerate perpetrators, only a small detention center used for petty thieves. That's why the Holy See relies upon the Italian government to prosecute serious crimes committed in Vatican City."

"Are there many crimes committed here?" the pope asked curiously.

"We actually have one of the highest per capita crime rates in the world," Keegan replied. "But that's because we have the smallest population in the world and hundreds of thousands of visitors. Visitors commit the vast majority of crimes and most are petty—pickpockets, minor assaults, stealing from the collection plate, that sort of thing. Although there was a double murder-suicide in 1998."

"Really. What was that about?" James asked.

"A newly recruited member of the Swiss Guard shot and killed the commander and his wife. Then he killed himself. There were all kinds of rumors as to the motivation, but no one knows what prompted the young lad," Mbuto said.

"There is no modern-day precedent for this type of crime—one committed by members of the hierarchy within the walls of Vatican City," Keegan said. "The canon lawyers advise that this is a 'case of first impression.' All the perpetrators, except Sicoli, have confessed, and with your approval, they will serve sentences of between ten years and life, depending on their knowledge and involvement in the murders. Of course, they will also be defrocked and excommunicated, and the terms of their pleas prohibit any media contact while they are in prison."

"No excommunications," James interrupted. "They'll need all the help they can get in prison. Don't take the sacraments away."

"Yes, Your Holiness. But what should we do with Cardinal Sicoli?" Mbuto asked. "The Holy See is not adept at handling a criminal trial of a cardinal for murder and conspiracy to murder."

Keegan added, "We could ask that Sicoli be charged and tried in the United States because his participation in the conspiracy occurred there. The FBI has agreed not to do anything unless we specifically make a request."

"Who knows about this report?" James asked.

"Only a few," Mbuto said. "Colonel Meire and Lieutenant Colonel D'Amore, the four FBI and MI5 investigators, two canon lawyers, and the three of us. No one else has seen the report, not even a secretary. Although there are many rumors about the incident, most are unfounded, but I'm told one of the rumors is pretty close to the truth."

The pontiff contemplated what he had heard. "There are enormous downsides to a drawn-out public trial. It could be turned into an international media circus," James said. "A Catholic cardinal and Catholic bishops using Catholic priests to assassinate the pope is a story we don't want to have to deal with for the next couple of years. We can handle rumors. We can deal with one-shot stories, a couple of days' coverage. But a multiple-year public trial could thwart all of our efforts. Who knows what effect months, perhaps years, of daily coverage might have on the Church?"

"It could turn you into a more sympathetic figure," Mbuto said.

"The assassination attempt engendered enough sympathy," James said. "I don't need any more of that."

"How can we escape a trial?" Keegan asked. "Sicoli murdered five people, and he tried to kill you."

"Perhaps we can't, Greg," James said. "But I think we need to try. We could threaten him with life and offer a lighter sentence if he admits his guilt. Maybe we just need to send him off someplace to pray and meditate—do some big-time penance."

"He must be held accountable," Keegan pressed.

The conversation continued. After further discussion about various alternatives, the pope instructed Mbuto to call O'Bryan in New York and direct him to take specific actions.

* * *

"You son of a bitch!" O'Bryan exploded. "You worthless piece of..." His voice trailed off as he tried unsuccessfully to contain his wrath. "How in God's name could you contemplate killing the Holy Father? What possibly possessed you? You must be completely out of your mind. Stark raving mad. An F-ing lunatic," O'Bryan raged.

Sicoli stood motionless in Cardinal O'Bryan's office on the tenth floor of the Terence Cardinal Cooke Building in Manhattan. He offered a slight grin, but did not respond.

"You murdered with premeditation," the six-foot-four and still-fit former high school football star fumed at the much smaller and diminutive five-foot-seven Sicoli. "In New York, we'd lock you up and throw away the F-ing key. You'd get a life sentence without any chance of parole."

Sicoli still did not utter a word.

"The cardinal secretary of state called me this morning, just before I ordered you here. He told me the Holy Father has asked me to offer you three options. If it were me, the only option you'd get is life in federal prison. But it's not up to me, so..." His voice trailed off again as he composed his anger.

"One," he said sternly, "you may clear your name by defending yourself at a Vatican trial. However, if the court convicts you, your punishment will be life without parole in an Italian prison.

"Two, you can come clean and admit to your involvement in this inexplicable plot and spend the rest of your life in prayer, meditation, and penance at a Benedictine monastery in southern California. For reasons I do not understand, you can maintain your status as a cardinal. However, if you ever leave the monastery campus or communicate with anyone outside the monastery, without specific authorization from the secretary of state or me, the FBI has agreed to arrest you. We will extradite you to Vatican City for trial. And, as you may recall, the Holy See no longer recognizes statutes of limitations."

"And my third option," Sicoli said smoothly.

"Three, you can admit your crimes to Italian authorities, voluntarily renounce your vows as a bishop of the Church, leave the priesthood, and be sentenced to thirty years in an Italian prison with the opportunity for parole. You'd be out in about twenty. However, if you were paroled and you ever entered any Church property, other than to attend Holy Mass, or if you were seen within five hundred meters of the Holy Father or any member of the College, your parole would be revoked. I encourage you to think about your options, Sicoli. You have six hours to decide."

"Is that all?"

"Yeah, that's all. Now get out of my office."

As Sicoli started to walk out, he turned and said defiantly, "Whatever I might have done, I have committed no sin. I have dedicated my life to the Church, and I will continue to do my best to protect her."

O'Bryan leaned back into his chair and shook his head. He thought it was a terrible mistake to offer Sicoli the option to retain his status as a cardinal of the Church, regardless of where he was sent. He had argued with Mbuto earlier that day, trying to convince the secretary of state to persuade the pope to take this option off the table.

"He's offering Sicoli the same options the Church offered the pedophile priests—a sentence of prayer and penance in a Church-run facility. And how'd that work out?" he had asked sarcastically. "This is going to come back and bite us, and bite us hard. I just know it."

Mbuto agreed with O'Bryan's assessment, but the pope had made his decision clear, and now they had their orders.

Later that day, Sicoli called O'Bryan and said simply, "I'll move to California."

"The lawyers will draw up the legal documents for your signature. You leave tomorrow morning."

Chapter Fifteen

"It's impossible for Flahvin to be a legitimate pope, because he was never a man of the Church," Cardinal Sicoli kept telling himself, as if he needed to continuously justify his actions. "Flahvin knows nothing about Catholic tradition. He has not dedicated his life in service to the Church. He was married for thirty years, God forbid! And he teaches heresy—married priests, homosexuality, birth control, women priests, and consorting with Jews, Muslims, and Buddhists."

Sicoli was convinced that he, himself, should have been pope. "I am the one who served the Curia for thirty years. I am the one who understands how the Church functions and works. I am the one who would lead the Church back to its principled, pre-Vatican II foundations. If it had not been for O'Bryan's antics causing a deadlocked conclave, the cardinals would have elected me, Manoles Franco Cardinal Sicoli, pope. That would have been the correct thing to do, and the best for the Church. But too many cardinals are spineless, unwilling to do what they know is right."

He felt no contrition for his previous actions. To the contrary, he was proud of what he and his colleagues had attempted, although deeply disappointed that the plan had failed. He was certain Flahvin was an imposter and the Antichrist.

Flahvin's decision to allow him to retain his rank as a cardinal had surprised Sicoli. He thought it demonstrated enormous weakness.

"A stronger and wiser man would have excommunicated everyone involved in the assassination attempt. If I had the power of the papacy, and anyone conspired to assassinate me, I would order each conspirator summarily executed. And I would do it in a manner where everyone would know who ordered the killings, but in a way that no evidence could possibly point to me."

Sicoli was both enraged and imprisoned at the monastery in the California wilderness. His commitment to rid the Church of the Antichrist endured, but he knew it would be far more difficult to orchestrate an effective action from this outpost. He was a brilliantly cunning and resourceful man, qualities that made him a successful prince of the Roman Catholic Church. But he knew he would need much more, given his current situation.

Holy Cross Monastery served as a retreat center for Catholic men. Once a month, except during the scalding summer, this tranquil campus offered a quiet and peaceful environment where one could get away from life's everyday demands and focus on the spiritual. Men came from southern California and western Arizona for private meditation, personal prayer, and Scripture study. This was a time to reflect on their lives and discern how they might be better Christians and Catholics.

By winning over the abbot, the monk in charge of the monastery, Sicoli strategized he would eventually have access to these men. Among them would be some who saw the world as he did. He would befriend those men, and they would become the foundation for his next offensive to remove the Antichrist.

The abbot did not know why the Vatican had sent Cardinal Sicoli to his abbey. He suspected Sicoli must have committed a serious wrong. The Vatican would not exile a foreign cardinal so far away from home unless he had committed a grave sin or somehow been heretical in his teachings.

Cardinal O'Bryan had encouraged the abbot to engage Sicoli in meaningful work that would be genuinely helpful to the retreat center, and not simply a drain on the abbey's minimal resources. "Perhaps he could labor in the field," O'Bryan had suggested.

The monk assigned Sicoli to work in the vegetable garden, but also offered him the opportunity to present one of the seven reflections during regular weekend retreats. Sicoli accepted both assignments. He agreed to describe the scriptural foundations and early history of the Church so the retreat participants might better grasp the full meaning of the words of the Gospel.

Every retreat began with dinner on Friday evening and closed with noon Mass and lunch on Sunday. Saturday's morning reflections focused on various topics, followed by individual prayer and meditation. After lunch, Sicoli offered his lecture on Church history. It was quite unusual for an Italian cardinal to be present at a retreat center such as this, but it was an unexpected treat for these men to be able to speak with and learn from a prince of the Catholic Church.

Sicoli began each reflection by acknowledging his views were conservative and based on tradition, although some might be considered controversial. He conceded he was not in tune with the progressive nature of the current Church, but emphasized the Church had always been conservative and opined that today's progressiveness and liberalism were an aberration. His reflection focused on the Peterine succession—how Jesus had selected Peter as the first pope, and how succeeding popes were carefully selected through prescribed processes.

"Sometimes, however, the electors fell victim to serving their own needs," he would say. "Sometimes they would select someone to fulfill their selfish interests." At some historical junctures, the electors' behavior had resulted in more than one pope, although he emphasized there was always only one legitimate pope. The others were imposters or antipopes. "On rare occasions," he argued, "impostors had sat on Peter's throne. But these travesties were always short-lived because subsequent conclaves corrected the previous debacle, and the new pope put the Church back on the correct track."

Cardinal Sicoli never specifically identified the imposters and never referred directly to Pope James or his election. Rather, he emphasized the importance of the pope being learned in Scripture and deeply devoted and committed to the organizational Church. He underscored that for the last one thousand years, only cardinals had been elected, because princes of the Catholic Church, by definition, were the only men who met all of the requisite criteria.

He also lectured about the second Vatican Council and the numerous ways it had negatively affected the Church. He explained his opposition to married priests, the vernacular Mass, and communal penance, and his fears of where the Church was currently headed—encouraging premarital and extramarital sex, artificial birth control, homosexuality, female ordination, abortion, fetal stem cell research, euthanasia, and a host of other social and religious ills.

It did not take long for those in attendance to glean Sicoli's ultra-conservative positions. The abbot allowed Sicoli to deliver his reflection because he believed all perspectives, from the most conservative to the most progressive, had value. As they listened, most of the men in the audience disregarded much of Sicoli's harangue. After a while, some got up and left, not wishing to waste their time. But a small number heard what they had been hoping to hear for many years, and Sicoli needed to entice just one or two with the expectation they would be enlightened and convinced by his arguments. At the end of the sessions, he invited all those remaining to come to his office to visit during the time scheduled for prayer and meditation. Generally, one or two men accepted and met with Sicoli, telling him how much they appreciated what he had said and how valuable they found it. It was a marginal minority. Sicoli knew he only needed a few good men.

As he visited with these extreme but faithful Catholics, Sicoli learned about their backgrounds, their occupations, their political viewpoints, and their religious beliefs. He would ascertain their level of conservatism, commitment to the Church as he understood it, and willingness to help him do something about its current horrific state. Occasionally, he would identify someone who could be truly helpful to his cause.

Sicoli encouraged the men to e-mail often and return for annual retreats. He formed personal relationships with a few, and in some cases, those relationships grew into devoted friendships. As their loyalty intensified, Sicoli would speak more openly about the gravely dangerous situation facing the Church. They discussed what Flahvin might be up to next, how his despicable actions had betrayed the Church, how dangerous he and some leading cardinals had become to the future of the institution, and the importance of stopping the travesty before it was irreversible. Sicoli knew what had to be done; however, he was not clear on how he would accomplish the feat. He would admonish his guests by concluding, "It's your sacred duty to expose, condemn, and end this treachery."

"What brings you to the monastery?" Sicoli asked the young man after one of his lectures.

"I'm worried about where the Church is goin', and I heard you are too, so I thought I'd come hear what you gotta say," Joseph Carlin replied.

"And what did you think about my session?"

"I think you're right on. When I was growin' up, I always liked traditional Catholic teachings. But, when I was in Afghanistan, I realized that if we don't defeat Islam, they're gonna take us all out. That's their plan, ya know. And I figure the only thing that will defeat Islam is fundamentalist Christianity. And that's kinda' what you talked about today."

"Interesting," Sicoli said. "But my primary purpose is not to defeat Islam, as you say. My purpose is to ensure the Catholic Church is true to its traditional beliefs."

"Yeah. And if we do that, Islam will be defeated because them and the Jews, Buddhists, and all other non-Christians are heathens. If Catholics are true to our beliefs, then all the other Christians will join up, and we'll so outnumber the rest that we'll win."

Sicoli wasn't sure he followed his new student's logic, but he was enjoying the conversation. "Which beliefs are most important to you?" Sicoli asked.

"Well, first we need capital punishment for any violent crime, and homosexuals should be automatically excommunicated or imprisoned. The Bible says we can use lethal force against nonbelievers and heretics, and wives should be submissive to their husbands, and women wearin' suggestive clothing is a mortal sin because it puts impure thoughts into men's heads. And the idea of married priests is just wrong. The pope never should've changed that. In fact, nearly everything Pope James has done is wrong. It's like he's not Catholic."

"What do you think we should do about that?" Sicoli asked.

"I don't know. I suppose he should be impeached or somethin."

"What are you doing now, Joseph?" Sicoli asked, intentionally changing the subject.

"Well, after I got out of the army, I went to community college in Modesto. But school ain't for me—too hard. That's not my thing. So I moved to San Diego, where I've had a few jobs—drove taxi, worked at a gas station, day laborer, was a farm hand—but none of them pay much. I'm workin' nights at a 7-Eleven now."

"How could you afford to come to this retreat?"

"My mom loaned me the money. She thought it'd be good for me."

"And what do you hope for your future?"

"I really want to get married and have kids, but women today don't want to follow the Bible and be subservient. So, I don't know when that'll happen. I'm sure not gonna find a girl at an all-men's retreat, though."

"How long were you in the army?"

"Ten years—I was in combat in both Iraq and Afghanistan."

"Really. What did you do there?" Sicoli asked.

"I was a sniper."

Chapter Sixteen

"**W**hat are the most critical and intractable issues currently facing the Church?" James asked the six men sitting around the large marble-top table in front of his office fireplace.

"Life issues have to be near the top of the list," one stated. "Abortion, capital punishment, stem cells, euthanasia—they all threaten the Church's position on the sanctity of life."

"We still don't have enough priests," another said. "So the role of the laity in church leadership needs to be encouraged."

"How we determine who is permitted to receive the Eucharist and the rules for excommunicating politicians for their stance on abortion, birth control, war, and peace are also vital."

"Emphasizing corporal works of mercy, and the issues surrounding spiritual and economic wealth and poverty."

"Respect for and encouraging reception of the sacraments. Too many couples just live together or only have civil weddings."

"We need to respect gays and lesbians and environmental stewardship."

"The most challenging of all is the question of female ordination."

James had gathered this group of friends and influential cardinals at the Vatican in order to seek their advice and counsel—Cardinals Mbuto, Keegan, O'Bryan, Diokno, O'Faolain, and Rodriguez, and Father Simmons to take minutes of the conversation. Five had been candidates for pope, each representing a different continent and a wide spectrum of opinions. Although none had been his competitor, each retained a popular following within the College of Cardinals and was deeply respected in his home country. Most important, all were fully committed to the mission of God's church on earth and loyal to this pope. Given the tragic events of the past few months and the realization that the assassins had come from within, now James instinctively questioned the allegiance of everyone in the hierarchy, and his definition of loyalty took on new meaning.

"I'm extremely pleased no one mentioned financial instability or corruption within the Curia," James said with a smile. He and his cadre of pro bono accounting firms had made considerable efforts managing the Vatican's finances and the financial health of the Church in dioceses around the world. He did not believe he had achieved success in other areas, but he knew he had turned the financial crisis around, although maintaining fiscal stability required constant vigilance. The Church was neither a frugal nor a fiscally prudent institution. Few in the hierarchy or at the parish level were schooled in basic financial principles. Although the accountants had made valiant efforts to rein in spending, there was still a strong propensity to spend whatever was collected. Cash reserves were a concept James continually emphasized, but his message was too often not heard, not understood, misinterpreted, or simply disregarded.

The many problems of the entrenched Curia had also been substantially resolved. He had reassigned most of the department heads and put term limits on all those he appointed in their place. Regular cabinet meetings were held to ensure that hierarchy leaders were effectively communicating with one another, and the concept of "fiefdoms" within the Vatican no longer held any currency.

James was intrigued by the litany of the most critical and intractable issues. The pope had the undisputed legal authority to address each of the varied issues raised by this assembled cadre without any outside consultation. However, James understood the practical and symbolic value of collaborative decision-making. It was in his interest and that of the Church that the clergy and laity appreciate the need for, and be supportive of, any significant changes.

As this ad hoc group of high-powered clerics discussed the major issues, they considered the possibility of calling a third Vatican Council to deal with all matters simultaneously.

"Church councils have tremendous might and authority, and their formal decisions are binding on all Catholics," Keegan advised.

"There have only been twenty-one councils in the past two thousand years, about one every century," Diokno reported. "The last one, Vatican II, was more than fifty years ago. Vatican I was in the late 1860s. Given the furious changes of the previous five decades, perhaps it is time for Vatican III."

"A council is one way to go," O'Bryan confirmed. "But perhaps a better solution is a series of bishop synods. In the last several decades, the Synod of Bishops has played a substantive role in the most important Church matters."

"One significant value of the synod is that they don't involve just bishops and cardinals. They can include other clergy and theologians as well," O'Faolain added.

"How do they work?" James asked.

"Ordinarily, each synod deals with one primary, overarching issue. They're not decision-making bodies. They're only advisory to the pope," O'Bryan said.

"Historically, the Curia has closely supervised the preparation of each synod and controlled the agenda, debate, and, for that matter, the outcome," Diokno said.

"But it doesn't have to be that way. We can ensure the Curia only plays an administrative function," Mbuto assured.

"How long do they last?" James asked.

"However long the agenda demands. But in my judgment, anything longer than three weeks is a waste of time," O'Bryan added.

"The debate is generally polite and respectful, in part because of your personal presence, but also because there is no advantage to offending anyone in the hierarchy," Rodriguez said.

"I don't want to hear just what others think I want to hear. I want the best thinking, seriously thoughtful arguments, and the most rigorous debate possible."

"Given the topics we've raised today," Rodriguez responded, "I don't think you have to worry about people just saying what they think you want to hear. Everyone will want to give you their best arguments in order to sway you to their view."

As the discussion continued, James concluded the more people sitting around the table or in the auditorium, the better. "I like the synod idea. They will involve more people, including a greater percentage of married clergy, than a council of cardinals. I want the perspective of married bishops and priests to be heard on all these issues."

As a lawyer, James appreciated the give and take of debate. He was also more democratic in his thinking than his predecessors had been, so he specifically instructed the Curia not to exercise the strict control it had in the past. Everyone understood that as pope, he would make any final decisions.

A series of five biannual Synods of Bishops was scheduled to address the most pressing and controversial matters facing the Church. For three weeks every other October for the next ten years, the Synod of Bishops would gather in Rome in the modern auditorium named after Paul VI, adjacent to St. Peter's. They would start with the least contentious issues in an effort to build momentum for change.

✳ ✳ ✳

That evening, in the solitude of his apartment, he opened a bottle of scotch. As he had done on so many nights before, he put a handful of ice cubes into a cocktail glass, poured the scotch over the crystal squares, and listened to the crackling. He sat back and enjoyed the whiskey swirling in his mouth. Two hours later, he was sound asleep and half of the pint-sized bottle of booze was gone.

When he awoke the following morning, his head pounded and his mouth was dry. He immediately took four Advil and a couple Alka-Seltzers, knowing that the sooner he medicated, the sooner he would feel better. He knew he drank far too much booze. What had been a social event when Vicky was alive had turned into a serious drinking problem since her death. A cocktail before dinner had transformed into a terrible demon that adversely affected his ability to live the life to which he had committed himself.

But his life in Vatican City was still just too unbearable. The incredible loneliness, the cold, ancient architecture, meaningless arguments with conservative cardinals, and the slowness of the bureaucracy all stretched his patience and aggravated his stomach. He often joked to his closest friends that living in the Vatican would mean he'd spend less time in Purgatory. The scotch helped him get through it all.

When taking the broad view, he enjoyed his work. Meeting with Catholics in their communities, learning about Church history, experiencing cultures not previously visited, and speaking to, inspiring, and motivating large audiences were wonderfully fulfilling aspects of this job. When he was involved in these activities, he never drank to excess. However, when imprisoned in the Vatican, scotch was a way out. But the booze demanded a high price.

Cardinal Keegan had spoken to him about seeking treatment. He had even suggested he take advantage of one of his trips to the United States to enter a Catholic treatment center reserved for Church leaders and the most famous Catholics. Many high-profile and well-known people had sought healing there without the media ever becoming aware. Keegan had offered to arrange for a five-week program; he was just waiting for the pope's OK.

James wrote in his journal that morning that he would seek help so that he would not need to drown his loneliness and despair in alcohol. He would tell Keegan to make the arrangements.

Mbuto and O'Bryan stood in the alcove off to the side of the auditorium. "Do you really think he's going to do away with the requirement of confession to a priest?" Mbuto asked his colleague.

"Based upon his questioning during the synod, I'd say he probably will," O'Bryan said.

James's first synod, held shortly after his second anniversary, had focused on the celebration of the Mass, the sacrament of reconciliation, and the Eucharist. Catholics believe that bread and wine are changed into the actual body and blood of Jesus the Christ through the process of transubstantiation during Holy Mass. However, the long-held rule was that even though Catholics were encouraged to receive the Eucharist as often as possible, only Catholics in "good standing" could receive. Prior to Vatican II, Catholics were required to confess an itemized list of their mortal sins to an individual priest in a confidential setting in order to receive the Eucharist. Vatican II offered the alternative to confess generally to a priest in a communal setting, detailing only to God the specific record of sins, although, the long-honored tradition of private confession had regained prominence in recent years.

After significant debate, James's first Synod of Bishops recommended that the Church explicitly teach that the healing nature of Holy Mass offers each participant the occasion for confession, reconciliation, and forgiveness. All are sinners, and God forgives all those who admit their sins, ask for forgiveness, and commit to sin no more. Throughout the Mass, the priest and faithful prayerfully acknowledge their sinfulness, and ask God for mercy and forgiveness.

While James did not change the law prohibiting a person who is "conscious of grave sin" from receiving the Eucharist, and did not modify the sacrament of reconciliation, he did eliminate the requirement that only those who had formally, privately, or communally confessed their sins could receive. The prevailing argument was that whether the person was qualified to receive the Eucharist should be a personal decision between an individual and God. The mere fact that someone showed up at Holy Mass and participated in the worship service was a strong indicator they were reconciled with the Creator, and thus were in the requisite state of grace to receive.

"None of us are sufficiently holy to receive the body and blood of Jesus the Christ," the pope's official statement read. "Yet, Jesus clearly states, 'Unless you eat of my body and drink of my blood, you shall not have life everlasting.' Thus it is inappropriate for the Church to decide who should be saved, because we believe that Jesus died to save us all. As Pope Francis said, 'The Eucharist is not a prize for the perfect, but a powerful medicine and nourishment for the weak.'"

Consequently, Catholics and non-Catholics alike were encouraged to receive the Eucharist. The only requirements were that the recipient be in spiritual union with Jesus the Christ and believe the Eucharist was genuinely his body and blood. Catholics were no longer required to confess their sins to a priest.

Consistent with the issue of formal confession of sins outside of Mass, this first "James's Synod" also concluded that Jesus' teachings substantially outweighed the reasons to continue the practice of excommunication, except for in the most severe circumstances. In one of his parables, Jesus taught that the Kingdom of Heaven is like a field of wheat and weeds. Because it can be difficult to tell the difference between these plants, Jesus advises to wait until harvest time to separate them, so as not to pull out the wheat while extracting the weeds. God will separate the wheat from the weeds when it is time. Thus, this synod concluded there is no need for the Church to judge who is worthy and who is not. God will do that in God's time. Jesus teaches, "Judge not, lest you be judged."

This was important, because excommunication had been used in the past to thwart scientific discovery and now was closely related to the secular politics of abortion and other life issues. According to settled canon law, anyone who participated in an abortion was automatically excommunicated from the Church, just as those who intentionally murdered another human being. This included attending physicians and nurses, as well as the woman carrying the child who willingly and intentionally requested that her unborn child be killed. Those excommunicated could rejoin the Church upon their repentance for their sins. The synod did not change this understanding. However, the remaining controversial question was whether this aspect of canon law also applied to politicians who voted for, or prochoice activists who supported, the legal right to abortion.

James was adamantly opposed to abortion, except in the rare circumstances when it was necessary to save the life of the mother. Life was sacred from the moment of conception until natural death because God created life. Most Catholics, the vast majority of clergy, and all the hierarchy concurred. However, James was unwilling to impose Catholic teaching on others through government legislation or edict. Not every religion taught that ensoulment began at conception. In earlier times, even some leaders of the Christian church had concluded sacred life did not begin until quickening, about the sixth month of gestation, although the earliest Christians had condemned all procured abortions.

"The words of Jesus, as recorded in Scripture, do not suggest his followers should force or impose his teachings on others," James wrote. "He commanded his disciples to 'go forth and teach all nations.' But he did not instruct them to use the weight of civil or criminal law to compel belief or behavior. Consequently, it is inappropriate for the Church to require Catholic government officials to support laws that prohibit abortion, capital punishment, euthanasia, or other life issues. Nevertheless, Scripture precludes personal participation in any of these acts, specifically Jesus' command to 'love your neighbors as yourself.' Active participation in abortion, capital punishment, or euthanasia amounts to grave and serious sin. Any person who actively and unrepentantly participates in any of these activities can no longer be a member of the Church."

This synod held that it was inconsistent with canon law to excommunicate politicians or activists because of their political stance on any issue. The question of the sinfulness of their political positions would be between them and their God. Further, local bishops could not deny political or government officials the Eucharist because of their public positions. It was in God's purview to separate the wheat from the weeds.

The synod concluded, "God alone separates the righteous from the sinners in God's time. The Church will only excommunicate those who affirmatively and publicly acknowledge that they are separated from Jesus the Christ."

In the third year of his papacy, James made his first "official" visit to the United States. It was a traditional papal expedition with public Masses at large venues, meetings with selected clergy and lay leaders, and appeals to the faithful to heed the call of the Holy Spirit to serve God's church as a priest, sister, or brother.

However, this trip was a logistical nightmare. Security was always heightened whenever a foreign government leader stepped foot on US soil, but for James, security was magnified several fold due to the enormous crowds and the persistent threats against his life. Bomb-sniffing dogs, surveillance robots, and heavily armed SWAT teams were ubiquitous. Clergy, the faithful, and reporters arrived at the events hours before the published start times in order to get through the multiple checkpoints and get a seat.

After greeting the overflow crowd of more than 140,000 at the University of Michigan football stadium in Ann Arbor, James began his homily with these words: "There is a historical debate among Christian theologians whether we are saved by faith or by good works. Well, I confirm to you today, Jesus saved every human being by his death on the cross. It is through our faith in Jesus the Christ that we are saved. Faith is a gift of God. But it is a 'use it or lose it' gift.

"So how do we use our faith so we do not lose it? We enrich it through daily prayer, Holy Mass, reading Scripture, and fulfilling the command of Jesus the Christ to love and serve others."

On this day, James wore his simple emerald-green vestments, with a dark green band down the front and back and the outline of a fish in ivory on the front, which represented Jesus, and on the back *chi-rho* ☩, the first two letters of Christ in Greek, superimposed one over the other. The fish was one of the earliest Christian symbols, and ☩ was allegedly a sign from God shown to Constantine.

He continued his homily. "These two latter activities—loving and serving others—are the equivalent of good works. We must do good works, just as we must pray, because Jesus commanded us to. That is how we ensure that we do not lose our faith. Just as prayer helps keep us closer to God, so do good works. By loving and serving others, we become closer to God. Just as sin separates us from God, serving others—and doing good works—brings us closer to God.

"Every person is a child of God. When you serve another, without any expectation of return or reward, you grow closer to God. There is no prayer more powerful than caring for one of God's children. It is a prayer of thanksgiving. When we serve others, God blesses us. Scripture teaches that to give is to receive. Whenever you experience the joy of serving, you are experiencing the ultimate joy of the blessings of Almighty God.

"Every one of us can make a difference in our family, our community, and our world. The failure to put forward an effort to make a constructive difference in the lives of our brothers and sisters tends to diminish our individual self-worth. This is especially poignant when we do not reach out to the poor, the disabled, the imprisoned, the elderly, the sick, and children.

"That failure causes us to turn inward. It disconnects us from the suffering of others. It tends to absolve us from our responsibility. This is the antithesis of what God calls us to do. Albert Schweitzer said it well. 'The only ones among you who will really be happy are those who have sought and found how to serve.'"

After Ann Arbor, James visited and preached in Dallas, Atlanta, and Washington, DC. While in Washington, the president of the United States invited him to the White House. There they discussed a wide range of issues, including peace and justice.

"The United States has been engaged in military conflict for forty of the last eighty years," the pope reminded the president during their visit in the Oval Office. He did not criticize the United States for being at war 50 percent of the time. Nor did he scold the president for money the United States allocated to military expenditures, as his predecessors had done to previous presidents. Rather, he reminded the president of former President George W. Bush's admission that he wished he had taken the opportunity to visit with John Paul II about the just-war doctrine.

"I don't want you, Madam President, to have the same regret as President Bush," he said.

President Mary Talbot was a Democrat, and firmly committed to world peace. She was well aware that this Catholic pontiff had resisted the draft, served time in a federal prison, and then volunteered in the US Peace Corps. She was sympathetic to his views because she too had concluded the Vietnam War was a colossal mistake. She also considered him a kindred spirit because the pope's son was a member of the US Congress, one from her political party.

However, Mary Talbot was not a pacifist. She was an honors graduate of West Point and had served in the Judge Advocate General's Corps, where she had risen to the rank of lieutenant general before being elected to the US Senate. She had won election to the US presidency as "A Strong Voice for a Strong Defense" of her country and its national interests. Moreover, she had studied the just-war theory at the Academy and later at the National War College. She remembered not being overly impressed. However, she was genuinely interested in the pope's take on the archaic concept and asked him to share his understanding.

"The primary test," James explained to the president, "is that the cause must be just. Correcting a grave public evil that violates the basic human rights of whole populations generally meets this test. Defense of aggression against national boundaries generally meets this test. Defending innocent human life meets this test. However, protecting a country's economy, defending economic interests, punishing those who have done wrong, or achieving material gain never meet the test."

As they discussed the basic principles of the theory, the president asked, "What do you do when your enemy clearly asserts up front that they intend to inflict irreparable harm, such as Saddam Hussein in Iraq, or recent regimes in Iran and North Korea?"

"There is a presumption against deadly force," the pope replied. "The underlying rationale is that human life is always sacred because God created all human life. The presumption against deadly force can be overcome when the cause is just, but generally only in self-defense. Preemptive strikes are prohibited, because until someone puts your, or another's, life in imminent danger, you cannot be certain what they will do."

"So your enemy tells you they are going to fly airplanes into skyscrapers, and you cannot do anything?" she asked incredulously.

"Braggadocio and saber rattling are as old as human life itself. Of course, you can prepare to defend yourself. You can defend if attacked.

But neither countries nor individuals are permitted to preemptively engage force that takes human life."

"If someone raises their fist at you, you're not allowed to strike them until they punch you in the face?" she pressed.

"The just-war doctrine allows you to defend yourself as soon as someone raises their fist at you. However, you cannot use force before they raise their fist. You cannot use force even if they declare they are going to punch you in the face. It is the distinction between talk and action. And sadly for us mere mortals, that distinction is not always obvious."

"What if you are engaged in a 'just war' and you know thousands of lives will be spared if nuclear weapons are used instead of slogging it out with conventional forces? Does your philosophy permit the use of those weapons?"

"Whose lives are being spared?" James asked. "Whose lives are taken? Weapons of mass destruction do not discriminate when it comes to who dies. All within range of a nuclear bomb die. I know this may not be what you want to hear," he said, "but the concept of proportionality does not permit the killing of hundreds of thousands of innocents in order to save thousands, or even hundreds of thousands of combatants."

When the meeting ended, President Talbot thanked the pope for coming to see her.

"You have a very difficult job," James said. "I appreciate that many of the issues you must address lie in the gray areas of life. If you prayerfully ask God for guidance, it will be granted. God blesses you!"

The White House held a state dinner for the pope that evening. Catholic government officials and renowned clergy, Catholic lay leaders, theologians of other Christian denominations, and leading Jewish, Muslim, Hindu, American Indian, and Buddhist religious leaders attended. Just prior to dinner, the president raised a toast to the pope.

"We are proud to call you an American. We are proud to call you our friend. We are proud to call you a man of God. We are proud to call you the Servant of the Servants of God. Ladies and gentlemen, I am proud to present to you the first American pope, James the First."

Everyone in the room stood and applauded. James thanked the president for her kind words, thanked the attendees for their warm greeting, and thanked the chef and waiters for their gracious service.

"There's quite a difference between being a Chicago lawyer and being pope," he quipped. "As a lawyer, I had to decide which dark blue power suit and what color tie I would wear each day. As pope, I'm not bothered with those decisions. I wear the same outfit almost every day of the week." The dignitaries laughed. "It was an hour drive on the freeway from home to my law office in downtown Chicago. Now my office is a five-minute walk from my apartment. I used to carry a billfold full of credit cards, driver's license, health insurance card, and lots of money. Now I don't even have a billfold, never drive a car, don't need health insurance, and have no idea how things get paid.

"When I practiced law, I tried to convince clients that our firm was the best one to serve them. Now I try to convince everyone that each of you are the best ones to serve each other.

"I attended Mass most Sundays. Now I say Mass every day. If I was in a hurry, or the Bears were playing at noon on Sunday, I'd sneak out of Mass early. I really can't get away with that anymore—too many people watching." Again, there was laughter. "And when I prayed before, I typically asked God for things. Now when I pray, I just thank God for everything.

"In that regard, President Talbot asked me if I would lead us in grace before we eat. I told her I'd be delighted." Everyone stood.

"In the name of the Father, and of the Son, and of the Holy Spirit. Bless us, O Lord, and these Thy gifts, which we are about to receive from Thy bounty, through Jesus the Christ, our Lord. And Lord, bless all in this room, especially my dear friend, President Mary Talbot. Amen."

CHAPTER SEVENTEEN

"**A**rrange it so I can spend time with children—orphans or kids whose parents can't care for them," he instructed Simmons during a planning meeting for his upcoming trip to South America. "Find a place in Lima where we can spend a half day meeting with the caregivers, administrators, and teachers. I want to make sure I do more than just meet dignitaries and wealthy contributors."

"Yes, Your Holiness, I'll get that on the schedule," Simmons assured him. The young aide knew that neither the Curia nor the prelates in Peru would be happy with the pope spending so much of his limited time visiting a children's home instead of schmoozing the wealthy, local celebrities, and public figures. However, he had learned from previous journeys that the pope could not be dissuaded when it came to children. James had visited orphanages, day care centers, failure-to-thrive clinics, and children's homes on every international trip. The Vatican powers and local bishops dissented, always in vain.

As leader of the Roman Catholic Church, James traveled to both familiar cities and places he had never before visited. During his first few years as pope, he preached in nineteen countries on five continents. Latin America was especially important to him. Central and South America comprised the single largest population of Catholics in the world—more than 40 percent of all the faithful. It was also a region of significant economic poverty, especially among indigenous people.

Of major concern was the enormous disparity between rich and poor. Several reputable journals declared Latin America as the most unequal region in the world in terms of individual wealth. Poverty and inequity always injured children the most.

A few weeks later, he was finishing breakfast in his room at the Marriott in Lima when the phone rang. "Good morning, Your Holiness," Simmons said. "It's time."

"I'll be at the elevator in two minutes." James took a last sip of orange juice, finished a glass of ice water, tied his shoes, and put his iPhone in his pocket. He was wearing his trademark plain light ivory cassock, white skullcap, and simple wooden cross that hung around his neck, resting on his chest. If it were not for the distinctive clerical garb, no one would have known he was one of the most influential men in the world.

As he exited suite 2414, two plainclothes Swiss Guards, together with a Peruvian security detail, accompanied him to the elevator where Simmons was waiting. When the elevator reached the main floor, Cardinal Rodriguez greeted him. The Peruvian police had cleared everyone out of the lobby, save the front desk staff. James walked to the reception counter and spoke to the hotel employees, shaking hands and thanking each of them for their service and assistance.

The motorcade lined up in the half-moon driveway at the hotel front entrance. Fourteen police motorcycles and eight police cars, four cars in front and four behind, six black Cadillac SUVs, and twenty-three eight-passenger vans waited. The hypnotic rhythm of the hundreds of flashing emergency lights foretold the importance of the convoy. Vatican and Peruvian bishops and priests, along with nearly one hundred members of the international and Lima media sat patiently in their respective vehicles. All were ready to move at the designated moment.

The large glass doors opened. A Peruvian agent escorted James out of the hotel to the second vehicle. The driver, a local police officer, and Colonel Meire were seated in the front. Cardinal Rodriguez got in the back on the driver's side, and Simmons rode in the third SUV. As the pope got in on the passenger side directly behind Meire, the agent closed the door, signaled the lead motorcycle, and tapped the roof of the vehicle. The motorcade immediately thrust forward. Four motorcycles led the way and four followed the SUVs. The remaining six bikes hovered near the second SUV, three on either side.

Hundreds of cars, trucks, taxis, busses, bicycles, and vans suspended their schedules as they stood still, waiting for the convoy to pass. Local people lined the streets and bridges that overlooked the Zanjon Freeway, hoping to get a glimpse of the eminent man the radio reported was in their city. As they heard the distant sirens getting closer, the excitement became palpable, but they were ultimately disappointed because of the darkened vehicle windows and the blurring pace at which the procession sped past. Previous popes had ridden in white glass-encased Popemobiles so all the faithful, as well as the curious, could see the Holy Father. But not James. The Vatican City assassination attempt and the hundreds of threats against his life had persuaded the Swiss Guard to protect this pope differently.

The first stop was the Estadio Monumental, the largest and most modern stadium in Peru, and the third largest in all of South America. Here the pope would say Mass at seven thirty and preach to the local people. In honor of the red and white Peruvian flag, he wore his white chasuble offset with a wide stripe of red fabric down the front and back, with an alabaster dove representing the Holy Spirit embroidered on the front and white roses signifying love stitched on the back.

Nearly half a million waited to see and hear him, although there was only room for seventy-seven thousand in the stadium—forty-seven thousand in the stands and box suites and another thirty thousand on the massive field below. There were large-screen monitors and speakers set up outside the stadium throughout the surrounding area for the other four hundred thousand people.

Jimmy Flahvin had always been an accomplished speaker; now he was becoming comfortable as a preacher. Years before, when he had been a member at Sacred Heart in Winnetka, Father Jack Thielin had asked him to become a lay preacher. There had been a limited time in the United States when some dioceses had allowed parishes to engage nonclergy in commenting on Holy Scripture during the homily at Sunday Mass. The Sacred Heart parish council had nominated Jimmy, and the pastor had agreed. But Jimmy was uncomfortable with the whole idea. He viewed himself as a sinner, not a preacher.

"I struggle just to keep my spiritual head above water," he told Thielin. He considered himself an "aspiring Christian," one who was trying to live a Christian life, but not to the level he wanted to be. He was not prepared to advise others on how they might fulfill their responsibility. So he had declined Father Jack's invitation.

Now he had no choice but to preach. He was Preacher in Chief. The more he preached, the more at ease he grew, and his homilies became better and better. Nevertheless, he did not preach at people. He was not self-righteous. He just spoke from his heart about what he believed and what helped him in his personal struggle to remain faithful in the midst of worldly temptation. Although he was not a theologian, he was a man of God. He offered awareness and practicality many cardinals, bishops, and even priests did not have. He was a common man, and the people identified with his commonality, even though they greatly respected and loved him as the Holy Father.

Whenever he preached in a country where English was not widely spoken, James would start with pleasantries in the local language before reverting to English. However, he wanted the people to hear what he said. So the Vatican hired the best translators in the world, many of whom came from the United Nations on short-term contracts. All were Catholics, honored to translate for the pope. The Vatican offered top wages, but few accepted money.

Prior to saying Mass, he met with the assigned translators. He asked them about themselves, explained in broad outline what he intended to say, and discussed in detail any difficult or complicated concepts he might raise. He told each translator that most people would not understand any of the words he spoke. They would only hear what the interpreter said. This of course caused frightful trepidation on the part of the translators.

Then he would always say, "That's why the Holy Spirit is here with us today—to make sure both of us communicate the Word of God. We will both do fine if we trust in the Holy Spirit. Will you trust in the Spirit?" he would ask.

The interpreter always answered, "Yes."

"Great! Then we're ready to rock 'n roll!"

On this day, the interpreter said, "I mean no disrespect, Holy Father, but I'm curious—why don't you write out what you want me to translate, to help ensure that I don't make any mistakes?"

The pope responded cheerfully. "Before you were born, there was a famous American bishop by the name of Fulton J. Sheen. He had a TV show. A reporter for *TIME Magazine* once asked him why he never used notes when he spoke on TV. Bishop Sheen replied, 'There's a story about an Irish lady who was watching her priest read his Sunday sermon. She turned to her friend in the pew and asked, "If he can't remember it, how does he expect us to?" That's why I don't read my homilies.'"

As was his custom, James blessed the interpreter before they went out on stage. The translator knelt as the pope raised his hand and made the sign of the cross while reciting in Latin, "*In nomine Patris, et Filii, et Spiritus Sancti.* Amen." Then, to the total astonishment of the interpreter, the pope knelt down.

"Would you bless me?" James asked.

Stunned, the interpreter did not know what to do. James gently instructed her. "Just bless me with the sign of the cross. You can say it in English or Spanish, whichever you prefer. Just say it like you mean it."

After a moment of hesitation to regain her composure, the interpreter raised her right hand and traced the sign of the cross over the man kneeling in front of her as she said, "In the name of the Father, and of the Son, and of the Holy Spirit. Amen." For this twenty-something woman, blessing the pope was beyond what any of her family or friends would ever believe. More importantly, she thought to herself, this was the most remarkable experience in her young life.

James stood and said, "Thank you."

"You're welcome," she stuttered.

"Well, let's go to work." He started walking out onto the immense stage to say Holy Mass, and the interpreter prayed fiercely that she would not make a mistake.

The Gospel for this day was the Parable of the Talents. James read the scripture and then explained what he had read.

"The apostles asked Jesus about the end times, and Jesus responded with a parable. The kingdom of heaven is like a man who was going away on a long journey. Before he departed, he called his servants to him. He gave each of them talents, which at that time was a particularly generous sum of money, equivalent to payment for many years of work by an ordinary laborer. In today's currency, it would be like receiving hundreds of thousands of soles. He gave one servant five hundred thousand soles, another two hundred thousand, and the third one hundred thousand. The master told the servants to invest the money wisely. Then he went on his way.

"When the master returned, he asked the servants to account for what they had done with the money he had given them. The man who received five hundred thousand soles invested wisely and returned one million soles to the master. 'Well done, good and faithful servant,' the master said. Then the man who had been given two hundred thousand came forward. He gave the master four hundred thousand soles. The master congratulated him as well and said, 'Well done, good and faithful servant.' However, when the man who was entrusted with one hundred thousand soles approached the master, he returned the one hundred thousand soles he had been given. This man had buried the money rather than investing it because he was scared of what the master might do if he failed.

"As is the case with most parables, there are many different ways in which this one can be interpreted," James explained. "One explanation concludes that Jesus represents the master in the parable. The apostles were asking about the end times. Jesus responds by sharing this parable about his leaving and returning later. He uses money as a metaphor for the love of God. Jesus assures each of us an abundance of the love of God. The question is not the measurable quantity of God's love. God loves each of us equally and immeasurably. Rather, the question is, what will we do with the love God gives us?

"Throughout the Gospel, Jesus explains how we are to share the abundance of God's love. He instructs us to love our neighbor as ourselves, to visit the sick, to give food to the hungry, to give drink to the thirsty, to clothe the naked, and to visit the imprisoned. Those who follow Jesus' teaching will enjoy an endless abundance of God's love.

"When Jesus returns, he will ask each of us to account for the love God has given us. Those who invest God's love by sharing it with their neighbor, caring for those in need, loving their enemies, and loving God above all things will be called 'good and faithful servants.' However, the person who takes the love of God and buries it—does nothing with it, does not invest it—will be thrown out into the darkness, where there will be 'gnashing of teeth.'

"So I encourage each of you today to invest God's love in your neighbor. Share it with all whom you meet. Do not hold God's love unto yourself. Freely give it away through generous acts of service to others. God's love is like the soles the master gave to his servants. It does not belong to us. God's love is given to each of us to share with each other.

"Invest wisely," James concluded, and then resumed saying Holy Mass.

From the Estadio Monumental, they traveled to the Presidential Palace to meet with the president of Peru. In the car, Cardinal Rodriguez looked over at James. "President Lopez is a good man, Holy Father. He is a strong advocate for the poor and is doing all he can to make life better for the indigenous people, especially in the rural areas." Interestingly, the Presidential Palace was just across the square from the Palacio Arzobisal, the cardinal's opulent residence.

President Lopez welcomed them at the grand arch and escorted the pope, Cardinal Rodriguez, and Fathers Charlie Martin and John Simmons into his spacious conference room, where key members of the president's cabinet waited. They met for over an hour, discussing the plight of the impoverished and how the Church and the Peruvian government might collaborate to help correct injustice and provide food, medicine, and education to the people. They agreed that Father Charlie Martin and the Minister of Family Welfare and Women's Affairs would work together to maximize the collective resources of both the Peruvian government and the Catholic Church.

Much to Cardinal Rodriguez's chagrin, the pope had committed the afternoon schedule to the Puericultorio Perez Aranibar, a children's home known as the PPA. No pope had been to Peru in over a quarter century. There were so many important dignitaries and wealthy people this pope needed to meet—major donors, politicians, business people, academicians—all of whom could help the Church as well as the destitute in Peru. Rodriguez had argued vigorously and persuasively with his Vatican colleagues that it was a senseless and unproductive waste of time for the Holy Father to spend an entire afternoon with orphans and abandoned children. His colleagues agreed, but none would take the cardinal's argument to the pope, because it would make no difference. James was the "children's pope."

So the pope's long motorcade drove from the government's palace to the "children's palace," arriving at the PPA in Magdalena, a suburb of Lima. The PPA was founded in 1930 by Augusto Perez Aranibar, a Peruvian dentist and philanthropist, who had agonized about the fate of Lima's "street children." Dr. Perez did not have any children, but he had dedicated his life to creating a "palace" for Lima's poorest. Using his own money and funds raised from wealthy friends, he built this sprawling ocean-side campus situated on the Pacific coast. Now one of the largest children's homes in South America, the PPA served six hundred at-risk kids ranging in age from newborns to seventeen. Most of the children were from *asentamientos humanos*—shantytowns comprised of squatters who moved their families from the highlands in hopes of a job and security near the city. But a better life was elusive. After time, many of these extremely poor parents, who tried so hard to survive on less than two dollars a day, asked the government to take their youngest children because they simply could not feed another mouth.

Maria Elena Aparcana, the PPA director, and her top staff greeted James and his entourage at the front gate. The director was a beautiful, trim, well-endowed woman in her mid-forties. Clothed in a simple black dress tied at the waist, she wore a white pearl necklace and pearl earrings. James found her striking and admired her beauty as she bent to kiss his ring. He tried to discourage her from performing the ancient ritual, but to no avail. He allowed his thoughts, for just a moment, to contemplate the possibility of what it might be like to love a woman like Maria Elena, and to live with her as he had lived with his lost love, Vicky. His thoughts were not of lust, although sex was never far from his imagination. He truly longed for the caring companionship of a woman. His days in the Vatican were lonely, and any meaningful relationship with a member of the opposite sex was prohibited. Why God would require him to be without familiar love and remain abstinent for the remainder of his life he did not comprehend.

After visiting briefly in Maria Elena's conference room, he was ushered into a clean, airy school cafeteria adorned with long tables and chairs. When the pope walked in, all the children rose and said, "*Buenas tardes, Padre Santo.*" James smiled at the healthy, happy faces.

"*Muchas gracias. Siéntense, por favor,*" he responded.

As the media pool photographer recorded his every move, James walked to one of the tables and crouched down between a little boy and girl, and asked, "Cómo estás?"

"I am fine," the little girl said.

"Well, you speak English very well."

"I like English," she said. James put his hand on her head and asked another child, parsing his words very clearly, "What is your name?"

"Jose," the boy responded.

"That's a very nice name. How old are you?"

"Nine," the boy responded.

Throughout lunch, James continued to go from table to table, speaking individually with the children. He could not visit directly with each one, but he made every attempt to speak to, hold hands with, or touch the head of every child in the room. A bell rang, indicating the lunch period was over. The children rose, picked up their plates and silverware, and placed them on a stainless steel counter in front of the kitchen.

Maria Elena asked if they could have a group photo. The children surrounded him as he knelt among them. A couple of the children laid their heads on his shoulders, others held his hands, and the rest moved in as close as possible, trying to touch his cassock. He knelt on the floor in their midst, and the photographer clicked off shot after shot. When the photographer was finished, the staff dismissed the children. As he stood up, fingerprints of brown peanut butter, grape jelly, crimson ketchup, and golden mustard spotted his once unadorned ivory cassock. The nun apologized profusely and tried to spot-clean his cassock.

"No, no, sister. This is exactly how I like it; plain white is such a boring color." He looked over at Maria Elena. "Where do the children come from?" he asked.

"Some are orphans, but most are from families who cannot support all their children." She hesitated for a moment. "They are Catholic families, Holy Father, and even though birth control is provided by the government, they won't use it because the Church forbids it. So they have more children than they can possibly care for on their meager earnings."

Her words deeply moved him. "Parents should not have to give up a child because they cannot support them," he thought to himself.

"May I visit one of the communities where the children come from?" James asked.

"Certainly," Maria Elena said, relieved at James's openness. "When would you like to go?"

"Do we need an invitation?"

"No, we go there all the time."

"Do we need to give them any advance notice?"

"No, we often go unannounced. The communities are very open. They know when we visit we come to help. It is a way we show our interest and care for others. Not many people visit shantytowns...only people who really care. The local people know this, so there is no worry."

"Can we go now?" he asked.

Cardinal Rodriguez, who was listening to the conversation, stepped in before Maria Elena could answer. "Your Holiness, it's a long drive, and we have an important dinner this evening."

Colonel Meire, who also was within earshot, added, "Holy Father, we have not secured the route or made any security provisions in the community. This could be very dangerous."

"Threats against me do not come from the poor and the powerless, Lukas," James said.

"Can we go now?" he asked Maria Elena again. She looked at Rodriguez uncertainly.

"Yes, of course," she finally said.

"Good. Then let's do it. John, call the organizers of tonight's event and tell them we might be a little late." He turned to Rodriguez.

"Cardinal Rodriguez, I understand your concern about the time. This visit might help me with what I need to say this evening. And Lukas, we both know I'm safest when no one knows when or where I'm going."

✳ ✳ ✳

When the pope's protracted caravan arrived outside the shanty-town, only ten people accompanied him into the community—Maria Elena, Cardinal Rodriguez, Colonel Meire and another plainclothes Swiss Guard, two officers from President Lopez's security detail, a videographer from CNN International, a *London Times* correspondent, a *Boston Globe* photographer, and John Simmons. Maria Elena had called ahead to alert the local priest that the pope was coming, and he met them at the entrance.

They were quite a sight as they strolled up the sand and stone gravel road of this dirty, impoverished community—James in his ivory cassock stained by children's food, the cardinal in his immaculate black cassock with red piping, the four security officers in their dark business suits and shades, the two priests in their standard black clerical garb, Maria Elena in her exquisite black dress and bright white pearl jewelry, and the pool reporters walking backward as they photographed and recorded the pope.

"This community is not as fortunate as some others," Maria Elena explained. "It does not have water, electricity, or sewage facilities. However, they are proud people and devoted patriots. You can see that by the little red and white Peruvian flags they fly over their humble homes."

Asentamientos humanos had crept into the hot and dry rural areas surrounding Lima in the 1940s, and had proliferated over the ensuing decades. The ultra-poor lived in makeshift communities, in temporary structures, on land they did not own. They constructed their homes from round wooden posts, discarded variegated cardboard siding, corrugated tin roofs, and corroding braided wire that tied it all together. The dirt-floor houses had no bathrooms and no running water. Any water they might have had to be trucked in and was stored in fading blue containers in front of the house, or at the end of the dusty road. An entire family often lived in one room, and straw mats, a single bed, three or four white plastic chairs, a few fire-blackened pots, and cast-off clothes comprised their total possessions.

Word spread quickly throughout the community that an extraordinary special guest had come to visit, and they crowded along the gravel pathway as the man in white passed by. Tears streamed from many people's eyes as they waved slowly, but out of deep respect, none approached the Holy Father.

James stopped first at the gray cement block church, still under construction. "We ran out of money, so the roof isn't completed," the local priest said, embarrassed that his church had no covering. The pope filed into a rough-sawn wooden pew in the rear of the church, knelt down, and prayed. The clergy and Maria Elena did the same. After a few minutes, James left the church. The priest took him to the home of Liliana and Jorge Rosario, longtime community residents.

Liliana was shocked that the pope would come to her small village, but she was completely overwhelmed when her parish priest informed her that the Holy Father would pay a visit to her home. With reverent graciousness, she welcomed the pope and the others into her one-room dirt-floor abode. The Rosarios owned only three plastic chairs, so she sent her eldest son to the neighbors to borrow a few more so all could sit down. She offered her guests some hot tea and cookies. The pope accepted both and settled into one of the chairs. As he sipped the tea, he visited with Liliana, Jorge, and the children while the local priest translated. He asked them about their life, their challenges, their hopes for the future, and how they survived day-to-day.

Liliana and Jorge were both thirty-three, and had three children at home. "Our two youngest girls, they're six and four, are at the PPA," Liliana confessed, tears welling in her eyes. "Two of our other children died, one shortly after birth and the other when he was four. It was from diarrhea and dehydration."

The priest explained that neither the father nor mother had any education beyond the fifth grade, although Jorge said he was a self-taught auto mechanic. He worked occasionally at a garage near the city, but it was only a few days a month. Every other day he walked the back alleyways of nearby affluent suburban communities in search of discarded metal, plastic, paper, and glass, which he sold for mere pennies to a local recycler. He also collected and traded plastic bottles and aluminum soda pop cans. Liliana volunteered at the day care center, even though her children no longer attended, and she was a mainstay at the community church. The older children went to school, but they often missed class due to illness. They had little food and no medicine. When the children got sick, all they could do was lie on the dirt floor of their home and hope their malady would pass quickly. There was a health clinic in the community, but its sparse medicine was available only for the most ill. The Rosarios lived on roughly two thousand US dollars a year—about one dollar per person, per day.

James had seen poverty many times before. However, he had never become immune to the deep grief that overcame him as he walked amid the abjectly destitute. Each impoverished person he met, every horrifying situation he faced, every desperate condition he encountered, pierced his inner being and struck a terrifying blow to the very faith that otherwise sustained him.

"How could God allow this to go on?" he would ask himself, even as he knew the answer.

The pope was the guest of honor to an overflow crowd at the Westin Hotel Grand Ballroom. Affluent Peruvians, along with Catholic, Jewish, and Protestant clergy and politicians and government leaders attended. The entire contingent of media who followed James around the world was also present. It was an elegant room of sparkling chandeliers, rich blue carpet, and floor-to-ceiling glass walls. Two hundred white linen-covered tables each held ten dinner and salad plates, shining silver and gold cutlery, crystal stemware, and light blue fragranced candles. Most of the men wore black tuxedos and starched white shirts, while the women dressed in a rainbow array of evening gowns and dazzling jewelry.

When it was his turn to address the gathering, James described in excruciating and vivid detail the *asentamientos humanos* he had visited that afternoon and the living conditions the Rosario family grappled with every day.

"This family is among the more than three billion people who live on less than two US dollars a day. Of those, half exist on only one dollar a day. I prayed in that simple, unfinished church this afternoon. I asked God, 'How can you allow this to go on? God Almighty, Creator of the Universe, why do you permit this?'"

He paused briefly, looking out at the audience. "I pray every day, most days multiple times. However, I seldom get a direct answer to my prayers." He paused again.

"Today was different. Today the answer was loud, instantaneous, and clear. It engulfed my being. I heard the Lord say to me, 'I don't allow this. You do!'

"'What do you mean?' I asked. 'How do I allow this? I'm not responsible for one billion people suffering from hunger every day. I do not cause twenty-six percent of the world's children to become physically and intellectually stunted. I do not permit children to languish and die from malnutrition and preventable disease. I am not liable for insufficient human and economic development and the resultant poverty,' I protested." The room fell silent. Even the sound of errant cutlery on china had ceased.

"But there was no answer. Apparently God had decided the conversation had ended." He looked intently across the packed room and, almost in a whisper, said, "I've come to realize I do allow this to go on in communities all over the world, every day.

He lowered his head and stared at the floor in front of him. Everyone in the audience, and all those at the head table, fixed their eyes on him as he stood at the microphone with his head bowed. When at long last he spoke, after nearly a minute of quiet, he asked, "Where is the joy of life when there is only pain and sorrow? God does not allow Jorge, Liliana, their children, and all their neighbors to live in abject poverty. I permit this to happen. The Catholic Church permits this to occur. The US government, the European Union, the People's Republic of China, and the

United Nations permit this to occur. This family's affluent neighbors all over the world permit this to go on.

"Poverty, illiteracy, hunger, preventable disease—we could wipe all these out in our lifetime if we just decided to do so. God has given us all the tools and resources we need. We have all the technology necessary so virtually every family can grow their own food. There could be sufficient health care, education, and opportunity for everyone, if we just decided we are going to make it happen. The question, of course, is who are the 'we'?

"Is the 'we' just me? Or is it the institution of the Catholic Church, or the UN, or the US, or China, or the EU, or the Peruvian government, or all of the above? Is the 'we' just me? Or is it all Christian believers, all Muslims, all Jews, all Buddhists, all traditional believers, all nonbelievers, or all of the above?

"Is the 'we' just me? Or is it all of us is this grand ballroom?" he asked as he extended his right arm and swept his hand from left to right across the entire room.

Simmons had heard the pope speak about poverty and hunger many times before, and the Holy Father was often animated. However, he had not previously seen this level of passion and 'depth of soul' commitment. Perhaps, the young priest thought, God really did speak to the pope today.

James continued. "The Catholic Church is committed to expanding our efforts one hundred times – one thousand times – over to obliterate hunger and poverty. We are committed to coordinate our efforts with all the great governmental powers and every willing religious institution on the planet. But that combined effort will not even dent the reality of human suffering and deprivation. Unless each of you, and all of Jorge and Maria's affluent global neighbors, decide to help, they are lost."

He paused again, and then said, "I've asked some of the good sisters to give each of you a simple printed card. You can pass them out now," he instructed. "Earlier today, President Lopez and I agreed to cooperate in an effort to stamp out poverty in Peru. Together, we will raise money and recruit volunteers to help the poor help themselves.

A nongovernmental organization dedicated to this effort will manage both the money and the volunteers.

"Each card you receive has a place for your contact information, and space to write your commitment to help rid Peru of hunger, malnutrition, disease, illiteracy, and poverty. You can indicate a specific financial contribution, or identify a specific action you will perform. We prefer that you do both. President Lopez, Cardinal Rodriguez, Vice President Hernandez, and PPA Director Maria Elena Aparcana have offered to collect the cards at the doors after the benediction. Please do not take the cards home with you. There is nowhere to send them. If you choose not to make a commitment, turn in a blank card. But I encourage you to make a generous commitment. Ask God for guidance before you start to write.

"God has been very good to each of us in this grand ballroom. God has entrusted each of us with tremendous talents, valuable gifts, and an abundance of love. God asks us to share those talents and gifts and love with others. Jesus specifically instructed us to love God and to love our neighbor. You know the truth of which I speak. Your decision to come here tonight demonstrates you know of, and have agreed to be bound by, this truth. God bless each and every one of you."

Sicoli ate dinner alone in his small room at the monastery. He was despondent. "Nearly six years have passed and the imposter stills occupies Peter's throne," he painfully admitted to himself. Although a patient man by nature, Sicoli's patience had worn frail. Now there were rumors from his informants in Rome that Flahvin was about to inflict even greater damage by overturning the long-term ban on artificial birth control, modifying the Church's strict opposition to abortion, sanctioning homosexual marriage, and allowing women to be ordained priests. And there was nothing he could do about any of it.

Most of Sicoli's Vatican supporters were now in jail, retired, or dead. "The few that remain are too weak and lack sufficient commitment to take action. They fear the repercussions if caught. They do not have the stomach to risk their lives or their careers to protect the Roman Catholic Church," he muttered to himself.

But Sicoli had followers from the weekend retreats. Some were powerful and wealthy men of conviction who knew how to get things done. However, they had no strategy—no plan. Sicoli knew what needed to be done, yet he was powerless to execute.

From the time he had been assigned to Holy Cross Monastery, Sicoli had questioned Flahvin's resolve. Now he realized the true viciousness of his adversary. Flahvin's lack of mercy was even greater than his own. For all practical purposes, Cardinal Sicoli was permanently incarcerated in isolation in a remote desert a hundred miles from nowhere.

"My day-to-day existence is worse than death," he wrote to a friend in the Vatican. "I am alive, but I do not live. My impotence overwhelms me. I have no power and lack any capability to right the grievous wrongs the Antichrist perpetrates." At times like this, Sicoli simply gave up, concluding there was no hope for his beloved church.

Then, to his complete delight, Joseph Carlin showed up at another retreat. Sicoli recognized him immediately and invited him to his office after his presentation.

"Joseph," Sicoli started the conversation, "when we last met you told me you were raised in a German-Catholic family and you joined the army immediately after secondary school."

"No, I joined up right after high school," Carlin said.

"Yes. You also told me you were a sniper. How did you become a sniper?"

"Well, durin' basic trainin', I qualified as an expert with the M16. My CO recommended me for sniper school at Fort Benning. I graduated with honors. I beat all the other guys—I shot ninety-nine."

"What does ninety-nine mean?" Sicoli asked curiously.

"To graduate, ya had to get a ninety hit rate at six hundred meters. That means you had to hit the bull's-eye ninety out of one hundred times. I hit the bull's-eye ninety-nine times out of every hundred. I'm really good."

"Yes, so it would seem. Then what did you do?"

"I was assigned States-side, where I practiced firin' my weapon every day. I honed my skills. I got promoted and got lots of medals. I was the best shot in the brigade. I can still put five rounds inside a circle the size of a quarter at a hundred yards," he boasted.

"Have you ever killed anyone, my son?" Sicoli asked.

"Oh yeah. After about a year, I shipped out to Iraq. Not much goin' on there, so I didn't have much chance to use my skills. Then I was deployed to Afghanistan. Snipers were in real demand there. Most snipers were used for recon. But our squad was assigned to take out Taliban leaders and communications operators. So me and my spotter, we'd get in full camouflage and sit way up on the side of a mountain lookin' down on the Taliban's camp. Sometimes we was a klick away. We'd just wait. Patience was the key. If you're gonna be a good sniper, ya gotta be really patient. When we saw one or two of them walkin' alone, we'd pick 'em off one by one. I got twenty-seven kills."

"How did you know which ones were the leaders?"

"You could tell. They was always tellin' the other guys what to do, and they walk differently," Carlin said.

"Really? They walk differently?"

"Yup. Like you. You walk different too, because you're like a general in the Church."

Sicoli smiled to himself. "How long were you required to be up on the mountain?" he asked Carlin.

"Oh, we'd stay sometimes two or three days before we get the right shot. Then we'd get the hell out of there."

"What did it feel like to kill?" Sicoli asked.

"It felt good," Carlin answered. "I was doin' my job, and I was doin' the right thing. The Taliban, man, they're really bad people. And Muslims are heretics. They needed to be taken out."

Sicoli recognized the opportunity Carlin offered. He stood out from all the others in temperament, conviction, and skill set.

"And what about God's commandment, 'Thou shalt not kill'?" Sicoli asked.

"God tells us not to kill good people. But the Bible tells us we're supposed to strike out against evil."

It was possible, Sicoli mused, that Carlin was damaged in some way, perhaps even mentally ill. But that wasn't important. This man was skilled. He was not afraid to kill. Sicoli was pleased.

Chapter Eighteen

At the suggestion of Secretary of State Mbuto, James traveled to Africa. Mbuto was from the south-central part of Tanzania, where he had first met Jimmy Flahvin when he had volunteered through Voluntares Globales serving the Evangelical Lutheran Church of Tanzania. Instead of employing an aircraft to fly the three hundred miles from Dar es Salaam to Iringa, they caravanned along the narrow paved road. That is how Jimmy and Vicky had traveled years before, and Mbuto wanted the Americans and Europeans who accompanied the pope to catch a glimpse of the economic deprivation and human suffering that was so readily apparent along the roadside.

While in Iringa, James visited his old friend, Lutheran bishop Richard Nyondo, and they reminisced about earlier days. At a dinner held in his honor, the pope told stories of his previous Tanzanian experience to the gathered crowd of several hundred.

"Bishop Nyondo invited me to his home village, along with a group of American visitors. His mother and father welcomed us warmly. My wife, Vicky, and the other visitors followed his mother into their dignified but humble house. I stayed with the bishop's father outside. It was evening, and a fire burned in a small open pit in the front of their home.

"His father motioned me to join him. There were a couple of three-legged, blackened wooden stools next to the fire. We sat down. His father did not speak any English. I did not speak Kiswahili or Kihehe. But we visited together for half an hour.

"The night was chilly. He beckoned me to sit closer to the flames. As I did, he picked up a hot coal with his bare hand and blew on it until it turned bright red. Then he placed it closer to where I was sitting. I felt the warmth on my feet and hands. I thanked him for his concern and generosity.

"We talked about the abundant stars, the bright moon, and the wonders of God's creation. I only spoke in English. He spoke Kihehe. Nevertheless, we understood each other because we both spoke the universal language of respect and friendship. I learned that night that differences in language need not be a barrier to human connection. We can connect with others by simply being present to the moment they offer.

"A few days later, all the American volunteers were invited to have lunch at Bishop Nyondo's home in Iringa. He invited a young Catholic bishop to join us. That's where I first met Cardinal Mbuto. As we ate, one of the volunteers asked if there was any competition between the two bishops for converts among the non-Christian Tanzanians. Bishop Mbuto quickly responded. 'No, there is no competition. We both learned long ago not to fish out of the same bucket.'"

Everyone laughed easily. "I remember when Bishop Nyondo met with our team of volunteers over dinner in the village where we were serving. A young unmarried couple was part of the team. During dinner, the young man asked Bishop Nyondo whether it would be offensive to the community if he and his girlfriend slept in the same bed. The young woman, her name was Kate, was visibly embarrassed. The young man was undaunted.

"'Well, Robert,' Bishop Nyondo said to him, 'That depends on your relationship. Do you love Kate?'

"'Yes, of course I love her.'

"'Do you want to spend the rest of your life with her?'

"'Yes, I do,' the young man replied.

"Bishop Nyondo then asked Kate the same questions. When she answered in the affirmative, the bishop looked at them and said, 'Well then, I pronounce you man and wife. Robert, you and Kate may now sleep in the same bed.'"

James laughed at the memory. "I remember how wide the young man's eyes were; I think his jaw even dropped. 'That's not what I meant!' he protested. And Bishop Nyondo said, 'Well, Robert, when that *is* what you mean, then you may sleep in the same bed.'"

When the laughter subsided, James continued, "I gained a great deal of respect for Bishop Nyondo and the Lutheran Church that day."

The pope, his entourage, and the media flew northwest across the African continent to Kotuku International Airport in Accra, Ghana, where government and Church leaders received James affectionately, just as the village chiefs and council of elders had received him forty years earlier. It was a traditional welcome. After they drove to Kwame Cardinal Abruquah's residence, where the pope would stay for the evening, they sat outside around a square wooden table. James was first served a glass of water, the traditional drink for one who has just arrived from a long journey. Then they had a glass of wine, a libation that is the traditional second drink after a voyage. They enjoyed a brief conversation, and then the cardinal suggested the Holy Father take his rest.

The next morning, they visited the rural coastal village where James had served while in the Peace Corps, an hour's drive east of Accra on the shore of the Gulf of Guinea. As his caravan maneuvered along the seaside road, he watched the women, both young and old, clothed in flamboyant multicolored dresses, walking on the hot pavement, carrying virtually everything and anything on their heads. He'd always been awed by Ghanaians' posture and agility—the facility to balance buckets of water seemingly without spilling a drop.

He remembered his Peace Corps years fondly. They offered a stark contrast to his previous four years in prison. But most importantly, they offered him a new appreciation of the simplicity and joyfulness of life, close-knit families, and a culture of ceremony, pageantry, multicolored garb, and ancient customs. Here, the ways of old were the ways of today. Amid the harsh realities of poverty, hunger, and disease, happiness and hopefulness were abundant. Gracious and friendly people demonstrated the awesome wonder of the human spirit and of the culture and community that supported it. The Ghanaians were a rightfully proud people who had much to offer those privileged to know them.

In this lovely, picturesque rural village that James had so many years before called home, fishing was the major source of income. Every day before sunrise, weather-beaten wooden boats cast off into the Gulf searching for their catch. Around noon, women and children gathered along the sandy shore waiting for their men to return. Hundreds of people dotted the beach as the boats arrived. If the netting was plentiful, all were happy. If not, they waited another day.

Cardinal Abruquah had briefed James that not much had changed during the past four decades in this part of Ghana. This was still an impoverished region. Although much of the country had progressed economically, all the poverty indicators were ubiquitous in this area, especially in the rural areas—insufficient food and nutrition, unbridled infectious disease, inadequate health care, devastating unemployment, excessive child stunting and mortality, substandard housing, and not enough educational facilities, staff, materials, or opportunity. Health was fragile, especially for children. Malaria was the number-one risk, and there was not enough medicine to treat all the sick. Serious drought struck all too often, and even during the rainy season, there might not be rain for several months. Times were difficult for most families. Countless women and kids resorted to simply buying every sort of inexpensive material good and hawking them along the roads and coastline, hoping to make some profit.

The consequences were immense. Food shortages, due to insufficient agriculture production caused in part by drought and inadequate irrigation, ineffective seeds, pests, lack of fertilizer, and post-harvest waste, ravaged the countryside. Tap water was limited—turned on only for a few hours each day. Electricity was rationed because the reservoir did not supply enough water to churn the turbines. There was no hot water, so people bathed out of a bucket or in the sea. It was a difficult life, especially for children.

When the caravan arrived that morning, James went straight to the village Traditional Council office. The paramount chief, an old friend who was just a teenager when Jimmy Flahvin was last there, received him enthusiastically. James remembered that the paramount chief was in charge of everything in these rural communities, including the schools and health clinics. Chiefs served for life, having been selected from one of three families in a complicated process that James had never fully understood. He and the chief spoke briefly about times long past. He greeted several other older men and women with whom he had taught and whose friendships he cherished.

While they were speaking, an elegantly dressed man approached. "Excuse me for interrupting," the man said as he shook the pope's hand. "You taught me English when I was in form one. You also taught me about the meaning of life, the value of education, and the importance of serving others. It was because of you that I went to college and then medical school. I'm now a surgeon in Accra, where I help save lives every day. There are no words available to express my deep gratitude." James was taken aback by the man's generous and affectionate appreciation.

"You are very kind. What is your name?"

"I'm Tommy Asamoah."

"Oh yes, I remember you. You were a very bright young fellow. And you had a brother who was one year younger, right?"

"Yes, Kevin."

"How is he?"

"Kevin died in a car crash several years ago."

"I'm sorry to hear that. I'll be sure to keep both of you in my prayers."

John Simmons interrupted their conversation, indicating it was time to get started. Out the rear door, a barren, sun-soaked expanse of flatland abutted the council building. There, local workers had erected a temporary outdoor stage. Thirty chairs sat on the weather-beaten platform in three rows of ten, under a blue and white striped canvas canopy facing a large audience of dignitaries, schoolchildren, and village folks. Five hundred people sat on folding chairs, and several thousand more stood waiting in the breezeless, hot morning sunshine.

The council of elders, dressed in traditional colorful robes, filed out of the building and up the stairs to the dais. Several bishops, priests, and local Protestant ministers followed. Then the paramount chief,

Cardinal Abruquah, Cardinal Mbuto, and the pope walked out to their places in the center of the first row. Before James sat down, a graceful young girl dressed in a bright sapphire, emerald, gold, and crimson dress, and an equally vibrant headdress, presented him with a bouquet of fresh, sweet-smelling flowers.

The program opened with prayer, first in English, the national language, and then in Ga, the local tribal language. Children quickly filled the narrow space in front of the stage, singing, dancing, and drumming. An all-male quintet sang Ghanaian songs in the indigenous dialect, and then a group of more than forty women, all dressed alike in blue and white dresses, chanted Christian hymns in both English and Latin.

The paramount chief read a speech welcoming the pope and thanking him for returning home to his village. The chief noted both James and he were young men when they had last met and that much had occurred during the ensuing years. "You have come a long way in forty years, my friend, making your way from the abysmal lows of prison life, to this little village, to the towers of Chicago, and now the City on the Hill. All of us who knew you when you served this community so many years ago assumed that God had great things in store for you. Now you serve the world as the servant of the servants of God. Ladies and gentlemen, I am proud to offer the podium to our dear and special friend, Pope James."

The audience jumped to its feet, excitedly clapping as they rocked back and forth. James thanked all gathered for their presence, especially under the hot sun, acknowledged several people in the crowd, commented on the remarkable changes in the village since he had last visited, and applauded both the children and adult choirs for their marvelous singing.

"It's wonderful to be back home in the land I love so dearly. This is a glorious day to be among so many friends. You welcomed me into your hearts forty years ago. You opened your homes to me. You taught me the ways of your culture. And you made me believe once again in the goodness of God's people. I've been blessed with a wonderful, exhilarating, and full life. But the days I spent in this village are among the best of my days. I'm very grateful to all of you."

The paramount chief presented him with a loose-fitting black and white traditional smock and a gleaming beaded necklace reserved for chiefs. He immediately put on the smock and necklace over his ivory cassock. The crowd applauded and cheered loudly. The principal elder proclaimed that now James was an honorary chief.

Before departing for Accra, the paramount chief, the village elders, Cardinals Abruquah and Mbuto, and the pope sat around a hand-carved teak table and drank a glass of water, as was custom prior to setting off on a journey. The council gave him a beautifully detailed handmade green chasuble and stole, and the secretary of the Traditional Council presented him with a written description of all that had transpired on this day. Then, holding hands, they prayed for his safe trip and the safe passage of all those who traveled with him.

As he was about to get into the black Range Rover, his eyes connected with those of a small boy in tattered rags standing alone off to the side of the crowd. James stopped, went over to the boy, knelt down, and asked, "What's your name?"

"I'm Jimmy," the boy said.

He put his hand on the boy's shoulder and said, "God loves you, Jimmy. Never forget that. God loves you." He wiped a tear from his cheek and returned to his car for the return trip to Accra.

James and Mbuto sat in the comfortable backseat of the Range Rover as the police-escorted caravan sped along. "It's the children, Jacob. We have to improve the lives of the children. One of our primary challenges, and the challenge of the Church, is to ensure that the greed and indifference of some do not deny them their own salvation, while simultaneously denying so many others the opportunity to realize the fullness of God's creation. But you know, Jacob, there are days like today, when I'm at a total loss how to do that. I'm not sure I even know where to begin."

On the final day of this papal visit, James traveled to the Elmina slave castle, several hours west of Accra and on the south shore of the Gulf of Guinea. This mammoth, white-walled structure with a bronzed-tiled roof was just one of several used in the trans-Atlantic slave trade during the fifteenth to nineteenth centuries.

He recalled telling Vicky about how deeply moved he had been when he had first visited the slave castles during his Peace Corps days. "It was unbelievable," he told her. "Man's inhumanity to man is staggering—and the Christian chapel was directly above the men's dungeon. How could people sell other people for money and then go pray in the chapel? What does that have to say about the Catholic Church?" he asked her rhetorically.

By some estimates, there were twenty major religions on the planet, most of which worshiped the Creator in one manner or another. As the leader of the largest denomination of the largest religion, James felt an obligation to open meaningful communication with all those who were willing to visit. James was aware of discontent among some of his cardinals and bishops, but he was unfazed. Mutual religious respect and understanding were too important to be bogged down in Church politics.

On numerous occasions, the pope met with leading Islamic ulema and grand imams, Jewish rabbis, the Dalai Lama, Hindu and Sikh gurus, Confucian scholars, and Native American medicine men. Sometimes the religious leaders met him at the Vatican; other times he traveled considerable distances to their homes, offices, or places of worship. While together, they discussed their respective scriptures and individual and collective roles in waging peace and promoting justice in the world. And they always prayed together.

James believed Jesus was the Son of God and the Messiah, that Jesus appointed Peter to lead his church on earth, and that, as pope, he was the direct descendant of Peter. However, James never intimated he might somehow be superior or privileged because of the numbers of his flock or the historical Catholic Church claim that it was the one true religion. He respected each person of faith and demonstrated genuine reverence with warmth and humility.

James met with Grand Imam Mehmet Ali Burakgazi and Rabbi Isidore Goldman on numerous occasions. They talked about their family experiences, discussed their hopes and dreams, and explained their religious beliefs. While together, the three men considered how the volatile situation in Israel and Palestine might be resolved non-violently. Their views differed widely; but they concurred that both Israel and Palestine must be independent nation-states living in peace and security with all their neighbors. How to achieve that end was the unanswered question.

They encouraged their fellow clerics to engage the synagogue and mosque as effective vehicles for mutual international understanding. Some of their colleagues embraced the idea, but most rejected it out of hand. While the grand imam and the rabbi expressed disappointment, the pope was undaunted. This process of reconciliation would take time—lots of time. Burakgazi and Goldman had developed a meaningful friendship, and friendship was essential to the resolution of intractable issues, because friends typically resolve disputes nonviolently. James was convinced that if these men could be friends, the Israeli and Palestinian people could become friends.

When meeting His Holiness the Dalai Lama, James was in student mode. He wanted to know everything about the teachings and practice of Buddhism. He yearned to understand the essence of Bodhisattva, the belief that enlightened beings, like the Dalai Lama, choose to be reborn to serve humanity by voluntarily delaying their own Nirvana, that state of being where one experiences perfect lucidity and clarity and the absence of all suffering.

He queried the Dalai Lama on the Bhikkshuni order and the rationale behind the prohibition of women being ordained in Tibet. And they discussed how the contemplative tradition of Buddhism dating to the fourth century before Christ related to and benefited from the methodical discipline of twenty-first-century science.

When it came to the question of the purpose of life, James examined the Dalai Lama as if he were a witness at a trial. The Dalai Lama had written that the purpose of life was to be happy. James opened a copy of *The Compassionate Life* and read aloud from the Dalai Lama's own words.

"You write, 'From the moment of birth, every human being wants happiness and does not want suffering. From the very core of our being, we simply desire contentment. Therefore, it's important to discover what will bring about the greatest degree of happiness. I have found the greatest degree of inner tranquility comes from the development of love and compassion. The more we care for the happiness of others, the greater our own sense of well-being becomes.'"

James closed the book. "Those are inspiring words, but they differ from the main ideas of Christianity, which is based on the twin principles of loving God and loving neighbor. For Christians, the purpose of life is to serve others. By serving others we are fulfilled."

"The end result is the same," the Dalai Lama observed, "but the process is different. Buddhists want to be happy, and they achieve happiness by serving others. Christians want to serve others, and by doing so, they achieve happiness."

Chapter Nineteen

" **F** or a long time now, there's been disagreement among theologians, bishops, and the laity regarding birth control," O'Bryan told the pope over dinner one evening in the papal apartment. "You know that the vast majority of Pope Paul's hand-selected commission members offered advice contrary to the conclusions of his final encyclical."

"I pushed Hoffman on that several years ago. I told him I didn't understand how Paul VI could conclude as he did, given so many of his handpicked people advised to the contrary. Hoffman's only response was, 'The pope has the sole authority to decide.'"

"Well, that is the case. You get the final word on this."

"How's that? I thought Paul VI's word was final."

"*Humanae Vitae* is not considered infallible doctrine, because Paul didn't promulgate it *ex cathedra*—from the chair. He never intended it to become doctrine, but rather a teaching appropriate for its time. He wrote it well before the spread of the AIDS virus, and the science of today is light-years from 1968. More important, many of the faithful never embraced it. Polls in the United States, Canada, and Europe consistently show that the vast majority of North American and European Catholics never have agreed with, or abide by, the birth control prohibitions laid out in *Humanae Vitae*."

"What do you think a similar commission of theologians, bishops, and lay folks might say today?" James asked his friend.

"Well, there is deep-seated resistance among the conservatives and traditionalists. They don't want any change in birth control, or anything else for that matter. It isn't just the hierarchy. As you so well know, while there are progressives and conservatives in the laity, most liberal Catholics departed for other denominations long ago. But there's some hope in Europe and the United States, where polls indicate that even the conservatives have made the 'progressive' decision on birth control."

"But what would the theologians say?" James pressed.

"The progressives would argue that the use of contraceptives is an individual decision of one's conscience, and its morality is based on a married couple's prayerful conversation with God. The conservatives will tell you that artificial birth control is always a grievous sin."

James appointed a commission comprised of cardinals and bishops representing six continents, as well as renowned theologians, priests, sisters, brothers, and laymen and laywomen. He did not select members based on their conservative or progressive views, but rather on their intellectual capacity and record of service to the Church and the people of God. He gave them twelve months to study the issue and report their findings and recommendations to the Third Synod of Bishops.

When the commission concluded its work, the result was virtually identical to the findings of those appointed by Paul VI. Of the ninety-eight commission members, only five found that artificial birth control was intrinsically evil. A few even reasoned that whatever mutually respectful men and women did in the privacy of their marriage was up to them; sexual relations in marriage could not be sinful. Most argued the use of artificial birth control was a matter of conscience for a husband and wife to decide—a moral issue only involving a man, a woman, and God. In addition, the overwhelming majority reported that the act of physical intimacy between a married couple was a gift from the Creator, intended not just for the procreation of children, but independently intended as an expression of love between husband and wife.

When the Third Synod was assembled, the bishops fiercely debated the findings of the report. They seemed evenly divided—half supporting the commission, the other half opposed. The agenda allocated three days for discussion; however, given the heat of the debate, Secretary of State Mbuto and Chief of Staff Keegan agreed to extend it for two additional days.

"I find it remarkably inappropriate that the Church would continue to describe artificial birth control as intrinsically evil, given all the theologians, cardinals, and bishops who have concluded in their judgment, in their good conscience, that it is not evil," the archbishop from Santiago, Chile, said. "More than fifty years ago, the vast majority of those appointed by Pope Paul VI came to the same conclusion as the vast majority of those appointed by Pope James. There are millions of Catholics who do not receive the Eucharist on Sunday morning, or perhaps do not even go to Mass because they believe they are in a state of mortal sin. We are the ones who tell them they are doing something sinful when our best theologians have concluded that is not necessarily the case. We must change this rule on birth control."

The bishop from Warsaw rose in response. "Pope Paul VI wrote, 'The teaching of the Church regarding the proper regulation of birth is a promulgation of the law of God Himself.' That was the definitive answer to this question decades ago. We cannot change the law of God, regardless of how many theologians might think otherwise."

"My brothers in Christ," Cardinal O'Faolain said, "lest we forget, it was only four hundred years ago when the Church condemned Galileo for heresy for opining the scientific principle that the earth rotated around the sun. At that time, the Church taught that the earth was the center of the universe and the sun rotated around it. The Church based its conclusion on sacred Scripture and the law of God. My dear friends, the only laws of God we know for sure are those written in Scripture and affirmed by Jesus. History shows that the Church has sometimes struggled getting the rules right. It is not possible for us to declare conclusively something is a law from God when it is not even mentioned or implied in Scripture. Jesus never addressed the rotation of the planets or the question of artificial birth control."

Cardinal Hoffman retorted, "The Church does not rely solely on Sacred Scripture in order to decide issues such as this. The Church is governed by sacred Tradition, the Magistrium and Sacred Scripture, all inspired by the Holy Spirit. As the Catechism so correctly states 'one of them cannot stand without the others.' Thus, we are required to adhere to previous teachings of the Church based on tradition."

Cardinal DeLuca then stood, straightened his glasses, and argued, "The Church has always taught that the purpose of marriage is procreation and every act of sexual intercourse must 'retain its intrinsic relationship to the procreation of human life.' *Humanae Vitae* makes it abundantly clear that there is an inseparable connection between the 'unitive and procreative' aspects of the marital act. Sexual intercourse that thwarts the possibility of conception of human life is contrary to this basic principle. Responsible parenthood is fundamentally grounded in this inseparable connection. Benedict XVI reaffirmed this when he wrote that Paul VI was 'prophetically correct.' It 'contradicts the will of the Author of life' to separate the unitive and procreative expression of the sexual act."

Cardinal Schmidt joined the debate. "The concept of unitive and procreative is not honored after menopause, or when couples who know they are infertile continue to have sexual relations. Yet the Church does not declare sexual relations between married men and women in these circumstances to be sinful."

"I'm a bit confused," Cardinal Villegomez admitted. "Is not the natural law of God clear? Does not the Creator afford a natural cycle, and has not the Church always taught that married couples can use the natural rhythm of this cycle to space births or, if necessary for legitimate reasons, control the number of births? If the answers are in the affirmative, then what is the reason for changing the Church's position on artificial methods?"

Cardinal O'Bryan was surprised by Villegomez's questions, so he attempted to respond. "The Church has encouraged the use of the natural rhythm method while condemning other means to control births. This raises the question of whether couples who employ the rhythm method, only engaging in sexual intercourse when they know conception is not possible, are beyond the bounds of the so-called inseparable connection between the unitive and procreative.

"If the principal reason to continue the birth-control ban is that the marital act must simultaneously honor both the unitive and procreative, then the natural rhythm method is as suspect as are so called artificial methods. If nature does not allow conception, there can be no procreation. If there can be no procreation, then our current rule should prohibit sexual intercourse during that time of the cycle. But we don't. In fact, we tell Catholic couples that they can freely engage in sexual intercourse even when they know there is no possibility of conception. And that is why we must change the Church's position on artificial birth control—because our teachings are contradictory and the faithful know we are inconsistent."

"If the Church reverses our long-held and strict opposition to artificial birth control, we should be prepared for the end of the Catholic Church as we know it," Cardinal Hoffman said ominously. "Such a reversal would put in grave doubt all Church teachings, everything from adultery to premarital and extramarital sex, to abortion, to the very fabric of the Ten Commandments."

"Cardinal Hoffman," O'Faolain said as he rose, "with all due respect, I believe you are exaggerating the potential consequences of adopting this report. Yes, there may be some clergy and laypeople who will be irreconcilably opposed to this change. However, our responsibility is to be true to Scripture—true to the Word of God. And if we cannot find anything in Scripture that tells us artificial birth control is intrinsically wrong, then we have an obligation to teach that. While the Church honors sacred Tradition and the Magistrium; when a particular rule or law is not founded on any scriptural reference, we are obligated to correct our ways. Moreover, every poll clearly shows that the people in the pews will welcome the recognition that this is a matter of individual conscience. Married couples need to decide this for themselves in prayerful conversation with the Creator."

De Luca rose again. "God is the Creator. It is up to God who is born and when they are born. Men and women are not at liberty to do as they choose—to decide when life should be created and when it should not. The act of sexual intercourse is limited to marriage and intended to result in human life. Man cannot legitimately frustrate the will of the Author of Life."

Unwilling to offer De Luca any credibility, O'Faolain could not help but reply. "The rules banning artificial birth control are not accepted by the population as a whole. The canon lawyers in this assembly are well aware of the Church's venerable tradition that even when a law is stated and promulgated, it is not valid unless it is received and accepted by the People of God. Catholics all over the world have made a judgment about this law's invalidity simply by not complying with its requirements. Today's discussion is not about abrogating a valid law. Rather we advocate the Doctrine of Reception because, although the law has been promulgated, the people have not accepted it. Consequently, the law opposing artificial birth control is without force."

Hoffman spoke again. "It doesn't matter how many people are sinfully using artificial birth control. What's wrong is wrong, even if everyone is doing it. And what's right is right, even if no one is doing it."

After more than five days of debate, Mbuto turned to Keegan. "I think everything that can be said has been said. We should end the debate."

"Everything might've been said, but not everyone has said it," Keegan responded. The debate continued through the night and into the next day. Toward the end of the sixth day, James indicated to Mbuto that he would speak. As was his style, he had not participated in the discussion up to this point, but he had listened carefully and taken copious notes. When he stood to speak, the auditorium was quiet.

"I thank all of you for your commitment to the Law of God and the role of the Church in faithfully teaching the law. I thank all of you for your participation in this important conversation.

"I have read the majority and minority reports from both the 1966 commission as well as the most recent one. I have thoroughly studied the encyclical *Humanae Vitae*, which I note Pope Paul VI issued on the feast day of St. James. I listened carefully to the discussion these past days.

"The Church has a clearly defined rule in opposition to artificial birth control. However, two esteemed commissions separated by more than fifty years have held there is no foundation to find artificial birth control inherently sinful.

"Rules of the Church are different from the laws of government and society. I know something about law as it pertains to the latter. Most governments strive to promulgate laws that maintain order. One hopes they also protect human rights. However, the ultimate objective of the rules of the Church is to enhance the spiritual growth and well-being of the faithful. Our mission is to facilitate mutual love among people by teaching the word of Jesus the Christ. We are commissioned to show by example and word the way to eternal salvation, which Jesus earned for each of us on the cross.

"Our authority to interpret Scripture and teach the Gospel comes from Jesus through the inspiration of the Holy Spirit. However, the Spirit is present in all the faithful, not just Church leaders. We have the authority to manage the Church, but we are not the Church. All baptized men and women are members of the Church. Every Christian plays an essential role in its mission. There are times when a large majority of the body of Christ does not abide by or comply with a rule promulgated by Church leaders. When that occurs, it is incumbent upon the leaders to reconsider the rule's authenticity, which is what you have done.

"We are in agreement that the primary purpose of married life is procreation. However, both commissions determined that the procreative responsibility applies to the totality of married life. That responsibility does not necessarily apply to each individual act of sexual intercourse. In fact, the most recent commission concluded that physical intimacy in married life is, in and of itself, a gift from God. That gift enhances and strengthens the marital bond, and by extension the entire family, independent from procreation.

"I remember a few years ago when Cardinal Rodriguez and I visited a shantytown on the outskirts of Lima, Peru. We met with a mother and father who had seven children. Two had already passed due to childhood disease. Their two youngest did not live with them. The parents were forced to turn their two youngest girls over to the government because they could not afford to raise them on less than one US dollar a day. The Church should not force parents to have children they cannot afford to raise. The Church should not force married men and women to abstain from the foundational joy of marriage because they cannot afford to raise children. It is an obligation for married couples to cooperate with the Creator in bearing and raising children. However, it is a matter of individual conscience for parents to participate in the decision of how many children they will raise and which methods they will use to initiate or prevent conception.

"In any case, as Cardinal De Luca so clearly articulated, it is God who decides how many souls will be created. God decides how many children are conceived and when. In the miracle of life, mothers and fathers collaborate with God, but they are only supporting players. God is the lead actor. God alone decides. It is simply not possible for men and women to thwart the Creator's will." The silence following James's comments indicated this was the end of the debate. The decision was clear.

Cardinal Hoffman asked the pope, "How will we convey this significant change in Church law to the faithful?"

"As a servant explains an error to his master," James responded. "Jesus teaches us that the one who rules should be like the one who serves. Therefore, we will convey this decision with humility.

"Admitting mistakes can be a positive sign. The faithful may well see this change as a symbol of renewed confidence. However, the findings in the commission's report advise us that most Catholics have already concluded the Church's position on this issue is wrong. Married Catholics acknowledged the error by simply ignoring the rule. This is a case where the followers led and the leaders finally caught up."

Although Sicoli had not settled on a specific plan to remove the Antichrist, he knew whatever the final strategy, he would need a reliable stream of untraceable money and multiple colleagues willing to help, no questions asked. Over the years, Sicoli had identified ten men, most of them from California, who might be helpful to his cause if the opportunity presented itself. One was an enormously wealthy executive from Long Beach. In an effort to spread the word about traditional Catholic principles, he had contributed sizable amounts of money to fundamentalist organizations and several right-wing political causes. He had provided Sicoli money as well. However, he did not want any of his contributions easily traceable. So, he had set up a private bank account for the cardinal in San Diego. On a regular schedule, he transferred money to Sicoli's account, generally under $1,000 in order not to attract either bank's attention.

Another supporter, Mark Nordby, was a gun dealer in Bakersfield. He was the most reactionary of all of Sicoli's American backers and held Flahvin in the highest degree of disdain. Every time the pope and the Synod of Bishops made any pronouncement of change, Nordby went ballistic, often calling Sicoli to complain about "how the church he loved was going straight down the toilet."

Over time, Sicoli gained the confidence of the abbot at the monastery. Eventually, the monk allowed him to accompany other priests on day trips into San Diego to buy supplies or conduct other business. Someone was always with Sicoli, as required by the Vatican. Occasionally, one of the younger priests allowed the cardinal to go off on his own for an hour or two. That is when he snuck into the San Diego bank to withdraw money from his personal account and perform other clandestine tasks.

After one of these outings, the young monk who drove Sicoli reported a strange incident to his superior. "Before doing the errands you asked of me, I dropped Cardinal Sicoli at the San Diego Central Library on E Street. When I returned three hours later, he wasn't out front, as we had agreed. I parked the car and went in to look for him. I found him on the third floor in a secluded area with another cardinal."

"How do you know he was with another cardinal?" the abbot interrupted.

"The man was wearing a red skullcap, just like Cardinal Sicoli's."

"Did Sicoli introduce you to the cardinal?"

"No. They were sitting at a table and Cardinal Sicoli had his back to me. I could tell that their conversation was very intense, and I didn't want to interrupt. But I got a good look at the cardinal."

"Did you recognize him?"

"No. He looked like he might be Mexican. I went outside and waited for them on the front steps. Cardinal Sicoli came out alone; I don't know where the Latino-looking cardinal went. I just thought it strange that Cardinal Sicoli would be meeting in the library reference room with another cardinal. Then, on the drive back to the monastery, when I asked him what he did at the library, he never mentioned the other man. He just said he was doing research for his next seminar."

"Well, it is a little strange," the abbot said. "But I wouldn't make too much out of it. They may have just run into each other and were catching up. Thanks for your report. You can go about your business now."

✳ ✳ ✳

Jimmy Flahvin had made many trips to Asia representing business clients. Now, as Cardinal Keegan and Father Simmons met with him in the papal study to discuss the itinerary for his upcoming tour to the Philippines, Vietnam, and China, James recalled a particularly moving meeting in Ho Chi Minh City nearly twenty-five years ago.

Minh Truan Nguyen was the coordinator of the Vietnamese-American Friendship Committee. After she and Jimmy had enjoyed a wide-ranging conversation about Vietnamese and American business opportunities, Jimmy asked Minh what she did during the war.

"My family was part of liberation movement in Saigon," Minh replied. "South Vietnamese and American government call us Northern sympathizer. We not just sympathizer. My father believe in one Vietnam. When I thirteen, my parent send me north to study. About five hundred set out to walk twelve hundred kilometer through mountain jungle along Ho Chi Minh Trail. American knew this trail used for troop and military supply, so American plane bombard trail. Of five hundred children who walk to Hanoi half die, most from injury cause by American bomb. I was one who live," Minh said, holding back her tears.

"After having lost so many of your friends to American bombs, why are you promoting Vietnamese and American friendship?" Jimmy had asked her pointedly.

"I met my first American in 1976," she said. "I could not look at him. My eye never left ground. However, I listen to what he say. He soldier in American War, and he say he sorry for war. When he say he sorry, I look at him. I could tell he sincere. I believe him. I thought, 'Perhap all American not bad.'

"Later, I meet foreign delegation and sometime escort them around southern part of my country. Some were American War veteran who return to Vietnam for different reason. I accompany one group of veteran to village in Mekong Delta. When old man saw American, he scream, say they kill his wife and seven children. Now he all alone, with no one to care for him. He want to strike American. I told old man about my experience. I too lost family and friend. When I say this, he calm down.

"The old man plight move American and they want to help. They tell old man they sorry, and ask what they can do. I advise they just give something to remember this day when American come and say they sorry, that enough. So one American veteran take off his shirt and give it to old man. Old man very happy. All villager appreciate symbolism of gift. American soldier ride back to hotel wearing no shirt. So you see," she said again, "I learn all American not bad."

James had never forgotten Minh's story. He told Simmons and Keegan about his meeting with Minh Truan Nguyen. "Try to locate her, John. Arrange a time when the two of us might meet during my time in Vietnam. She has a common name, so it might be difficult locating her. Nguyen is as common in Vietnam as are Johnson, Smith, Kelly, and Garcia combined in the United States. Start with the Ministry of Foreign Affairs. Do the best you can, John. I'd really like to see her."

The day prior to leaving for Asia, James issued a Papal Letter, formally instructing Catholic clergy not to lobby for political issues or governmental entities, and forbidding clergy from encouraging the faithful to take up the banner of one political party or another.

He wrote in part, "Holy Scripture provides no evidence that Jesus instructed his followers to attempt to impose his teachings on others, by government edict or any other means." His rationale was clear: government should not mess with the things of God, and in turn, the Catholic Church would not mess with the things of politics or government. "Government policy belongs to Caesar, whether the policy relates to capital punishment, abortion, poverty, education, climate change, or any other issue. Love of neighbor, Holy Scripture, prayer, the sanctity of life, all creation—those things belong to God."

Nevertheless, James had no problem addressing the adverse effects of public policy when, in his judgment, they affected the things of God. Consequently, he was an outspoken critic of capital punishment, greed, governments that abused the human rights of anyone, abortion, unjust wars, and anything that contributed to the destruction of the natural environment. So while his papacy would not oppose or be involved with political or legislative processes, James was fully engaged in public policies that affected God's creation.

He did everything in his power to influence the hearts and minds of the men and women who had the power to affect these issues, and he encouraged all Christians to do the same. Ordering the clergy not to lobby government officials on one hand and yet encouraging them to influence their hearts and minds on the other, was, James realized, a subtle distinction.

At every opportunity—every homily, every speech, every meeting with a head of state—James asserted, pursuant to sacred Scripture, his understanding of what God wanted from each of us. It mattered not if he was addressing a Christian, Muslim, Jew, Hindu, Buddhist, Confucian, Indian, agnostic, or atheist; his posture and message was always the same.

"This is what God wants us to do," he would say. He never said, "This law is bad." He only affirmed what God would have us do based upon passages from the New Testament.

During his trip to China, James visited Shanghai, Xi'an, Kunming, and Beijing. This country of 1.4 billion people counted only 12 million Catholics, half of whom worshiped in underground parishes. There were no official ties between Chinese Catholics and the Holy See due to government edict. However, in deference to this pope, the government-controlled Chinese media announced the scheduled locations where James would say Mass, and the Chinese came out in droves in all four cities, filling the venues to overflow capacity. The Curia had thought the opportunities to proclaim the Gospel of Jesus the Christ in China would be limited. They were all happily surprised.

While in Beijing, James met with the chairman of the Chinese Communist Party, who was also the president of China and the most powerful person in this most populated country on the planet. They exchanged pleasantries and gifts. He gave the chairman an ebony crucifix crafted in China five hundred years earlier. The chairman gave the pope a beautiful miniaturized replica of a general from the Terracotta Warriors entombed near Xi'an.

During their conversation, James addressed the issue of the sanctity of life. He explained his views on why every life is precious in the eyes of the Creator—why taking life, other than in self-defense or in the execution of a just war, is an abomination against God. Why capital punishment is not self-defense and thus an abomination. How God looks with mercy and love upon those who constructively amend their ways. He never mentioned the thousands of Chinese who waited on death row. He did not criticize the Chinese government for its brutal policies. He did not ask the chairman to end capital punishment.

The chairman queried him about his belief in a creator, the value of deterring violent crime, the justification of permanently removing murderers and other deviants from society, and the absolute power of the state to protect law-abiding citizens. It was a lively discussion, but the pope continued to emphasize that human life was sacred because God created every life. Interestingly, he did not ask the chairman if he believed in God. The fact many men and women were atheist or agnostics saddened James, but he interacted with everyone assuming they believed in the Creator.

Seven months after this historic meeting, the Central Committee of the Chinese Communist government announced that it had amended its long-standing policy of sentencing its citizens to death. They reduced the number of capital crimes from twenty-six to one: premeditated murder. The rationale given for this radical, far-reaching change was that every Chinese citizen had intrinsic value in and of himself, as well as to the collective.

✳ ✳ ✳

Joseph Carlin attended several retreats at Holy Cross Monastery over the next several years. During those days in the desert near the Salton Sea, Carlin and Sicoli engaged in lengthy conversations denouncing Flahvin. At one meeting, Sicoli told Carlin that James Flahvin was the Antichrist. Carlin was skeptical, but the cardinal was a persuasive man. After all, Sicoli was a prince of the Catholic Church, learned in Scripture, and obviously authorized to speak at a Catholic retreat center. And Carlin knew that numerous recent changes in the Church were in total opposition to what he had been taught. Birth control was a mortal sin. Married men could not be priests. Catholics did not say the Protestant Lord's Prayer. Homosexuality was an abomination. Women were subservient to their husbands. James had changed all of this and more.

"If what you say is right and the pope is the Antichrist, then we gotta do somethin' about that."

"That is correct, my son."

"Well then, maybe I'll become a soldier again. Except this time, I'll be fightin' for the Catholic Church."

Chapter Twenty

"**W**e have an idea I think you'll like," Keegan told the pope during one of their regular meetings. "Jacob, John and I think you should make a two-week trip to the United States where you would preach in six major cities."

"It'd be promoted as the Religious Heritage Tour," Mbuto added. "We'd limit the cities to those with Christian names—Los Angeles, San Francisco, San Antonio, St. Louis, St. Paul, and Notre Dame. You would say Mass in the largest public venue in each place. Hundreds of thousands of people would come out to see you, and you would get significant international media coverage. This trip offers a great opportunity to build on the enormous successes you have made over the past nine years."

"Six cities in fourteen days seems more like a political campaign than a Religious Heritage Tour. Wouldn't it be better to do fewer cities?"

"Six is really the minimum," Keegan argued. "It has to be a huge effort because the objective is to completely own the US and international media for two full weeks. You will be able to deliver six vital messages that will be heard 'round the world."

"What makes you think we could fill six major venues, almost back-to-back? Don't you think US Catholics have seen enough of me by now?"

O'Bryan chimed in. "You're the most popular public figure in all of North America. Not only will Americans come in droves, but Mexicans will help fill the stadiums in LA and San Antonio, and Canadians will flock to St. Paul. We could do ten cities, if you were up to it. Trust us. This'll be the biggest multistate event ever held in the United States by someone other than a president, and it will raise lots of money for the poor throughout the world."

Given the magnitude of this trip, the Curia set the itinerary well in advance in order to reserve the appropriate facilities—generally football or baseball stadiums. In Los Angeles, James would say Mass at the Coliseum, in San Francisco at AT&T Park, the Alamodome in San Antonio, Edward Jones Dome in St. Louis, the Minnesota Vikings Dome in St. Paul, and Notre Dame Stadium in Notre Dame, Indiana.

In the seclusion of his room at the monastery, Cardinal Sicoli read a private e-mail on his iPad. "Pope to Tour US" was a subject line that caught his attention. A friend in the Vatican had advised him of the pope's upcoming trip months before it was publicly announced. The e-mail detailed the itinerary. "This is our opportunity," he whispered to himself. The occasion of Flahvin traveling throughout the United States offered his sniper protégé numerous prospects.

The next day, Sicoli contacted Carlin, and they met a week later on one of his day trips at a secluded area of the San Diego Library. The cardinal quietly told his friend of the inside information about Flahvin's visit to the United States, scheduled for little more than a year away. "Now we can finally resolve this disaster that has afflicted the Church for nearly a decade," Sicoli whispered.

During the following several weeks, Carlin examined the architectural plans of the various stadiums online—readily available to anyone who knew what to look for. At "sniper school," Carlin had learned the basics of building construction and architecture, and what to look for in determining an optimal concealed position. That course of study now served him well. He knew he would need an accessible location with an unobstructed view of the target while being sufficiently hidden so as not to jeopardize the mission. He concluded the Vikings Dome offered the best opportunity.

Carlin and Sicoli met again at the library, where Carlin reported his findings and the cardinal agreed that St. Paul offered the best venue. Sicoli then excused himself for a moment and immediately called Peter Johnson, one of his supporters who ran a large sports facility in Phoenix.

"Peter, I need a favor," Sicoli said.

"What is it, Your Eminence?"

"I have a friend, someone who has come to our retreats at the monastery. He may be moving to St. Paul, Minnesota, and needs a job. He is not skilled, but he has experience as a maintenance worker, although he is willing to take any position. I remember you telling me one of your colleagues is the executive director of the football stadium there. I thought perhaps he could use your name as a reference."

"Sure, I'd be delighted to help. What's your friend's name, and when's he going there?"

"Ah, his name is not important. But if someone from the Vikings Dome calls you about a man applying for a job who has used you as a reference, I would appreciate you putting in a good word for him."

"That's a little hard for me to do, Your Eminence, if I don't know his name."

"It is better that you not know, Peter."

Sicoli returned to the isolated table where Carlin patiently waited. "You will need to move to St. Paul and get a custodial job at the Vikings Dome," Sicoli instructed. "Use Peter Johnson as a reference."

"Who's he?" Carlin asked.

"He is an important friend of mine, and if you use his name, you will get the job."

"OK."

"You will need an automobile to drive to St. Paul and get around while you are there."

"The stadium's actually in Minneapolis. They just call it St. Paul because they're twin cities or somethin'," Carlin corrected.

"All right. Minneapolis, then. Here is twenty-five hundred dollars to buy a used vehicle to get you to Minneapolis."

"That don't seem like enough to get a good car," Carlin objected.

"It is enough for the car you need."

"OK. If you say so."

"We need to be careful how we communicate. I will use disposable cell phones that are not registered. You use public pay phones. I have set up an obscure website that only you and I can access. I will periodically post the number, date, and time when you should call me. Scan the website every day for messages. Understand?"

"Got it."

Suspecting the custodial work would not pay much more than minimum wage and wanting to ensure that Carlin didn't feel the need to get extra work, Sicoli gave Carlin $12,000 cash he'd withdrawn from the bank over the previous few months. "The job will not pay enough to cover all your expenses," Sicoli explained.

"I'll need a high-powered rifle, a special one that I can take apart and reassemble inside," Carlin said.

"I have already spoken with a gun dealer I know in Bakersfield. He can sell you such a rifle. I will put his name and address on the website. You stop at his store on the way to Minneapolis. Call him the day before you go to his store. Arrange a specific time. He will take care of you personally. He does not want any of his employees involved."

"OK."

"Rent a one-bedroom apartment in Minneapolis. Make it inexpensive. Your lifestyle must look like someone earning minimum wage. Find several telephone booths where you can speak privately. Call whenever the code shows up on the website. Your instructions will be clear."

"What happens when the pope dies?" Carlin asked.

"Flahvin is not the pope," Sicoli said with anger and frustration in his voice. "He is the Antichrist. He is an imposter who is destroying the Church. Never forget that." Sicoli took a deep breath and composed himself. Speaking more slowly and deliberately, he continued. "When Flahvin dies, the College of Cardinals will conduct a conclave. At that conclave, they will elect me pope."

"That'll be great," Carlin said enthusiastically. "Will you get me a good-paying job?"

"Yes, you will be taken care of. Now, no one else knows our plan, Joseph. Other people will help. But no one else knows the plan. Do not discuss it with anyone. If even one other person becomes aware, or grows suspicious, both of our lives are in danger. If we are not successful, the Church is lost forever."

"I get it, Excellency. I get it."

They agreed they should no longer have any personal contact. All future communications between the two men would be through the Internet and on untraceable phone calls.

"Are you sure you can do this, Joseph?" Sicoli asked, looking for affirmation.

"I've told you before; I got no problem doin' my job. This is no different from Afghanistan. Bad people gotta go down."

Father Simmons showed the consecrated women into the pontiff's formal study. Sixteen women representing women clergy from the Americas, Europe, Asia, and Africa sat at the large conference room table when Pope James entered the room. They immediately stood. He walked around the table greeting each sister as they introduced themselves. He then sat in the center of the oval-shaped table and thanked the nuns for travelling so far to meet with him.

"Holy Father," the leader of the group started, "the pressing issue of insufficient numbers of priests continues to plague the Church. Although the addition of married priests has increased the overall numbers, it has not resolved the problem. Because of your policies and embracing style, many Catholics have returned to the Church, and the number of converts is way up. Now there are substantially more people attending church, which is a very good thing. However, additional active Catholics have increased the need for even more priests. The actual shortage today is greater than when you first became pope."

"I guess there are plusses and minuses in everything, Reverend Mother," James smiled.

"Yes, Your Holiness. This may also be an answer to our prayers. Perhaps this is the time to reconsider the Church's long-standing discriminatory opposition to female ordination."

The nuns and pope devoted the remainder of the hour to discussing the difficult yet vital question of women priests. James had considered this issue for many years and was positively inclined to review the Catholic Church's position. He concluded the meeting by telling the nuns, "I will appoint a commission to study the question of female ordination. After the commission provides me its written report, I will bring it before the Synod of Bishops. We will then see where that process takes us. Thank you again for coming to see me."

The sisters were elated. Although the pope had made no commitment, he had agreed to reconsider the ban on female ordination, something no pope had ever agreed to do. James selected conservative, moderate, progressive, and liberal representatives from all continents of the faithful, and named three members to lead the commission—a European theologian, an Asian cardinal, and an African laywoman. For several months, the commission met, debated, and concluded the Church should amend the tradition of an all-male clergy. They delivered their report to the pope.

James carefully reviewed their justification. After much prayerful consideration, he rejected their report and sent it back to the commission leaders under seal with specific instructions not to disseminate either its conclusions or its contents. In his cover letter, he invited them to come speak with him about his decision.

When they met in the papal offices two weeks later, the European theologian expressed surprise and dismay at the pope's action. "We thought our conclusion was what you wanted, Your Holiness."

"That's why I cannot accept your report. It is not your conclusion I disagree with. Rather, it is the lack of adequate foundation for your argument. You did not carefully, effectively, or competently explain why we should change what some claim is a two thousand-year-old tradition. It is far less important what I may want than what we believe God wants, and what Catholics worldwide will conclude is right.

"Reconvene the commission. Address this issue as if I am adamantly opposed to any change. If the commission concludes change is still appropriate, then make arguments that will convince the Synod of Bishops and me that this is the right thing to do. Then and only then will the People of God recognize it as such."

The commission reconvened, studying Scripture, the early writings of the Church, past and current theologians' commentary on the issue, the rationale and conclusions of other denominations on ordaining women, and the change in societal status of women in various cultures over the millennia. They debated the arguments pro and con and carefully reconsidered their rationale and conclusions. It was an arduous task, but they had to get it correct. They rightfully assumed that if they failed to be sufficiently convincing the second time around, it could be years, perhaps decades, before this or any pope might entertain the question.

When they submitted their second report, James was finally satisfied. He ordered the Synod of Bishops to convene. There was a single item on the agenda. The schedule allowed commission leaders two days to present their methodology, rationale, and conclusions. Ten days were allotted for debate. After the opening prayer, the pope made a brief statement.

"The sole responsibility of this synod is to address the question of whether the Roman Catholic Church will ordain women. Should God's church recognize that women have the full and complete rights, authority, and responsibilities of male clergy? This is not just an issue of a shortage of priests. This is an issue of whether Jesus the Christ intended to restrict clerical duties to men. Did Jesus prohibit women from being ordained for all time?" James sat down and listened intently to the commission's presentation and the full synod's debate.

Cardinal Tamborino was the first to speak. He spoke with uncompromising authority. "The Church has spoken clearly and consistently on this issue. When the Church of England was considering ordaining women, Pope Paul VI wrote to the archbishop of Canterbury. His letter read in part that the Church 'holds that it is not admissible to ordain women to the priesthood, for very fundamental reasons. These reasons include: the example recorded in the Sacred Scriptures of Christ choosing *his Apostles* only from among men; the constant practice of the Church, which has imitated Christ in choosing only men; and her living teaching authority which has consistently held that the exclusion of women from the priesthood is in accordance with God's plan for his Church.' This body and this pope have no authority to ordain women because it is contrary to the will of God."

Cardinal Schmidt rose and was recognized. "We tread on dangerous ground when we start talking about what is or is not the will of God. In my study of Scripture, I do not find anywhere that Jesus discriminated based on gender. We all know that immediately after his resurrection he appeared to women before addressing the apostles. That intentional act goes a long ways toward demonstrating the importance of women in the eyes of the Lord. Moreover, in the first-century Christian Church, women and men performed significant and equal roles. The writings of Paul and Luke tell us that women were teachers, preachers, missionaries, prophesiers, and church leaders. Unfortunately, the Church slowly, albeit understandably given the contemporary culture, regressed to earlier inequitable times.

"But discrimination is unacceptable today. Discriminating based on gender is no different from discriminating based on race. People in societies all over the world perceive discrimination on any basis as morally wrong. How can we persuade others that the Catholic faith is the true faith when they conclude our ethical standards fail to meet the accepted norm?" Schmidt sat down.

"We do not disagree with the basic equality of male and female. However, men and women are as different today as they were two thousand years ago. If Jesus had wanted women to be leaders of his church, he would have selected a woman as one of his apostles. It is no more complicated than that," Cardinal DeLuca stated.

Cardinal O'Faolain stood. "I beg to differ with my brother in Christ. This issue is far more complicated than my esteemed colleague suggests. During Jesus' time, women were neither considered nor treated as equals to men. Nevertheless, Jesus consistently regarded men and women as equals, sometimes to the consternation of his fellow Jews.

We all know that Jesus only chose dark-skinned, Aramaic-speaking married men of the Jewish faith as his apostles. Yet the Church has not made race, ethnicity, or language criteria for ordination. On the other hand, we have established many other conditions for ordination. In our time, a priest must be university educated, have a master's degree in divinity, and may only be ordained after thorough psychological examinations. None of the apostles could have met these rigorous criteria. The rules for ordination have changed because times have changed."

"Given the clear words in Holy Scripture, I am deeply troubled by the very purpose of this synod," Cardinal Hoffman said. "St. Paul writes in First Corinthians that, 'Women should keep silent in the churches, for they are not allowed to speak, but should be subordinate, as even the law says. But if they want to learn anything, they should ask their husbands at home. For it is improper for a woman to speak in the church.' How can we be discussing women becoming priests when Scripture says women should not even speak in church?"

"That passage has intrigued scholars over the centuries," Cardinal O'Bryan responded, "but we've come to understand that Paul was writing only to the women in the Corinthian church. He was speaking about wives who interrupted the worship service with questions and conversation. We know he was not addressing all women in all churches about all conduct because he writes in Galatians that 'There is neither male nor female. For you are all one in Christ Jesus.' And Scripture records that women prophesized in other churches. Paul is simply addressing particular unbecoming conduct by a group of first-century women as their roles were understood at the time."

"I've never read that passage any other way than its clear meaning," Villegomez retorted.

Becoming impatient with his so-called protégé, Schmidt rose. "If women were really prohibited from speaking in church by Holy Scripture, what would you do with female lectors, women directors of choirs, nuns who offer reflections on Scripture or make financial pleas for the missions, women who teach the Word of God to children during Mass, and the plethora of other activities in which women are involved? If you took this to the extreme, women could not even be Eucharistic ministers because they would be prohibited from proclaiming the sacred words, 'The Body of Christ.'" Exasperated, Schmidt sat down.

"This is not the Catholic Church in which I was raised," Villegomez said under his breath, but for all around him to hear.

Many were greatly surprised by Villegomez's response. It was utterly inappropriate for a prince of the Church to say such a thing in public, but especially in the presence of the Holy Father.

In an effort to move the conversation along, Cardinal O'Faolain said, "We've been commanded to 'go forth and teach all nations.' Part of our responsibility is to bring the joy of Christian hope, faith, and love to all people. However, a male-only clergy inhibits our ability to fulfill the Lord's scriptural directive because there are not enough men who choose the priesthood. Women are a magnificent resource offered to the Church by the Creator. It is up to those of us sitting in this room today to either employ this resource or to continue to squander it."

The debate continued. Cardinal Hoffman was recognized again. "In St. John Paul II's 1994 Apostolic Letter entitled 'Reserving Priestly Ordination to Men Alone,' he wrote, 'Wherefore, in order that all doubt may be removed regarding a matter of great importance, a matter which pertains to the Church's divine constitution itself, in virtue of my ministry of confirming the brethren (cf. Luke 22:32) I declare that the Church has no authority whatsoever to confer priestly ordination on women and that this judgment is to be definitively held by all the Church's faithful.' With all due respect, given those words, what purpose is there to this debate?"

"St. John Paul wrote what he wrote, but he purposely did not speak *ex cathedra*," Cardinal O'Bryan said. "There is absolutely no indication he intended this doctrine to reach the high standard of infallibility, as required by canon law. St. John Paul II was a brilliant man, and he chose his words with considerable care. He wrote 'the Church has no authority.' That was a present-tense statement at the time of his apostolic letter. The necessary prayerful consensus of the People of God had not been achieved in 1994. Consequently, because of tradition, the Church had no authority to ordain women at that time. However, he clearly understood that his words would not bind this synod of bishops or this pope.

"This is a different time. The changes the Church has enacted over the last few years would have been inconceivable only a few decades ago. The Church concluded these changes were based upon the prayerful consensus of the People of God, and we believe the consensus achieved is the will of God. The People of God have reached another consensus. Poll after poll and survey after survey have clearly shown that Catholics favor the ordination of women, a result consistent with the vast majority of the members of the commission. The People of God have spoken. We should return to the tradition of two thousand years ago of fully engaging both men and women as leaders, teachers, and preachers, as practiced in the early Church."

"I apologize, but I'm a little confused," Villegomez said a bit sarcastically. "Are you saying the will of God has changed? Or are you suggesting that St. John Paul II concluded that even though it was the will of God to ordain women, the Church could not act because the consensus of God's people had not yet been achieved? Let me state my question a different way: Is the Church bound by the will of God, or is the Church bound by public opinion polls?"

As was the case in previous synods, Mbuto and Keegan allowed the discussion to go on for the full period allowed by the agenda. They agreed with James that everyone who wanted to speak should have the opportunity to make his argument and be heard. It did not matter if others had already made the same point umpteen times. Everyone would have the chance to persuade his colleagues, and the pope.

At the conclusion of the tenth day of the debate, Mbuto declared, "The allotted time for discussion of this vital issue has expired, and this concludes this portion of the work of this Synod of Bishops. We will recess and reconvene at a time determined by the Holy Father."

Shortly after his final meeting with Sicoli, Carlin went to a local car dealership and paid $2,600 cash for a used, older-model Toyota Camry.

The following morning, he drove north to Bakersfield to meet with the gun dealer. The proprietor took Carlin into a back room and opened an oblong black metal case. Seventeen components were meticulously set in individual molded polystyrene cavities.

"This weapon can be easily assembled and disassembled. It's the best I got, and one of the best ever made," Mark Nordby puffed. "The assembly instructions are in the box and they're straightforward. The scope's a 3.5x-10x 50mm and has all the necessary adjustment controls—elevation, windage, magnification, illumination, and parallax compensation with audible click stops and easy fingertip turrets. You properly calibrate each of these controls, and if you're any good at all, you ain't ever gonna miss. I can show you others if you like."

Carlin assembled the weapon. Nordby was impressed at the ease with which the young man put it together. Carlin liked its feel; the weight was right and the stock fit him well. "This one," he said. Carlin bought twelve boxes of ammunition. He put the black case and cartridges in the trunk of the Camry and got started down the road.

He arrived in Minneapolis two days later. The following day he applied for a job as a maintenance man at the Vikings Dome sports facility and used Peter Johnson as a reference. A Super 8 Motel in Roseville was home until he got a call telling him he was hired and to report to work on Monday. On his first day on the new job, Carlin went to the HR department and filled out all the necessary papers. He asked the HR manager if she could provide proof of employment so he could rent an apartment. She readily complied. After work, he went to an Internet café to check Sicoli's website. The coded message indicated he should call on Friday evening at six.

He found an inconspicuous apartment not far from the stadium, a clean but colorless single bedroom with kitchen and adjoining living area for $575 a month. Carlin moved into his new place and used some of the money Sicoli had given him to purchase a forty-two-inch flatscreen television, dark blue cloth recliner, used wooden kitchen table with one chair, a single bed, dishes and cutlery, and some linens. Even after he moved everything in, the place still looked barren and sad.

At the Vikings Dome, Carlin's job was to help clean up after events and do general janitorial maintenance. A sophisticated computer-controlled system adjusted air distribution to inflate the translucent Teflon-coated fiberglass roof. Twenty-four blowers encircled the interior of the stadium and pumped air through steel vents to ensure sufficient air pressure to hold up the roof. One of Carlin's jobs was to clean the ducts. Every week he would clean two of them, first shutting off the air to those particular vents, and then climbing inside with a large vacuum cleaner, removing any dirt or debris.

He found a pay phone in one of the hotels not far from his apartment. Promptly at six o'clock on Friday, he called Sicoli.

"Where are you calling from?" Sicoli asked.

"I'm across the street from City Center, in Minneapolis," Carlin responded.

"You call from a phone booth?"

"Yes, sir, as you instructed."

"Anyone else around?"

"No, sir."

"Did you get the job?"

"Yes, Excellency."

"Good. Any problems?"

"Everything is fine. No problems."

"Good. Look on the website in ten days. There will be another message to call me."

Carlin didn't work on Saturdays, so he assembled the sniper rifle and took it to a firing range to sight it in. He found it to be a remarkable weapon. The scope was particularly effective. It magnified the target by a factor of ten and easily allowed him to adjust for all the variables—distance, temperature, and wind. Carlin knew the effectiveness of the scope, more than anything other than him remaining completely steady, determined the accuracy of his shot.

The paper target was three hundred meters down field. He made the necessary scope adjustments, rotated the power ring so that the upper torso of the black body image was in full view, superimposed the crosshair on the center of the head, took a half breath, held it, and squeezed the trigger. He was pleased. The bullet passed directly through the forehead.

A couple of days later, he went on the website and saw his instruction to call Sicoli at seven thirty on Friday evening. He called as instructed.

When Sicoli answered, he asked, "Where are you?"

"Across from City Center."

"Is that where you called from last time?"

"Yes, sir," Carlin responded.

"Joseph, listen carefully. Every time you call, you must use a different phone at a different location. Pick out pay phones at four or five hotels. Use them randomly. Never call from the same phone twice in a row. I will list different cell phone numbers on our webpage. Use our code to know which number."

"Got it."

"You get the rifle?"

"Yes, sir. It's a great weapon."

"Good. Go to a firing range and practice. I found a good range on the Internet near—"

Carlin interrupted. "I've already done that."

"Already done what?"

"I've already taken it out to sight it in and get its feel. It handles real nice."

"Now listen carefully, Joseph. This is very important," Sicoli said sternly. "You cannot do anything unless I specifically order you. Understand? You wanted to test out the rifle. I appreciate that. However, you can only do what I tell you to do and where and when I tell you to do it. This is critically important. If we are going to be successful and protect the Church, you must do it my way."

"I'm sorry, Excellency. It won't happen again."

"I hope not, Joseph. The entire Church is depending upon you following my directions." Clearing his throat, Sicoli continued. "There is a firing range in Pine County, seventy-five miles north of Minneapolis. You can practice there in relative secrecy. Take Interstate 35 north to the Pine City exit and turn left. There are signs that will direct you to the firing range. Go there tomorrow afternoon. Plan to arrive around four o'clock. Very few people will use the firing range at that time. Do not show your rifle to anyone.

"Just to make sure, go to a sporting goods store in Minneapolis and purchase a deer-hunting rifle. Buy two similar cases, one for the deer-hunting rifle and one for the sniper rifle. Take both to the firing range. Practice with the sniper rifle when no one else is around. If anyone shows up, put the sniper rifle into its case, and use the deer-hunting rifle. Do you have any questions about what I have told you?"

"No, sir."

"Very good."

James issued an apostolic letter entitled "The Ordination of Men and Women." He recalled the Synod of Bishops, and in assembly explained his decision and rationale. "The book of Genesis tells us, 'God created man in his own image...male and female he created them.' We conclude from this that both male and female are made in the image of God. Consequently, God has either no gender or both genders. Theologians construe that although God incarnate came in the form of a male, Jesus the Christ, there is nothing he did as a man that he could not have done if God incarnate had come as a female. It may have been more difficult, given the gender discrimination of the times. However, the daughter of God could have been baptized by John, preached the Sermon on the Mount, consecrated bread and wine at the Last Supper, been crucified on a cross, and raised on the third day. For reasons we cannot know, God came to earth in the form of a man. But that choice did not alter God's decision to create male and female in God's own image."

He concluded his remarks this way: "There is legitimate concern among some that ordaining women will fatally divide the Church. To you I say with all the compassion and empathy I can muster, I have heard your voices and respect your views. However, we should never conclude that we cannot do the will of God because it may jeopardize the unity of the Church. The role of the Blessed Mother, apostolic succession, geocentrism, slavery, racial integration, interracial marriage, married priests, and artificial birth control were all seminal issues. Some Church leaders forcefully argued that modifying traditional teachings would invariably and irreconcilably split the Church and result in her extinction. We now know that was not the case. The Church must always address controversial and potentially divisive issues in a manner consistent with the teachings of Jesus the Christ. Moreover, we seek the prayerful consensus among the People of God, regardless of the possible ramifications.

"From this day forward, both men and women who meet the necessary qualifications for the priesthood shall be ordained by their bishop as priests in the Roman Catholic Church."

Carlin noticed a new message on the website from Sicoli. This time the coded telephone number differed from the one used in the past. On the appointed day and time, Carlin dialed the number.

Sicoli always made certain he was somewhere in San Diego when Carlin called, never at the monastery. On this day, he was near the Navy Broadway Complex when he answered and asked, "Where are you?"

"At a public pay phone at the Westin Hotel."

"Good. Did you practice with your rifles?"

"Yes, sir."

"All right. Every two weeks, go to a different firing range and do the same thing. You must regain all of your skills as a marksman."

"I got those skills, sir. I never lost 'em."

"It is necessary to practice. Practice, practice, practice. There will be a long time between your final practice and when you execute."

"Excellency, I'm a professional. I've been trained to do what I do. I'm best in my class. I got twenty-seven kills. No one's better than me. Don't worry. And you don't gotta tell me everything I do."

"Remember, Joseph, when you told me I am like a general? Well, I am a general. I am your commanding officer. Follow my orders. The entire Roman Catholic Church depends upon our actions. I depend upon you. I support you. But you must know your orders. Follow them explicitly. Understand?"

"Yes, Excellency. I'll accomplish the mission."

Carlin took his weapons to different firing ranges when few others were present. After every session, he brought the rifles back to his apartment, took them apart, cleaned them thoroughly, and put them back together. He did it so often that he began doing it in the dark.

A few weeks later, Carlin saw Sicoli's message on the website, and went to the Marriott at City Center for the phone call.

"He will be coming soon. Get the rifle into the stadium now," Sicoli said. "Make sure it is securely stored. Find places to hide all the parts. Places no one will ever look. Take one piece each day so as not to arouse suspicion. All the components must be inside by sixteen August. That is eight weeks before the imposter arrives. That is enough time before security starts tightening up."

"I gotta get some other things in there too."

"What else do you need, Joseph?"

"Well, I gotta eat, so I need MREs for a couple of days."

"What on earth are MREs?" Sicoli asked.

"That's military talk for meals ready to eat. I'll get 'em at a surplus store—do it all the time. I also need somethin' to hold my piss and a breathin' device."

"Why do you need a breathing device?"

"No matter how well a mission is planned, shi—ah, stuff can always go wrong. If they think they cornered me, they're gonna use gas. This thing is similar to what firefighters use when they're in hostile environments, only much smaller. It'll allow me to breathe."

Carlin was a reliable soldier and Sicoli trusted his judgment on tactical issues. Each day for the next month, Carlin did as Sicoli ordered. He reported for work at the Vikings Dome, and every day for three weeks, he carried a single component of his high-powered sniper rifle into the stadium. The smaller pieces he wrapped in waxed paper and tucked in his lunch bucket, sometimes inside his sandwich. The larger ones—the scope and the barrel—he taped to his legs. He hid the parts in a variety of places inside the stadium. Some he attached with duct tape to the backsides of office filing cabinets, which rested up against walls. Others he hid in suspended ceilings. No one ever suspected a deadly weapon was stored in this public arena awaiting the Holy Father's arrival.

CHAPTER TWENTY-ONE

"**Y**ou're not going to believe this," Keegan reported to James one morning. "The National Organization of Women wants you to address their annual convention. They're holding it in LA while you're there on the Religious Heritage Tour."

"That's interesting," James replied.

"Best we can tell, no bishop has ever been invited to speak to an official gathering of NOW members, primarily because of the rift over abortion. That is their major issue. Their whole purpose is just to ensure all women can have legal abortions."

"Why do you think they've invited me?"

"It can't be for anything good. The Church has been a longtime outspoken critic of NOW, and the Curia is opposed to any interaction with them. They do not want you to give NOW any credibility. I don't think you should do it either, but I know I have to bring these things to you."

James was intrigued. "What's your objection, Greg?"

"I think their motive is to engage you in a public debate. We don't need that. Or worse, when you're done speaking they'll mock you and the Church."

"Couldn't we agree to some rules up front?" James asked.

Against the advice of both the Curia and his closest advisors, James directed Keegan to obtain assurances from NOW's president that if the pontiff spoke, he would be treated with the utmost respect and the event would not be turned into a debate or a prochoice demonstration. Keegan got the agreement in writing and an unconditional authorization from NOW that the Church could share the agreement with the media at its discretion.

When NOW's president, a baptized but nonpracticing Catholic, introduced Pope James to the convention, the fifteen hundred delegates welcomed him politely. He thanked the president for her introduction, and thanked the convention for inviting him. Without wasting any words, he immediately addressed their differences.

"My religious belief is that all human life is sacred because we are created by God in God's image. Each of us is a reflection of God. Human life is sacred from the earliest moment of conception until the final breath. Except for the rare exception when a mother's life is in imminent danger, abortion is always a grave sin. Catholics do not recognize any difference between aborting a five-day-old fetus, killing a five-day-old baby, or executing a fifty-year-old man.

"However, we acknowledge there is no general consensus on this issue. There are Christian denominations and other religions that do not believe sacred life begins at conception. Unfortunately, science has not yet proven our belief is truth.

"Jesus instructs believers to 'go forth and teach all nations.' However, he does not tell us to use government edict or law to impose our beliefs on others. Government's role is to legislate for the public good within the political arena. Governments make laws to ensure order, right wrongs, and prevent injustice. That is good. However, religious organizations should not use government law to impose their beliefs on others, regardless of the righteousness of their beliefs. This applies not just to abortion, but to all government issues. Religious organizations have many other tools with which to oppose wrong and promote good. Prayer, rational argument, education, and support for those in need are all effective means by which we can and should live our beliefs.

"However, when it comes to abortion, there is a point when religious differences and beliefs give way to medical science, and the legitimate right to life trumps all others. This point arises when a baby can live outside its mother's womb. When a child can draw breath, albeit with assistance from medical technology, the child has achieved the universal right to life. For a fetus today, science confirms that occurs during the twenty-first week of gestation. Given the ever-changing progress of medical science, it is possible that at some point in the future that moment will be earlier in the life of the child. Consequently, all governments should ban all abortions during the twenty-first week and beyond as a matter of public policy, unless the mother's life is at imminent risk.

"In addition, there are many who agree that earlier abortions should be rare or nonexistent. Consequently, public policy should also advocate for, and financially support, abstinence, contraception, assistance for women in troubled pregnancies, prenatal care, and adoption. Unfortunately, governments around the world have failed to adequately promote, or financially support, these initiatives.

"So I come here today to advise you that the Catholic Church is going to take an active and positive role. We will address the emotional, physical, financial, and spiritual needs of women, especially those with children and those who are pregnant. The Church will offer care for mothers and their children, born and unborn, in all ways possible. We will dramatically increase our financial assistance for health care, prenatal care, well-baby care, and day care. And we will sympathetically encourage and compassionately facilitate adoptions.

"We recognize that self-esteem—a true belief in self and a genuine concept of love, love of self, and love for others—is missing among some women. We recognize that some women falsely believe that just because a man told her he loves her, he will always be there for her. We are going to counter that false belief by providing a sense of hope and a renewed belief in the human spirit. We will demonstrate love that is life-giving to all—love that requires a personal commitment to reach out and help others.

"And we will teach boys and men of all ages to fully respect women. The Catholic Church will work to prevent spousal abuse, female genital mutilation, and rape. We will teach men to fulfill their responsibilities as fathers from the moment of conception. The Church will encourage all to love and support those in need.

"I call upon all who support life to reach out to and help young girls, mothers, and pregnant women. I call upon all Catholics, all Christians, and all those involved in the pro-life movement to put their political arrows back into their quivers. I call upon all of you in this room to pray for the sanctity of human life. Pray for all women in need as you take constructive practical action to correct society's ills that result in the unjust taking of life."

When he finished, there was polite but no enthusiastic applause. Every woman in the room was an advocate for the legal right to terminate a pregnancy. The Catholic Church had always opposed that legal right, and while the pope had indicated a change in tactics, it was clear the Church had not changed its fundamental position.

Most women in the room were advocates for supporting women in unwanted and rape-induced pregnancies. The Church had previously been lukewarm toward those goals. Most women in the room were advocates for social policies that reduced unwanted pregnancies and abortion. The Church had not been a leader on those policies either. For most women in the room, words were not enough.

But some women were moved. A handful sought James out after his speech and expressed their appreciation for the significant steps he mentioned toward helping women in need. The headline in the *Los Angeles Times* the following day accurately reflected the organization's reaction: "NOW Gives Pope Cool Reception."

On the second stop of the Religious Heritage Tour, James accepted an interview by the *San Francisco Chronicle*. The reporter pressed him about the Catholic doctrine of papal infallibility.

"This is one of the most misunderstood doctrines in the Church," James explained. "First, it's not the pope who is infallible. God is infallible. Sometimes God speaks through the pope. Christians believe the Holy Spirit inspired the prophets and Gospel writers, thus making the Bible the Word of God. So too, Catholics believe that God speaks to all of us today, sometimes through the voice of the pope. However, it is quite rare when God speaks to all of us simultaneously and infallibly through the pope. There have only been a handful of occasions in the past two thousand years.

"Second, there are specific conditions that must be met for this doctrine to apply. The declaration must be a serious matter of faith and morals. It must be binding upon the universal church. And the pope must speak *ex cathedra*, that is, in his official capacity as the immediate successor of St. Peter."

"Has God ever spoken to you so that you've declared something to be infallible?" the reporter pressed.

"God speaks to me just as God speaks to you. However, I have never spoken *ex cathedra*. As I said, infallible statements are rarely proclaimed. Nevertheless, this doctrine is one of the unfortunate causes of Christian disunity. Most Protestant theologians hold that everything necessary for salvation is contained in Holy Scripture. Catholics disagree. We believe God did not stop speaking to us in a formal way with the concluding statements of the New Testament."

It was a foolproof plan, Sicoli ruminated. "Unlike the failed bombing in Vatican City, no one involved in this effort really knows anyone else involved. Only I know everyone. No one can point fingers at me, because no one except Carlin is aware of the plan. And in the unlikely event Carlin is apprehended, he will not divulge any aspect of the plot. But Carlin will never be captured; he'll either get away scot-free, or be killed." Sicoli hoped for the latter.

Oh, someone might inquire whether Sicoli knew Peter Johnson had recommended Carlin for a job in Minneapolis. But he would deny any knowledge and simply suggest that Carlin and Johnson must have met at the monastery. The monastery's records showed that both of them had attended the same retreat. The only plausible incriminating connection was Mark Nordby. The Bakersfield gun dealer had insisted upon meeting Carlin face-to-face at his shop. Nordby might put one and two together after the event and conclude he had sold the gun that killed the Antichrist. However, Nordby would never say anything. He was as opposed to Flahvin's illegitimate papacy as anyone. Moreover, it was extremely unlikely law enforcement could trace the rifle back to Bakersfield because

Carlin had filed off all the serial numbers. And, if by some incredible miracle of science they did make a connection, it would merely be coincidental that Sicoli knew both the gun dealer and the killer. In fact, as was the case with Johnson, Carlin and Nordby had attended the same retreat, and they must have met there. If anyone attempted to connect all the dots, it would be easy to explain the connections were all circumstantial. It was sadly unfortunate that Cardinal Sicoli happened to know the deranged man who assassinated the Holy Father. It was indeed a foolproof plan.

"All of us are sinners, I among you," James told a crowd of over one hundred thousand people in San Antonio. "Scripture tells us this and our daily lives confirm it. Nevertheless, God forgives us if we repent. True repentance is not just feeling guilty for your bad behavior. Repentance is the decision of the will to change bad behavior. Forgiveness follows repentance. Our redemption was earned on the cross for those who commit to change their behavior and ask for forgiveness.

"St. Peter offers us a wonderful example of repentance. Peter was very special to Jesus. Yet I am particularly struck by how often he failed Jesus. But when Peter repented, he was forgiven. Throughout the Gospels, Jesus uses Peter as an example that all repentant believers are saved. Even when we deny our faith, or sin multiple times, God always forgives the repentant.

"Try to imagine how Jesus must have felt when Peter behaved as he did. At the Last Supper, as he washed the feet of the apostles, he came to Peter. Peter protested. He did not want his master to wash his feet. Jesus had taught his disciples to be servants of all. Yet, when Jesus tried to demonstrate this teaching by the acceptable custom of washing their feet, his chosen leader protested. Jesus unequivocally admonished Peter. He said, 'Unless I wash you, you have no part with me.' Peter quickly repented. 'Lord, not only my feet, but also my hands and my head.' Jesus washed Peter's feet. Peter was forgiven.

"After supper on that last night, before Jesus prayed in the Garden of Gethsemane, he asked his apostles to stay awake and watch. Peter fell asleep, as did the others who were with him. Imagine how Jesus felt when he came back to discover his key lieutenants could not stay awake for even an hour.

"When his enemies came to the garden to seize Jesus, Peter grabbed a sword and cut off the ear of one of them. Imagine how Jesus felt after he had preached peace and nonviolence for three years, and Peter, his chosen leader, used force and violence at this final moment.

"Peter was Jesus' best friend. He assured Jesus that he would never leave his side. Imagine how Jesus felt when Peter denied he even knew him on three separate occasions during the Christ's most trying hour. When the cock crowed, Peter knew he had sinned and asked forgiveness. When Jesus rose on the third day, Peter was the first apostle to whom he appeared. Peter had repented. He was forgiven.

"Feeling bad, sorry, or remorseful may be helpful, but in and of itself, that is not repentance. Deciding to change your behavior and then changing—that is repentance. Scripture acknowledges that Peter sinned. Then Peter devoted the rest of his life to spreading the Gospel. In the end, he too was crucified—hung on a cross, upside down. Peter demonstrated true repentance. Peter received complete forgiveness.

"Jesus' message was simple: 'Repent and be saved.' Change your behavior by loving God above all things and loving your neighbor as yourself. This is the teaching of Jesus the Christ. This is the message of redemption."

According to plan, a week before the pope was to say Mass at the Vikings Dome, Carlin went to work as usual. Throughout the day, he carefully collected all the components of his weapon from their hiding places. One by one, he carried the parts to a secluded, predetermined vent. He turned off the air compressor, climbed inside the dark space, and securely duct-taped each piece to the wall. Because he was the only maintenance person responsible for cleaning the vents, Carlin was not concerned that anyone might locate the weapon. By the end of the day, he had completed this task and turned on the compressor.

At 5:00 p.m. the day before James was to arrive, Carlin again turned off the compressor to this one vent and crawled in to the end. From that vantage point, he could see the entire football field below. As he looked out the opening, he saw hundreds of workers assembling the stage and putting chairs on the field for special guests. There were also twenty-some security personnel with German shepherd dogs, scrutinizing the stadium for contraband.

Carlin had brought food in a brown paper bag for that evening's dinner and MREs for the next day. He thought it might be chilly, so he had brought a military-issue aluminum-coated plastic "casualty" blanket as well. In the pitch black, he quietly cleaned off the tape residue and assembled his weapon as he had done so many times before in the darkness of his small apartment.

He felt prepared—much like he had in Afghanistan before an important mission. He had attended Mass the day before, praying that he would be able to carry out his assignment effectively and professionally. Now he suppressed all emotion, fixating on the task at hand. After eating dinner, he lay inside the vent with his rifle alongside him, headphones covering his ears as he listened to music, and drifted off to sleep.

Like with the other venues on this tour, James celebrated Mass to a standing-room-only crowd at Edward Jones Dome in St. Louis. He started his homily with a quote from Corinthians:

"'Eyes have not seen and ears have not heard what God has in store for people who love Him.' Loving God is one of the two great commandments Jesus gave us. Loving God requires a daily commitment because evil is always present in an effort to distract us from genuinely loving God.

"We have been taught that life is a struggle between the forces of good and the forces of evil. Sometimes we may let down our guard. Sometimes we may even believe that evil is not present in our lives. That is a foolish notion. I pray that you not be fooled. There is no doubt that evil is constantly present in our world and in our lives.

"We know evil when someone flies a passenger jet into an office building, killing thousands. We know evil when a priest sexually violates a child, leaving the innocent marred for life. We know evil when the priests' superiors cover up or delay taking corrective action. We know evil when children have no food to eat, no home to sleep, no lessons to learn, no parent to love or to be loved. We know evil when people are threatened or killed because of their skin color, race, religion, nationality, heritage, gender, sexual preference, age, or tribe. We know evil when people are enslaved, tortured, trafficked, aborted, abused, disowned, segregated or executed. We know evil when chemicals, war, or greed threaten God's creation. And we know evil when a man is brutally crucified on a cross, nails pounded into his wrists, and a spear thrust into his side. Evil surrounds us. It is an unfortunate part of our daily lives. Evil surrounds us.

"But goodness also surrounds us. It too is a part of our lives. We know goodness when someone teaches a child about the wonders of life. We know goodness when someone provides food for the hungry, clothes for the naked, shelter for the homeless, or medicine to the sick. We know goodness when someone embraces the infirmed, the imprisoned, or the abandoned. We know goodness when someone grows food, builds homes, or manufactures products that are needed, fairly priced, and safe to use. We know goodness when someone defends the defenseless and offers hope to those in despair. We know goodness when someone adopts an unwanted child and cares for her as his own. We know goodness when an employer pays a fair wage, provides needed benefits, and offers a safe place to work. We know goodness when someone plants a tree, waters a flower, or protects the environment. We know goodness when Almighty God raises the crucified man from the dead in demonstration of forgiveness of and love for all humanity.

"Evil and goodness are present every day in all of our lives. Given the choice, we prefer to reject evil and embrace goodness. We have that choice. It is an everyday choice. We can choose goodness over evil today. When we do, we find our love of God grows and our love for our neighbors grows as well. So I have a prayer for you today. When day-to-day life gets in the way of love and beckons you toward evil, be motivated by the words of Scripture: 'Eyes have not seen and ears have not heard what God has in store for people who love Him.'"

The next morning James arose feeling good. However, as he looked in the hotel bathroom mirror, he saw a much different man than the one elected pope nearly ten years earlier. Time and the stress of the job had taken their toll. His hair was still full and thick, but now it was nearly all gray. His trim 192 pounds had swelled to 210. The weathered face, slight curve in his back when he stood, the slowing walk, lack of energy, perpetual tiredness, and array of daily medicines all spoke of a man who had aged beyond his years.

After dressing and eating breakfast in his room, he met Simmons and the security detail at the elevator, rode to the lobby, greeted all the hotel staff, slowly walked out of the building into one of the several waiting black limousines, and caravanned to Lambert-St. Louis International Airport.

Dawn was still breaking as people gathered in front of the Vikings Dome gates. Some were taken aback by the level of security and scrutiny. Everyone went through two sets of metal detectors, and all handbags were meticulously examined. The nuns' metal rosaries consistently set off the detectors, causing added consternation among security personnel.

The lower sections of the stadium filled first, then the upper two levels. The ground floor between the end zones was reserved for VIPs— clerical hierarchy of all faiths, current and former political figures, education leaders, wealthy businessmen and women who had contributed generously to the Church, friends of the pope's family, and those who knew somebody who had access to the highly sought-after tickets. By eleven, the facility was filled to capacity with people dressed in all hues of the rainbow. Some wore suits and ties or dresses and heels, but most dressed comfortably in casual slacks, jeans, or trousers with colorful tops or shirts, yellow being the principal color.

Waiting patiently is a challenge for large crowds, and this was no exception. Further, the sports arena atmosphere made this event feel more like a political rally than the prelude to a worship service. Before long, the packed crowd was doing the Minnesota wave—one section at a time, standing and cheering with arms in the air and then sitting down as the motion moved around the stadium left to right. A few minutes later, the folks in Section 222 started chanting "Jimmy, Jimmy, Jimmy, Jimmy," and the entire flock joined in.

When the crowd saw his plane land at Minneapolis-St. Paul International Airport, broadcast by local television stations on the giant Arbitrage screens, they screamed, whistled, and applauded. Watching in anticipation as he walked out of the Boeing 737 and down the stairway, cameras captured him kneel and kiss the ground, as he did at every stop around the world, and as St. John Paul II had consistently done decades earlier.

"After all," James often said, "the ground is the source of God's creation—from which all life comes and to which all life returns." As he knelt, the crowd roared its approval. The pope stood, greeted local dignitaries, blessed the children who sang to him, and walked to a black SUV into which he reclined in the back passenger seat. Through the tinted windows, the television screen showed him taking a long drink of water from a plastic bottle and the vehicle, led by a police escort, whisked away. Words ran across the large screen: "Pope James expected at the Dome in 15 minutes."

Carlin was oblivious to all that was occurring beneath him. He had been awakened by the noise below when people first entered the sports ground, but he did not look out of the dark opening, concerned that someone might see him. Sicoli had issued clear instructions: he was not to do anything until Flahvin started his homily during Mass. Then, only after he had spoken for at least one minute, and the entire audience was certain to be focused on his words, was Carlin to move toward the field-side opening in the vent.

James's security detail knew there were many with motives to assassinate the pope. Insiders who thought he was taking the Church too far, too left, too fast. Outsiders, like Muslim extremists, who saw him as the symbolic leader of the Crusaders. The demented, who wanted to rid the world of the Antichrist. The crazy, who wanted their names in the history books.

James was an engaging and open pope, thus requiring security personnel to protect against a variety of assassination methods. Suicide at the altar, a security guard traitor, a hand grenade thrown from the audience, a patient sniper in a building along the motorcade route, a massive bomb planted in the arena or his hotel, anthrax in the ventilation system—there was no end to the possibilities.

The Secret Service took every precaution to protect this most important of world leaders. Hundreds of police and private security officers were on watchful duty. Everyone who entered the stadium was searched and searched again. German shepherd dogs were ever present as their handlers suspected everyone of foul play. Even the air space was protected. No private planes were allowed within thirty miles of the Vikings Dome, and two F22A Raptor fighter jets ensured that no one would even think about attacking from the air.

When James walked out onto the makeshift sanctuary, all stood and applauded. On this day, he wore his lavender vestment, offset by a wide band of deep purple down the front and back of the chasuble. A simple cross, embroidered in light beige, adorned the front band, and the crown of thorns decorated the back. These symbols memorialized the passion and crucifixion of Jesus the Christ.

As he stood at the center of the platform, James began the sacred worship service with the simple words, "In the name of the Father, and of the Son, and of the Holy Spirit. Amen."

Following the Scripture readings for the day, he opened his homily. "We are all sinners because of our human condition. All of us are works in progress. God is not done with any of us yet. This is the true gift from Jesus the Christ. As long as we repent for our sins, do our best to amend our life, perform appropriate penance, and serve others as Jesus commanded, God's infinite mercy will keep us in good stead. That is the great gift of redemption. Jesus died for us, knowing we will continue to fall short of what God desires. He taught us about prayer, fasting, good works, and the sacraments. Every one of us can become stronger and more brilliant in our spirit life and overcome the darkness of—"

There was only one shot. The bullet struck above his left eye. One hundred thousand watched on the stadium screens as the pope's body crumpled to the floor of the vast platform. The natural noise of the stadium retreated into horrified silence. They had heard a crack and saw him stagger briefly, then fall. The others on the stage—priests, bishops, nuns, and altar boys and girls—instinctively threw themselves to the floor in self-protection. He lay motionless on the red-carpeted deck for only an instant before his bodyguards sprang to his side. Then thousands of people screamed. Some ducked for cover while others ran in pandemonium. There was no second shot. There would be no second shot.

People stood up to see what had happened, mesmerized by the altar and the large television screens. Doctors tried frantically to revive him, as other doctors in the audience quickly gathered around the foot of the stage, ready to offer help. A bishop knelt by James's side and performed last rites.

Emergency vehicle sirens cried out in the distance. A nun near the front, close to the stage, recited the Lord's Prayer, saying it aloud. Immediately, all those around her joined in. Those in her section prayed with her. Now, thousands in the stadium prayed in unison. The shrill sirens grew closer. The faithful repeated the sacred words. They watched and prayed, many gasping as men in official white and blue uniforms wheeled out a stretcher. They lifted him up and placed him on the white pad. The paralyzed crowd continued their unified prayer. Swiss Guards pushed the stretcher off stage. All one hundred thousand prayed aloud. Clergy, physicians, and altar boys and girls formed a procession behind the stretcher. The words were numbing, soothing, angelic.

When they put him in the ambulance, Father Simmons turned to one of the attending physicians. Before he could ask, the doctor simply said, "He's still breathing. That's a good sign. We won't know more until we get him to the hospital."

It took less than two minutes for the ambulance to travel the eight blocks to the Hennepin County Medical Center. News of this magnitude spread at lightning speed, and a team of hospital gunshot trauma specialists had already assembled. The paramedics hurriedly wheeled him in into the ER where the team had gathered. Only doctors and nurses were allowed in the room as they fought frantically to save the life of the most important patient any of them had ever served.

As the spontaneous procession left the stage, Cardinal Keegan returned to the podium where James had stood mere minutes before. He tapped the microphone. The praying stopped. With tears running down his cheeks and his baritone voice trembling, he announced, "Ladies and gentlemen, the pope has been shot. Please pray for the Holy Father." Wiping his tears, Keegan turned and walked away.

Men, women, and children shrieked in pain. Thousands held their heads in disbelief. Others collapsed into the arms of those around them. Tens of thousands cried. Many just slumped into their chairs, praying silently.

Then, a Servite sister with a strong, penetrating voice sang "Amazing Grace, How Sweet the Sound." Others joined. Through tears and sobs, choking back deep grief, tens of thousands sang verse after verse of the eighteenth-century hymn of faith and grace.

Gunfire interrupted the hymn. People scrambled for the exits as more shots rang out. As they rushed out of the stadium, the audience found a growing crowd gathering outside on the plaza. People were coming from all directions. Soon, the crowd assembled in a prayer vigil for the man who had brought them hope for their church, peace in their lives, and a closer relationship with Jesus the Christ. The devoted were subdued, ambling slowly to the stadium entrance from which the pope's ambulance had just screamed away. Flowers, cards, balloons, and rosaries were laid gently at a makeshift memorial. Some knelt and prayed. Others just touched the building, and walked away.

Sicoli's plan called for Carlin to wait a second night in the vent high above the stadium floor. The next morning, after securely duct-taping the weapon and all other stuff he'd brought with him to the side of the vent, Carlin would slip out. He knew the building would still be crawling with FBI, Secret Service, and local police. However, because he was an employee, wearing his stadium worker's uniform and appropriate identification, Carlin believed he could bypass all law enforcement. There would be no telling evidence that he was in the vent because he wore gloves at all times and wiped down the weapon, leaving no fingerprints; and once he turned the ventilation system back on, all hairs, clothing fibers, and gunshot residue would be blown away by the tremendous force of air, thus leaving no trace evidence. He also wore a Weeables, a waterproof urine container he would empty in one of the restrooms and dispose of when he returned to his apartment. Moreover, as Sicoli had told him, if his DNA ever were found in the vent, he would advise the cops that he climbed inside every vent when he cleaned them, so it should be no surprise that his DNA might be found.

In the meantime, however, law officers were huddled around the stadium's sophisticated security imaging system, reviewing every impression, from every frame, from every camera. Within ten minutes of screening video on multiple screens, they saw what they were looking for—a flash of light coming from one of the vents at the exact moment of the shooting. They presumed it was the flare from a weapon.

Thousands of people lingered in the stadium, so police exercised extreme caution. They immediately sent a SWAT team to the area of the suspicious vent, and quickly discovered the air had been shut off. They did not know if the shooter was still in the cavity, or if he had already fled. They took no chances. The officer in charge shouted up toward the vent, "Come out with your hands up."

Carlin was stunned, but remained silent. His military training had taught him how not to be captured in a situation like this. Given what he'd originally thought was a remote possibility that someone might detect his presence, he lay on his stomach, weapon in hand, facing the direction through which he had entered. If anyone were going to come get him, they would have to come through that small opening. He did not want to die, but he understood the realities of combat. If he were captured, his punishment would be far worse than death.

Several moments passed, and the officer yelled out again, "Come out with your hands up." Carlin made no sound, no movement. A minute later, he saw a flashlight and the silhouette of a man's head. The light struck him in the face and he immediately squeezed the trigger.

The bullet hit the officer in the head. Killed instantly, the man dropped to the floor below.

The SWAT team had cornered their killer, but at a terrible price. They threw in a canister of gas, and Carlin put on a pair of goggles and his miniaturized self-contained breathing device. He made no sound. The police were frustrated. They wanted to capture the killer alive, but he was not cooperating. After Carlin wounded a second police officer, they knew they had no alternative but to take him out.

The authorities evacuated the building. Then they did something Carlin had not anticipated. They turned off the blower to the vent that was immediately across the field from the one where he hid. Two police sharpshooters with high-powered laser-equipped rifles climbed into the vent. All the lights in the stadium were turned off; the sharpshooters put on night-vision goggles and pointed their weapons at the vent eighty yards across the field. When Carlin saw the red laser beams, he twitched, and when he moved, they fired. He died where he lay.

When the police were sure the killer was dead, they removed his body and identified him. The FBI got a warrant to search Carlin's apartment. There they found something Sicoli had not anticipated—a box of recordings. Joseph Carlin had digitally recorded every conversation with Cardinal Sicoli from their second meeting at the San Diego Library until the final phone call, three days previous. Carlin had left a simple note that read, "If you find these, I'm probably dead. Let my mother listen so she'll know I was followin' orders from the Catholic Church."

Chapter Twenty-Two

The crush of media engulfed every entrance to the hospital as the world sought to learn the fate of the "children's pope." As at the stadium earlier in the day, a vigil of thousands grew to tens of thousands, then hundreds of thousands. People came to pray, to be close, to hope, to weep.

The pope's children rushed to Minneapolis on board the mayor of Chicago's private plane. They stayed with Keegan, Simmons, and a small gathering of other clergy in a specially arranged waiting room at HCMC. It was still and serene as they quietly prayed for their father, mentor, and friend.

The bullet had struck the pope's left side of the brain. There was massive damage and blood loss, but there was still hope. Others had survived similar wounds, the trauma team reminded themselves as they operated. They refused to give up as long as there was hope. His heart stopped beating; they resuscitated and continued their work on his brain, relieving pressure and fluid buildup. The heart stopped again; they resuscitated once more and resumed their efforts. When his heart stopped for the third time, they tried again. Nothing could be done. James was pronounced dead at 9:30 p.m., after nearly nine hours in surgery.

The doctors informed Cardinal Keegan and the pope's children. Keegan offered to tell the media and the crowd; the children were grateful. So for the second time on this day, Gregory Cardinal Keegan, in his deep baritone voice, addressed the throng of men and women who so loved his friend.

"I have the worst possible news. The Holy Father is dead. Please pray for the repose of the soul of our dear friend and brother in Christ, Jimmy Flahvin, Pope James the First. Eternal rest grant unto him, O Lord, and let perpetual light shine upon him. May his soul and all the—" He could not finish. Sobbing uncontrollably, he was unable to get through the rest of the traditional prayer for the dead. He turned and stumbled back into the hospital.

Pursuant to state law, the medical examiner performed an autopsy, determining the cause of death as a single gunshot wound to the forehead, left side, front to back, through and through. A few hours later, HCMC released the corpse to the archbishop of the archdiocese of St. Paul and Minneapolis. The archbishop's staff arranged for James to be taken to a local Catholic mortuary.

Cardinal Keegan called Secretary of State Mbuto in Rome. "He died a few moments ago," Keegan reported.

"I know. I saw you on television. I know how close the two of you were. I'm very sorry."

"He was your mentor, and he admired you more than you'll ever know. I'm sorry for both of us."

"What are we going to do without him, Greg?"

"I don't know, Jacob. I don't know. When will you get here?"

"I fly out in a few minutes. Should be there by six in the morning."

Tradition, custom, and canon law spelled out in specific detail the process the Church followed when a pope died. The non-theological authority immediately, but only temporarily, passed to the Vatican secretary of state. Cardinal Mbuto executed the pope's death certificate and ordered locks installed on his private apartment and his office. Tradition also called for Mbuto to immediately remove the pope's gold ring from the fourth finger of his right hand, and in the presence of other cardinals, smash it with a hammer to thwart any possibility of authenticating forged papal documents during the interregnum. However, because Mbuto did not arrive in St. Paul until early morning the following day, this part of the process was delayed.

When Mbuto arrived, a police escort drove him to the mortuary where he paid his respects. Kneeling down in front of the closed casket, he steadied himself by placing his hand on the wooden box, closed his eyes, and prayed. After several minutes, he stood and asked the attendant to open the casket. In the presence of several other cardinals who had arrived overnight from around the world, and adhering to centuries-old tradition, he removed the Ring of the Fisherman from James's hand. The cardinal secretary smashed it with a heavy hammer.

Mbuto turned to the assembled cardinals. "Pope James will not be interred in St. Peter's Basilica. Instead, he will be buried alongside his wife in Maryhill Cemetery, north of Chicago, as he instructed. We will conduct the funeral mass at the St. Paul Cathedral because there is no cathedral sufficient in size in or near Chicago."

"That's the only good news today," Cardinal Keegan said softly. "Given the tragic events that have occurred here, it will be healing for the people of Minnesota to have this pope's life celebrated in their capital city."

✳ ✳ ✳

A federal judge authorized the FBI to listen to the recordings found in Carlin's apartment. It did not take the agents long to figure out who Sicoli was and where he lived. Less than twenty-four hours after the assassination, FBI agents swarmed Holy Cross Monastery in southern California and arrested Manoles Franco Sicoli without incident. He was charged with conspiracy to murder, accomplice to murder, and murder in the first degree.

Sicoli waived his right to an attorney and confessed to his involvement in the killing. He argued the righteousness of his act, but the police and federal prosecutors did not care about his self-absorbed reasons. They were, however, interested in certain e-mails on his iPad, especially those that appeared to have originated from the Vatican. After several hours of questioning, Sicoli acknowledged that he had received inside information from a colleague in the Curia, Juan Carlos Cardinal Villegomez.

* * *

All four children quickly agreed to honor their father's wishes to have a traditional Roman Catholic papal funeral celebration, save for the pomp and ceremony he so disliked. The clerics respected the pope's wishes that it be a simple service, with interment at Maryhill Cemetery, where the Vatican had long ago constructed a burial place on the cemetery grounds in preparation for this day, in compliance with the Holy Father's request.

Tradition called for nine days of mourning. Cardinals, bishops, and other clergy from over the world flocked to Minnesota to celebrate the funeral rites. Global media outlets descended upon the metropolitan area. All the ceremonies that would normally occur in Vatican City took place in St. Paul.

The St. Paul Cathedral was among the most magnificent churches in America. Inspired by French cathedrals, this enormous Beaux Arts structure, adorned with its copper-clad dome, sat high on a hill facing the commercial center of St. Paul, as the wondrous Mississippi River flowed on its right and the grand, Renaissance-style secular buildings of state government dominated to the left.

James's body lay in repose in closed casket for public viewing for four full days. Local police estimated that over four million people came to the great church to pay their respects during those ninety-six hours, but less than half actually had the opportunity to pass by the casket at four abreast. Among those expressing their condolences were presidents, prime ministers, kings, queens, senators, governors, and other representatives from across the globe. Some distinguished officials came to pay their genuine and heartfelt respect, others because of the historical significance of the passing of a pope, and still others merely for the photo opportunity to be recorded in the presence of a genuinely great man.

On the day of his funeral liturgy, more than three million people turned out. The cathedral accommodated about three thousand in the pews, and another thousand standing. The remaining mourners gathered outside, masses of people stretching north to the Historical Society and state capitol grounds, east down the hill in front of the great church, south to the freeway, and west along Marshall, Dayton, Selby, and Summit avenues. Minnesota's governor and mayors from across the state offered police for security, and loudspeakers were set up so as many as possible could hear the proceedings, although most watched on their smart phones or tablets. Thousands of local priests, nuns, and Eucharistic ministers spread out among the vast crowd, offering Holy Communion to everyone who wanted to receive.

Cardinal Keegan, who had served in this archdiocese as both a parish priest and a state prison chaplain, and Pope James's friend for fifty years, celebrated the Requiem Mass. An Irish bagpipe corps played "Amazing Grace," and an African American women's choir sang "How Great Thou Art." Cardinal Mbuto offered the homily, and Rev. Robert Jacobson, Rabbi Isidore Goldman, and Grand Imam Mehmet Ali Burakgazi all presented eulogies.

"James and I have a different theology," the grand imam said. "A different set of beliefs, and we practice a different religion. Nevertheless, we always understood we are brothers serving the same God. He treated me as his brother. When he wrote me, he started his letters, 'Dear Brother.' So today I mourn the terrible loss of my beloved brother."

After Mass, the pope's hearse carried his casket from John Ireland Boulevard, named after the first archbishop of St. Paul, down Kellogg Boulevard, named after the former US secretary of state, along the Mississippi River to Union Depot. The entire contingent of 116 Swiss Guards in their formal multicolored dress uniforms surrounded the hearse and escorted the body on foot in close-order drill. Hundreds of thousands of mourners walked the two miles to the train station behind a parade of black limousines.

At Union Depot, the most senior members of the Swiss Guard tenderly and with solemn respect placed the casket on a US government train. The 167 cardinals present boarded and accompanied the pope on his final journey, along with his children and grandchildren. The president of the United States and many members of the US Senate and

House of Representatives also rode the train that day. In deference to the family, Keegan and Mbuto allowed Jimmy Flahvin's friends, classmates, fellow prisoners, former coworkers, and Winnetka neighbors to ride the train as well. Protestant, Jewish, and Muslim clergy were also onboard, as were the Italian prime minister, the Chinese president, Isidore Goldman, and Mehmet Ali Burakgazi.

James's children didn't want this last trip to become an overly somber event, so as the train rocked and swayed, they walked up and down the aisles of the passenger cars, greeting friends, bishops, cardinals, and elected officials, telling stories about their dad—the taller the story the better. They sang songs, spilt tea, and shared some Irish whiskey. Given the traditions of the Roman Catholic Church upon the death of a pope, the customary Flahvin Irish wake had been postponed, but this train ride offered the opportunity for a traveling Gaelic celebration.

The funeral train wound its way from St. Paul along the Mississippi River to Winona, across to the Wisconsin Dells, on to Milwaukee, and down the shore of Lake Michigan through his hometown of Winnetka. In every community, both large and small, urban and rural, thousands and sometimes tens of thousands greeted the procession as it slowly chugged along. The train made no stops and took on no additional passengers; however, the trip required four hours more than scheduled because of all the folks along the track.

When the train pulled into Morton Grove, Illinois, at eleven in the morning, well behind schedule, the twelve youngest cardinals, all in their late forties and early fifties, and all appointed by Pope James, removed the precious cypress coffin from the white railway carriage. They tenderly placed it on a casket gurney and rolled it to a white hearse.

Mourners had waited hours for the arrival. Those in apartments across the street from the station filled their balconies with family and friends as they watched the casket move from train to hearse. Many held rosaries, their lips silently moving as they said the repetitive prayers. Fifty busses in the adjoining parking lot, and four hundred cars authorized to park up and down the residential streets, waited reverently to join the motorcade. Thirty-two motorcycle police in teams of four led the hearse as it pulled away from the station and took a right-hand turn onto Elm Street, then an immediate right onto Lehigh Avenue. They crawled slowly on to Lincoln, driving past St. Paul Woods, crossing the railroad tracks they had just come down, and turned left onto Dempster. The solemn procession drove west to the Village of Niles. The police had blocked off traffic going both directions, and the roadway teemed with several million along the five-mile route from the train station to his final resting place. Turning left onto Milwaukee Avenue, the imposing caravan processed into Maryhill Cemetery.

A dark green metal picket fence enclosed the multi-acre burial ground, a relatively modern graveyard first opened in 1959. The police escorted the procession through the front gates into an urban forest. Chirping birds and roaming deer shared the grounds with religious statuary and the faithful departed. Off to the left was a shrine to Mary, Queen of Peace. Further to the right was a shrine to Our Lady of Guadalupe. Inside the main chapel, visitors were greeted by a mosaic of our Lady of Czestochowa. Straight ahead, and directly in front of the mausoleum, an oversized bronze sculpture of John baptizing Jesus welcomed all who entered.

Shortly after becoming pope, James had decided to be buried in this cemetery named in honor of the mother of Jesus and close to his home in Winnetka. When asked why he did not want to be buried in St. Peter's with the other popes, he would tell a childhood story about his mother. She was asked one day by a Protestant friend why Catholics prayed to Mary when they could just pray to Jesus. Jimmy remembered his mother saying, "The most important person in Jesus' life was his mother. I guarantee you; he'll listen to her before he ever listens to me." Then the pope added, "I want to do everything in my power to have the mother of Jesus rooting for me. So I'll be buried in the ground that honors her name."

The Chicago archdiocese had set aside Section Fifty of Maryhill, an immense, undeveloped wooded area of the cemetery, across the road and south of the chapel. This was reserved for the pope and his family. The Church had anticipated thousands of people would visit his grave, so they had made appropriate arrangements, clearing a large open space surrounded by pine, maple, and oak trees. However, no one had expected this day to come so soon, and certainly not in the manner in which it had.

In accordance with his wishes, Vicky's body had been relocated to the area. The black cloth-covered inscription on the granite block that would sit next to hers and atop his grave simply read, "James - a Servant to the Servants of God."

Five million people crowded into Maryhill on that bright sunshiny day and along the roadways leading to the gate. As in St. Paul, there were dignitaries from all over the world. James had left specific instructions that the working class, as well as the poor of Chicago, be encouraged to intermingle with the powerful on this day. So the area closest to the gravesite, which would normally be set aside solely for VIPs, included some of the poorest Americans, all dressed in their finest clothes.

When all finally gathered at the plot, US Senator Matthew Flahvin spoke into a microphone that echoed through speakers across the expansive acreage. He reminisced about his father and mother, and the love they shared for each other. He concluded with these words: "The man you call 'Holy Father,' 'Your Holiness,' and 'Pope,' my sisters and brothers, our spouses, and I call 'Dad.' To our children, he's just 'Grandpa Jimmy.'

"We are numb. We are spent. We have no more tears to shed. We have no hope to survive this ordeal if not for the love of all of you. Your presence here today is a gift beyond all gifts. We thank you from the depths of our souls.

"Throughout the ages, the corrupt, the depraved, the insane, and the perverted have assassinated and executed humble religious leaders. For reasons we will never comprehend, those who teach and live peace and love are too often in the line of fire. Mahatma Gandhi, Martin Luther King, Oscar Arnulfo Romero, and now James the First are just a few of the recent many.

"My dad was the most likely to be a wonderful father, the most likely to be a loving husband, and the most likely to be a good friend. But he was the most unlikely man to be pope. Nevertheless, he changed the Church. Emphasizing the inclusiveness that Jesus proclaimed, and refocusing her on the principal message of Jesus—love of God and service to others—he changed the Church, hopefully forever.

"In the past week, everything that could be said about my dad's life has been said. There really are no more words to say. As sad as this day is for our family, for the Church, and for the world, we rejoice in knowing that Dad is now where he should be, back home with Mom in the loving presence of the Creator."

EPILOGUE

I tell you this story on the two hundredth anniversary of the birthday of Pope James. Every subsequent pope has honored James's specific request not to be considered for canonization. Nevertheless, twenty-three years after his death, on the celebration of his one hundredth birthday, Pope John XXV proclaimed he would forevermore be known as James the Great.

So this is the story and the legacy of James the Great, the first North American pope. I am able to share this story, in large part, because my great-great-grandfather explicitly released the cardinals who elected him from their vow of secrecy regarding the proceedings of the election. And because of his extensive personal writings, including daily journal entries that started when he was imprisoned, and all the family stories that have been passed down generation to generation.

James the Great served as pope for ten years. He was an international man of vision, purpose, compassion, intellect, charm, humor, and holiness. He studied the life of St. Peter and attempted to lead the Church in the manner and style that he believed Peter would lead. Scripture suggests that Peter was a collaborator and consensus builder. He did not exercise power for its own sake, but recognized the contribution each believer made in the name of the Holy Spirit. As he did at Antioch, St. Peter listened carefully to all his colleagues and to all their arguments. Only then did he speak the deciding word. James the Great tried to follow Peter's example, recognizing that the gifts of the Spirit were endowed to all believers. His principal responsibility was not to state the law but rather to speak the consensus of the People of God.

James was never venerated, in part by his own insistence and humility, and in large measure because Jesus is the only true leader of the Church. There have been thirteen popes in the 123 years since his death; four have been North Americans and three were women. His immediate successor, James II, was formerly known as Jacob Cardinal Mbuto, his secretary of state.

Many positive changes ensued because of James the Great's leadership and that of his immediate successor. When James was elected pope, women were not permitted to be ordained; today more than 50 percent of priests, bishops, and cardinals are women. Prior to his pontificate, there was a critical shortage of Catholic clergy, especially priests. There is no shortage today, in large measure because he included women in the ranks of the clergy. Now in many dioceses there are waiting lists of young men and women hoping to enter seminary. And many married people are members of the Catholic clergy, something that was virtually unheard of prior to his papacy.

James's primary effect on Catholicism was following in the steps of Pope Francis I by making permanent the change in emphasis from ritual and grandiose ceremony to caring for the poor and forgotten. Millions of people carry on the work James initiated, all in the name of Jesus the Christ. Today the Catholic Church has schools, universities, children's homes, clinics, hospitals, and senior centers in more than two hundred countries, where those less fortunate receive daily food and nutrition, health and hygiene education, medicine and patient care, and excellent formal education and job training, all for the price of their commitment to serve others. The money to run these facilities comes from donations, mostly from people and their extended families who were at one time themselves beneficiaries of the work of the Church. The number of those suffering from economic poverty and illiteracy has decreased sharply across the world, as has the growth in population due to increased education and health care.

Some of James's impact was realized during his lifetime. After he spoke to the affluent in a community, they often heeded his call and contributed to the needs of the destitute. For example, after a dinner speech to the wealthy and powerful in Lima, Peru, which I have included in this manuscript, many of the affluent Peruvians in attendance, most of whom had never previously visited an *asentamientos humanos*, offered to volunteer at one of the shantytowns. The wealthy volunteers worked with, and under the direction of, impoverished community leaders. Both the volunteers and local people reported that they learned from and about each other. The church in Liliana's and Jorge's community was completed. In addition, electrical and potable water systems were installed, a sewer system constructed, school and household gardens established, community streets paved, the elementary school library equipped, the health center expanded, sufficient medicines donated, and the stench of sewage and the wild dogs disappeared.

Most important, the well-educated and economically prosperous suburbanites discovered, as James the Great hoped they would, that regardless of their superior education and extraordinary difference in wealth, they were far more like their impoverished neighbors than they had ever imagined. Out of that discovery, deep and lasting friendships were born. Some of the business-owning volunteers hired some of the local people. Others provided funding so the shantytown children could go to college. With increased employment and educational opportunities, the shantytowns began to flourish. Most notable, families from both communities shared holidays and celebrated baptisms, *quinceañeras*, and weddings together.

Upon reflection years later, many were amazed at the sweeping, tangible results from this one dinner with James the Great. Cardinal Rodriguez, the archbishop of Lima, wrote in his memoirs about how he had tried to dissuade Pope James from visiting the Puericultorio Perez Aranibar and how the pope simply did not listen to him. "Pope James dismissed my pleas to meet individually with the wealthy and powerful because he knew better things would come to pass by his sharing a meal with those impoverished but worthy children."

Membership in the Catholic Church grew dramatically during James's tenure, and it continues to grow to this day. More than 60 percent of the world's population call themselves Christians, and two-thirds of them are Catholic—four billion people. In addition, virtually all Christian denominations actively participate in One God, One Church, the ecumenical organization started by James the Great.

So on this day, we celebrate the two hundredth birthday of Jimmy Flahvin—James the Great. His life was one of many contradictions. He often called himself "a lowly sinner." However, he showed all of us that repentant sinners are great in the eyes of God.